ALSO BY MELISSA GOOD

Dar and Kerry Series
Tropical Storm
Hurricane Watch
Eye of the Storm
Red Sky At Morning
Thicker Than Water
Terrors of the High Seas

Tropical Convergence

Melissa Good

Yellow Rose Books

Port Arthur, Texas

ISBN 978-1-935053-18-7
1-935053-18-3

First Printing 2009

9 8 7 6 5 4 3 2 1

Cover design by Donna Pawlowski

Published by:

Regal Crest Enterprises, LLC
4700 Highway 365, Suite A
PMB 210
Port Arthur, Texas 77642

Find us on the World Wide Web at
http://www.regalcrest.biz

Printed in the United States of America

Chapter
One

THE CONFERENCE ROOM was almost full, every seat at the long table taken except for the one at the head. Late afternoon sunlight poured into the room, resisting the valiant efforts of the several ton air conditioning plant to alleviate its effects, and after a moment of shading his eyes, Mark Polenti got up and walked over to the glass panel. "Son of a bitch." He lowered the shades. "You could cook a damn egg on this thing."

"No kidding," Peter Prescott, one of the IT group leaders, agreed. "I start sweating just thinking about going out to my car."

With a shake of his head, Mark returned to his seat. The MIS—Management Information Systems—manager picked up and flipped his pen, settling back in one of the leather chairs that ringed the table. "Long damned summer."

"Mm."

"Yeah."

Agreement chimed in from around the table full of assorted technical managers. "I wouldn't go outside for ten minutes longer than I had to," Peter added. "Man, I see those freaking tourists on the beach and you can just see them frying like turkeys at Thanksgiving."

"You got that right," Mark snorted.

The door to the conference room opened, and they all turned. Eyes opened wider as the newcomer commenced to dance inside, jiving to a song apparently audible only to her as she made her way across the room and ended up bouncing into the chair at the end of the table.

Relatively short, but sporting a lithe muscular build, the woman placed a leather folder on the table, then shrugged out of her neatly tailored blue jacket and draped it over the back of the chair, before she leaned on the padded surface in a jaunty finish to her dance.

"Hi, guys." Kerry grinned at them. "Is today not an awesome day, or what?"

The operations department heads all looked at each other, and then peered down the table as their blond leader sat down. Kerry was dressed in a no nonsense business suit, with an impeccably pressed cream-colored silk blouse, but her pale, summer-cropped hair was so tousled it appeared that she had stuck her head out of some car window on the way back from lunch.

"Um." Mark cleared his throat. "Yeah, it's okay," he allowed. "We got the espresso machine working again, at least." His eyebrows quirked. "Did you...like drink a couple cups to celebrate or something?"

"Nope." Kerry laced her fingers together in front of her on the table. "Guess again."

"Did we make our numbers?" Peter hazarded a guess.

"Yes, but that's not why I'm jazzed," she replied.

"Did your dog have puppies?" Ellen Jasmine chimed in from across the table, her weathered face wrinkling up in a grin.

"No, no, no." Kerry waggled her hand. "No puppies, no kittens, and neither Dar nor I are pregnant so don't even go there." She danced a little in her seat. "C'mon, c'mon...we've only been talking about this for a month."

Mark made a face. "Don't tell me you're all whacked about going to the technology convention."

Kerry grinned widely.

Her audience wasn't sure whether to laugh or groan. "Jesus." Mark covered his eyes. "Man, I thought I was the primo geek in this place." He pointed at Kerry. "Not any more. You win. I give."

Kerry opened her leather folder, and chuckled. "Actually," she glanced around and lowered her voice, "I could give a gopher's wazoo about the convention. I've been waiting to go back to Disney World with Dar since forever." Her face creased into a grin again, her summer tan emphasizing the bleached lightness of her hair, and the vivid green of her eyes.

"Ahhhh!" Ellen laughed. "Now I get it!"

"Augh...Orlando in July? Kerry, you're gonna regret it," Mark objected. "Not even the Mouse could get me up there in this weather."

"You," Kerry pointed at him, "have obviously never done Disney with Dar." She pulled out her agenda. "Now, let's see where we are this month." She smoothly switched gears, her voice dropping a few notes and becoming more businesslike. "Okay, I've got some good news, and some bad news."

The room settled down, and became more serious. Around the table, eyes met in mild apprehension. Even though most in the room trusted Kerry, and all liked her, they also knew exactly where her loyalties were.

"Let me get the bad news out of the way," Kerry said. "First of all, let me make it clear that in no way do I, or Dar for that matter, hold anyone here responsible for the fact that twenty percent of our contracts up for renewal this quarter did not sign." She looked up, meeting the eyes facing her squarely. "Our service was not in question, nor was it a factor in the signings."

Mark exhaled. "Fuckin' lowballers."

Kerry's expressive face twitched a little. "For the record—when sales brought the final numbers to the table, it was Dar who drew the line and said we would not counter bid them. Okay?" She gave them a moment to absorb the words. "Dar said she would not trade off our service levels for paper numbers. We decided we couldn't provide acceptable levels of response for the dollars they were suggesting." She paused. "I agreed wholeheartedly."

Bodies relaxed around the room, falling back into the leather chairs with faintly audible squeaks.

"Kerry, that's an amazing thing to hear," Ellen said, in a serious tone. "I have a friend who works for our friends out west, and last time something like this happened, they took big time heat for it."

Kerry rested her chin on her hands. "Dar would never let that happen," she said. "But let me tell you, those meetings in Houston last week weren't pretty."

"Yeah, I bet," Mark muttered. "But, Kerry, I saw those freakin' numbers. No way in hell those guys can deliver what they said they would."

His boss shrugged one shoulder lightly. "Time will tell. But in the meantime, we have twenty percent of our budget we need to find funding for, or else lose it. That means you all need to look *very* carefully at your books and see if we have room for slack," she warned. "If we have a repeat next quarter, things are going to get very tight around here."

Everyone nodded in grim understanding.

"Now, on the bright side." Kerry changed gears again. "We did make our service numbers. In fact," she smiled warmly, "we exceeded them. I'm very proud of that, and so's Dar." Her eyes twinkled a little. "And so, even though I know you all must have heard about the salary freeze..."

Mark cleared his throat. Ellen looked away out the window. The rest of the table found something to study that didn't involve middling height blond women. Everyone knew how much Kerry hated office gossip, and wise people didn't bring it up in her presence.

"It doesn't apply to us," Kerry finished quietly. "I've processed the first of this quarter's raises and bonuses, and they should be hitting your work lists by the time you get back to your offices." She almost smiled at the instinctive gasps at the unexpected statement. "Please let your people know that we appreciate all the hard work they've put in this year, and we hope they continue through the rest of the year."

For a very long moment there was silence around the table. Then Mark rocked forward and thumped his elbows against the table. "Holy crap, boss. My socks are still bouncing off the walls here," he said. "Aren't the rest of those guys gonna be pissed?"

Kerry leaned back in her chair, extending her legs and crossing them at the ankles. "Well." She steepled her fingers and tapped the tips against her chin. "First off, no one should be talking about it." One blond eyebrow cocked meaningfully. "But second, if someone has a problem, direct them that way." She jerked her thumb sideways, in the general direction of Dar's office.

"Not to you?" Ellen asked, curiously.

Kerry's nostrils flared slightly. "Dar's orders," she replied briefly. After another moment of silence, she nodded. "Okay, so, next on the agenda..."

Her staff shifted around the table and leaned forward, sorting their own papers and relaxing. Kerry took the opportunity to silently evaluate them, absorbing the air of surprise at her last statement. They knew her to be a fierce defender of her own prerogatives, and one of the very few people in the company not only willing, but also able to stand up to their legendary Chief Information Officer.

Of course, Kerry had the inherent advantage of being married to and living with Dar and while that didn't quite diminish her courage, it at least made it understandable to everyone in the room.

Ah well. Kerry folded her hands over her stomach, twiddling her thumbs idly. Everyone would get over it in a few days, and after all, there was Disney World to contemplate.

It wasn't that she was making light of the company's troubles — they weighed on her shoulders more than most. But as she'd told her staff, the troubles hadn't been laid at their doorstep, and the best thing they all could do right then was keep doing their jobs.

And that meant putting on a good show at the convention. "Everyone ready for the trade show, since I mentioned it?"

"Advance team's packed and itchin'," Mark replied, checking something off on his agenda.

"Who's in charge?" Kerry asked. "You going?"

Mark glanced up at her. "Peter. He's buds with Eleanor's chief whiner. They get along great."

"He the one with the pierced eyebrows?"

"Eh..."

"Good choice." Kerry spun her papers. "Okay, tell me what didn't come in on time this week."

"DAR, LISTEN."

"I'm listening." Dar Roberts selected a colorful dart from the case resting on her knees and let it fly, grinning in triumph when its point buried itself in a new wall mounted target. "I'm not hearing anything but bilge wash so far, but I'm listening."

"Bilge wash? You been out on that boat of yours again?" Alastair McLean chuckled.

"Been around my daddy," Dar replied, launching another dart. "Alastair, we've been around and around with this. We both know there's no damn good answer."

A long sigh issued through the phone.

"I've put as much pressure on every supplier we have, pushed as hard as I could, got everyone down to the lowest cost they can do without losing money," Dar said.

"I know that."

"Cut our costs to the bone. We don't have any padding, not one area that I can point to and say fluff."

"Dar, I know that too."

Dar thwacked another dart in the target, nailing the bull's-eye. "So why are we still on this call? What else do you want from me, Alastair? Want me to sell my desk? Have Kerry bake cupcakes and run a raffle for you? What?"

Another long sigh. "You could can those raises."

"No."

"Dar."

"No," Dar repeated firmly. "Take it out of my check if you want to. Those people deserve it."

Her boss grunted. "Hell of a time for you to be turning into Robin Hood."

The inner door to Dar's office cracked open, and a shaggy blond head poked inside. Dar's face responded with a wide grin, and she twirled a dart in silence, pointing at the phone and mock aiming at it. "Me, Robin Hood? Get out of here. I value my people as much as you value yours."

Kerry snapped her fingers in silence, and then pointed at Dar, biting her lip.

"Ahem." Alastair cleared his throat. "Walked into that one didn't I?" he admitted. "All right, but please, Dar, try to drum up something good at the convention, will ya? I need something other than bad news for the board meeting next month."

"Do what I can."

"I know I can count on you Dar," Alastair concluded. "Good luck."

The line clicked off. Dar rolled her eyes, as she waited none too patiently for Kerry to cross the carpet and arrive at her side. "Hey there."

"Hi." Kerry sat on the edge of Dar's desk, dangling her feet and allowing her moderate heels to slip off. "He sounds worried."

"He is," her partner agreed.

"You don't sound worried."

Dar flipped another dart at her board, a newly christened present from Kerry. "Wanna know the truth?' She searched Kerry's face intently. "I don't know how much I really care."

Kerry reached over and ran her fingers through Dar's thick, dark hair, moving the slightly shaggy bangs out of her pale blue eyes. "Yeah, I know," she murmured. Dar's tanned skin was a shade darker than her own, and there were several sun-lightened streaks in the locks her hand stirred.

Dar's lashes fluttered and she fiddled with a dart. "Ah, I still do care." She half shrugged. "I just can't take the whole thing so damn seriously anymore."

"It's okay," her partner said. "I have to admit I'm more excited about going back to Disney World with you than I am about the convention, so don't feel bad."

Dar peeked up at her. "Really?"

Kerry grinned wholeheartedly. "Yeah. I keep trying to figure out how we can run the display scenarios from our PDA's." She scratched Dar behind the ears with her fingertips. "How'd you like to go up a little early to check out the convention center?"

Dar slid open the flat drawer at the front of her desk and withdrew a folder, dexterously opening it with her thumb and displaying the contents.

"Mmm...I think those are plane tickets." Kerry cooed in delight.

"I think you're right," Dar agreed. "C'mon." She got up, curling her arm around Kerry's waist and drawing her up as well. "Let's go get some bags packed, Yankee."

Kerry amiably returned the hug, resting her head against Dar's shoulder and reflecting on her lover's surprise at finding their bags already packed. "Hey, Dar?"

"That's me."

"If we get a memory upgrade for my Palm, I really think I can run the data apps."

"While we go down the water slides?"

"Yeah."

Dar walked her toward the door, considering the question. "You'll need a waterproof case for it," she finally concluded. "I think the dive shop has them in blue."

Kerry only chuckled, as they walked through the door, and headed for the elevator.

AHH. KERRY CLOSED her eyes, and exhaled, enjoying the slight chill of the condo's air conditioning against her recently showered skin as she lounged on the couch. She could still faintly smell the spices of their stir-fry dinner in the air, and feel the ache of their joint sparring session in her upper arms.

Life was good. Even though she wasn't entirely sure she was going to really catch on to kickboxing, she found she loved every minute of the classes they were taking for it. It was a new skill for Dar as well, and the learning process felt exciting and fun.

Besides, Dar looked so cute in boxing gloves.

"Hey, Ker?"

Kerry opened one eye, and rotated it around toward Dar's bedroom. "Yeah?" She wiggled into a more comfortable position flat on her back on the couch, and waited.

"Think a T-shirt'll be okay on the plane?"

T-shirt. Kerry considered the question with due seriousness. "Tank top," she disagreed. "Like that nice pale blue one you had on the other day."

The faint scuff of bare footsteps intruded into the living room, accompanied by their maker. "What?" Dar queried, putting her hands on her hips. "The damn planes are air conditioned, Kerry."

"I know," she agreed readily. "But I really love you in that tank top, and if you get too cold, I can always warm you up." She studied the tall, lithe figure in its worn jeans and bra. "Or you could go like that."

Her lover sauntered over and took a seat on the edge of the couch, draping her arm over Kerry's hips and gazing affectionately at her. "Does that mean you'll wear your new suit on the plane then?" she asked, with a grin.

"The gray one?" Kerry hazarded. "Dar, it's sorta see through."

Dar grinned.

"Hm." Kerry slid her hand up the inside of Dar's thigh. "Nah, let's save it for the wave pool," she conceded. "I am so looking forward to this trip." Her face creased into an easy grin. "I have such cool memories of the last one."

The blue eyes twinkled brightly. "Me too," Dar said. "I wish we didn't have the stupid convention to deal with, but I guess it's as good an excuse as any to spend a week up there." She leaned a little against Kerry. "You all packed? Dad picked Chino up while you were in the shower."

"Yep, I'm all set. One medium-sized case full of fun clothes, and a garment bag for the monkey suits. You all ready? I'll go start up the buggy."

"Just have to put my shirt on." Dar leaned forward, smiling as Kerry's arms slipped around her neck and they kissed. After a few moments of increasing intensity, she braced herself and slid around, stretching out half beside, half over Kerry's body.

It was a good size couch, and they had a lot of practice fitting on it together. Dar kept up the kiss as she slowly eased her hand under the fabric of Kerry's cotton shirt, tracing a path up the center of her belly and ending up curling her fingers around the curve of Kerry's right breast.

Even after a year and a half, her body's reaction to Dar's gentle touch still grabbed Kerry right in the guts, making it hard to think straight. Kerry returned the attention, easier for her since there was nothing between her partner and herself except the thin silk of Dar's bra.

She loved the way Dar's body fit her hands. "We're gonna miss the plane," Kerry whispered, circling Dar's navel with her index finger.

"We can drive." Dar bit her earlobe gently. "My folks and I used to all the time."

Kerry lost herself in the rich scent of Dar's skin. She paused, and then poked her partner in the ribs very gently. "Know what?"

Dar went nose to nose with her, licking her lips with an attentive tongue. "What?"

"Let's drive." Kerry undid the top button on Dar's jeans. "It'll be fun." She let the rest of her thoughts drift away, burned off by the heat of passion igniting in her guts. "You... me..."

"Corn dogs on the turnpike. Yeah." Dar laughed softly. "I'm all for it."

Kerry laughed with her, and savored the touch of Dar's bare skin. She loved how Dar felt, loved the silky texture of her skin, and the light twitches of her reactions as Kerry's hands explored her.

She loved the low hum of approval when it tickled her ear, and the pressure as Dar slid her thigh between Kerry's and tugged off her shorts.

And you know, sometimes life just rocked.

TWO HOURS LATER, they were sitting side by side in Dar's Lexus, tooling down the Florida turnpike as the last of the sun disappeared behind the pines bordering the road. Kerry had the passenger seat pushed all the way back, and her bare feet propped up against the dashboard while Dar leaned back in a relaxed attitude with one hand on the wheel.

"Y'know, I think this really is a good idea," Kerry commented. After they'd been companionably silent for a few minutes, she chose a new CD to listen to. "We need a car up there anyway, and with all the time getting to the airport in Miami, and from the airport up there, it's probably a wash."

"Uh huh." Dar reached behind her, and removed a bottle of YooHoo from the cooler in the back seat. "And we've got better in-flight refreshments."

Kerry slid the CD into the drive and leaned back, circling one knee with her arms. She watched the passing scenery, and decided most of the state of Florida had a lot in common with parts of the state of Michigan in terms of flat terrain and boring horticulture. "Is it like this all the way up?"

Dar glanced around in the twilight. "Pretty much," she admitted. "We used to leave at 4:00 a.m. to get up here. Dad always said there wasn't nothing to look at, no sense in wasting sunlight on it," she recalled, shifting the car into the left lane to pass a dawdling truck. "You go on road trips much?"

Kerry laid her head back against the seat. "Not with my family, no," she replied, in a quiet tone. "But when we went to camp in the summer, yeah. All of us in the bus. That was kinda fun." A brief flash of civilization whipped by, a lone white house facing the road with an old, half-rusted bus in front of it. "It wasn't really a wild and crazy camp—it was from my school. But Angie and I counted the days till we went there and we were always sorry to leave."

Dar moved to the right again, and settled back. "Where was it?"

"Up in the mountains," her partner replied. "We had these precious little cabins with maid service twice a day, and a valet to do our laundry. You know." Her eyes slid sideways. "Well, no, you don't know, but I look back on it now, and realize how bloody damn pretentious it all was."

"Eh." Dar chuckled a little. "I went to the Y camp one or two summers, but when I got old enough, I went to the summer programs on base."

Kerry's lips twitched. "No valets, huh?"

"No." Dar shook her head. "You had kids who grew up on a military base, who had that mindset to begin with, and who lived in that culture. We did war games, camping, hunting..." A smile appeared. "I had a blast. It was one of the few times I remember just being really..." She paused.

"Happy?" Kerry guessed.

"Content," Dar amended. "Accepted, maybe." She moved to the left again to bypass a Lincoln Town car. "I was so damn sure that was the world I wanted."

"Well." Kerry swiped the bottle of YooHoo and took a swig. "I never felt that way at camp. I was just glad to be out from under my parents' eyes. It was all so damn fake. They had comportment classes, for Pete's sake."

"What?"

"How to walk, talk, and greet people without tripping and dumping your bad white wine on them," Kerry translated. "That and lanyard making. Jesus, do you know how many lanyards I made? Every damn color in the rainbow and let's not talk about the potholders."

Dar snickered. "You and I come from such different planets," she said. "Only thing I made in camp was a belt from old ammo cartridges I collected on the base and rifle webbing someone had thrown away." She glanced at Kerry, watching the corners of her mouth curve up in a smile. "I'd have taken a potholder and used it to wipe my..."

"Dar!"

"Hey, you know what choices you have out in the bush?" Dar said. "Now you know where I got my dislike of camping from."

Kerry burst out laughing. "Oh my god, you have no idea how funny that is. In our camp, one summer, they got the wrong toilet paper delivered. It was that brown craft paper kind of stuff they usually have in really bad rest stops?"

"Ow."

"Yeah." Kerry nodded, still chuckling. "Well, me, the little rebel that I was, stole a case of it, and led the rest of my cabin in TPing the lead counselor's house so badly you couldn't even see the door." She did a little dance in her seat. "Oo...oo...the little bitch turned red as a tomato and didn't talk to us for a week!"

"Troublemaker."

"Angie was so pissed at me." Kerry snickered. "But that woman already hated my guts so..."

"Why?" Dar asked, curiously.

Her partner paused in mid-thought. "I have no idea. She made me really uncomfortable. I figured she was trying to get something from my parents," Kerry said. "She gave me the creeps."

Dar watched the Lexus' powerful headlights carve up the road ahead of them for a long moment, and then she turned her head toward Kerry. "How old were you?"

"High school," Kerry replied. "Why?"

"Hm." Dar tapped her thumb against the steering wheel. "Ever think maybe she was interested in you?"

Kerry's brow creased. "Well, yeah—I mean, I said she was, Dar," she replied, then paused when she watched Dar's eyebrow hike up expressively. Realization hit, and she inhaled in slight surprise. "Oh. You mean...that kind of interested? Like...romantically?"

"Uh huh." Dar returned her attention to the road, flicking her eyes to the passing sign and noting its contents. "Wouldn't surprise me. You were cute in high school," she drawled, with a slight smile. "I've seen pictures."

Kerry remained absolutely silent for a few minutes, sucking absently on the neck of the YooHoo bottle as she watched the shadowed trees flash by. Finally, she snorted a little, half surprised and half disgusted. "Never would have crossed my mind," she admitted. "I think I...Brian and I had just started going out. I wouldn't even call it dating. It wasn't that serious. I probably would have freaked out if she'd..."

"Tried to seduce you?" Dar stretched out her free arm and laid it over Kerry's shoulders. "She'd have been an idiot, given your folks, but..." She scratched Kerry's neck with her fingertips. "You were really an adorable kid."

Kerry blushed slightly. "You know, I really never even thought anything like that. By that time, I'd learned just how far people would go to get in with my father, I just..." She exhaled. "Assumed she was more of the same."

"Well, maybe she was." Dar sensed her partner's discomfort. "I was only presenting another point of view." She tugged on Kerry's earlobe. "Want a pit stop?" She pointed to a sign indicating a rest stop ahead. "It's all commercial now, but I can show you where they used to sell the tackiest Florida souvenirs this side of Key Largo."

Kerry relaxed, and finished off the chocolate soda. "Sure," she agreed. "We've got plenty of time."

Dar signaled and pulled to the left, preparing to leave the highway.

After a second, she glanced at Kerry, not surprised to find herself being studied by those sea green eyes. She winked at her partner and was rewarded by a grin, which she returned.

The ride was turning out to be a darn sight more interesting than she'd remembered it.

PEOPLE WERE SO funny. Kerry leaned against the wall and watched some of their fellow travelers walk by. They were pretty much oblivious to everything on their way to get food, or drinks, or relieve themselves, and yet virtually every other one of them paused to look at the figure studying the turnpike map on the wall.

Of course, Kerry was doing the same thing, but she felt she had an innate right to, since the sleek body wrapped in faded denim and cotton tank top belonged to her partner. Dar's jeans were the old, ripped ones Kerry had found way back when for their biker school reunion. She had her tank top tucked in them and boy, she looked good.

She'd recently gotten her second summer haircut, and it left most of her shoulders bare. The last few months of their life had been a lot of work, true, but almost every weekend spent down at the cabin and their new gym classes had given Dar a deeper tan and added a little more muscle to her tall frame.

Mm.

The rest stop was an interesting combination of retail outlet and tourist hard pitch. Kerry wandered around in the main lobby, examining the racks of leaflets as she sucked on a cone full of frozen strawberry yogurt. Florida was definitely both tourist driven, and eclectic, and she riffled through advertisements for things as varied as a mystery house where things ran uphill, to Monkey Jungle, to Weeki Watchee. "Paladar?"

"Yes?" Dar's voice erupted from right behind her, even after all this time making Kerry jump. "You rang?"

"What the heck is a Weeki Watchee?" Kerry selected the lurid pamphlet from the rack and held it up. "It looks like a mermaid farm."

"Sorta," Dar agreed. "It's a place where mermaids give shows, and sell trinkets."

"Mermaids?" Her partner eyed her. "Not manatees?"

"Mermaids," Dar assured her, pointing at the colorful page. "Women in fish tail costumes with big breasts."

Kerry stared at the advertisement. "And people go there? Really?"

"Well." Her partner examined the ad. "They have nice gardens, too, and I think a snack bar."

Kerry giggled, and wandered off, shaking her head. The rest stop was a relatively small place, with a central lobby that had restaurants off either side, and a set of surprisingly clean restrooms. There was also a gift shop, where you could, if for some reason you had forgotten to purchase candy oranges or bright pink flamingo Christmas lights somewhere else, obtain those last minute gifts to bring back home with you.

Hm. "Snow globes." Kerry selected one and shook it, amused by the white plastic flakes drifting down on the palm trees and beach. A flash of motion caught her eye and she glanced to one side, spotting her own reflection in the mirrored back of the display case.

The neatly pressed, carefully ironed and tucked prep she'd once been now was gone. Kerry felt her eyebrows lifting as she reviewed her cutoff, ragged shorts and long, faded T-shirt.

Correction, long faded T-shirt that didn't even belong to her. She'd also let her hair grow out longer than usual, not really out of control, but giving it a touch of shagginess she hadn't had since she'd been small. The overall effect, given her tan and the sun bleaching of her already pale locks, was that of a beach rat caught out shopping.

"So, rat...get shopping," Kerry cheerfully directed herself, toasting her reflection with her yogurt.

She spotted a stuffed alligator and picked it up, finding herself smiling at its toothy cotton visage. She tucked the toy under her arm and continued browsing. To her booty, she added a package of chocolate covered orange slices and a T-shirt before she dropped it all down on the counter and removed her wallet from the back pocket of her shorts. "Hi."

"Hi," the cashier replied. "Yawannalotta?"

Kerry blinked. "Excuse me?"

"Yawannalotta? Big this week."

At a total loss, Kerry instinctively looked around for her native guide, who plunked down a twenty dollar bill on the counter. "She'll take three," Dar pronounced, "and take the rest of this Floridiana out of that."

"Three of what?" Kerry whispered.

"Sure." The cashier took the money and rang up Kerry's purchases. She gave Dar back some change, then punched in some numbers in a black machine nearby and handed over the resulting pink and white tickets. "There ya go. Ya'll have a great old day."

"Thanks." Dar took the tickets, the change, the bag, and a totally befuddled Midwesterner and hauled them all out of the gift shop and out into the lobby. "Here. Put your Lotto tickets away. If you win on 'em, I get ten percent."

"My what?" Kerry took the tickets and examined them. "Oh!" She nibbled her cone. "Jesus, you know in all this time down here I never bothered to buy one of these things?" She followed Dar outside, trading the stinging chill of the air conditioning for the warm soup of the night air. "Thank you for buying my junk, sweetheart. You didn't have to do that. I've got my wallet."

Next to them, a minivan with Dade County plates had just parked, and the side door slid open allowing a gaggle of children to emerge. They bolted for the doors to the building, with a harried looking woman chasing after them. In the back of the van Mickey Mouse droppings were squeezed into every square inch.

A man got out of the driver's side and shut the door with an air of martyred exhaustion. He glanced at Kerry and Dar and gave them a civil nod before he trudged after his family.

Dar watched him go. "Think it'd be cruel to tell him he's going in the wrong direction?"

Kerry peered after him, then glanced at the big "Northbound" sign over the door. "What if he isn't, and that's all just from last time?" She pointed at the van. "And you didn't answer me about buying my stuff."

"Uh huh." Dar unlocked the Lexus, tossing the booty inside on the rear seat. "You bought dinner." She glanced at the van again. "Mom had a point."

"About?"

"Only one." Dar pointed at her chest and slid into the driver's seat.

"Ah. Hm. Yeah." Kerry got in on the passenger side and settled comfortably into the big leather seat. "That restaurant was pretty good, wasn't it? I really liked those spices they used."

Dar sucked up a mouthful of milkshake and set her cup into its holder before she started up the car. "It was pretty good, but yours is better," she said. "I like those crunchy things you put in."

"Peanuts?" Kerry chuckled. "Or do you mean the water chestnuts?"

"Whatever it is." Dar backed carefully out of the spot she'd parked in, and navigated her way through the parking lot and past the massive truck park. "I like it." She let an aggressively speeding Volvo pass them by, and then got into the merge lane to return to the turnpike.

"Careful, Roberts. If it's the water chestnuts that's almost a vegetable."

"Pfft." Dar stuck her tongue out. Once on the road, she leaned back in her seat and relaxed, enjoying Kerry's nearby presence and the prospect of spending the long trip at her side.

It was quiet. The roads were nearly empty now that they'd left the more populated part of Florida, and at the end of the drive there was some serious fun waiting for her.

Life was good. Dar tapped the side of her thumb against the wheel and nodded a little to the music coming out of the speakers. "So, what did you think about that bird theory?"

Kerry had shed her sandals, and now had her bare feet propped up on the dashboard again. "Dar, did you know that it's pretty darn likely you'd have been tied to a tree and beaten to death by the teachers at my high school just for thinking about the bird theory?"

Dar looked at her. Both eyebrows shot up. "What did they have against birds?"

"Nothing." Kerry neatly nibbled an exact circle around her cone.

"But boy, did they have a problem with Darwin."

"Ah."

"Mm." Kerry agreed. "You know something, it's funny, but I think that was the first time I found myself questioning the absolute nature of my religion," she mused. "I remember seeing something—on PBS, I guess—about species evolution, and the way they explained it, it just made so much sense, Dar."

"Uh huh. Always pissed me off they insisted on calling it the theory of evolution instead of the science of it," Dar agreed. "I had this argument with someone on base about it and the woman wanted to have me jailed for heresy."

"Mm." Kerry nodded. "That's about what happened to me when I went into school the next day and started asking my teachers about it. Hooboy." She finished up her treat and dusted her fingertips off. "But you know, for me it never caused a problem if I bought into evolutionary science but still believed in God, and in Jesus and the Bible," she continued. "Seeing the exquisite wonder of how life works, how could anyone not believe in a higher power?"

Dar stretched her arm across the divider and let it rest casually on Kerry's shoulders. "It's easy for people to get stuck in a narrow view, Ker. You know that. Even those guys, the scientists—they were practically fist fighting over the idea that dinosaurs evolved into birds...and it's so structurally obvious." Dar's voice grew a touch more animated. "All you have to do is look at those carnivorous dinosaurs, and look at an ostrich, and it's right there in your face."

"Dinosaurs into birds, lizards into snakes, proto-hominids into us..." Kerry mused. "Whoops...guess I'm going to hell for that last one. Again." She chuckled. "Hey, what did you think about that one we saw the other night about humans being water mammals during their evolution?"

The theory was an interesting one, Dar conceded. "Navy brat's the wrong person to ask about that," she joked. "I always assumed I was some kind of freak otter." Her face grew faintly introspective. "For me, the water was always home."

"Yeah," Kerry agreed, with a smile. "You're so natural underwater. I thought of you when I was watching that show. I wish I felt that comfortable."

"Give it time," Dar advised her. "I've been diving since I was two."

Leaning back, Kerry tipped her head to one side and regarded the thick, black night sky. It was fun to just sit and talk. Dar had an active, intelligent mind and she was as curious about many things as Kerry was. Keeping your mind in a learning state, she'd realized, made you a lot better at whatever you did. You were always open to new ideas, and new ways of looking at things. "Hey Dar?"

"Yeeeesss?"

"Wanna play 'what is it?'"

"Okay." Dar grinned. "You start." She gave Kerry a few microseconds. "Animal, vegetable, or mineral?"

"Would I pick a vegetable for you to guess? Give me a minute."

Dar drummed her fingers on the wheel and waited, humming under her breath, already anticipating the game. Would it be an animal? Kerry liked animals. She'd pick a strange one though.

Platypus duck, maybe?

Chapter
Two

THEY ARRIVED AT the convention center later than Dar had originally planned. The building was lit on the outside though, and there were both security guards, and a stir of motion about the place that reassured them.

Dar strolled across the front courtyard, approaching the doors and making eye contact with the guards. "Evening," she greeted the first one cordially, as she removed her ID from her back pocket and offered it up.

The man studied the card, and then glanced at her. "Dock entrance is round back," he told her politely.

One finely arched dark eyebrow lifted. "Excuse me?"

"Construction workers enter in the back," the guard clarified, still with careful politeness.

Dar looked down at herself, then up at the guard. "Do I look like a construction worker to you?"

"Yes, ma'am," the man replied. "You can enter in the back."

Kerry covered her mouth to keep in the laughter threatening to burst out. The expression on her lover's face was so priceless.

"This is not funny," Dar told her, testily.

"C'mon." Kerry swallowed her amusement, taking Dar's arm and starting for the rear of the center. "No point in arguing with him, Dar. Call the convention services group in the morning and have the entire company fired." She let her voice raise slightly, enough to know that the guard would hear her.

"Do I look like a construction worker to you?" Dar ignored the speech, turning and giving her an indignant look.

"Absolutely not," Kerry reassured her. "It's must be the tank top and ripped jeans, sweetie. Orlando is obviously not ready for CIO's in less than pin stripes." She took Dar's arm again and patted it. "C'mon." Out of the corner of her eye, she could see the guard's eyes turning into round saucers. "I bet if you really tried, you could get the entire convention services company kicked out. Wouldn't that be fun?"

Dar's eyes narrowed suddenly. "You're having fun freaking the guard out, aren't you?" she uttered, in a low voice.

"Yes." Kerry smiled charmingly at her. "Give me two more minutes, and he'll need a change of shorts." She waggled her fingers at the man. "He deserves it for being a prick butt with the vision of a rhino in the dark."

Dar snickered, her humor restored. She draped her arm over Kerry's shoulders and headed toward the rear of the building, leaving the hapless guard behind them. Her ego was still stinging from the man's remark, though, and she was self aware enough to know it.

"Jerk." Kerry held the gate open that lead into the loading dock and waited for Dar to pass through. "What could he be thinking, Dar? Let's just say it was true."

"What?"

"Shh. Let's just say you were one of the setup crew," Kerry pacified her prickly partner. "It's nearly midnight. Who cares if you go in the front door? Who's gonna see you, the cleaning staff?" She closed the gate behind them and followed Dar toward an open loading dock door, the sounds of hammering and banging clearly audible inside.

"I don't know, and I don't give a damn," Dar grumbled, as they crossed from the warm night air into the cooler, but musty smelling building. Lit by fluorescent lights, and featuring a poured concrete floor it resembled the inside of a warehouse more than anything.

Which, of course, it basically was. Kerry's nose wrinkled at the scent of mildew coming from a set of draperies dropped in a pile near the door. "Nice."

"Maybe they'll have a sledgehammer I could borrow," Dar muttered.

"Dar." Kerry patted her on the behind. "Would you relax? He was full of horse poots. Don't tell me you're getting so sensitive in your old age."

Her partner scowled dourly.

"Okay." Kerry could see a pile of people ahead of them, all busy. She took hold of Dar's arm and pulled her to a halt barely inside the loading area, out of sight of the main room. "Sweetheart." It really wasn't like Dar to be so sensitive, and Kerry sensed a moment taken here would pay off in the long run. "Did that really bother you?"

Her taller partner leaned against the wall, and scrubbed one hand through her hair. "Stupid, isn't it?" she admitted, lifting her eyes. "Just hit me the wrong way, I guess... and I don't even have the excuse of it being that time of the month."

Kerry tucked her fingers into the waistband of Dar's jeans. "Listen, I asked you to wear this because I think it's really sexy." She tugged a little. "And I didn't marry a construction worker." She paused, considering. "Though, I would have if you'd been one."

"Would you?" Dar grudgingly smiled.

"Absolutely." Kerry gazed up at her. "You know I would."

Dar's expression gentled. "I know." She looked down. "And given I picked a pair of boots to wear that I used when we were painting the cabin, I guess he might have had a point."

"Hm."

"Tank top, ripped jeans, paint splattered hiking boots...all I need is a tattoo and I could pass as a very good butch stereotype."

Okay, crisis over. Kerry relaxed, and smiled. "Nah, you'd need leather pants for that."

"I have those," Dar reminded her. "But you'd have to arrest me to get me to wear them in summer." She bumped Kerry's knee with her own. "C'mon. Let's go see what the kids are doing, and get the hell out of here."

They walked through the open garage door and into the convention center, pausing for a moment to catch their bearings. The room was huge, and it was full of nerds. The smell of new computers mixed with the scent of old coffee was almost overwhelming.

"Whoa." Kerry rubbed her nose. "What a zoo."

"Uh huh." Dar stretched to her full height, reviewing the room. It was laid out in regulation trade show fashion, with wooden frame booths stretched in orderly rows interspersed with larger displays custom built by some of the bigger companies. "Ah. There we are." She pointed to a familiar logo banner, half hung, half draped over some metal pipe supports.

"Nice spot." Kerry followed her between two wooden stalls, ducking as a technician struggled with a projection screen and almost clocked her in the process. They walked through piles of equipment cases, and emerged into a more open area that held the ILS display.

It was definitely one of the bigger ones. It held pride of place in the center of the largest open aisle and spread out in a series of ovals to either side.

Four of their techs were on ladders trying to lift up and bolt into place the steel tube framing the marketing department had designed, and as they watched the heavy structure tilted precariously to one side. Without a word between them, Kerry and Dar reacted, leaping forward to help.

Kerry grabbed the nearest ladder, which had started to tip over, while Dar used her greater height to reach up and take hold of the steel frame, taking its weight as the techs fought to regain control over it. "Whoa!" Kerry grunted, throwing her body against the ladder as it threatened to come down on top of her. "Take it easy, guys!"

"Damn it!" the tech on her ladder cursed. "This piece of shit was built by freaking Gumby!"

"All right, hang on." Dar grabbed the ladder and climbed up several of the steps, hoisting the frame with her as she walked. "Get that end on there, Bruce."

The tech on the next ladder blinked, only then realizing who it was addressing him. "Holy crap!" he blurted. "When'd you get here, ma'am!"

"Just in time, apparently," Dar grunted. "You gonna bolt that into place, or are we all going to end up with our asses on the concrete? I can't hold this forever."

Kerry could hear the tension in her partner's voice, and beneath the worn denim, she could see Dar's legs straining to keep her load balanced. With Dar's weight on the ladder, though, it no longer threatened to tip over and she shifted her grip to wrap her arm around Dar's calves in a secure hold.

"Okay...okay...almost got it." Bruce panted, extending himself out on his ladder to put a socket wrench on the bolts that Dar was holding even. He ratcheted them quickly, muscles jumping under his skin as he tightened the grid into place on one end. "Done!"

Dar relaxed her hold cautiously, relieved when the structure seemed likely to stay in one place. She flexed her fingers and shook her arms out glancing up at the tech still perched on the steps above her. "Why the hell are you guys doing this?"

Bruce finished bolting down the other end of the structure then scampered down the ladder. He was of middling height, and lightly built, with wide brown eyes that had a perpetual look of astonishment in them. "We gotta get the booth up ma'am." He paused. "Don't we?"

Dar got off her ladder, and dusted her hands off as the tech above her gingerly climbed down as well. "They don't have a setup crew here?" She looked around, aware now that at many booths around them conspicuously corporate T-shirted crews were struggling to assemble the structures. "What the hell? Kerry, didn't we contract for this to be built?"

"Well," Kerry cleared her throat, "I don't have the paperwork in front of me, but I'm willing to bet I didn't expect our setup staff to handle the carpentry."

"Hmph."

Kerry ducked out from under the ladder and joined her, as the rest of their techs gathered around. "Hi, guys," she greeted them with a smile, keeping an eye on Dar who started investigating their surroundings like a large, suspicious house cat.

"Hey, boss." The one nearest her returned the smile, his blond head not topping her own by much. "What are you guys doing here? Mark said you'd be up in a few days."

"Eh." Kerry put her hands on her hips. "We decided to come up a little early. Did they say why no one was here from the production company? You guys shouldn't be doing this. Dar's right. We pay big bucks to have someone else come in to do it."

"Well," Bruce sidled over to her, "we got here a couple hours ago, and the guy in charge told us if we wanted anything else put up, we'd have to do it," he said, with a tiny shrug. "Everyone here was bitching for sure, but what could we do?"

"Call?" Kerry eyed him, spreading her hands out in question. "It's not like my cell phone number's a secret."

The blond tech next to him winced. "We didn't want you to think we were whiners. It's not that much to do. Get those pipes up so we can start cabling. Not like the other guys, they're trying to get that wood together without hardly any tools."

"Mm." Kerry shook her head. "The guys in charge, they still here?"

"No way." Bruce snorted. "They took off and left the guards out front. Bunch of...um..." He remembered whom he was talking to and his voice trailed off.

"We met them," his boss muttered. "They didn't make a very good impression on us. Hey, Dar?"

Her partner had wandered over to the next booth, and was talking to its occupants. She held a hand up to acknowledge Kerry's call, but continued her conversation. "Well, anyway, we can help you get set up," Kerry told the techs. "What's up next, those poles over there?" She pointed.

Dar returned before they could get started, and she didn't look happy. "The Lucent guys say they heard the center didn't pay their setup crew for the last convention or something, so they walked," she reported. "They're pretty torked. According to their lead tech, the center basically told them they could wait until tomorrow, when maybe they'd have some workers, or do it themselves and shut up."

"Nice," Kerry muttered, "very professional."

Bruce nodded. "That's what they told us too," he agreed. "So we talked about it, and decided to see what we could do. We didn't want you guys to get here and not have stuff ready."

Dar sighed. "So instead, you get to have us show up and help you haul cable. It'll make a good story back at the office. Let's go. Faster we do it, faster we get out of here."

Kerry walked over and claimed a spool of cable and a wrench. "Are those the switches over there?" She pointed at a stack of brown cardboard boxes with a familiar label on them. "Cody, why don't you start unpacking them."

"Speaking of..." Dar turned, and then tipped her head back. "Let me guess. They didn't pull any Telco drops, did they?"

"Nope," Bruce said. "That was going to be a real problem," he admitted. "Mark didn't send any WAN guys up here."

"Not a problem anymore." Kerry tossed Dar a punch down kit, which her partner fielded with consummate grace. "I think the jack boxes are over on that pole, Dar." She nudged Bruce toward the remaining not-yet-hung structure. "Let's go guys—move those ladders over."

Dar removed a pen from her pocket and scribbled down the jack numbers on the pole Kerry had spotted. She paused when she saw several people standing near the back entrance watching them.

None were familiar, but if she squinted, she could make out the logo on the nearest one's shirt. "Ahh," Dar murmured, "our low-balling adversaries." The faintest twinkle appeared in her eyes, as she stuffed the bit of paper she'd written on in her back pocket, and headed for the

Telco room, which they'd passed on their way in.

Two of the newcomers walked on past her into the room, sparing her only cursory glances. The other three remained at the entrance, talking amongst themselves with sour looks on their faces. They absently returned Dar's nod of greeting, then dismissed her as she walked by and continued talking to each other.

"I'd love to take off, but I want to wait till ILS gets their system set up, and then see what we can find out about it. Those guys look like they'll talk our ears off." The one nearest the booth—a well-built man with thick, black hair who had the air of a manager—pointed toward the ILS area. "Maybe we can recruit some of 'em...I heard they're looking at layoffs."

The other man laughed. "Typical. Cut the people who do the real work and protect the do-nothing executives."

He probably would have stopped, if he'd bothered to turn around and see the ice blue eyes drilling unseen holes in the back of his head, but his attention was focused on the booth and so he missed the rude gesture as well.

"You go for the guys. I'll take that babe with the cables." The shorter man also laughed. "I'll give 'em one thing, they hire for looks. She's hot."

Dar glanced at the kit in her hands, and opened it, selecting a pair of needle nose pliers and studying them, wondering how much jail time she'd incur if she pulled the bastard's gonads out with the tool. Then she sighed, and put it back, turning and continuing on her way with commendable restraint.

Work before pleasure. Their time would come soon enough.

"HERE YOU GO, guys." Kerry eased back into their booth, cradling a half dozen cans of soda in a pouch made from the long tail of her T-shirt. The techs gathered around her shyly selecting their choices as Kerry stood in their midst. "C'mon, they're cold."

"Thanks, ma'am." Bruce sat down on a switch, wiping his brow.

Two hours had gone by, and they'd finished the structure of the booth only to realize the center had turned off its air conditioning.

It had rapidly gone from relatively comfortable to stuffy to stifling before Dar had hoisted her pirate's pennant and found the A/C control room. She got busy picking the lock and flipping switches inside until the units turned themselves back on.

Now the air was sluggishly circulating again, and Dar had gone back to methodically hacking her way through the unlabeled circuits in search of the one they'd ordered.

"Okay." Kerry sat down with her own soda and opened it, taking a long swallow before she continued. She was sweaty and covered in dust, and her knee ached where she'd banged it on the corner of a switch, but as she looked around at their progress, she was satisfied. "Once we get the line up, we're pretty much done until the servers get here tomorrow."

The techs looked tired, but relieved. "Think the circuit'll be up tonight?" Bruce asked.

"Oh, I'm sure it will." Kerry leaned back and extended her legs, crossing them at the ankles and regarding their bare length studiously. "Even if Dar has to run a fiber cable all the way to Miami, it'll be up." She looked up at her troops, with a grin. "I have faith."

The four techs grinned back.

"Thanks for stopping by and giving us a hand, ma'am. That was really cool," Cody said.

"No problem." Kerry glanced to one side as a motion caught her attention, and stopped speaking when she spotted a pod of their competitors approaching. She watched them as they came over, observing the booth with intent eyes. "Hi."

"Hi," the man in front greeted her with a friendly grin. "You guys sure have been busy."

"Hasn't everyone?" Kerry replied. "What a mess, huh?"

"Yeah," the man agreed. "We're going to wait for some help tomorrow to put things up, but I guess you folks decided to do it yourself, huh?"

Kerry glanced around at their booth. "Looks like it," she agreed. "We can take off and go to sleep in peace now."

The man stuck his hands in his pockets and chuckled. "Yeah, I'm sure you guys have to be careful about that. I hear things are up in the air for you. You don't want to take any chances, huh?"

The techs all looked at Kerry, who looked at the man with gently inquisitive green eyes. "Pardon me?" she asked.

"Ah, c'mon, we've heard about your problems...hell, we caused some of 'em!" The man laughed. "No hard feelings. In fact, you guys look pretty bright. Interested in coming over to the other side?"

Kerry's eyebrows lifted. The rest of her troops remained prudently quiet, apparently quite satisfied to let her do the talking. "I have no beef with who pays me," she said. "What about you folks?" Her eyes shifted to her techs.

"We're fine," Bruce replied. "No gripes here," he added, as the rest of the techs shook their heads.

"Now, come on." The man lifted both hands up. "Here you are, sweating like pigs, busting your humps to get this all running, and the guys who make the big bucks are sitting on their asses in some leather chair in a penthouse. That how you like things?"

Bruce giggled, his eyes fastened on Kerry's disheveled figure, which had started taking on distinct lines of angry tension. "Ah huh..."

"That's not how our company works," the man said, apparently oblivious.

"That's not really how our company works either," Kerry replied in a quiet tone.

"Yeah? When was the last time you saw your boss pick up a cable?" the man countered. "I bet you never have."

Kerry's lips twitched into a reluctant grin. "I bet you're wrong," she said, as she spotted Dar's distinctive figure approaching the group. Her lover looked harassed, but triumphant, and she brushed past the intruders as she picked up an interface cable and shoved it into place. "We up?"

"Son of a bitch piece of shit, half-assed infrastructure," Dar growled, plugging in their router and booting it up. "I'm surprised the damn sixty-six block wasn't put together with grape bubble gum."

"So, we're up." Kerry interpreted the cursing. The techs all clapped and whistled.

Dar studied the lights, and then grunted. "Yes." She dusted her hands off and gave the two strangers a dour look. "Excuse me." She sat down next to Kerry and examined the palm of one hand, which was covered in dust and scraped raw. After a second, she looked back up at the men. "You want something?" she snapped.

Caught off guard, their jaws dropped. "Ah, no, just visiting. Listen, you guys take it easy, okay? Come talk if you're interested in what I had to say." The man in front lifted his hand and waved it. Then he stepped forward and offered it to Kerry. "My name's Robert Caustens, and I'm the director of IT, for Telegenics."

Kerry readily took his hand and gripped it. "Kerry," she replied. "Nice to meet you. Hope you get things straightened out."

The two men left.

"Jesus." Kerry shook her head. "How unprofessional was that?"

"He pitch you?" Dar inquired, her eyes flicking to the rest of the techs in question.

"Yes, ma'am." Cody nodded. "Said we shouldn't work for a company where the big shots stay up in their ivory towers." He blinked at Dar, keeping a straight face. "It was pretty funny."

Dar extended her boots, and let her scraped hands rest on her knees. "You know, that's just damn hilarious." She glanced at Kerry. "Are we supposed to be in a tower? How come you didn't tell me that? What the hell am I doing here covered in dust then?"

Kerry patted her on the shoulder. "They forgot to put that in our contracts, honey."

Dar sighed. "And how come he didn't pitch me?"

"I dunno, boss. Maybe you scared him." Kerry took Dar's right hand and turned it over. "I think you have a splinter here. Let me get it out."

"Thanks." Dar relaxed. "Okay, let's get cleaned up here, gentlemen, and get the hell out of this damn garage."

Bruce got up and straightened the router, while the rest of the techs began tidying up the space. Kerry bent her head over her task, straining to see clearly in the annoying florescent light.

"Are those the guys who took those accounts?" Cody asked Dar, shyly. "That everyone was so pissed about?"

"Mm." Dar nodded. "They're an upstart company. Only came onto the scene this past year, targeting a bunch of contracts coming up for renewal. Not just us. We got slammed pretty bad, though our other friends..." Dar pointed to the right, where another of their bigger rivals was setting up. "Lost a couple too."

"Are they that good?" Bruce asked.

"They're that cheap," Dar replied. "That's their pitch — that they're lean and mean, and they can service the contracts at a lower cost." She regarded Kerry's pale head. "Which on a small scale they can, if everything runs perfectly.

"Like when does that ever happen?" Kerry muttered.

Bruce was mounting the switch they'd brought into a rolling cabinet with a locking door, as Cody helped him. "But they tell that to everyone," he said. "So — they can do it for one company at one time, but they can't do it for all their companies every time."

Dar produced a warm, sexy grin. "You got it," she complimented him. "It's like the stock market. You can't get hung up over the short term."

"The sales guys are worried," Cody commented. "I heard them talking in the lunch room."

"I know." Dar nodded. "It's not a comfortable situation. But panicking won't solve it. Our difference in the market is the quality of our work. If we stoop to their level, we risk that. It's not worth it."

The techs studied her with solemn faces.

"There." Kerry straightened, smoothing her thumb over the roughened skin on her partner's palm. "That wasn't a splinter, Dar, it was metal," she said. "And it might have been rusty. We should go get you some first aid."

"Thanks, Dr. Kerry." Dar gave her an affectionate look, bumping her shoulder lightly. "Well, I think we're done here. Let the marketing wonks crawl all over this place in the morning." She glanced at the techs. "You guys got a ride to your hotel?"

"Um...I think there's a shuttle," Bruce said, hesitantly, checking his watch.

"C'mon." Dar got up, clasping Kerry's hand in her own and hauling her up as well. "It's gonna be crowded, but we'll get there." She straightened to her full height, looking around. Most of the crews had given up and left, and they were virtually alone in the cavernous chamber, only a few other teams still making desultory attempts at completing their set ups. "Good job, everyone."

Bruce peeked up at her. "Ma'am?" he said. "I think you all did most of it."

"Us?" Kerry drawled in response. "Nah. We're up in our ivory tower, remember? In our nice leather chairs, eating...um..."

"Quiche." Dar patted the rolling case. "Or caviar."

"Ick." Kerry's nose wrinkled. "I'll pass. How about a pizza, instead?"

The techs all chuckled, as they followed their two leaders toward the back door, after Bruce double checked the locks on the rolling cabinets. They passed a few stragglers, but didn't see any of their friends from Telegenics, and the area they'd been setting up in was dark and quiet.

Outside was dark and quiet too. The guard at the back door watched them as they left. They circled the building and headed for Dar's lonely looking Lexus. Buzzing came from crickets in the bushes ringing the parking area, and Dar made her car chirp in response as she remotely unlocked the doors.

"Someone want to let Kerry sit on their lap?" Dar asked, as they reached the car.

Four sets of stunned eyes faced her in such evident shock it made her smile. "Didn't think so." She opened the rear hatch, and shoved their bags over. "One of you in here, the rest in the back. It's not a long trip."

"You're so bad." Kerry opened the front passenger door.

Dar watched the crowd pile in, and then she opened her own door, pausing when a motion across the parking lot caught her attention. A car was parked near the front door of the center, and as she watched, two figures got out and headed for the guarded front door.

Dar blinked, and leaned forward a little. Despite the distance and the darkness, she recognized them both, a knowledge that brought a faint grimace to her face and a knot to her stomach.

"Dar?" Kerry called her.

"Yeah." Dar slid into the driver's seat. "See that?" She pointed to the two figures. "Recognize them?"

Kerry peered through the glass. "Um...not really...oh." She sat up. "Isn't that Michelle Graver?"

"Uh huh." Dar nodded. "Sure is."

"Didn't she go into business on her own? You told me that, I thought."

"Uh huh," Dar said again. "Found herself a new partner, apparently." Her face could have been cut in ice, the angles were so cold. "They might even deserve each other." She started up the Lexus, and put it into gear. "Looks like Shari's finally found a kindred spirit."

Kerry's jaw clicked shut audibly.

Dar pulled out of the parking spot and drove slowly past the parked car, which bore a blazon on the driver's side door. She chuckled humorlessly as she read it, and heard a sound of mixed consternation and disgust come from Kerry.

"Son of a bitch." She picked up speed and drove past the front door, where the guard was courteously opening the glass for the two women. "Telegenics."

"Holy crap," Kerry uttered. "You have got to be kidding me."

"Now isn't that a kettle of stinking fish." Dar tapped her thumbs on the steering wheel. "Why is this such a damn surprise?"

"Something wrong, boss?" Cody asked hesitantly from the back seat.

"Oh, no." Kerry leaned back in her seat and crossed her arms. "Everything's peachy." Her eyes slid to Dar's profile. "Juuuust peachy," she repeated. "You don't think they'd mess with our stuff, do you?"

Dar paused at the exit to the lot, leaning on the steering wheel and considering. "No." She continued her turn, moving out onto the main road. "They probably don't think they need to right now."

"But you'll set up a monitor when we get to the hotel."

"Yeah," Dar muttered. "We better send someone in early to check the setup. Just in case."

Kerry sighed. "This is going to suck."

"Oh, yeah." Dar smiled grimly. She relaxed, and leaned back, the knots in her gut easing. "Ah, hell with them. Wait till they see the wreck their booth's in." She changed the subject, aware of the techs listening.

"And the wreck ours isn't in." Kerry grinned.

"It would almost be worth being there to see their faces. Almost," Dar acknowledged, glad of the car's cold air conditioning against her, and looking forward to the shower she knew was at the end of the ride.

Kerry reached over the seat divider and laid a hand on her knee, the green eyes full of a promise she knew was also waiting there.

To hell with them. "Let 'em sweat. I turned off the A/C before we left."

Kerry muffled a laugh. The techs joined in, not really sure what was going on, but willing to follow Kerry's lead anyway.

They drove on into the night, leaving the blazing lights of the convention center behind them.

"THANKS." DAR PASSED the valet a tip, shaking her head when he went to remove her luggage and Kerry's from the back. "No, that stays with us." She shut the hatch and walked around to the driver's side door.

"Aren't we staying here?" Kerry laid one hand on the frame of the car door, giving Dar an inquisitive look. "I thought we had reservations." She glanced up at the tall, respectable looking hotel they were parked in front of, having let the techs out.

"No." Dar got in and closed the door, waiting for Kerry to do likewise. "I have other plans."

"Ah. Okay." Kerry got in and leaned her elbow on the seat arm, watching her partner's profile as Dar pulled out of the Marriott's driveway, and headed back out onto the mostly empty roads. "I see." She evaluated the half hidden smirk, and decided whatever Dar's plan was, she'd appreciate it. "Telegenics. Big surprise, huh?"

Dar snorted. "You'd have thought the detail analysis Mark did would have tossed THAT little bit of intelligence up to the top. Did we miss it?" she wondered. "No way. He'd have flagged it, at the very least."

"Yeah, I don't get it," Kerry agreed. "How did that slip past? Maybe not Shari, but definitely Michelle should have been in the filters. Right?"

"I don't..." Dar paused, as she thought. "Maybe not, Ker. Did we consider them a business threat? Personal pain in the ass for us, yes, but for the company?"

"Good point." Kerry reached idly over and pushed a bit of Dar's hair back behind one well-shaped ear. "I'd say they targeted us, but you know they didn't. There've been other companies hit by them too."

"Exactly." Dar nibbled her lower lip a she thought. "Didn't think Shari had any interest in the IT field."

One of Kerry's blond eyebrows lifted. "I'd say she had a very significant interest in a specific part of the IT field," she remarked dryly. "Maybe she saw an opportunity to poach two eggs in one cup."

Dar looked at her. "You calling me an egghead?"

They both laughed, relieving the tension. "Ah." Dar shrugged. "So it'll make it interesting. Helps, sort of. At least I know some of their motives and more than one of their tactics." She wrapped her hands around the steering wheel and flexed her fingers. "A tisket a tasket..."

"Pair of bitches in a basket." Kerry warbled back at her, joining Dar in another round of pretty darn close to giddy laughter. "Jesus, it's late." She finally sighed. "I'm losing it. We're losing it." Her fingers curled around Dar's bicep, and she leaned her head against her shoulder. "So, where are we going?"

"Same place we went last time," Dar said, "for a lot of reasons," she went on, evidently realizing Kerry was staring at her. "First off, if I want to ravish you on the balcony, then I really don't want to worry about someone whose paycheck I sign watching from the next one." She cleared her throat. "Second..."

"Ahahahaha." Kerry reached over and covered her mouth. "Whoa. That one's enough for me."

Dar smiled, feeling the pressure as Kerry's fingers gently tweaked her skin. After a moment, she was released. "I want to wake up with you wrapped around me, and not have you almost pass out from the horror of it all."

"Ahhh." Kerry chuckled softly under her breath. "Oh, do I remember that." She half covered her face with one hand. "If I could have crawled through the floor of that room, I would have." She reminisced wryly. "You have no idea how I almost levitated off the bed when I woke up—only thing that kept me from freaking out was knowing I'd wake YOU up if I did."

Dar turned onto the access road that led to their destination. "I think I knew, even in my sleep," she said. "I was dreaming about snuggling."

Kerry peered at her from the corner of her eye. "Were you really?"

Dar nodded. "It felt wonderful. Then I woke up, and it was gone. I was pissed."

"I remember." A slow smile crossed Kerry's face. "You said it was a hangover." She paused. "Wait a minute—how did you know? I never did ask you that...was it only a lucky guess?"

Dar reached out and riffled her fingers through Kerry's pale hair. "You left evidence," she replied. "But yeah, it was half a guess. You were acting like you'd gotten caught in the cookie jar."

"Hmph." Kerry managed a dignified look, which swiftly dissolved into a sheepish grin. "I felt really, really stupid."

Dar pouted.

"No, not..." Kerry drew her knee up and wrapped her arms around it as she watched the quiet streetlights whisk by. "I felt like I was out of control... like I had my heart pinned on my jacket lapel or something."

"So..." Dar drawled, "my hoodwinking you into sleeping in my bed didn't clue you in that I wasn't in any better shape?"

Kerry thought about that for a while as they drove through the vast Disney property, toward the large, white, spread out Grand Floridian hotel. "Did you?"

"I enticed you with chocolate," Dar reminded her, with a smile. "Remember?"

How had she ended up in Dar's bed, anyway? They'd been watching the news, and she'd gotten sleepy. She remembered the sweet taste of hot chocolate on her lips, and then the cup had been taken and the covers pulled up around her.

"I could have gotten up and gone to my own room," Kerry mused.

"Uh huh," her partner agreed. "You could have."

"But I didn't want to." The memory surged sweetly over her. "I wanted to stay there with you. I didn't want to be alone."

"Me, either." Dar skillfully navigated the big Lexus into the driveway of the hotel, pulling up at the stately Victorian styled portico and putting the car in park. "I wanted you to stay there with me."

"Ah, I see." Kerry had to smile.

A valet trotted alertly out to meet them. "So I wanted to come back here, and revel in the fact that what I felt that morning..." Dar opened the door and gave the valet a slight smile, then ducked her head back inside the car. "Was dead on real."

Kerry felt, and suspected she looked, slightly wide-eyed at Dar's sudden and somewhat unexpected headlong dive into rampant romanticism. "Okay, honey," she agreed. "I'm all for it!'

Dar's face split into a grin, and her eyes twinkled before she disappeared again and went to open the trunk for the valet. Kerry sat for a moment, and then simply shook her head, opening the door and hopping out.

The hotel hadn't changed. Kerry drew in a breath of warm air scented with night jasmine as she joined Dar in walking toward the door. This late, it was very quiet, a soft hint of music from the speakers and the clatter of cleaning crews was all that accompanied them to the door.

A blast of chilled air met them as they entered, and they strolled across the beautiful lobby that almost succeeded in bringing them right into another world. Kerry allowed herself to be entranced, and she spent a few minutes simply looking around at the soaring ceilings as Dar worked out the details of their room.

"Let's go." Dar put a hand on her shoulder, and smiled.

Kerry took her hand and held it as they walked from the front desk, and strolled across a silver ribbon of their own memories.

"MM. PRETTY." KERRY gazed outside, watching the small, blinking lights as a boat crossed the lake toward the pier in front of the hotel.

Or maybe it was the back of the hotel. It was hard to tell, though the views on this side had it all over the ones on the other side. Kerry leaned against the chilled glass, her breath fogging it slightly as she exhaled. Below them, she could see a few, lone figures walking down the paths, and on the end of the pier two figures sat together, apparently simply enjoying the view as she was.

She watched them lean together, against each other. It made her smile because she knew exactly how good that felt.

Her shoulders ached, and she felt tired from the long day and their active evening, but she wasn't sleepy. Behind her, she could hear Dar rattling around in the bathroom and she spent a moment contrasting the reality of her now, with the memories of the past.

It was almost too disparate to compare. Then, Dar's every motion, every sound had flicked against her unsure awareness, making her heart jump.

Now, they made other parts of her jump, and her heart merely beat calmly, waiting for its other half to finish fussing and come to join her. Kerry could already feel the warmth of Dar's touch and she divided her attention—half to the glistening castle seen in the distance past the glass, and half in the reflection of the room behind her, waiting.

Dar finished arranging their toiletries and re-entered the room, watching Kerry press her nose against the glass sliding door. "I think I remember being suckered into those pretty lights last time I was here."

She flexed her bare toes against the carpet. "By that same look, too."

Kerry had turned and was grinning at her. She was draped in her old, worn Pooh T-shirt, her hair damp from the shower they'd shared. "You didn't take much suckering," she said. "It was just a tiny appeal to your pride, and presto." She snapped her fingers. "Instant monorail ride."

"Oh yeah?"

"Oh yeah." Kerry cheerfully nodded. "Although I did keep trying to convince myself I was doing it to help you relax, and it was for your own good."

"Mm." Dar stretched her body out, popping her shoulders into place. "It was."

"For your own good?"

"Oh yeah." Dar joined her at the glass and slid an arm around her as Kerry turned and they gazed out over the dark water, to the brightly lit theme parks beyond. "I'm damn ticked."

"At me?"

"At those stupid pieces of horse manure." Dar's eyes narrowed. "They're putting a damper on my fun plans, and I don't like it."

Kerry reached over and gave her a rub on the belly. "We can still have fun. We got our stuff done tonight, didn't we?" she asked. "Any reason why we need to be there tomorrow for them to put the froo froo up?"

Dar considered. Then she grunted. "No," she answered. "We're not supposed to be here for another day and a half."

"Exactly," Kerry agreed. "So you, me, and a pair of Florida resident park hopper passes are going to go have a wild and crazy time tomorrow."

"Hm. Do we have those?"

"Yeees." Kerry smirked. "Since I knew you weren't going to let me put the hotel on my card." She batted her fair lashes at her partner. "So get your bathing suit ready, Dardar."

For an answer, Dar moved a bit of Kerry's hair out of the way and gently kissed her neck. "Want some hot chocolate?" she uttered into the smaller woman's ear.

"No." Kerry's eyes closed. "I want you." She let her hand slowly glide up Dar's thigh. "I wanted you the last time I was here, but I couldn't have you."

Dar laughed softly into her ear. "Kerrison, you had me from day one." She slipped her arms around Kerry, and guided her toward the bed, turning in lazy circles as they smiled into each other's eyes. "But I wanted you too."

"You did?" Kerry felt the edge of the bed hit her behind her knees, and she ended up sprawling over it, with Dar's body crouching over her.

"I did." Dar's lips nipped across Kerry's pulse point.

"Oh, baby. You had me." Kerry laughed weakly. "Body, heart, and soul. Just like you do right now."

Dar paused and rested her weight on her elbows, studying her partner. Kerry's hands were already under the fabric of her shirt, stroking her skin with gentle, knowing fingers, and she could see the honest passion in those eyes gazing back at her. "How'd I get so lucky?"

"You got lucky?" Kerry's brows arched.

Dar smiled and lowered her head, kissing the waiting lips.

"We could really recreate this, and turn the news on," Kerry suggested, between light kisses across Dar's collarbone.

"Try it, and I'll bite your fingers off," Dar replied.

"Oo."

THEY BOTH WOKE at the same time. Kerry heard Dar take a sudden, irregular breath, as she opened her eyes to see the early morning sun pouring through the window. Once again, she was sleeping half on her side, half on her stomach, and snuggled tightly up against Dar's body.

Oh, but what a difference. Kerry smiled. This time she had no urgent desire to levitate herself off the bed in pure shock, and her heart didn't attempt to emerge from her ears with its hammering.

This time her welcome was sure, and the shoulder her cheek was resting on was as familiar to her as her own pillow.

Well, it often was her own pillow. Kerry slid one thigh up over Dar's and gave her a squeeze, humming low in her throat as sleep slowly cleared from her eyes. "Morning, sweetheart."

"Eeurrgh." Dar made a purring noise in return. "Morning to you too." She rubbed Kerry's back with her fingertips. "And what a pretty one it is." She turned her head and watched the sunlight creep across the floor, still tinted coral instead of the bright white yet to come.

It would be yet another in an almost endless series of summer days, hot and sticky, the morning fair with the ever-present possibility of thunderstorms in the afternoon as the earth struggled to throw off the sun's heat.

Water parks in the morning, Dar decided. Then maybe a visit to Epcot in the afternoon, since the technology park offered up lots of indoor attractions to escape the heat, and possibly the rain as well. "You up for dinner at the Living Seas?" she inquired. "I love that tank."

The sea green eyes brightened. "Oo...yeah." A nod. "Good idea."

Dar smiled contentedly. "I think that sounds like a plan," she said, as she arched her back to stretch it out, lifting Kerry a little with her before she relaxed again under the covers. "Damn, I'm glad we got all that crap squared away last night. If I'd walked in there today with nothing done, heads woulda rolled."

Kerry traced an idle pattern on Dar's ribcage. "So the only reason you didn't was because there were no heads to roll?"

"Hm." Dar grunted after a moment's silence. "You know something? I really don't know." She lifted one arm and settled her hand behind her head. After another short, pensive silence, she shrugged. "Ah...probably faster if I did it myself anyway."

Kerry nodded slightly. "I had the neatest dream last night," she related, changing the subject. "You and I were getting married."

Dar's eyebrows twitched. "Um...aren't we?"

"Yeah, I know we are married, but not... I mean, it was this whole ceremony with rice, and flowers," Kerry felt Dar start to laugh. "You and me in pretty gowns."

"Don't tell me white ones." Dar groaned.

"Sure," Kerry cheerfully agreed. "You looked gorgeous. You had this lace sheer neckline thing on and..."

"Kerry." Dar tapped her on the shoulder. "You need some coffee or something?"

"No, why?"

"Just wondered."

"Anyway. We were in this beautiful cathedral, with stained glass windows, and everyone was throwing bags of rice at us..."

Dar half sat up, bringing Kerry up with her and displaying the considerable strength of her abdominal muscles. "What?"

Kerry tumbled and rolled into Dar's lap, peering up at her as she lay on her back across her partner's legs. "What?"

"Bags of rice? What was this, a Cuban wedding? Were there bags of beans too?" Dar queried, tossing her head back to clear the disordered hair from her eyes. "Five pound bags? Ten? Fifty?"

Kerry folded her hands over her bare stomach. "Sweetheart." She twiddled her thumbs. "Yankees don't like to whip out their dustpans during a wedding. We wrap a pinch of rice into a cloth bag and toss that at newlyweds," she informed her lover. "It's supposed to be good luck.

Dar put a fingertip against her nose. "It's supposed to be for fertility, so you'll have lots of babies," she corrected her in a wry tone. "Leave it to Yankees to conveniently forget *that*."

"Mm...we didn't forget it." Softly glinting green eyes peered up at Dar. "It was so nice. All our friends were there, and Chino had a hat on...your dad was in a tux."

Her partner smiled in reflex. "You have cute dreams."

"I had one the first time we stayed here too," Kerry admitted. "Remember you were saying you did? Before we woke up? So did I." She sat up and pulled her legs up crossed under her, pushing her hair back with one hand.

"It didn't have rice in it, did it?" Dar leaned on one elbow, facing her. The sheets draped loosely over her body, exposing roughly half of her torso and all of the length of one long leg.

"No." Kerry leaned her elbows on her knees. "I didn't remember it until way after we left Orlando. It was you and I up in a tree."

"A tree." Dar sniffed reflectively. "I like trees," she allowed. "What kind of tree?"

A shrug. "I have no idea. But we were up in it, looking at the sky." Kerry glanced at the sheets, drawing her finger over the soft surface. "I remember being so happy, a strange feeling for me back then."

Dar laid her hand on Kerry's knee. "And now?"

"And now?" Kerry laughed, a light, joyous sound. "Oh, my god, Dar. What a question." She peeked up into her partner's eyes. "Do I sound like a babbling idiot this morning or what?"

The blue orbs twinkled. "Wanna have breakfast here, or go find some hapless characters to harass?" Dar rubbed the skin under her hand gently.

"Here." Kerry rolled over onto her side and stretched out on the bed. "Banana stuffed French toast?" she suggested. "Then we can grab our swimsuits and go look for trouble." With a quick twitch, she yanked the covers off Dar and scrambled back off the bed with them as her partner rose to the challenge and chased her.

She almost got away and then her feet got tangled up in the sheets. "Augh!"

Kerry hopped madly to free them, bouncing all over the room and nearly causing Dar to cough up an eyeball laughing. At the last hop, Dar got an arm around her and they both fell, hitting the carpet and thrashing around with the sheet winding itself around them.

"Ee!" Kerry squirmed, as long, ticklish fingers attacked her bare ribs. "You punk!"

"Yeah? Takes one to know one!" Dar grappled with her, the fabric tangling around them and winding them tighter together. "Auarrgguhhh!!"

"Ooooo...gotcha!" Kerry wrapped her arm around Dar's calf and attacked the inside of her knee, feeling the powerful limb jerk in response to her tickling. "Ahahahahahah!!!!"

Buzz.

Dar's head popped out from under its wrapping of cotton. She glared so intently at her cell phone the leather cover nearly shriveled.

Buzzz.

One long arm snaked out and snatched the instrument, but then paused as Dar took a moment to catch her breath before she opened the phone. "What?" She snarled into it.

"Oo." Kerry wiggled up and poked her head out into the open to listen. "Rambunctious interruptus. How rude."

"Well, good morning to you too, Dar. Always such a pleasure to talk to you." Eleanor's voice held equal parts sarcasm and amusement. "Were you up?"

Dar's pale blue eyes slitted. "Yes," she said. "You get assigned wake-up call duty this week? I thought Alastair was gonna invest in software to do that."

The VP of Marketing chuckled. "Oh, there're parts of you that never change, aren't there? It's a relief really...like death, taxes...you know?"

"Eleanor, what the hell do you want?"

"Is Kerry there?" Eleanor asked, giving up on her torment.

Dar gave her cell phone another evil look. "It's a quarter to seven in the morning, I'm in my hotel room, and I'm not dressed. What do you think?"

A pause. "Well wouldja put her on the phone, please? She's at least civil before coffee."

Kerry fell forward against Dar's chest, laughing helplessly, covering her mouth to keep Eleanor from hearing.

"She's occupied at the moment." Dar gazed down at the blond woman draped over her. "What do you want?"

Eleanor sighed audibly. "Okay, okay—there are a lot of really ticked off people here, Dar," she said. "I'm about to head into a meeting with ten of our fellow exhibitors."

"And?" Dar nuzzled Kerry's hair, nibbling its softness. "If the hall's screwed up, what do you want from me? It's not my fault." She leaned back against the bed, sliding her free hand around Kerry's now still form. "And it sure as hell isn't Kerry's fault."

"No...Jesus, all right! I'm coming!" Eleanor sounded more than exasperated. "Listen, Dar...bottom line, these guys want to know who you paid off to get our booth up. Nothing fancy. They're frustrated, and out of time, and they want to get it all done so...who gets the check?"

Dar grinned at her cell phone. "Me."

"What?"

Dar smirked. "I didn't pay anyone off, Eleanor. I went...sorry...we went in there last night and made it happen."

"You?"

"Me," Dar confirmed. "Tell them I take credit cards. What do you think, three, four thousand a minute? What's my time worth?" She chuckled. "I tell you what, it's gonna take them the whole goddamned day to pull the circuits, because the nitwits who installed them didn't label the damn things. I had to check them one by one and let me tell you, I was raising the roof in that Telco room cursing."

"Oh, my god." Eleanor muffled a laugh. "Everyone thinks you bribed the management company."

"Hah." Dar looked down into Kerry's expressive eyes. "We don't need to bribe anyone to execute the technology we're responsible for implementing."

"Can I quote you?" Eleanor sounded gleeful. "Please?"

"Sure." Dar lowered her head and brushed Kerry's lips with her own. "Just don't raffle me off. I'm busy."

"Rats. I could have recouped the outlay for the damn convention,"

Eleanor mock sighed. "When are you coming over?"

"We're not." Dar moved her head up a little, so their combined breathing wouldn't echo over the phone. "I have other things to do today. I put my time in last night."

"Oh. Well, okay." Eleanor sounded a little off-balance. "I thought you'd want to be here to see the fun."

"I make my own fun." Dar watched Kerry bite the inside of her lip to stop from laughing. "Call me if you need me, but you better the hell really need me."

"Okay," Eleanor sighed. "I'll call you later. "

"Bye."

Kerry closed the cell and tossed it on the bed. "C'mon nerdmeister. I hear a banana calling my name." She got a last tickle in, laughing as Dar rocked backwards with her in her arms. "Score one for the geek squad."

The sun poured into the room, painting it silver, splashing across the carpet and catching on tan skin and tangled dark and light hair.

Dar broke off for air, rubbing Kerry's nose gently with her own. "Score two."

"Was Eleanor upset?" Kerry asked, after a moment. "About us not being there?"

Dar shrugged. "I don't care if she was," she said. "It's not my job to set up the full color hand outs and fluff the stress balls." She kissed Kerry. "I wasn't supposed to be there this soon anyway."

"True." Kerry returned the kiss, sliding her hands up along Dar's sides. "But with Telegenics there, not to mention our friends, maybe she thinks every opportunity counts."

"Maybe she does." Dar paused and gazed down into Kerry's eyes. "Then she should do her job, and promote the company to everyone in the building, right?"

Kerry hesitated, and then nodded. "Right."

Chapter
Three

KERRY CLIPPED HER cell phone to the waistband of her shorts, and slid her sunglasses next to it. She studied the result in the mirror and decided that, plus the tucked in tropical fish T-shirt, was acceptable.

She had the bathing suit she'd purchased the week before, a relatively sedate aqua green one-piece, with a racing neckline, on underneath her clothing.

Shopping for bathing suits had gotten a lot more fun since she'd started living with Dar, that was for sure. She'd always been nervous about what she looked like in them before, so many years of her family's criticism stuck in her head making her shy about putting them on in public.

But Dar lived in the water, practically. If she wasn't on the boat, she was in the pool, or on the beach and Kerry realized after they'd started going out that she was going to have to get over it if she wanted to share that lifestyle.

She remembered the first time she'd gone shopping for the beach with her mother, after she'd gotten old enough to really be conscious of her body, and her figure. She'd wanted a two piece like all her friends, and she'd been treated to an hour of critique on why she couldn't possibly wear one because of what the press would say about her not quite shed layer of baby fat.

Jesus. Kerry met her own eyes in the mirror and winked at herself wryly. What a horror show that had been.

So she stayed away from bikinis, even though she knew, with her new, buff physique and her tan, she could now wear a bikini in rather grand style.

Dar said she looked sexier in the sleek, one-piece solid color functional ones she tended to wear, so who needed a bikini anyway? Dar only laughed when she suggested to her partner than she wear one herself.

Ah well.

"Right." She gave herself a nod, and then looked up as Dar appeared behind her in the mirror, already decked out in her wraparound shades and sleeveless cotton shirt and shorts. "Would you mind?" Kerry handed Dar the sunscreen.

"Never." Dar sprayed some of the tanning lotion on her hands and started working it into the exposed portion of Kerry's skin. "Want to pull your hair back?"

Kerry moved her pale locks out of the way, so Dar could get the oil all the way up the back of her neck. "You think it'll stick?"

"For a while." Dar glanced at the bottle. "Theoretically waterproof, but we'll take it with us. I don't want to get toasted, and I know you don't either."

"Nuh uh." Kerry simply stood in place, enjoying the strong hands giving her a massage in the process of protecting her hide. "Dar, can I ask you something?"

"Sure."

"Aren't you at all curious as to what those two are up to?"

"No."

Kerry looked up into the mirror, watching her partner's face as she worked. Dar's expression was relaxed and calm, and when the blue eyes lifted and met hers, there was no evasiveness in them. "Really?"

"Nah." Dar shook her head. Then she half shrugged one shoulder. "I mean, I guess I don't want to see them run us out of town, and I guess we're going to have to sit down and really analyze what they're doing...what their plan is...if they've really got something different that we can't compete with, that sort of thing."

"But you don't care that it's them?"

"No."

"Hm."

"Do you?" Dar studied her for a moment. Kerry's face twitched a little, her jaw muscles bunching as she considered. "You think it's personal?"

Kerry took the oil and capped it. She gestured for Dar to turn and precede her from the bathroom, and didn't speak until she'd tucked the bottle into the small pack she'd planned on carrying and fastened it around her. "I think it might be, yeah," she admitted, as they walked to the door and exited into the hallway. "But maybe that's only my green eyes talking."

Dar touched the button for the elevator, maintaining a thoughtful silence.

They walked through the lobby, and out to the bus stop. Kerry removed her sunglasses from her waistband and settled them firmly onto her nose. They took a seat together to wait for the correct bus, wincing a little as their bodies had to adapt from the air conditioned comfort of the hotel to the sauna-like heat outside.

"I think I just realized somewhere along the way this past year I grew up," Dar said, out of the blue. "Maybe they do have personal motives, but I don't give a crap. I don't have time in my life for their dramas."

Kerry flicked an adventurous love bug away from her bare knee. She could already feel sweat gathering under her light clothing, and she was looking forward to the cool kiss of the water at their current destination.

She'd realized the past year that though she chose to live in the subtropics, she didn't much like breathing swamp air most of the time and saved her excursions in the summer for the early morning and late evening hours. "That's an interesting point of view."

Dar shrugged. "Would you rather go to the convention center and mess with them?" she asked bluntly. "You having second thoughts about our being out today?"

"No." Kerry shook her head. "That's not it at all, Dar."

"Then what's the problem?"

Did she have a problem? Kerry frowned, feeling the edges of her own temper prickle. "Did I say I had a problem?" she asked, half turning to face her partner.

Dar merely raised her eyebrows, folding her arms across her chest in mute eloquence.

Kerry exhaled, looking up as their bus approached. "I don't have a problem. I want to make sure my job is covered." She got up and started for the door. "We get paid a lot of money to do what we do. I don't want to think I'm blowing that responsibility off."

"Blowing what responsibility off?" Dar asked. "You weren't supposed to be here today, remember?"

"I know," Kerry admitted. "I guess maybe finding out what we found out last night...what if they start something?"

Dar climbed up after her, and they took seats near the middle of the bus. Dar stretched her legs out and studied the neatly folded half socks peeking over the edge of her sneakers. "Hmph."

Several other guests filed in behind them including a family with three or four children, all wide-eyed and excited as their parents corralled them in the back. Dar watched them for a few minutes, and then she glanced at Kerry's profile.

Kerry looked back at her at the same time. "If it is personal, and they are gunning for us, it's going to sting them like hell if we don't show up."

Dar grinned like a pirate, her eyes twinkling. "You think?"

"It's like we don't consider them a worthwhile threat," Kerry went on, giving her taller companion a poke in the shoulder. "You're too freaking smart for your own good, Paladar."

"You're not so bad yourself." Dar leaned back. "If it makes you feel any better, yeah, my gut instincts were to go over there and just run roughshod over everyone, micro-managing every detail like a concierge on steroids," she admitted. "But strategically, since we're already a jump ahead of them, it makes sense to steer clear and let them all scramble."

"Mm."

Dar gazed at the roof of the bus. "And it's a great rationalization for me to just do what I want to do anyway." She cleared her throat. "Which is spend the day having fun with you."

"Ah." Kerry surrendered with a wry chuckle. "Is this a case of the action plan having two parallel goals?" she asked. "Or are we simply coming up with good excuses for ourselves?" After reviewing her words, and the stillness of Dar's face, she held a hand up. "Okay, truce. Scratch that."

The bus trundled over a myriad of bumps in the road, and eventually pulled into the water park. The door opened, and through the heat Kerry caught a whiff of sun warmed concrete and chlorine. She followed Dar down the steps and stayed behind her a step as they walked toward the entrance.

Well, screw it. With a shake of her head, Kerry increased the length of her strides and caught up to her partner, deliberately bumping her with her shoulder.

Dar looked at her, then bumped her back. "Done wrestling with your conscience?"

"Mm." Kerry patted her cell phone. "If they need us, we're here," she concluded. "Besides, what the heck could happen at a trade show before it even opens?"

They showed their passes at the gate and were admitted, the sounds of splashing and laughter already beginning to surround them much as the scent of the water did. They secured a locker and Kerry stripped off her shirt and shorts, stuffing them and the rest of her gear into the small space. Save the phone, which she snapped into a waterproof housing before looping the lanyard on the case around her neck. Then she picked up her towel, and joined her now swimsuit-clad companion as they headed out into the sun.

DAR HOISTED HERSELF out of the wave pool for the nth time, shaking herself free of a spray of chlorinated water as she waited for Kerry to join her. Kerry was heading her way, towing a body board behind her with a big grin on her face. "Nice one," Dar complimented her.

"Yeah." Kerry exhaled, raking her fingers through her drenched hair. "Next stop, Hawaii." She sat down on the edge of the pool to catch her breath, tipping her head back to observe the sun's slant in the sky. "Know what?"

"It's lunchtime," Dar responded. "Want to do the big slide one more time before we grab something?"

Kerry accepted the offered hand up and stood, looking around at their surroundings. The park wasn't busy at all, not nearly as much as it had been the last time they were there. It was the heat of summer now, though, so that wasn't unexpected. However, it had made it all the more pleasant to not have to fight the crowds and stand in long lines. "Sure," she concluded. "Let me just get a towel and wipe my eyes. The water's killing them."

Dar lead the way back to the chair they'd taken possession of, picking up Kerry's towel and handing it to her as she lifted her own and dried the largest of the water droplets off with it. Now, instead of being oppressive, the sun felt good and warm on her back, and she felt pleasantly tired from all the activity.

Out of habit, she checked her phone. No calls. With a grin, she checked Kerry's, which was also devoid of any missed calls. She admitted to herself that curiosity was beginning to prick her softly, wondering what, if anything, was going on in the trade show.

"Why don't you call?" Kerry had been watching her, and now she produced a knowing grin.

"Would it make you feel better if I did?" Dar countered.

Kerry took a seat on the beach lounger, and extended her bare legs out, crossing them casually at the ankles. "Yes." She waggled her fingers. "Dial, your Nerdiness." She arranged herself more comfortably on the lounger and put her sunglasses on, then folded her hands over her stomach.

Dar chuckled, but unzipped the case and flipped the phone open. She dialed Eleanor's number and waited. It rang twice, and then was answered.

"Yes?"

"Is it a convention yet?" Dar asked.

Eleanor chuckled nastily.

"That's what I thought. Need us for anything?"

"Only as icing on the cake. Having fun?" Eleanor asked.

"Yes, we are," Dar affirmed. "Glad everything's going okay there."

"Dar, did you know who the principals were in Telegenics?" Eleanor asked suddenly. "The operational team, I mean? Not the money people?"

Dar exhaled. "Yes," she answered evenly. "Always nice to have old friends in the business, huh?"

"Mm," Eleanor grunted. "Well, I think they figured to have a little competition with us here. My sources tell me they were involved in why we had no staff here last night."

"Ah." Dar smiled humorlessly. "That would explain why they showed up to the offices as we were leaving," she said. "So they thought they'd throw a wrench in, eh?"

"Apparently." Eleanor sounded so very smug. "They were looking to be the big shots and come riding to the rescue this morning. Terribly disappointed, apparently, when they discovered we were already providing that role by generously lending out our resources to help all our friends and enemies get their gear running."

"Aww."

"Terribly disappointed to not find you here."

"Double awww." Dar chuckled. "They can kiss my ass."

"That would be playing right into it, no?" Eleanor quipped. "But just so you know, they left, and one of the boys heard them saying they were going to go looking for you. The short bitchy one apparently had some idea of where you might be."

Dar's ears pricked up and she very slowly turned her head to scan her surroundings. She didn't see anyone she knew, but there were a lot of areas she couldn't see, either. "Nice," she muttered.

"You do make charming enemies, Dar." Eleanor sighed. "Anyway, they left us alone, so thank God for that. You will stop by tonight to make sure everything's a go for tomorrow, right?"

"We'll be there," Dar responded quietly.

"Good. Later!" Eleanor hung up, her voice already rising to talk to someone as it vanished into the cellular ether.

"YOU WERE RIGHT. There they are." Shari leaned on the balcony of the restaurant, gazing pensively down across the forest of chaise lounges.

"Seem to have an affinity for water," Michelle Graver commented, biting off the words with sharp precision. "I remembered they spent time here last time."

"During the Vista bid?" Shari asked.

"Exactly."

"Mm." The bigger woman turned her attention back to their subjects. As she watched, Dar wrapped her towel around her neck and took a seat on the lounge next to where her blond companion was lying. But instead of joining her, the tall woman remained upright, just looking around.

"She always been that good looking?" Michelle asked, curiously.

Shari thought about it. "Eh." She shrugged one linen covered shoulder. "The potential was always there, but there was so much crap covering it you'd never have guessed." She snorted slightly. "She sure kept herself in shape though. Damn sight better than I did."

"Mm." Michelle nodded. "She's into karate, or so I hear."

"Not karate." Shari shook her head. "Some other weird thing. Not surprising. She grew up on that navy base and it screwed her head up royally. Half the time I thought she was psycho."

"Doesn't look it now," Graver observed, noting the elegant lines of Dar's profile. "If you hadn't told me what her background was, I'd never have guessed it."

"No," Shari conceded. "She cleans up all right. Now, at least." Her eyes drifted over to the other chair's occupant. "So she's still with the little blond rat, huh?" She mused. "Wonder how she's managed to get her to stay around."

Michelle turned her head to give her companion a look. "Don't sell our young blond wasp short. She's got brains," she said. "And from what I hear, she's got a set of well taken care of, exquisitely dentured fangs beneath all that sweet Midwestern bullshit," she added. "The few times I had to deal with her, I respected what she did for me."

A shrug. "Whatever." Shari stared down at the two with an almost obsessive look. "Never thought it would last, especially if she's got brains. Who could live with an animal like Dar?"

"She could have changed," Michelle suggested. "I never got the sense that she was anything but sharp, and damn ruthless. When she took that bid group apart it made my heart go pit-a-pat, that's for sure." She considered. "Her reputation's not built on BS, Shari. I know you've been on the sales and development side, but I haven't."

"Leopards don't change spots." Shari shook her head. "But she's the key to ILS all right. She's the cornerstone. You see what she did last night? Busted my ass, but that's Dar all over." She snorted in disgust. "Here I figured we'd make a little stir, and get a face off this morning between her and us."

"It was a good plan," her companion allowed. "Let the clients see our style differences, head to head. I never figured on her showing up last night."

"No." Shari's lips wrinkled. "Or her turning grease monkey on us. Though I should have remembered that side of her. Used to drive me nuts."

"Mm." Michelle nodded thoughtfully. "She makes things happen. I said that when I met her and nothing I've seen since contradicts that. So," she watched their subjects, "Now she's going to be gunning for us. We lost our surprise."

"So." Shari watched Dar draw one leg up and circle it with both arms the muscles under her tan skin rippling visibly even at this distance. "Okay, maybe we need to rethink our strategy. It would have been good to have been able to get in there today and make points, but we didn't."

The shorter woman raised a ginger colored eyebrow at her. "No. And I will have to give the ILS team their credit, those people know how to show off, and they know what they're doing."

"Pah."

"Shari, don't discount them," Michelle warned. "Just because we've had some successes, and have a little advantage right now, don't forget they're the big player here."

"That's their problem. They've been around too long, doing the same thing the same way too long," Shari said. "They can't react fast, and they're conservative as hell. You saw the strategic readouts on them I gave you, right?"

"True," Michelle said. "But I will tell you one thing, Dar never struck me as conservative."

"She is," Shari said. "What we have to do is keep the pressure on them, and throw her some curve balls. If we can do it in front of everyone, we can knock some of that mystique off."

Michelle looked doubtful, but intrigued. "Go on," she said. "That might work."

"Let's go have lunch," Shari suggested. "Get out of this damn heat. I'd forgotten how much I hated it."

They turned and strolled toward the door. As they reached it, Shari paused and glanced back over her shoulder. By design or chance, Dar's head was turned, and she was staring right at her from behind silvered shades.

Though she was far away enough to know the dark haired woman couldn't see her, Shari shivered anyway, and hastily ducked inside. "Psycho," she muttered, closing the door behind her.

"I LOVE EPCOT," Kerry said, as they strolled through the main entrance to the park. "I think it's my favorite place here."

"Me too," Dar agreed. "Not just because it's nerd heaven, either. It holds my interest more than the other parks."

That was significant, Kerry decided. Dar had a surprisingly limited attention span, something that she'd found out over time much to her bemusement. If you wanted her help, you condensed your problem down into its essentials, and got it in front of her in squarely black and white terms. Then she would review it, decide, and give it back to you sometimes in a matter of minutes.

Anything longer than that, or heaven forbid, if someone chose to do a PowerPoint presentation to make their case, and you lost her. Kerry had seen it happen more than once. Her lover would let her head rest on one hand, and start sketching, occupying her restless mind with something more interesting than whatever the person presenting was saying.

Which brought up an interesting question. "Hey, Dar? Were you hyperactive when you were a kid?"

Dar turned her head and focused on Kerry, away from the dancing fountains they were walking toward. "Was I?" She mused. "I don't know. I was a pain in the ass child, that's for sure. Just ask my mother."

The scent of pastry distracted them both and Dar steered Kerry toward a bakery shop in the central plaza. They walked up the steps and into the shop, getting in line as they reviewed their options. "Mm." Kerry eyed a chocolate mousse. "Another reason I like Epcot. Good food."

"Uh huh," Dar agreed, making eye contact with the cashier and pointing at the mousse. "Two, and two cappuccinos, please," she said. "Yeah, I think I was."

"Huh?" Kerry had her mind on the pastries. "Think you were mousse, hon?"

"Hyperactive." Dar deftly evaded Kerry's attempts to pay for their treat and plunked down a handful of bills instead. "Probably my parents had no clue, but when I look back now and think of how I was, yeah. Why?"

"Just curious," Kerry answered. "I noticed you're so restless a lot of the time when you're at work, so I wondered."

Dar picked up the tray with their treats and nudged Kerry toward a table. "Either that or it was all the damn chocolate I ate." She sat down and handed over Kerry's mousse, taking her own and commencing a methodical attack on it. "Okay. Let's grab some dinner reservations, then we can wander around in this part for a while."

"Okay." Kerry licked her spoon. "First stop, Test Track. Vroom, Vroom."

"Vroom, vroom," Dar agreed with a smile, daubing a bit of mousse on Kerry's nose. "You got it."

IT WAS GETTING on to evening, and the raw heat of the day was moderating slightly as the breeze picked up. Kerry plucked at the front of her shirt, glad to feel the cool touch of the air and she was wishing the sun would drop faster and bring on the twilight's relief. "Whew."

"Yeah." Dar ambled into the path of a mist gun, letting it spray her with a fine fog of water. "Let's go find something indoors."

They stopped in front of the reservations kiosk, and Dar poked at the touch screen looking for what she wanted. "Reservations... reservations...World Showcase, no...Ah. Living Seas. Here." She reviewed her choices. "Time...what do you think, seven? If we can get it?"

"Oo." Kerry put a hand out and grabbed her partner's wrist. "Hang on...what's that?" She pointed. "Scuba reservations?"

Dar's eyebrows shot up. She punched the required button and leaned forward, with Kerry pressed against her side in curiosity. "Whoa," she said. "Never saw that before." She studied the announcement. "Dive in the Living Seas. Tropical fish, turtles, sharks. Hmm." Her eyes turned to Kerry. "Wanna do it?"

"You need to ask?" Kerry said. "Scuba diving in the gazillion gallon aquarium? Sign me up!" She watched as Dar indicated their interest. After a moment, a real person appeared on the screen. "Hi."

"Hello!" The face smiled back at them. "How can I help you?"

Having punched a specific button, Dar had more or less expected the operator to know what she wanted. "We want to go dive in the Living Seas."

"Great!" The woman replied. "Would that be for today?"

"Yes."

The woman did something on her end that involved typing. "Great," she said again. "We have spaces available at five thirty. How's that?"

Kerry checked her watch. "It's five now," she said. "Sounds perfect."

Dar bounced up and down on the balls of her feet happily. "Do it," she instructed the woman. "What do we need?"

The woman typed for a while, then she looked up. "Okay, you'll need bathing suits, and of course, you do have your certification cards?"

Dar nodded. "Yep, we do."

"Terrific! Go to the customer service center at five-fifteen, and they'll take it from there." The woman smiled broadly. "Excited?"

"Yes." Kerry forestalled Dar's answer. "Thanks!' She watched the woman sign off, and then she turned to Dar. "Oh, this is going to be so cool."

Dar grinned as she requested their dinner reservations. "Yeah," she said. "It's not like we haven't been diving in more exotic places, but this'll be different all right." Finishing, she put her hands on Kerry's shoulders and directed her toward the service center. "Let's go."

THERE WERE SIX others in their group of eight, Dar discovered. They were a diverse bunch ranging from resort certified divers with very limited experience, to two others like Dar herself, experienced dive masters out for some fun.

After a solemn introductory session, and the paying of the fee, they all trooped through an unmarked gate, going from the public part of the theme park, into the work area guests typically never saw. Dar more or less ignored the chattering around her and spent time looking around at the facilities, which were well kept and spotless, though far less ornate than the theme park areas themselves.

They walked past administrative offices, and across a service roadway to the rear part of the Seas exhibit, which featured a huge marine system serviced by entire buildings full of pumps and water treatment equipment.

Inside the exhibit, they moved carefully around huge pipes and up several flights of narrow stairs to a small classroom. Once there, they were given release forms and refreshments while they filled them out. "When was the last time we dove, Dar?" Kerry chewed the end of her pen. "Tuesday or was it last Thursday?"

"Thursday." Dar was busy scribbling. "You were nearly bitten by that cranky parrot fish you kept chasing down."

"Ah. Yeah." Kerry finished writing and signed her name to the bottom of the release, dating it neatly. "I was just trying to take his picture. You'd think he was a TV star in LA or something."

"Maybe that barracuda that kept following me was his agent." Dar slid Kerry's form out from under her hands and gave both to the khaki clad man giving them directions. "Here you go." She sat back and regarded their fellow divers as the guide collected all his paperwork, and checked off sizes for their gear.

"Okay, guys." The man finished and gave them a sunny grin. "Next, we go down to the locker rooms and suit up. Your gear bags are on the benches. When you're done, walk out into the hallway and I'll meet you there to take you up to the dive platform. Okay?"

"Good deal." Kerry stood and followed Dar as they left the room, traveling down a short flight of stairs to another in a seemingly endless series of pale blue corridors. Touching the wall, she could feel a distinct vibration, and the scent of water seemed to penetrate even the thick concrete. The air was also damp, and combined with the chill of the air conditioners, rather refreshing after being outside.

The locker rooms were surprisingly plush. Kerry's eyebrows rose as she noted the well-equipped showers, complete with shampoo and soap. "Hey. Nice." She complimented them, as Dar sorted out their respective wetsuits. "Almost like home."

"Here." Dar tossed Kerry a suit, moving forward as one of the two other women walked past her to the changing booths. The other woman followed, leaving Dar and Kerry in the main room together.

They exchanged looks, and then Kerry pointed to one of the changing booths. "After you, little fishie. Give me a hand getting this thing on?"

Dar grinned knowingly. "Sure," she answered in an offhand tone. They entered the same space and closed the door, as Dar draped the two wetsuits over the partition wall. "We don't use these much."

"Nope." Kerry removed her shorts and T-shirt, leaning forward and giving Dar a kiss on the navel as she did the same. "Too hot most of the time." She removed her still dampish swimsuit and slid it on, grimacing at its clammy touch. "Someone's going to invent instant suit dryers some day. Brr."

Dar adjusted the strap on Kerry's suit, then ducked her head and nibbled her neck, running her hands over the sheer fabric lightly to warm it. "That better?" she inquired, into Kerry's now bright pink ear.

"Much." Kerry rubbed the bridge of her nose, as the surge of heat from her guts felt like it was going to produce steam off the dampness. "Thanks."

"Anytime." Dar put on her own suit and adjusted it, then she picked up Kerry's wetsuit and held it up for her. "Squiggle."

Kerry stepped into the shortie suit and tugged it up over her thighs and past her hips before she stuck her arms into it and straightened. "I always feel like a penguin in one of these." She remarked, as Dar pulled the neoprene into place and zipped the back. The suit was restrictive, and she spent a moment moving her arms and adjusting the half sleeves as Dar got into hers. "I ever tell you that you look really good in a wetsuit?"

Dar paused in the process of pulling on a sleeve and peered at her. "I look good as a penguin? Thanks, Ker. You're a peach." She tugged the neoprene over her muscular shoulders and stretched her arms out;

grimacing as the stubborn fabric pulled overly taut before it grudgingly inched into place.

Kerry pulled her zipper up and gave her a pat on the side. The thick rubber outlined Dar's body sleekly, and despite the overwhelming scent of carbon, she did find it kind of sexy looking. "You don't look like a penguin, sweetie. You look like a superhero."

Dar looked down at herself, then up at Kerry. "I think you're the one who needs glasses, Kerry." She laughed. "C'mon. Let's go see some fish." She picked up their clothing and opened the booth door, waiting for Kerry to exit before she moved toward a set of lockers where they'd been assigned a top one for their things.

The two other women had already exited, and when Dar and Kerry opened the door they found most of the rest of the group waiting. They joined their guide, now also suited up, and stood quietly as the last of the group finally ducked out of the men's locker room.

"Okay, let's go up." The guide turned and lead the way, past anonymous blue doors and up another set of stairs before he reached a door marked "Stage Entrance". "Okay, we're going into the Living Seas now, so everyone suck it up and look good."

Before anyone could react, the guide opened the door and they were greeted with a blast of chilly air. Past the entrance they could see the inside of the public pavilion filled with guests, some of whom were now glancing their way curiously. "Oh...hm," Kerry murmured, as they filed out and started across the carpeted floor. "Boy, that could be embarrassing."

Dar merely kept walking wryly hoping she didn't bump into anyone she knew.

They traversed the main floor and got to the central area, where a huge tube with Plexiglas windows showed a diver's lock-in area. For a moment Dar wondered if they were really going to lock through, then the guide took them to a door in the rear and they disappeared into a stairwell leading up.

The scent of water was much stronger here, to the point that Dar could almost feel the salt collecting on the back of her tongue as they walked upwards. At the top of the circular stairs a door opened, and they walked out onto a steel platform.

The aquarium was laid out below them, the entrance to it a huge circular room crisscrossed with steel catwalks to give access to the water's surface. There were huge slings and cranes over the water, and equipment for servicing the giant tank was clamped everywhere. Here, rather than the public viewpoint of an entertaining, safe, cheerful show was instead the rig of a professional marine habitat and an air of scientific matter of factness.

Dar found it fascinating. But they were being herded down to the launch area, so she dismissed it and followed Kerry down to the lower platform where the divers would enter the water. Already, eight sets of gear were perched on the side, neatly arranged. Very professional, she noted approvingly.

"Okay." The guide faced them. "We're going to gear up, and get in the water. I'll lead you around in the tank, and let you know when it's time to interact with the guests. Now, you know a big part of this is being part of the show, so make sure you have fun with it."

Kerry swiveled her head and looked up at her partner, whose eyebrows were crawling almost into her hairline. "Uh oh."

"Part of the show?" Dar mouthed in outrage.

"You'll get to interact with our guests in the observation bubbles, and at the restaurant. Isn't that great? The guests love it. They think you're one of us, so let's get going!" The guide took the first woman's arm and started moving her toward the gear.

"Wait a minute," Dar started to protest, but fell silent when Kerry put a hand on her arm. She glowered at her partner, but found herself pinned by warm green eyes, and a gently entreating expression and knew she was going to dissolve under it the moment she saw it. "Kerrrryy..."

"It'll be fun," Kerry insisted, taking her arm and tugging her toward the gear. "C'mon, Dar, didn't you always want to work at Disney World?"

"No." The taller woman scowled. "I don't do the Wal-Mart greeter, Kerrison."

"Just pretend they're more fish to look at," Kerry soothed her. "It'll be fun."

Dar snorted, but reluctantly followed her down onto the platform, blinking a little as the cold water hit her feet. "If I kiss you underwater, think they'll throw us out?" she muttered.

"Dar."

"Heh."

KERRY SLOWLY SANK into the water, letting herself submerge as she looked around her at the inside of the tank. Beside her, still visibly glowering even through her mask, Dar was doing the same, her hands folded over her stomach as she remained at the vertical beside Kerry.

Kerry poked her. Dar turned her head and waited, her eyes fastened on Kerry from behind the glass panels.

"I love you," Kerry signed with her hands, watching intently until she saw the flow of bubbles change as Dar smiled around her regulator. After a glance at the guide, Dar signed back the same message, and then she appeared to relax, tilting back and finning lazily around in a circle as the rest of the group descended.

That left Kerry free to simply float and watch the fish surround her, an explosion of sea life greater than any she'd experienced so far, even in the prolific Caribbean. The water was crystal clear, and though the corals were fake, the colors made the fish stand out in vivid waves.

It was very different than ocean diving. For that, you needed to take into account the waves, and the currents, and the visibility was often not that great due to floating debris. This was a complete departure—like having the best parts of a dive set before you without the nasty parts you had to live with.

How Disney, Kerry mused, as she put a hand out curiously toward a large parrot fish circling nearby. It drifted closer and nibbled her skin, a ticklish sensation that made her nose wrinkle. She felt a tug on her arm, and turned to see the guide motioning them all on toward the main part of the tank.

The water was cold, but the shortie wetsuit kept her warm enough until her body started adjusting to it. Kerry gently bled some of the air from her BC and sank a bit, moving down toward the bottom. She stayed back a little then, watching the rest of the group as they explored the first large fake coral structure.

Dar had relaxed enough to take up her usual diving posture, her buoyancy completely balanced, her arms clasped lightly in front of her as she dolphin kicked in a slow circle around the coral. She slowed, and a cloud of fish surrounded her, coming closer than they ever would in the wild. Dar went still, only her head moving as the silvery bodies brushed hers, and behind the glass Kerry could see those pale blue eyes widening.

Cool. Kerry smiled, wishing she had her underwater camera with her. A motion caught her attention, and she turned her head, her own eyes widening as a long, sleek gray form swam toward her. She stayed completely still as the small shark nosed at her fins, then moved on with a negligent flick of his tail. She watched it swim off, and then she turned to find Dar gazing at her, one hand lifted with its thumb up.

Kerry responded positively, and swam over to join her partner as they followed the group toward a large circular rock. The guide had all the divers swimming up through it, she realized, emerging at the top where there was a cameraman filming each one as they popped up. Ah. She got into line amiably. A videotape offering must be in the near future.

Dar was in front of her, so she put her hand on the taller woman's hip, holding herself in place as Dar started forward, towing her along. They both reached the circular hole together, and Kerry pressed close to her partner as they slid through, their gear barely clearing the rocks. On the other side, the cameraman caught them, giving them a big thumbs up as they both swam free of the enclosure and tumbled into somersaults in front of him.

Heh. Kerry took the lead now, heading downward to where the guide was pointing out something behind a rock. When she got closer, she saw it was a huge turtle, and she settled down cautiously next to it to get a better look.

Dar hovered above her, studying the animal with interest, then motion caught her eye and she looked up to see faces pressed against the Plexiglas wall next to them.

Several people waved at her. Dar lifted a hand and hesitantly waved back, surprised when the smallest faces started moving as their owners jumped up and down. Curiously, she drifted closer, and watched the children point at her.

She pointed back. They squealed, their mouths opening and closing. With one eyebrow raised, Dar decided to try something more interesting, and she inverted herself neatly, flipping her body over and hanging in the water upside down with bubbles trailing up the length of her.

A crowd had gathered now, and she was apparently the center of attention. Dar glanced down, to find Kerry sprawled over the floor of the tank, flippers crossed at the ankles, watching her with great amusement.

The turtle decided he was being upstaged, and lifted up his flippers clawing through the water as he drifted past Dar and nudged her with his foot.

Dar drew her knees up and somersaulted over him, and then dove for the tank bottom as the rest of the group came wandering over. Kerry caught up with her and gave a playful tug on her weight belt, then she found a school of yellow reef fish to focus her attention on.

Another tug. Dar sighed, a plume of bubbles rushing up toward the surface, but then she looked over at her partner and lifted her hand in question.

Kerry pointed at her, and then closed her fist, and then she held both hands together and rocked them. *I love you.*

Dar removed her regulator and stuck her tongue out, then pulled it hastily back in as the cold water surprised her with its sting. She put her regulator back into her mouth and bit down on the mouthpiece, sucking in a breath of cool, dry, rubber-scented air. Gathering the remaining shreds of her dignity, she rolled over in the water, looking around as the guide motioned them on.

Ahead of them were more floor-to-ceiling plate glass windows, with people behind them. Dar edged closer, realizing she was seeing the interior of the restaurant where they would be eating dinner.

As she floated down past the first window, her eyes focused on the people beyond it and felt a shock going up and down her spine as she recognized the faces. She half turned to find Kerry, only to have warm fingers clamp down on her wrist as Kerry eased in next to her.

Inside the glass, outlined in the eerie aqua shadows from the water, were Shari and Michelle. Seated in one of the best viewing tables, neither was paying attention to the sights. Instead, they were talking animatedly over full plates of dinner, as Michelle pointed her fork at Shari to make a point.

Shari put her glass down and shook a finger playfully at her, and they both laughed.

Dar made a hand sign. Kerry nodded. They both turned and swam a little ways off, floating in mid tank as they watched the rest of the group wander past the main windows. After a moment, Kerry pointed to the tank floor, and then lifted her hands suddenly, pushing them upwards in a rush.

Behind the mask, her partner's blue eyes twinkled mischievously. Dar glanced around. She and Kerry swam slowly down to the bottom of the tank, drifting inches off the ground as they made their way to the wall. At the base of the wall they paused, neither breathing. Dar held up one finger, then two, then three.

At the third, they both shot up past the window, exhaling a huge exhaust of bubbles that sounded like thunder around them.

Dar heard, even through the window, the clattering sound of dishes being dropped. She angled up and over with Kerry next to her like a limpet, diving down to another part of the exhibit and exchanging friendly waves with two small boys in identical Mickey Mouse ears.

After a few moments, Dar peeked over her shoulder, watching as two waiters hastily tried to clean up the two tumbled plates of food, while Shari tried frantically to wipe the red wine off her jacket. A snicker escaped her, causing a cloud of bubbles to emerge from her regulator, and she shifted her jaw, biting down on the rubber as she tried to control her laughter.

It was childish, she acknowledged to herself, as she saw Michelle throw her soiled napkin down in disgust.

But it was fun. Dar resolutely turned her head toward her waiting audience, and proceeded to make a face at them, blowing bubbles as they pressed their faces against the glass.

Kerry rolled onto her back and rested her hands on her belly, twiddling her thumbs as she grinned. Then she hastily rolled back over and paid attention to the little boys, as the two women suddenly turned and looked out the viewing port, pointing and yammering at the harried looking waiter.

Dar drifted down to her knees in the shell bottom holding out her hands and playing pat a cake with the smaller of the two boys. He was squealing in delight, his eyes sparkling with excitement as he slapped the Plexiglas from his side, his mother looking on with a smile.

Kerry peeked past Dar's shoulder, hoping her features were obscured enough by her gear as she spotted the figures in the window peering at them. For a moment, she thought her eyes met Michelle's and she was busted, but after a split second the figures looked elsewhere, finally pointing toward two of the male divers who were chasing each other in and out of the coral.

Aww. Kerry felt a sense of guilty enjoyment. She turned her back on the window and fastened her eyes on her partner instead, who was now swimming slowly away from the restaurant panes, coming alongside one of the small gray sharks.

Kerry followed her, falling into her usual position at Dar's shoulder as they came alongside the next big coral formation, settling slowly to the bottom on their knees as an entire school of brightly colored fish swirled around them.

She tipped her head back and spread her arms, feeling the fins brush her fingertips. Ahead of them, most of the group was clustered near the clear Plexiglas tube, amusing a host of guests snapping photos. Kerry decided it was their turn to be on stage, and she stayed where she was, playing with a curious, small angelfish nibbling at the side of her mask.

Her heart was still beating rapidly from their prank. She wondered if Dar's was, noticing her partner was merely drifting around the rock formation, turning slowly along her length as she took in the inside of the tank. Casually, she reached up and closed her hand around Dar's bare ankle, feeling the steady flutter of her pulse beneath her fingertips.

Dar looked over at her, and waggled her flipper, giving Kerry a thumbs up and a wink clearly visible even behind her mask.

Heh. Kerry released her and undulated her body, diving down toward the bottom of the tank to have an up close and personal introduction to another big turtle plodding along.

This was fun. She touched the turtle's shell, drifting back a little as it stopped its methodical chewing of algae and peered at her with its fathomless black eyes. Had the turtle seen their joke?

Did he think it was funny, too? Kerry scratched him on the side of his neck, charmed by the creature's gentle regard.

Then the turtle winked at her, and swam on, searching for new patches of algae to consume. Kerry leaned on her elbow, and then turned her head as something nudged her. Expecting to see Dar, she saw a shark instead.

But since it was a Disney shark, the animal, rather than eating her, merely bumped her with its nose and slid past her, letting her trail her fingers over its sandpaper skin.

Incredible. Kerry grinned. Simply an incredible day.

"THAT WAS AMAZING." Kerry wiped her face with a towel, wishing for a glass of anything to clean the taste of rubber out of her mouth. "Dar, can you believe we got afrrff." Suddenly the taste of rubber was made irrelevant as Dar swung the door shut on their changing cubicle and kissed her, effectively cutting off what she intended on saying. "Mm."

"Shh," Dar whispered into her ear, jerking her head toward the next cubicles where the two other women on the dive were getting out of their gear. "Yeah, I can't believe we got so close to those fish either," she added, in a louder tone. "Incredible."

Kerry made a twirling motion with her fingers, unzipping Dar's wetsuit and peeling the neoprene off to reveal Dar's tanned shoulders. "Did you see that shark?"

"Mmhm." Dar stripped off the suit and stepped out of it, hanging it over the wall of the cubby and leaning in to start the shower running. "We've seen most of those things before, but never in one place, and never so damn clearly."

"Yup." Kerry peeled out of her own suit and added it to Dar's, then removed her swimsuit and hung it up as well. She stepped into the shower as Dar got naked and joined her, and bowing to the close confines of the small space, she made the most of it by putting her arms around Dar and hugging her.

Dar pressed the button on the shampoo dispenser, and used a handful to lather Kerry's hair for her. She scrubbed the thick, pale strands as Kerry simply stood quietly, her fingertips running up and down Dar's back in a lazy rhythm.

The water pounded down on them, warming them after the long immersion in the cold tank, and the chilly walk down from the diver's lock. Dar rinsed the soap out of Kerry's hair, and knelt, resting her chin against Kerry's thigh as Kerry returned the favor.

Her skin felt a little tender, and the long day's exertions had started to spread a slight ache through her body. She was looking forward to a nice dinner with Kerry, and then sliding under the covers with her back in their comfortable room. Then a thought occurred. "Oh, crap."

"Something wrong?" Kerry leaned toward her. "Did I hit the sunburn on your neck?"

Dar sighed. "No. I just remembered I promised Eleanor I'd stop by the convention center tonight and make sure everything's all right for the opening of the show tomorrow."

"Oh." Kerry ran her fingers through Dar's hair, removing the soap from it as her partner tipped her head back and looked up at her. "Well, that won't take long. We can...oh, crap."

"Mmhm. We have to go back and get the car," Dar said. "We took the bus and monorail." She sighed again. "Oh well. We'll just have to go do it." With that, she rested her hand on Kerry's tensed thigh and stood, reaching for the shower controls to turn them off. "After dinner."

"Absolutely. I'm hungry enough to have started chewing on those turtles down there and that would have been a shame because they were adorable," Kerry agreed, as she followed Dar out of the shower and handed her partner one of the two large towels they'd left waiting.

The other two women had already finished dressing, and they heard the door close as they dried off. "Not real friendly, huh?" Kerry peered in the direction of the exit.

Dar lifted herself up on her tiptoes and peered over the partition, making sure they were alone in the room. "No." She nipped Kerry's ear playfully. "Did you see the crosses? They're from a Kansas seminary."

Kerry stood quite still, enjoying the tingles brought on by Dar's teeth. "And?" She patted her partner's body dry with her towel, removing impudent droplets from between her breasts. "Did they guess we're gay or something? What clued them?"

"Beats me." Dar watched Kerry lean closer and kiss a few more droplets away. "Maybe it's our haircuts."

Kerry looked up at her, one eyebrow arching sharply.

"More likely it's the way we look at each other." Dar grinned. "Or the fact that we spend more time dressing and undressing each other than all the rest of them combined." She ruffled Kerry's wet hair. "C'mon. Let's get our T-shirts and our certificates, and go eat."

Kerry toweled her head vigorously, and reached for her clothing, dismissing their unfriendly neighbors with a shrug. Not everyone, she reminded herself, accepted their lifestyle as easily as their friends or Dar's parents.

In fact, she mused, as she pulled on her shorts and fastened them, most people who were not gay really didn't seem to be comfortable with the idea, at least at first. What she'd discovered, however, was that after a while, even the most wary generally got used to it, and then they forgot about it.

That was pretty much what happened with her and Dar at work. In the beginning, there had been many people who had avoided her like the plague unless they had to come to her for something.

Now, however, she very seldom got what she referred to as the 'ew—gay cooties!' response. People generally treated her like anyone else, and that really was all she ever could have asked for.

With a satisfied sigh, she shouldered her small bag and followed Dar out of the changing room, setting down both of their wetsuits in the marked hamper. She ran her fingers through her hair to put it in some kind of order, and rubbed a little remaining water from her eyes as Dar opened the door into the hallway and they joined the rest of the group.

"Okay." The guide reappeared, with two of his buddies carrying a clipboard and a pile of bags. "I've got your shirts and your guaranteed frameable certificates here...anyone interested in getting the video? We've got it inside, and it's just twenty bucks. The money goes toward the marine sciences institute here, so we can keep doing these kinds of services."

"We'll take one," Kerry spoke up ahead of the others, who agreed and nodded.

"Great." The man smiled at her. "Hey listen, did any of you see anything weird happen in the tank? Like around the windows to the restaurant?"

Kerry felt Dar inhale, and she instinctively took a step closer to her, caught flatfooted by this new danger of revelation. Had any of the others seen them? And if they had, would they tell? She let her eyes slowly drift around the group, and then fastened them back on the guide.

Everyone had a puzzled look. Even Dar had manufactured a nice one, cocking her dark head to one side and lowering her eyebrows.

"Okay, well, I didn't see anything either, but somebody inside the restaurant swears they had someone scare the poo out of a couple of people at one of the window tables, so...I had to ask. Probably was a fish." The guide dismissed the entire affair, and went about passing out their goodie bags.

"Whew," Kerry muttered under her breath.

"Mm." Dar returned the guide's smile and took her booty. "Thanks...that was great."

"Hey, thanks yourself! You were great," the guide responded. "You were a real trooper with the kids. They loved ya! Got any yourself?"

"Just a dog," Dar responded. "Glad I was a hit."

Kerry took her bag. "It was really fantastic," she complimented the guide. "I had a great time."

"You're a good diver," the man responded. "You've got great buoyancy control. You dive a lot huh?"

"I do, yes," Kerry agreed. "Mostly in the Caribbean and South Atlantic." She smiled at him. "This was really cool."

"Thanks! Tell all your friends." The man smiled back, and moved on. "Your tapes'll be out in a minute, and after that, my buddy John here will take you back out to the lobby. Hope you all had a great time!"

"Yes!" the group responded in a chorus.

Dar rested her forearm on Kerry's shoulder, and they both relaxed as the guide left and the rest of the group milled around waiting for their videos. "This was nice," she remarked. "Totally Disneyfied, but nice."

"Uh huh," Kerry agreed. "And at least they don't pipe "It's a Small World" at you through underwater speakers." She guided Dar toward the doors, where a new staffer had appeared with a stack of plastic videotape cases. "C'mon, let's go."

Dar took the tape from the woman and they escaped into the Living Seas, blending into the sparse crowd and heading for the exit. As they passed through the doors, Shari and Michelle entered from the other direction, pausing to look around intently before moving on.

Chapter
Four

DAR DIDN'T EVEN bother with the front door this time. She
pulled the Lexus around to the back and parked in the loading dock,
hopping out and slamming the door as Kerry did the same. They
strolled over to the entrance in companionable silence and ducked
inside.

It was much less chaotic and much more organized, Dar noticed at
once. She paced slowly down the aisles of now completed booths,
giving the odd security guards now on duty an amiable look as she
passed them.

The ILS booth was in the center of the room, and she circled it
entirely once before she entered the neatly made up space. "Nice," she
commented to Kerry, who was checking out the locked case full of
routers and switches. "Everything look good?"

Kerry walked to one of the sets and brought it up, coding in her
password and running a few quick commands. "Looks very good," she
said. "Decent throughput."

Dar leaned against the center column with her hands in her shorts
pockets, admiring the contrast of Kerry's sun-gilded skin against the
white cotton of her shirt. The sleeves were rolled up, and the shirt was
tucked into her worn denim shorts and Dar found the whole picture
quite appealing. "Know what?" she drawled.

"What?" Kerry looked up inquisitively.

"You're gorgeous."

Kerry's sunburn deepened several shades, and she glanced around
the room before she produced a grin. "Um...thanks," she murmured.
"What brought that on?"

Dar shrugged. "Merely an observation. Are we getting a two meg
download?"

Kerry blinked. "What?" Her brows creased for a long moment
before she realized what Dar was talking about. "Oh...um." She looked
back at the screen in confusion, and then punched a few more keys.
"One point eight."

"Good enough," her partner decided. "We're streaming locally
anyway. At least I hope we are. Check to see if the marketing nitwits
downloaded the mpegs." She wandered over to the far side of the booth,
examining the colorful brochures curiously as Kerry bent over the
console again.

A door slammed. Dar lifted her head at the sound, turning and peering across the center toward the front of the room. She spotted the two figures and barely stifled the impulse to grab Kerry and disappear, reasoning that they'd have to face off against their two adversaries sooner or later.

But there was no point in rushing the confrontation, so she merely went back to examining the marketing literature.

"Dar?" Kerry's low voice reached her.

"I know," Dar answered calmly. "Just do your thing."

Kerry sat down in the nearest seat and continued her parsing, examining the file structures of the presentations they'd sent out from the office earlier that day. Her ears were perked, though, as she listened to the footsteps wandering through the hall, which would, she knew, eventually end up right where they were.

She grinned a little, and cracked her knuckles.

MICHELLE STOPPED AS she reached the edge of the booth and waited for the two women inside it to look up.

When they didn't, she cleared her throat. "Well, well."

Kerry glanced up from her screen. "Oh, hi." She greeted their guest cordially. "C'mon in."

Michelle availed herself of the invitation and stepped inside the booth, circling the desk Kerry was at and taking a seat on the edge of the console. "Hello, Dar." She peered at the booth's second occupant and paused.

"Hi." Dar rested her chin on her fist and looked up briefly, then went back to studying the settings she had been investigating. "How's it going?"

Somehow, it wasn't the reception Michelle seemed to have been expecting. "Damned good, actually. Bet you're surprised to see me here."

"Not really." Kerry finished checking her screen, and moved to another one. "You guys get everything taken care of? We heard there were some problems last night. I thought your booth looked pretty well together."

"Our booth?"

"Mmhm..." Kerry indicated the Telegenics display a few rows down. "I like the LCD scrolling–it's nice." She tapped a few keys, and clicked twice with her mouse, reviewing the results. "There, that's better. Did you adjust that, Dar?"

"Uh huh," Dar responded. "Put prioritization in and filtered out some of Mark's crap."

"So you liked our stuff, huh?" Michelle decided to go with the flow of the conversation. "Glad to hear that. We worked hard on it, just like we've been working hard on getting new accounts around here. You must have noticed that too."

Kerry sat back and gazed thoughtfully at Michelle, then she turned her eyes to Dar, who had looked up and was now twiddling her thumbs at her workstation. Dar shrugged. "Are you? Well, congrats, then," she replied.

"So, you didn't notice we took eight of your accounts from here?" Shari stepped around the pylon and confronted them, leaning on the counter right above where Dar was sitting. "Hello, Dar."

"Hi," Dar responded, without budging an inch. "Business is business, I figure. You win some, you lose some." She tipped her head back, meeting Shari's eyes evenly, feeling her guts clench.

After a long moment, Shari looked away first, ostensibly turning her attention to Kerry. "That the way you see it too, Ms. Stuart?"

"Is there any other way?" Kerry queried. "We've got lots of competitors."

Michelle and Shari exchanged quick glances. "Well, that's great," Michelle said. "Frankly, we were hoping you'd feel that way. I mean, yes, we're competitors, but we've all got a lot in common, don't we? It'd be nice to do some friendly networking for a change." She smiled at them. "Matter of fact, we were hoping you both would be here today. We checked in a few times, but didn't see you around."

"Nah." Dar leaned back and extended her long legs, crossing them casually at the ankles. "We came in and did our part last night. We've been relaxing all day."

"At the parks?" Michelle smiled again.

"Like you were, huh?" Kerry indicated the Goofy shirts they were wearing. "It was a beautiful day, wasn't it?"

Shari glanced down at herself, and her face twisted into a half grimace. "Yeah, well, we love shopping," she muttered. "Never can have too many of these."

Dar slid her hand up, covering the grin that threatened to appear on her face.

"Listen." Michelle wrested control of the conversation back. "We really dropped by to make sure things were ready before we headed back to our hotel. You two free for breakfast tomorrow? Maybe we can chat then."

I'd rather eat Donald Duck jello eggs on toast with a pack of mimes. Kerry hesitated, trying to recall what their schedule was for the following day. The convention started at ten, so... She looked at Dar, reading the resigned set of her eyebrows and the faint twitch on either side of her mouth.

Kerry wrinkled her nose slightly, and saw the wry twinkle appear in Dar's eyes. "I think we're free for breakfast, aren't we? Unless you promised Marketing we'd meet with them." She gracefully gave Dar an out anyway, and waited for her decision.

"I can't take Eleanor before coffee," Dar replied. "Yeah, we're free." She glanced up at Shari. "Where are you staying?"

"The Sheraton across from here," Shari answered warily. "But their restaurant is pitiful."

"Ours isn't," Kerry said. "Why don't you meet us there? It's the Grand Floridian." She flipped off the monitor she'd been working at and stood up. "They've got great banana stuffed French toast." She let her hands come to rest on her hips and cocked her head at them. "Eight all right? We get up early."

Dar folded her arms over her chest, content to let Kerry hack and slash her way through with her charmingly piratical good manners. "Yeah, that's early enough to miss the characters. I don't want to scare Pluto again," she remarked with an easy grin.

Michelle appeared as though she'd sucked on a sour orange. "Sure," she finally agreed. "We'll meet you there." She got up and stepped out of the booth, giving Shari a backhanded slap on the arm. "C'mon. Let's get out of here."

Kerry perched next to Dar's seat and watched them leave, casually leaning her wrist on her partner's shoulder. "I think we scored," she remarked as they walked through the entrance and out of sight. "You were right, Dar. That was exactly how to handle them. Good call."

"Oh yeah." Dar closed down her connection and stood, stretching her body out. "Round one to Roberts and Stuart, Ding ding," she added. "But now we've got round two at eight a.m. tomorrow."

"Yeah." Kerry sighed. "What a way to ruin perfectly good French toast." She slipped her arm around Dar's waist as they walked together toward the rear door. "You know, Dar, I really don't like Shari."

"Oh, really?" Dar opened the back door and held it as they exited.

"Really." Kerry took a breath of the warm, humid night air. "In fact, I'd like to take a set of cat five crimpers and clamp the end of her nose with them."

Dar looked at her. One eyebrow lifted. "What would that do?"

"Make her scream like a cat in a blender," Kerry replied, with a firm nod. "Start my day off just right."

Dar's nostrils flared. "Remind me not to piss you off, okay?" She draped an arm over Kerry's shoulders.

Kerry chuckled and shook her head.

"THANKS." KERRY SCRIBBLED her name on the room service check and handed it back to the waiter, then closed the door after him as he slipped out into the hallway. On the table near the window he'd left a tray, which had a large white china pot, two cups, and a plate full of chocolate dipped strawberries.

Kerry inspected the tray, lifting the lid on the pot and sniffing appreciatively. "Mm." She put the lid back down and dusted her hands off, turning her back on it and heading for the bathroom.

Dar was inside, applying aloe to her shoulders which were a deep, burnished color half tan and half sunburn. Kerry took the bottle from her and smeared the stuff across her back, rubbing it gently on the patches between the straps of her swimsuit. "You got toasted, honey."

"I feel it." Dar seemed embarrassed. "Next time remind me to put my damn sunscreen on after I get out of the water, willya?"

"Sorry. Thought you had." Kerry winced at the red marks. "My fault. I should have checked when I had you put some on me."

"Your fault?" Dar chuckled softly. "I could have remembered when I was putting some on you." She flexed her arms and turned, taking the bottle and putting a little on her fingers. Then she carefully painted Kerry's face with it, tracing the pink skin over her rounded cheekbones. "You got a little toasted too."

"I sure did." Kerry let her hands rest on Dar's hips. "But you know what? I had a great day. The dive was stupendous, and scaring the poo out of those two was so choice."

Dar grinned. "Yeah, it was," she admitted. "A little juvenile, though."

"So was their trying to make trouble last night," Kerry stated. "And so was their showing up tonight and trying to bait us. So there."

"So there." Dar leaned over and kissed her, tasting a hint of lip balm as she explored Kerry's mouth. "I am starting to wonder now what they're up to, though." She added, "The bitchiness I understand. Them being nice is scary."

Kerry took her hand and tugged. "Well, let's give 'em the benefit of the doubt, Dar. You never know — maybe they decided to grow up too."

"Mm." Dar followed her willingly. "Like us, you mean?"

"Exactly." Kerry paused and indicated the tray. "So, grownup. Wanna share some hot chocolate and berries with me?"

They walked to the table hand in hand. Dar gazed down at the treats with a smile, picking up a piece of apple garnish and taking a bite of it. "What more could any woman ask for?" she inquired around her mouthful of apple.

"Share." Kerry stood on her tiptoes and closed her teeth around the apple slice, and they both nibbled toward the center, giggling as their noses bumped and they fought over the last scrap of it.

"Whoops." Dar rolled her tongue around a small, hard point. "Seed."

"Where?" Kerry caught the pink appendage in her teeth, surprising Dar into releasing the seed into her mouth. "Ah! Got it!" She pulled back and swallowed the seed sticking her tongue out a few times like a lizard. "Mm."

Dar laughed. "Did just swallow that?"

"Yup." Kerry picked up a strawberry chaser and bit into its chocolate shell ruthlessly. "I heard a story once that if you swallow an apple seed it makes the tree of knowledge grow inside you."

"Um."

"Here. Don't think about it. Just eat." Kerry offered her half a strawberry. "It was a goofy story, but it's better than the other one I heard."

Dar chewed her berry contentedly. "That it makes you healthy, wealthy and wise?" She hazarded a guess.

"That it makes you pregnant."

Dar spit a bit of berry halfway across the table and nearly inhaled the rest of it. She covered her mouth as a laugh erupted from her.

Kerry patted her back solicitously. "Told you it was goofy. You'd be surprised at what you end up being taught in Sunday school that far north, honey."

"Jesus...remind me to throw some of our education outreach budget up there, will you?" Dar buried her face into Kerry's shoulder. "Before they start teaching Cabbage Patch creationist theory."

Kerry gave her a kiss on the head and exhaled happily, patting Dar's cheek when she lifted her head up. "Will do." She brushed Dar's cheek with her lips. "But they threw the book away when they came up with you."

Dar poured out two cups of hot chocolate, lifted hers, and clinked its edge against Kerry's when she picked her own up. "Here's to us." She looked into Kerry's eyes. "To hell with everyone else."

Kerry took a sip, and gave a kiss. "I'll drink to that anytime."

DAR SETTLED HER balance, gripping the bar on the weights with both hands at shoulder width and pressing her back against the weight bench. Slowly, she lifted the barbell clear, and lowered it, pushing it away from her with the same deliberation until her arms were straight.

It was very quiet in the hotel's gym, not surprising since it was before dawn. Dar lowered the bar and pressed it up again, keeping an even rhythm until she'd done it ten times. Then she set the weight back on the bar and let her arms drop.

"Ouch." She flexed her shoulder carefully, reaching over to probe the tightness she could feel still in the joint. It had mostly healed after her injury, but getting a full range of motion back and evening out the strength between her two arms was proving a long and, to her, tedious process.

But a process it was, and she slid down, fitting her legs under the leg press and flexing her thigh muscles to steadily lift up the weights she'd set on it. Aside from their new kickboxing classes, she'd felt the need lately to reaffirm the power she'd taken years to build into her body and she'd started doing a little more weightlifting than she had been for a while.

There wasn't any real reason for it. Dar folded her hands across her stomach and counted silently. Just a phase she was going through, apparently, figuring maybe her running and other efforts were getting her bored at the moment.

Breakfast was also on her mind. As she exercised, Dar went over the possible tacks she could take in their next fencing match with Shari and Michelle. Should she give them the benefit of the doubt and assume maybe they did want to bury the hatchet? Maybe Kerry was right.

Dar slid up on the bench and switched back to the chest presses. Maybe she was letting the personal side of the issue get in the way a little too much. After all, Shari wasn't anything she needed to worry about now. She'd passed her years back in the business strategy arena. She was a successful corporate executive, and she had the stable loving relationship Shari had been so sure she hadn't been capable of.

So it was her game, match, and set, and she had nothing to fear from either her ex-lover, her ex-lover's company, or the breakfast they were going to have in just a few hours.

Right. Dar let the bar drop again, and braced her legs, beginning a set of sit-ups, contracting her torso muscles in a more rapid rhythm. So why did she have knots in her guts?

For a few long moments she turned the thoughts off, concentrating on the exercise instead. Then her eyes lifted and met her reflection's gaze from the mirrors on the wall and she saw the wry lift of her own lips. "I think that whole 'grown up' crap wasn't a hundred percent now, was it, Paladar?" She addressed herself in a mocking tone. "Still smarting from that first blow off, huh?"

Just the articulation seemed to help. The knotted feeling inside her stomach eased, and she felt her body relax in response to it. "Redneck squirt fraud." She stuck her tongue out and slowed her motion, turning the last crunch into a rise to her feet as she ambled over to the leg press with a sigh. "Turn off the hormones, turn on the synapses. Think about what you've got right now."

She loaded an extra plate onto the bar and got under it, lifting it up onto her shoulders carefully and pausing to set her feet. With a deep breath, she went down with the weight, then straightened her legs and eased back up.

She did it again, reveling in the reassuring sense of control as her body responded smoothly. *You are the energy in this, Dar.* She reminded herself silently. *They want something from you. That means you have to drive the situation to your advantage.*

I can do that. Her inner voice responded. *We can do that.*

Dar studied the far wall of the gym. *I hope.*

THE NEXT MORNING started off charmingly enough, Kerry reasoned, as she surveyed the chocolate kiss resting squarely on her navel. Dar was nowhere to be seen, but she concluded the kiss could not have come from a Disney waiter, so she unwrapped it and popped it into her mouth as she slid from under the covers and got out of bed.

A rumble of thunder caught her attention, and she glanced outside the window, where a gray, drizzly day met her eyes. "Hm." She lifted her T-shirt from the back of the chair and slipped into it, turning to check the clock by the bed. "Six thirty."

She poked her head into the bathroom, and deduced by the one neatly hung, but still damp towel over the shower bar and the distinct, lingering scent of their body wash that Dar had taken her morning scrub and gone out to do...

To do what? Kerry scrubbed her teeth and ruminated on that for a while. Dar hadn't mentioned going out before meeting their unwelcome breakfast guests, so what was her partner up to?

The answer came quite unexpectedly when the door to the room opened. Kerry stuck her head out and spotted Dar entering, dressed in a pair of sweatpants and a cutoff cotton shirt. "Hmph."

"Morning." Dar greeted her with a cheerful grin. "Ready for breakfast?"

"Nph," Kerry pointed her toothbrush at Dar. "Wherf yof gop?"

"Gym," Dar replied. "I woke up at five, and couldn't go back to sleep."

"Hmph." Kerry disappeared, going to the sink and rinsing the toothpaste out of her mouth. "You could have woken me up. I'd have gone with you." She wiped her lips and returned to the doorway.

Dar stripped out of her sweatpants and slipped past her, giving her a kiss on the back of the neck. "I know. But I was doing heavy presses, and I know you hate those."

"Mm." Kerry wrapped her fingers in the fabric of Dar's half shirt and followed her like a puppy toward the shower. "That's true, but I didn't have to do them and I do like watching you when you do."

"You looked too cute to wake up." Dar removed her shirt and sports bra, then tugged on Kerry's T-shirt. "Share a shower with me?"

Mollified, Kerry removed her shirt and stepped into the shower as Dar adjusted the spray. "Thanks for the kiss, by the way." She picked up the scrubber, still damp from its earlier use, and squeezed some gel onto it.

Dar joined her. "No problem." She stretched both arms out and flexed her hands. "I thought you'd want to get as much sleep as you could, since we're starting early, and it's gonna be a long day."

Kerry stifled a yawn and managed to not quite suppress a rueful grin. "Yeah," she admitted. "Now I wish I hadn't been such a smart mouth and suggested breakfast at the crack of dawn." She scrubbed Dar's chest industriously. "Though, it was worth it to see their sour pusses."

Dar slid her arms around Kerry and held her for a brief moment, giving her a hug before she released her again. "You know what?"

Cautiously, green eyes peered up from between a few wet strands of pale hair. " Are you going to make me blush again?" Kerry asked.

"Not that I minded the compliment," she added.

"It was true." Dar exhaled contentedly. "But what I was going to say was that I'm sort of looking forward to this damn breakfast."

Kerry gave her a light scrub around the belly button. "Why?"

"I just am," Dar replied, stroking Kerry's cheek with the backs of her knuckles. "We may even have fun at it."

We just may. Kerry chuckled silently to herself. She had always fiercely defended Dar, even from the first. Now, faced with someone who had quite deliberately hurt her beloved friend and lover, Kerry found a very unexpectedly fierce protective instinct rearing its head inside her.

Kerry finished her washing, and they stepped out to dry each other off. She wanted to kick Shari's ass and the violence of the thought almost surprised her.

Almost.

DAR RELAXED ON the bench in the lobby, stretching her legs out and leaning back as she watched Kerry circle the pretty atrium examining the birds. Arriving a little early, they settled in to wait for their guests, as the rain continued to drum on the plate glass windows.

She hitched one denim covered knee up and rested her ankle on its mate, examining the little blue and white cross stitches on one side of her sneaker. It was cool in the lobby, and she briefly wished she'd put on a long sleeve T-shirt instead of a short sleeved one, but considered that the writing on the front of it was probably worth a little chill.

Kerry returned from her impromptu bird watching and took a seat next to Dar, kicking her heels out a little listening as her sneakers squeaked a bit on the newly polished floor. "Nice weather," she commented.

"Mm," Dar agreed, with a nod.

"Hope they got caught in it." Kerry went on, in a mild voice.

"Your wish to the god of thunder's ears." Dar pointed through the window. "Nice work."

Kerry peered through the rain-streaked glass to see Shari and Michelle running awkwardly through the rain to get to the door from the parking lot. "Heh," she chuckled. "Must be tough running in those heels."

"Mmhm," Dar agreed. "Must be."

The two reached the doors and entered, their smart and well-fitted business suits spotted with rain, which also glistened in droplets on every square inch of them. Both shook their hands in disgust as they looked around.

"Hi." Kerry waved. "Over here!"

Dar waited for them to walk over before she uncrossed her legs and stood. "Morning," she greeted them briefly. "Dining room's that way."

She turned and headed for the steps, clearly expecting them to follow.

"Good morning," Michelle greeted Kerry in a polite tone. "Lovely weather." She glanced at Shari, who merely started off after Dar. After a second she started walking as well, and Kerry fell into step next to her. "So, is this where you start the good cop, bad cop routine?"

"Hm?" Kerry cocked her head. "What routine?"

Michelle shook her head and snorted. "Never mind." She exhaled. "Looks like the convention's going to start on time, if anyone comes in this mess, that is."

"I think they will," Kerry said. "But in any case, the people who we really want there are already here, and with this weather, they're really more likely to attend the con than skip out and go to the parks. So it works in our favor."

Michelle glanced at her, and then made a small sound of grudging agreement. "So how are things otherwise?" she asked. "We tried to get into Vista, but I heard they signed a long term with you this year."

"True." Kerry motioned Michelle ahead of her as they reached the restaurant. Dar and Shari were already at the server's stand, waiting for them so they could be seated. "We were able to put most of their stuff up on our new net, and it meant a good cost savings for them if they signed now. So they did," she continued, as they followed a uniformed woman to a table near the front.

They sat down across from each other, Kerry neatly slipping in next to Dar as the woman handed them their menus. "Thanks." She let hers sit, already knowing what she was going to order.

And what Dar was going to order, for that matter. She watched Dar fiddle with her fork, and then she shifted and leaned forward, bringing her knee into contact with her partner's. "So, how are things with you?" she asked Michelle. "Are you having fun doing this start up?"

"It's been a blast," Michelle responded amiably. "Until this week, that is. I forgot how lousy the weather was here this time of year." She took her napkin and attempted to dry herself. "Or maybe I deliberately blocked it out of my memory."

"I've gotten used to it down south," Kerry said. "I remember the time I saw my first tropical thunderstorm I thought the world was ending."

Dar chuckled.

"But we have lots of plans for the future," Michelle concluded. "How about you?"

The waiter arrived and stood poised, a look of polite inquiry on his face. "Ma'am?" He addressed Michelle first. "Would you like to order?"

"I'd like to be put through the spin dry cycle," The short redhead answered. "But I'll take a continental, please," she added. "Coffee, wheat toast."

The waiter scribbled for a moment, then shifted his gaze to Shari. "Ma'am?"

"Juice and a bowl of whatever dry cereal you have," Shari answered shortly. "Skim milk."

Kerry folded her hands together on the table and made eye contact with the waiter as he looked inquiringly at her. She shifted her gaze to Dar's profile, and then looked back at him. "Two orders of French toast with crispy bacon, coffee, and two large glasses of milk, please."

The man beamed at her, and took the menus she handed over. "Be right back."

Dar leaned back and rested her elbows on her chair arms, steepling her fingers together, then folding them inward. "We have plans for the future as well," she allowed. "We've recently started development work on G2 of our net."

Shari frowned, but Michelle blinked and sat forward. "But you put it up only last year," she objected. "You can hardly have a baseline yet."

"We've got one," Dar replied. "I've projected out five years, and with current trends in applications development, I'll need a G2 in twenty four months at the very latest. We short wired some whole development cycles in firmware."

"Impressive." Michelle nodded, with a serious expression. "But if your projections come short, it could be an expensive white elephant."

Dar's expression remained relaxed. She flexed her fingers a little, the lights catching on the ring she wore on her third finger as they moved. "It's circular." She shook her head. "Right now, we've provided a pipe for some companies that allows them to triple their production cycles. That's speeding up their demand, which they'll come back to us for. No one else can do it right now."

"So your marketing hype says," Shari interjected. "But there's more to it than expensive hardware."

"The system capabilities aren't hype," Kerry said. "Or else the accounts of ours you targeted for conversion wouldn't have been the external and programming services ones. You didn't go after anyone with our infrastructure."

Shari looked over at Kerry, her eyebrows lifting slightly. Kerry gazed back at her with a mild expression. "Contracts are contracts," she countered. "We only started with those."

Dar chuckled. "And service is service. What's gonna happen the first time one of them calls you up and wants their contract expanded on the spot to new coverage, or they move to a different system that you don't have?"

"We can handle that," Shari answered quickly. "We've got the best people in the business...some of them were damn glad to come over from you, in fact."

"If they came from us, they weren't the best in the business." Dar let her chin rest on her fist. "We don't let the best go."

"Maybe they got tired of the same old same old then," Shari shot back. "We've got a whole new attitude about what we do. People like that."

Michelle took a breath and gave her companion a look. "Hey. We're supposed to be networking. Not boxing," she said. "Of course we picked certain arenas to compete in. We're not stupid," she added. "But we are in an expansion mode."

The waiter returned and poured their coffee, giving them all a moment's break. When he finished and left again, Shari leaned back. "Michelle's right," she conceded. "It's been a tough startup, and we're damn proud of the progress we've made."

Kerry stirred her coffee and took a sip. "Well, you can thank us for making it easier than it might have been," she spoke up. "A lot of accounts that I go in on the bid teams for, who've never worked with us are still not sure if women can handle IT, you know. The accounts you worked with already know we can."

Michelle and Shari exchanged glances. Shari tilted her head to one side, and her lips quirked. "Never really considered that," she allowed.

"Mm." Michelle nodded briefly. "That's a good point. I was on the other side for a long time, and I never had any doubts myself..." She chuckled self deprecatingly "But I remember sitting at intercompany seminars with lots of old boys who did."

"Yes." Kerry's lips tensed into a half smile. "I lived with one for many years." She rested her hand on the table, her wrist brushing Dar's crossed knee. "We've worked hard for what we've achieved too."

The waiter came back again, this time with a big tray. He placed their breakfasts down, then came to the front of the table and straightened up. "Anything else I can get for you right now?" he inquired. "Everything all right?"

Kerry inspected her plate of French toast, while Dar picked up her glass of milk and took a long swallow. "Looks great," she complimented the man. "Thanks." She picked up her fork and knife, cutting off a piece of the fragrant toast and dipping it neatly into some syrup before she put it into her mouth.

It was quiet for a few minutes, as everyone concentrated on eating. Dar typically sliced her toast into manageable squares then put her knife down, and selected the closest square to liberally drown in syrup.

"So you don't think we can compete with you on services?" Shari asked, after a long moment's silence. "I think you're wrong."

Dar glanced at her. Then she went back to eating. "You can think whatever you want."

Kerry took a sip of her milk. "We have contracts go other places all the time," she commented. "Everyone wants to get the best deal for their company, after all."

"Exactly," Shari agreed. "You can't compete with us on pricing."

"No." Kerry wiped her lips. "We don't disregard our pricing model."

"That's why we got all those accounts," Shari said. "So don't say we can't compete."

"You got those accounts because I allowed you to have them," Dar spoke up, keeping her attention on her French toast. "I was the one who elected not to counter bid. I don't undersell delivery."

Kerry glanced up, and caught a surprised look on Michelle's face, and a stunned one on Shari's. "Like I said, it happens all the time," she remarked. "We have another category of accounts we call rebounders." Her eyes twinkled a little. "So you better make sure you perform for those customers or you won't have them for long."

"We definitely know how to take care of our customers." Michelle recovered. "But listen, like I said, we're not here to box. We've got a lot in common, and there's no sense in us squabbling all the time."

Dar looked up from her plate, looked at Michelle, then at Shari, then exchanged glances with Kerry before she chuckled and went back to eating.

"Sounds good to me," Kerry said diplomatically. "I'm looking forward to the start of the convention. They have some interesting panels this year, don't they?"

"Always love those panels," Michelle grimly agreed. "Right Shari?"

"Yeah. Love 'em."

"THAT WASN'T VERY successful."

Dar leaned on the inner balcony, watching a bird fly across the inside of the huge lobby. "Not for them, no," she agreed. "But I sure had fun."

Kerry looped a finger into Dar's belt and tugged. "Let's go change, sweetheart. We're due at the convention in forty minutes." She turned and started walking, towing her taller companion behind her. "You know, Dar, I don't know that antagonizing those two was a really good idea."

Dar sighed aggrievedly. "Kerry I didn't antagonize them on purpose. I just answered the damn questions. Did you want me to lie?"

Kerry unlocked the door to their room and pushed it open. "I mean, I don't like them either, but we could have had a truce during the show. I don't really want to spend the next two days dodging darts."

"Yeah, I know." Dar trudged past her and kicked her sneakers off, pulling open the closet door to expose the neatly pressed business clothes hanging there. "Sorry." She pulled her T-shirt over her head and tossed it over the back of the nearby chair, unbuttoning her jeans with one hand, and sliding out of them.

Kerry leaned back against the dresser, watching her partner for a few minutes. She pushed off and walked over to her, pressing her cheek against Dar's bare shoulder for just an instant. She dropped a kiss on the same shoulder and slipped past Dar, drawing her fingernails along Dar's back as she headed for the bathroom.

Dar almost let her get out of reach, then at the last minute she extended one long arm and caught Kerry's sleeve.

Feeling the tug, Kerry stopped and half turned, her brows lifting in question. Her searching eyes found something in Dar's that made her walk back over and lean against her, waiting in silence as her partner's jaw muscles worked briefly.

After a little silence between them, Dar lifted one hand and gently traced the curve of Kerry's jaw, an unusually sad look on her face.

"What?" Kerry asked, in a low tone. "It's Shari, isn't it?"

Dar's lips twitched slightly. "It's idiotic," she replied. "I can't be nice to her, Kerry, no matter how I try to rationalize it."

Kerry leaned into her touch. "I know she hurt you."

Dar blinked a few times. "She almost made me miss out on meeting you," she replied quietly. "Kerry, I hate her. I can't pretend I don't." She exhaled, feeling a sense of almost absurd relief from saying the words, and even more so when she saw the understanding in Kerry's eyes. "I know this is business, but I can't do it."

The cell phone still clipped to Dar's discarded jeans buzzed, but Kerry took both of Dar's hands in hers and ignored it, looking her partner squarely in the eye.

Her breath almost stopped in her chest, seeing an expression on that face she'd never seen before. Then Dar blinked, and it was gone, but Kerry knew she'd gotten a glimpse of the confused young woman who had gotten kicked in the head by love all those years ago.

It stirred a feeling inside her, deep and powerful, and she pressed her body against Dar's, slipping her arms around her partner's sturdy form and pulling Dar close. "I understand." She tilted her head to look up. "We'll deal with it. You be as nasty as you want to be. I'm right there with you." Her arms tightened. "I'm right here for you."

Dar sighed. "Boy I must sound like a nitwit," she murmured softly.

"Never," Kerry replied.

"Yeah, I do." Dar rested her cheek against Kerry's head. "But what the hell. They expect me to be an asshole. I'll live up to their expectations." She half chuckled, a tiny, wry sound. "But no more breakfasts. I'm not wasting one more cent of my expense account getting indigestion."

Kerry dropped her hand down and gave Dar's belly a rub. "Did you really?"

A sigh. "Yeah," Dar admitted.

"Okay." Kerry took a deep breath. "Here's what I'd like you to do. Will you think about it at least before you start making those grunting noises?"

Caught in the actual act of preparing to do just that, Dar cleared her throat instead. "Um. Sure."

"I'd like you to crash here for a bit, and let me show my title off at the show for a while." Kerry said. "Would you do that for me?"

"I don't need you to do that."

"No," Kerry agreed. "But I'd like to anyway. Please?"

Dar considered the request seriously. Her first instinct was to refuse, and she mulled that over as her fingers sorted through Kerry's hair, watching the gray illumination outside catch light and dark shadows in the soft locks. The pros and cons sorted themselves out as easily, and after a brief pause, she nodded "All right."

Kerry smiled at her.

"On one condition."

The green eyes rolled. "Always a condition."

"If anyone asks you where I am..." Dar clasped her hands and put them behind Kerry's neck.

"Mm?"

"You tell them you wore me out last night and I had to take a nap."

Kerry produced a noise somewhere between a sneeze and a cough, both of her eyebrows hiking up. "Dar!"

At last, her partner laughed softly. "Just kidding," she relented. "Actually, I'm going to boot up and start some deep research on Telegenics." Her brows contracted. "If we missed who was behind them, we might have missed a lot more. You know how much I hate surprises."

"Sounds like a plan." Kerry plucked at the waistband of Dar's briefs, a spiffy blue pair covered in grinning goldfish. "You could lay out on the balcony in these. Everyone would think it was a swimsuit. No one would know."

"I would know," Dar objected. "My daddy didn't raise me to show my drawers in public, you pithy little Yankee." She nudged Kerry a little. "G'wan. Eleanor is probably getting so nervous her eyelashes are touching her navel."

Reassured by her partner's tone, Kerry moved to the closet to get her suit out. When she turned, Dar had tugged a pair of shorts on and was sprawling onto the bed, already pulling her laptop over to her.

Satisfied with her plan, Kerry grabbed the hanger with her suit, a new silver blue one with a deep aqua silk blouse that she'd picked up not long before. She spent a moment attaching her favorite pin to the lapel, and then studied the results.

It would do. She glanced over her shoulder at Dar, whose half bare body was vividly outlined against the white sheets and spared herself a moment of envy, and then she started dressing for the show.

"Hey, Ker?" Dar interrupted her. "You should keep that T-shirt on."

Kerry paused and glanced at the garment. "Oh, that'd make a great impression, Dar." She laughed, a touch embarrassed. "Were you thinking I could open my jacket and flash anyone who pissed me off?"

Dar rolled onto her side and crossed her ankles. "Hm."

"I was joking." Kerry tossed the shirt at her, landing it on her head and watching in amusement as it draped half over her face and obscured one pale eye. "I'm not wearing a shirt that says RTFM to a trade show."

Her partner wiggled a sock covered toe at her. "Yeah," she agreed. "You'd spend your whole damn time explaining what it meant."

Kerry chuckled, removing her jeans and reluctantly replacing them with the austere, straight-line skirt that came to a respectable knee level and the light, silk shirt that was thankfully sleeveless. She tucked the blouse into the skirt's waistband and buckled the integrated belt, picking up her shoes and taking them to the bed with her as she sat down to put them on. "I think I like the one you have better," she said. "The programming one?"

Dar chuckled. "I like the 'no, I won't fix your damn computer' one myself." She rested her head on her fist and ignored her laptop screen. "Hey, Ker?"

Kerry fastened her watch around her wrist and stood, turning to face the bed. "Hm?"

"Thanks."

"For?"

The visible blue eye twinkled. "Being my best friend."

Kerry picked up her jacket and walked over to the side of the bed, leaning over to kiss Dar on the lips. "And what a pleasure it is to be that," she whispered, nudging aside the still draped shirt so she could look into both eyes. "I'll give you a call when it's time for you to make your grand, triumphant entrance, okay?"

"Okay," Dar agreed. "Have fun."

Kerry shrugged into her jacket, twitching the light linen fabric straight and fastening the single button. It was cut somewhat low, accentuating her tapered physique, and she gave Dar a wink as she accepted the frankly admiring gaze turned on her. "Look okay?"

"You look better out of it," Dar replied. "But it'll do for now." She watched Kerry check her image in the mirror, then pause to clip the cell phone to her belt. "Give them heck."

"Do my best." Kerry went to the door, looking back as she opened it and leaned against the jamb. "Will you..."

"Keep my eye on the pipes?" Dar swiveled her laptop around, displaying a screen full of jumping gauges. "Nah."

Kerry grinned and ducked out the door, letting it slide shut behind her.

Dar let the echoes fade before she turned the laptop around and minimized the displays, bringing up another screen and keying in a terse request. "All right...let's see what the hell we've got here," she muttered to herself. "Before anyone other than me realizes how frigging embarrassing it is that I let these guys stomp all over us and didn't even pay attention to it."

She set the request to run and lay back against the pillows. After a few moments the silence of the room started bothering her and she reached for the television control, flipping on the room's set. After browsing her choices, she settled on ESPN and let it run in the background as she opened her mail program.

The inbox filled with black lines that she glanced over, dividing her attention between the headers and the women playing volleyball on the screen. After a few minutes, however, she abandoned the mail and watched the game, tucking Kerry's discarded T-shirt under her head as she put it down on the pillow. In her peripheral vision, a thin line of alert gauges winked reassuringly green.

IT WAS A short trip, but Kerry was glad it was over. Driving through a downpour heavy enough to drown lobsters with nervous tourists wasn't her idea of fun at any time. She was more than happy when she parked Dar's big Lexus near the front of the building and bolted for the door.

A small crowd was milling there, and as she ran her fingers through her hair to shed the rain from it, the guard spotted her company badge and politely cleared a path. Kerry gave him a gracious nod then realized belatedly it was the same guy as the night they'd arrived. Her face crinkled into a wry grin as he held the door for her. "Thanks," she addressed him pleasantly. "Sure beats coming in the construction entrance."

He froze, but she didn't give him a chance to answer as she strode inside and headed for the show hall. Now, the lights in the outer lobby were on, and a buzz of conversation filled the high ceiling'd space. Banners were strung across over the doorways and company representatives were everywhere, passing out marketing gimmicks and the occasional business card.

It was all too familiar to Kerry. She'd attended more than her share of trade shows on behalf of ILS, and as she made her way through the crowd and was recognized, she returned the greetings with pleasant good manners.

It was ironic in the extreme that her early training in her father's household now served her so well, making her responses gracious and automatic and completely forgettable. Kerry excused herself from between two of her major distributor's sales directors and escaped into their booth, giving the techs and the salespeople a brief wave. "Hi guys."

"Kerry!" Mark appeared from apparently nowhere, dressed in a crisp company shirt and black pleated slacks. "Glad you're here."

"Uh oh." Kerry brushed a last droplet off her sleeve. "What's broken?"

Her MIS manager put his hands on his hips. "Does it have to be a bad thing that you're here?" he asked plaintively.

"No," Kerry smiled at him. "True disasters wait for Dar." She glanced around at the crowd. "They about to open the doors? Lot of action going on around here."

"No shit," Mark agreed. "Hey, you know who's here?" His voice dropped, and he moved closer to Kerry.

Kerry gave him a wry look.

"Guess you do."

"We had breakfast with them." Kerry ran her eye over the interior of the booth, and gave the approaching Eleanor a quick smile. Everything looked ready, and she exhaled out that tiny bit of apprehension still tensing her guts from their abandonment of the prior day. "Morning, El."

"Good morning to you too, Kerry." Eleanor was in a good humor. "Fricking weather's going to knock us on the ass for a while, but that's a good thing. Start slow, less bull." She leaned against the counter next to Kerry. "Where's Rambo's worst nightmare?"

"Chilling." Kerry watched a group of salesmen from their biggest network equipment supplier break out of a huddle and make a beeline for her. "She'll be by later."

"Good." Eleanor spotted a slow, but steady flow of people into the room. "Let's keep them waiting... I know there's at least four big talkers around who were looking to meet her." Eleanor brushed her hands together. "All right folks — it's showtime. Let's go get 'em."

Mark eased back in next to her as the marketing people cleared out, starting to filter through the crowd with their bags full of ILS stress balls and the rather clever little beanbag monitor perchers that resembled a cartoon Rottweiler theoretically watching over you. "Man, there were people talking all over the place today," he told Kerry. "Those lowballers were telling everyone they're the new power players around here."

Kerry scratched her nose. "They do talk a lot," she agreed.

"They came over here talking shit, but I ran them off," Mark added. "Pain in the asses."

"Mm." Kerry folded her arms across her chest. "They tried to recruit us the other night."

Mark laughed. "Yeah, the boys told me," he agreed. "Bet he's going to crap when he finds out who he was talking to."

Kerry spied their little friend in question and chuckled under her breath. 'Yeah." She pushed off from the console and strolled off. "I bet he is."

THE SOFT CHIME of her laptop slowly penetrated Dar's idle, formless dreams and after a few moments of confusion, she opened her eyes, blinking them a few times to regain their focus. "Umph." She lifted a hand and scrubbed her face, putting her head down and almost letting the warm comfort of her pillow reclaim her.

One hand lifted and touched her track pad, and she studied the results of her query in silence. One eyebrow slowly lifted. She rose up on one elbow and typed another request in one handed, rolling the pointer over and clicking to submit it.

She'd slept for two hours, and she felt like she could sleep for a few more. Maybe it was the weather. Dar peered over her own shoulder at the window, which was still being lashed by rain. It was dark inside the room, and cool—perfect day for staying in bed.

Well. Dar shifted a little. *That's exactly what she was doing, wasn't she?* Lazily she rolled over and stretched her body out, peering up at the television. The volleyball game was over, replaced by a gymnastics competition. She watched the girls tumbling in their intricate routines, and idly imagined Kerry participating when she was younger.

One of the girls stood at the edge of the mat, her tongue sticking out a little as she concentrated and Dar found herself smiling, knowing Kerry would have likely been doing the same thing. She did, when she was focused on something, often without realizing it.

It was really cute. Dar put her hands behind her head and indulged in a little daydreaming. It was interrupted, however, by the room's phone ringing. Dar turned her head, frowning as she judged how long Kerry had been gone. She picked up the phone and put it to her ear. "Yes?"

"Ms. Stuart?"

"You had a fifty-fifty chance and you blew it," Dar replied.

"Oh, I'm sorry, Ms. Roberts?"

"Yes?"

"I have a package here at the front desk for Ms. Stuart. Is it all right for me to send it up?"

Package? Dar was puzzled. "Sure," she answered, trying to recall what package Kerry might have been expecting. It didn't come to her, so she put the phone down and got up, walked to the bathroom and ran some water to wash her face.

She was patting her skin dry when the door knock came, so she tossed the towel down and went to the door, opening it to find a short, curly haired boy standing there with the promised package. "Hi."

The boy blinked and swallowed, then held out the package to her. Dar took it, watching bemusedly as he turned and sped away, disappearing around the corner of the hallway in mere seconds.

"Huh." Dar closed the door and glanced down at the box, only then realizing she was still in just her bra and jeans. An embarrassed chuckle forced its way out and she covered her face with one hand, wondering if she was due a smack to the head to get her brains working again.

She dismissed the bellboy and examined the package instead. It was relatively small, but heavier than she'd expected for its size. The label on it was addressed to Kerry, sure enough, at the hotel address, but the return address was...

"New Zealand?" Dar repeated. "Who in the hell do we know in New Zealand?" Several major accounts, of course, but she didn't think Kerry knew any of them personally, and besides, the box was from what appeared to be a business.

Dar walked over to the table and set the box down, then dropped into the chair next to it and folded her arms across her bare belly. She was curious. One hand lifted and she thunked the box with her finger, hearing a sturdy solidity inside.

Hm. Dar picked the box up and brought it close to her face, sniffing it. Cardboard. "Okay." She examined the wrapping, which was very thoroughly taped. After a moment, she put it back down and drummed her fingers on the table.

She could probably open it. Kerry probably would not mind, since the object had been sent to their hotel room and it would be logical to assume Dar would see it anyway.

"Okay, how would you feel if she opened it and it was yours?" Dar asked the empty room. "Would you care?"

Would she? Dar drew one knee up and circled it with both arms, taking a rare delve into her own psyche.

"No," she finally spoke frankly. "I wouldn't give a damn, which means Kerry probably would. So leave it alone," She got up and left the package where it was, returning to the bed and plopping back down beside her laptop.

But now that she was up, she felt restless again. So though she put her computer up onto her lap, she also dragged the phone over and picked it up.

"Room service," the tinny voice answered promptly.

"Hi." Dar tapped a command into her mail program. "Can you send me up a really big pot of coffee, a jug of milk, and a bowl of chocolate ice cream?"

Silence.

"Hello?" Dar frowned at the phone.

"Yes, ma'am — that'll be one pot of coffee for... how many people?"

"One person who really likes coffee," Dar replied. "Whatever your biggest one is."

The sound of writing. "Okay, and a jug... is that like a glass?"

"No." Dar glanced at the first mail in the box. "If I wanted a glass, I'd ask for a glass. Just bring me a half gallon, or whatever."

"Our biggest. Gotcha," the room service clerk replied. "And our biggest bowl of chocolate ice cream?"

"You're catching on," Dar said.

"That will be about fifteen minutes."

"Thanks." Dar hung up the phone and settled back, plumping the pillows up behind her and resolving to at least get some work done. After a few minutes though, she found her attention wandering from the mundane mail on her laptop and focusing on the television. An extremely cute blond girl was on the balance beam, and as Dar watched, the kid did a back flip and missed.

"Ouch." Dar winced, as the small body hit the bar, then the mat. She got up immediately, but she was obviously stunned, and wavered as she tried to get back on the bar. "Hey! Stop her, you creep!" she instructed the girl's coach, visible just on the side of the floor exhorting her.

The girl put her hands on the bar and boosted herself up, getting her feet under her and standing up. But as she started to walk, she lost her balance again and fell in a heap on the mat, this time staying there.

Dar was surprised at the outrage she felt as the coach yelled, faintly audible, for the girl to get up. "Stupid son of a..." she barked at the television. "Go help her!"

The coach did not. However, as though hearing Dar, one of the other competitors, a taller girl with dark hair did rush over and kneel next to the fallen gymnast even though her costume indicated she was on a different team.

The coach yelled again, but the dark haired girl looked up and yelled back angrily, and then people began rushing onto the floor and surrounding them both.

"Mm." Dar returned her attention to her mail. "That's better. You go, kid." She typed in silence for a moment, then the irony of the situation struck her. She looked back up at the screen in time to see the tall gymnast helping the shorter one off the mat, their arms wrapped around one other.

Dar chewed her inner lip and then she smiled, making a mental note to check the ESPN website later and find out who the kids were. There was, she suspected, a story in there somewhere. Her eyes shifted to the table, suspecting there was a story inside the box too.

With a sigh, she went back to her typing. As she finished one mail and found herself checking the television before going to the next, she recalled something Kerry had said. "Restless," Dar murmured under her breath. "Yeah. More like scatterbrained."

KERRY WALKED UP in back of Mr. Slimy, giving him a smile as he sensed her presence and turned to face her. "Hi."

"Oh! Hi...um..." The man's eyes dropped to her corporate badge. "Kerry wasn't it...ah."

'That's right," Kerry replied. "And you can do me a big favor by cutting the crap out and stop wasting my people's time."

He actually took a step back. "Hey, wait a minute..."

"No, you wait a minute." Kerry squared her shoulders and gave him a direct stare. "They're too smart to do anything but laugh at someone who would go behind their boss's back and approach them like that. If you'd do it to me, you'd do it to them. None of my people like stupid games."

The man blinked. "Look, it was nothing more than business as usual, Ms. Stuart. Don't tell me you don't do it."

"I don't do it," Kerry shot right back at him. "And if you do it again, you're going to have to explain to my boss why you're annoying my staff."

He held up both hands. "Okay, lady. Okay." He took a step backwards into Telegenic's booth. "No problem...I get the message."

Michelle Graver suddenly appeared around the other side of the booth. "What message?" She glanced at Kerry, one ginger eyebrow lifting at the blond woman's aggressive stance. "Problem, ah... Kerry?"

Of the two of them, Kerry found it much easier to tolerate Michelle, for some probably not too noble reasons. "You have slime bags working for you," she informed her. "I'm over it. He doesn't know how to take no for an answer."

Michelle gave her manager a look, and he ducked away, disappearing into the interior of the booth. Then she turned back to her visitor. "Ah. Tried a little poaching, huh?"

Kerry put one hand on her hip. "He tried to recruit me and Dar."

Both of Michelle's eyebrows hit her hairline with an almost audible crack. "Ambitious," she murmured under her breath.

"Not really. He had no idea who we were."

"Ah." Michelle cleared her throat. "Sorry." She grinned slightly. "We are pretty aggressive. I won't apologize for that." Her eyes drifted, then went back to Kerry. "Breakfast was fun."

For a moment Kerry didn't answer, as she wavered, deciding how to respond. Then she relaxed her stance a trifle. "What did you really expect?" she asked.

Graver exhaled, and half shrugged. "Damned if I know," she said, giving her head a slight toss to take the edge off the comment. "Let's see if I can start over. Buy you a cup of coffee?"

Good cop, bad cop. Kerry almost smiled. "Sure," she agreed,

Michelle turned and led the way toward the snack bar on one side of the convention hall. "Nice turnout. Didn't expect that with the rain."

"We did." Kerry let her arms drop to her sides and lengthened her steps, secretly enjoying the sensation of having someone shorter than she was have to keep up with her. Dar was such a beast that way—she didn't do it on purpose, but her legs were so much longer than Kerry's she always felt like she was having to take a little hop to keep up.

"Did you?"

"Orlando is full of distractions." Kerry arrived at the snack bar and pointed at the coffee, then held up two fingers. "However, most of them are outdoors. We're not." She leaned on the counter and faced Michelle. "I'm glad I got my fun in yesterday."

Michelle took one of the cups the server offered them and indicated a small table nearby. She led the way over and sat down, waiting for

Kerry to take the seat opposite her before she spoke. "Listen." She leaned on one elbow. "This is a...touchy...kind of situation, I know that."

Kerry's eyebrows twitched.

"We really didn't want this to turn into a war."

"Sure you did." Kerry cut her off, but in a remarkably mild tone. "You came in here setting the stage for us to clash."

Michelle sighed.

"Well, you did. It's not my fault," Kerry said. "I wasn't the one who tried to pay off the convention staff not to help set the place up, and I wasn't the one who sent my lackeys around trying to steal other company's employees."

Michelle eyed her. "You're not as nice as you used to be," she remarked. "Dar must be rubbing off on you."

Far from taking offense, Kerry produced a sunny grin at that. "Thank you." She sat back and sipped at her coffee, waiting for Michelle's next salvo. In the mean time, she let her eyes scan the room casually, spotting ILS's marketing team doing their thing in the aisles. Eleanor had the vice president of technology of one of their biggest clients by the lapel, and she made a point of making eye contact with Kerry as she cruised along with him. "Ah. Sorry to cut this short, but my services are required."

Michelle was nothing if not tenacious. "Okay. Can we try all this again at dinner tonight? Call me a stinkweed, but I still want to try and make this work. We can all learn from each other."

Kerry crumpled her cup and tossed it into the nearby wastepaper basket. "Thanks." She stood up and braced her hands on the table, leaning on them a little. "But no thanks. We've got plans for tonight and I promised Dar she wouldn't have to deal with any more indigestion from you guys." She straightened and turned, walking away without a backward glance.

Michelle got up and dropped the half unfinished cup into the garbage can. "Well, I think I've wasted enough time for one day," she commented to the receptacle. "Don't you?" With a snort, she followed Kerry out onto the floor.

DAR HAD TRADED her unorthodox loungewear for a pair of cutoff overalls and a polo shirt, and left her laptop behind as she investigated the hotel. She'd answered all her mail that she felt needed answering, and ditched the rest of it, losing interest in the weightlifting that had been showing on ESPN as well.

So here she was, sauntering around the lobby in her bare feet, watching the tourists mill around giving the still stormy weather evil looks. The interior of the hotel was a pristine white, and the whole décor was one of lightness and elegance.

Dar found a comfortable and mostly empty corner and selected a seat in it, leaning back against the cool fabric as she watched the world go by for a few minutes. There were families here, but she saw a lot of couples, too, walking together or sitting and talking around her.

Her own visits here in her youth had been very different. Dar propped her leg up with one ankle on her knee and rubbed the prominent bone with her thumb. They hadn't been rich. Far from it, in fact. The best her father could manage was one of the ratty little motels on the strip in Kissimmee or, memorably, the camping ground inside the park itself.

Fort Wilderness. Dar smiled to herself. She'd loved that place. It had been full of pine scent and horses, and she had spent hours with her father swimming in the manufactured swimming hole on the side of the lake.

It had been one of the best vacations ever. Only four days, a long weekend leave before his next deployment. Yet it was one of the few times Dar could remember where they'd all been just...happy together.

They'd slept in the back of Dad's truck, under the nylon tent and sweated like pigs. It had made the lake that much sweeter.

"Excuse me."

Dar looked up to find a man standing next to her, peering down. "Yes?"

"Are you Dar Roberts?"

A prickle of surprise rippled up and down her spine. "Yes," Dar replied briefly. "Why?"

The man sat down and extended a hand, which Dar ignored until he awkwardly withdrew it. "My name is Peter Quest. You don't know me."

"You're right. I don't. What do you want?" Dar gave him a direct look.

"I'm looking to do a little business, Ms. Roberts. I was told you would be someone I could talk to," Quest replied. "I was at the trade show this morning looking for you, but they told me you weren't around."

"So you decided to walk around Disney hotels asking people at random if they were me?" Dar asked. "Nice."

The man shook his head and chuckled. "No, I had a picture of you," he admitted. "Hope you don't mind."

Dar set her feet on to the floor and leaned forward. "I do mind," she spoke softly. "So you better explain why you're stalking me before I kick your ass right out that door into the rain, buddy."

Quest eased back away from her. "I beg your pardon, Ms. Roberts. I'm making a big mess of this, and I'm sorry. I really meant no harm. I just wanted to talk to you." He licked his lips. "I've got a business proposal I think you might be interested in."

Dar was on the verge of booting him anyway, when Alastair's

words echoed into her memory. New business. "Okay," she replied instead, relaxing again into her chair. "I'm listening." Her head cocked slightly, and she pinned the man with a sharp stare. "Start talking."

"Um..." Quest visibly gathered up his scattered wits, confused by her change of attitude.

'Well?' Dar inquired.

The man held up one hand, and then took a breath. "Okay," he said. "Tell me. How do you feel about cruise ships?"

Dar's eyebrows knit fiercely. "Cruise ships?"

"Yeah." The man went on more confidently, producing a big smile. "Cruise ships."

"Well." Dar paused to think. "I'm an IT professional. Why would I think anything about cruise ships? We don't have anything to do with them."

"Ah." Quest rested his elbows on his knees. "Well, that's where I think I can change your mind then. We want you to have a lot to do with them."

Dar studied him. "Okay. Go on," she said. "I'm listening."

KERRY COULD FEEL a headache building, and she subtly put her hand behind her neck and rubbed it as she listened to Eleanor's smooth pitch. Their booth was now crowded with interested onlookers, most peering at the network monitor screens prominently displayed at each corner. They were showing a real time display of their systems, mirrored from the big monitor Mark had in the operations center down in Miami.

Out of long habit, she found herself keeping an eye on them, also, because the colorful, bouncing screen represented things wholly her responsibility. At work, she had a twin of that screen mounted on a flat panel display in her office and she knew every graph like it was written across the back of her hand.

"Ms. Stuart?"

Kerry turned, vainly trying to keep her nostrils from flaring as she recognized Shari's voice. "Yes?"

The husky woman leaned on the edge of the booth. "I'll make this short and sweet." She kept her voice low. "Michelle's a decent sort, and she really has an idea that your company and ours can help each other."

Kerry simply waited in silence.

"Leave me out of it," Shari continued, after it was evident she wasn't going to get an answer. "I know Dar has a problem with me."

"You're wrong. She doesn't have a problem with you," Kerry interrupted.

Shari rolled her eyes. "Okay, fine. She doesn't have a problem, but it's not really likely that we're going to start being pals any time soon, how's that?" She gave Kerry a sarcastic look. "She never did have a handle on dealing with people. It's nice to know nothing's changed."

The burn of anger didn't surprise Kerry this time. It almost felt good, in a way, because she knew the emotion was based squarely in the love she felt for Dar. "You know what?" Kerry finally spoke. "I guess you're still the same asshole you were back then too. She doesn't have a problem, but that doesn't really matter to me because I have a problem with you. So do me a favor and go find someone else to hover over. Okay?"

Shari fell silent and looked at her for a second before she straightened and took a step back. "O...kay." She lifted both hands and dropped them. "Nice to have the air cleared."

"It will be, as soon as you leave." Kerry felt slightly abashed at letting her temper get the better of her. "Excuse me." She moved over to where Eleanor was bidding her latest victim farewell. "El?"

"Hm?" Eleanor turned. "Oh, hey Kerry. You ready to go get some lunch? My snappy patter's wilted."

The thought of lunch made her slightly sick to her stomach. She was shaking inside that much. "Actually, I was going to tell you I'm heading back to the hotel to pick up Dar. I'll get something there." Kerry looked around. "We've got a nice crowd going. I figured it was time for the ubergeek to show up."

Eleanor smiled knowingly. "Go on." She nudged Kerry. "See you after lunch."

Kerry signaled to Mark that she was leaving, getting a thumbs up from him as he stood guard over the locked switch box. Feeling that everything was relatively well in hand, she turned and started to work her way out of the room.

Even the rain outside didn't deter her. She cleared the door and stepped out into it, almost welcoming the wash of warm water that plastered the hair on her head and quickly dampened her clothes. She reached the Lexus and triggered the door lock, opening the driver's side and sliding inside with a sense of relief.

It smelled like leather tinged with the faint hint of Dar's usual perfume, and Kerry sat there for a minute breathing it in.

She took a moment to remember the first time she'd ridden in this car, in a rain not unlike the one she'd just escaped from, but with little other similarity.

It had been one of the most miserable nights of her life, and one of the most wonderful. Kerry leaned back in the comfortable seat and ran her fingers through her wet hair, pushing it back off her forehead. "You know what?" she mused. "A navy sweatshirt sure would feel good right about now."

With a sigh, Kerry shook a few droplets of water off her hands and started the car up, shifting smoothly into reverse and backing out of the parking spot she'd chosen. If she couldn't have a navy sweatshirt, at least she knew where to find the next best thing.

"NO." DAR SLUNG her leg over one chair arm, leaning on the other. "I'm not interested."

Peter Quest looked puzzled. "You're not?" he asked. "I don't understand. You're a services company, we're looking for someone to come in and install, maintain, and run networks on all our ships. What's the problem?"

"I'm not in the business of being part of a circus," Dar replied. "Why don't you just throw open the business for bids? Plenty of companies around who'd be willing to tender. Why sneak around making secret deals to have people come in?"

Quest looked around carefully, and then lowered his voice. "It's really complicated." He said. "Listen, can we go somewhere more private...like the bar?"

Dar's eyebrow lifted. "No," she said. "My partner's going to come back through here looking for me and damned if she'd look there," she told Quest. "So talk, or take a hike."

The man exhaled. "You're a difficult person, Ms. Roberts."

Dar shrugged. "So I've been told. But then, you came looking for me, not the other way around."

"Okay, here's the deal," Quest went on. "My company, American Visions, intends on being the first American cruise line in decades," he said. "We've gotten hold of four ships, and we're having them rebuilt to US specifications in New Zealand."

New Zealand again? Dar almost let herself get sidetracked. "Yeah?"

"But it's all hush hush. If we can bring them into the States by January, we can grab a big segment of the homeland cruise market. If those four make it, we have eight more waiting overseas to join the fleet."

Dar looked at him. "Hush hush?" she repeated. "They're cruise ships. What do they weigh...seventy, eighty thousand tons? How the hell do you hide them?"

Quest looked around again. "We're not revealing who owns them," he said. "And they'll get their final paint in San Diego. Anyway, seventy percent of the refurb stuff needs to be US, and that includes the technical infrastructure."

"And?"

"And if we throw open bids, chances are people we don't want to find out about this are going to find out, because they'll send spies in to figure out what we're up to."

Dar braced her chin on her fist. "So what if I'm a spy?" she asked.

"Your company has no connection with the business," he answered readily. "Neither do the other three American companies we asked to compete for the contract...and I've got some friends in the government who tell me you can keep your mouth shut."

Dar shook her head. "Still not interested," she said. "I don't know that we want to get involved in this. It sounds irregular."

"Well..." Quest replied. "It really isn't, it's just business. I have to get some government paperwork straightened out and that's why it has to be kept quiet. You understand? It's political."

Dar frowned. "We have a lot of government contracts," she said. "I don't think we want to be a part of it." She paused. "Who else are you asking? Maybe I can give you some names to talk to."

Quest gazed at her, biting the inside of his lip. Finally he leaned forward a little. "Advanced Tech, KDC, and Telegenics."

"Ah." Dar's expression didn't change, but a dark sparkle lit in her eyes. "Interesting choices."

"Telegenics talks a good game. They've been wooing my director over another contract, so..." Quest shrugged. "Anyway, since you're not interested, let me stop wasting your time." He straightened up in his seat, and half turned, pausing as one of the figures walking across the lobby caught his eye. "Sure must be raining outside."

Dar watched the object of his attention, an unconscious smile appearing on her face. Even drenched, Kerry had her head held high, and despite the rain dampened clothes she had an innate grace as she approached that attracted more eyes than Quest's. "Mm."

Quest started to stand as Kerry closed in on them, but she gave him a polite smile as she dropped into the chair next to Dar's and leaned on its arm. "Hi."

"Hi." Dar rolled her head to one side and indicated her somewhat unwelcome visitor. "Kerry, this is Peter Quest, Mr. Quest, this is Kerrison Stuart, my partner."

Kerry extended a hand politely, and gripped his, then released him. "Mr. Quest."

"Nice to meet you," he replied. "Well, Ms. Roberts, as I said, no sense in wasting your time. I'll leave you to get on with your day."

He turned and walked out, leaving Dar and Kerry behind as he disappeared.

Kerry remained silent for a moment, and then she turned to Dar. "So, what was that all about?" she asked. "Someone propositioning you, since you're hanging out in such cutely provocative clothing?"

"Hardly." Dar pushed herself upright. "Let's go upstairs and I'll take your clothes off while I fill you in." She stood and waited for Kerry to join her. "You look like a..."

"Drowned rat?" Kerry sighed, getting up and following her partner. "I feel like a drowned rat that's been hit on the head with a brick." She rubbed her neck. "I'm not having a good day."

Dar slipped her arm around Kerry's back, ignoring the dampness. "Problems at the show?" she asked. "You should have called me."

Kerry sighed and fell silent, taking solace in the comfort of Dar's close presence. "Not the show," she admitted after they'd entered the elevator. "I got pegged by both our new little friends and I think I lost it with them. They pissed me off."

"Uh oh." Dar chuckled softly. "Did you draw blood?"

"It's not funny, Dar," Kerry muttered. "I told them both off."

Dar slid her keycard into the door and opened it, then held it open as Kerry entered. She followed her inside and closed the door, blinking as she realized housekeeping had been in and cleaned the room while she'd been gone. Somehow, they'd managed to make the bed and place the laptop in its exact position where she'd left it. "Glad I locked the screen."

Kerry took off her jacket and laid it across the back of a chair. She didn't look up when Dar came over to her, but as a pair of a warm, strong hands touched her neck and began to massage it she turned her head to the side and brushed the nearer one with her lips. "So what was that guy all about?"

"Had an offer I refused," Dar said.

"Mm. Been that kinda day."

"I may call him back, but I wanted to talk to you first." Dar replied, keeping up her rhythmic kneading. "You had lunch?"

Kerry shook her head. The ache in her head was fading, and she felt the tension draining out of her at Dar's skilled touch. She unbuttoned her skirt and let it slip down, kicking it off to one side and almost tripping as Dar started mixing a few playful nips along with her massage. "So you don't mind if I blew out any possibility of us being civil to our booth neighbors?"

"Nope." Dar blew in her ear. "You saved me the trouble." She slid her arms around Kerry. "Besides, it might work to our advantage if we end up competing head-to-head with them for a new services contract."

Kerry stopped in mid motion and looked over her shoulder. "What?"

"How do you feel about New Zealand?"

Kerry's brows knit. "New Zealand?" she asked. Wh..."

Dar chuckled. "Let's get some lunch, and I'll explain the whole damn thing," she said. "And you can tell me what happened with Heckle and Jeckle."

"Mmph." Kerry half turned in Dar's arms and snuggled up to her, plucking at one of the catches on her overalls. "That's the best deal I've heard all day." Her eyes fell on the table. "Oh." She blinked. "Did that come for me?"

"Uh huh." Dar waited expectantly. "Gonna open it?"

Finally, a smile appeared on Kerry's face, along with a devilish twinkle in her eyes. "Nope."

"No?"

"We'll never get to have lunch." Kerry gave her a quick kiss, and slipped out of Dar's grasp, heading for her suitcase to get a change of clothes.

Dar looked at her, then turned and looked at the mysterious box.

Both eyebrows crawled up into her hairline and a delighted grin appeared. "Ah hah." She folded her arms. "Couldn't we call room service instead?"

Kerry merely chuckled, and shook her index finger at her partner.

Chapter
Five

IF ANYTHING, THE hall was even more crowded when they re-entered it. However, the rain had slowed at least, so they were only lightly misted with dampness as they passed from the warm humidity into the chill of the hall.

Kerry ran her eyes over the throng and spotted Mark making his way back from the snack bar "Mark!"

The MIS manager recognized the hail and paused in mid stride, turning and giving them a wave as he saw them approaching. "Hey."

"Everything okay?" Dar asked. She'd reluctantly traded her comfortable overalls for a well-fitted business suit, and she was aware that her distinctive appearance was already attracting attention from several people in the nearby stream of attendees. "Looks like a good crowd."

"Smooth so far, jefe." Mark nodded. "The marketing goons were looking for you a few minutes ago...some kinda presentation or something."

Dar frowned and looked at Kerry. "Was I supposed to do one? Someone forget to tell me?"

Kerry was equally surprised. "Not that I know of," she replied. "I didn't see your name on the schedule, Dar. I would have mentioned it."

"I figured you would." Dar straightened, and peered over the crowd, finding Eleanor standing near the entrance to the hall. "Let me go find out what the hell's going on." She made her way forward, easing through the packed lobby with surprising ease.

"You know something? I'm getting really tired of having perfectly good meals ruined by bullpoop." Kerry shook her head and started after Dar, finding it quite a bit tougher to get through the crush than her taller partner.

She reached Dar's side in time to see her take up a belligerent stance, however, and deftly avoided Dar's elbow as the taller woman planted her hands on her hips. "What's up?"

Eleanor looked more amused than worried. "Oh, her nibs doesn't want to go show off, that's all."

"That is not the point," Dar growled. "Where do you get off volunteering me for a dog and pony show?" She kept her voice low, but the anger behind it was real.

"C'mon, Dar. I thought you'd love it...you and a couple other geeks up there talking over everyone's head. What more could you ask for?"

Eleanor protested.

Dar glanced around, spotting a small vending room off to one side. She took hold of Eleanor's arm and turned, pulling the smaller woman with her as she started for the alcove. Biting off a protest, Eleanor did her best to keep up, as Kerry slid up on the opposite side of her and helped clear the way with brief smiles and somewhat charming 'excuse me's.'

"Hey. If you two are gonna put me in cement boots, lemme call home first, okay?" Eleanor said, in an exasperated tone as they reached the room and entered it. "C'mon now. This is business, Dar!"

"Yeah." Dar whirled and let her temper ignite. "It's business."

Eleanor took a step back out of pure instinct. "Now, Dar." She held up both hands. "Take it easy. I'll go tell them you're not interested. I don't need a screaming match with you in here."

Dar held her eyes with fierce intensity. "I wasn't going to scream."

"Whoa, whoa, whoa." Kerry stepped between them, putting a hand on Dar's back. "Hang on, guys." She kept her voice gentle. "Let's do a zen break here."

Dar swiveled her head around. "Zen break?"

Kerry's objective was to break Dar's single-minded focus, and she congratulated herself silently on doing it in one try. It wasn't easy, and despite their relationship she always held her breath when she did it. "Dar, you're right."

"Damn friggen straight I am." Dar snorted. Eleanor sighed audibly.

"But that aside, would it really tank you to do it?" Kerry asked. "You and some nerds...talking electronic gears and sprockets...sounds like more fun than listening to Jose's repetitive bs all afternoon."

Dar scowled at her. "Kerrison."

Mild green eyes watched her. "Would it?" Kerry asked, relying on the simple logic of her argument. "I mean, yeah, I know how you feel, Dar. I would feel the same way if someone volunteered me for something without me knowing." She turned to Eleanor. "You didn't do that, did you?"

"Crossed my mind," Eleanor admitted.

Kerry's eyebrows hiked up. "Eleanor, that really is inappropriate," she said. "We don't work for you."

"Yeah, yeah." The other woman held up a hand. "Look, I'm sorry," she said. "I honestly didn't think you'd give a damn, Dar. You've got to be here anyway, I figured you'd have some fun."

"I make my own fun," Dar growled. However, she straightened a little and moved closer to Kerry, relaxing her posture. "Damn it, Eleanor, don't do this shit to me." She poked the other woman in the shoulder, and then brushed past her. "Or I'll make sure your entire department works on scratch pads with VGA screens."

Out of Eleanor's line of sight, Kerry gave her partner a pat on the butt, and then watched as she stalked across the lobby and ducked inside the hall. Her head then turned to regard Eleanor. She put her hands on her hips. "What was that?"

Eleanor shrugged. "You know, I didn't even think about it," she admitted. "These days, we forget sometimes what Dar used to be like. I just got reminded. I'll remember next time."

Kerry was at a loss for words briefly. "Oh, I don't know, Eleanor...I mean..."

"Don't you dare say it," Eleanor cut her off. "Don't you dare say she hasn't changed, Kerry. We both know differently. You remember what it was like when you first started. You remember walking into meetings representing ops and having people cheer."

Kerry did remember that. "Mm." She nodded briefly. "Damn, I hated the place," she admitted. "I wanted to just throw up most afternoons."

Eleanor had the grace to look uncomfortable. "Anyway, it's been a huge difference, and even though some things probably got done faster the old way, I wouldn't trade for it. I used to dread staff meetings." She peered back into the lobby, which had started to empty. "She isn't intimidating the entire industry anymore, and yeah, we probably lost out because of it, but I don't care."

Kerry's brow creased. "You don't really think that, do you?" she queried. "That we lost sales because Dar isn't screaming at everyone all the time?"

"Well." Eleanor turned and leaned one shoulder against the wall. "It's tempting, isn't it? Easier to think it's because of that than because Jose and I aren't doing our jobs." A sardonic look crossed her face. "Nah, I don't really think that. The market's just turned toward smaller companies right now. Everyone thinks it's better economics."

"But it really isn't." Kerry relaxed. "In the long run."

"Mm." Her companion gave a half shake of her head. "Doesn't help my quarterly earnings statement though." She gave Kerry a wry look. "Want to go hear the old grump blow the new kids on the block away? They have no idea I volunteered her."

An irrepressible grin appeared on Kerry's face. "You've got a mean streak yourself, El." She gestured toward the hall. "Sure, let's go."

DAR PAUSED AT the edge of the open space, reviewing the small group of men clustered on a single step mini-stage. Two she knew slightly, senior technical managers in the industry she'd met earlier that year at a networking function, and three others whose names she'd heard around. All men, all in their thirties, all with that air of not quite management about them that technical people did tend to have; pleated chinos with sports jackets, or workmanlike suits.

Dar halted briefly to shed her annoyance at Eleanor, and then she eased her way through the last line of watchers and took the one step up onto the platform. "Afternoon, gentlemen."

The five men and the moderator turned at the sound of her voice. The two men who knew who she was immediately took on what Dar had always thought of as the 'smelling the dirty diaper attitude', and she realized it had been quite a while since she'd seen it.

It made her smile.

The moderator stepped forward and extended a hand. "Ah, Ms. Roberts. Glad you could join us."

Dar gripped his fingers in hers then released them. "Anytime," she drawled, turning her eyes on the two men nearest her. "Hello, John. How's that experiment with consumer grade switches going?"

The man she addressed winced. "We...ah...well, we went a different route with that one, Dar. Thanks for asking!" He turned to his companion. "Ted, you know Dar Roberts, don't you?"

"Uh...sure." Ted extended his hand gingerly. "We bumped into each other at the IEEE conference a couple months back...great presentation you did there."

"Thanks," Dar replied graciously, giving the other three a brief nod as the moderator made introductions. "So what's the deal with this? We talking about IP v6, or something really earth shattering like the latest security holes in SNMP?"

"Eh...hah." The moderator finished putting some stools in place for his guests. "Well, securing our networks was the topic...ah yes."

"Mm." Dar claimed the last stool on one side and settled onto it, letting her eyes run idly over the crowd as the rest of the speakers got into place. She spotted Shari's distinctive features near the back but let her eyes pass right over her, settling instead on the blond woman now perched on a nearby booth.

Kerry gave her a thumbs up. Dar rolled her eyes and crossed her arms, but directed a wink her partner's way nonetheless.

"Okay, folks." The moderator clapped his hands. "Let's get this debate going."

"Debate?" Dar chuckled. "Eleanor screwed up again. She picked the wrong one of us."

John leaned closer. "Sorry, did you say something, Dar?"

"No," Dar replied.

"The question we're posing here..." The moderator glared surreptitiously at them. "Are our networks safe?" he asked. "With all the stuff we've been hearing in the news lately...Internet sites hacked, credit cards stolen, drive by hacking...are you all worried? Are your networks safe?"

Dar watched the speakers glance at each other, waiting to see who was going first. "That's an idiotic question." She threw out the sentence to stir up a little fun.

"Wh...what?" the moderator stammered.

"That's an idiotic question," Dar repeated, a little slower for him.

"Do you really think anyone here is going to stand up in front of potential customers and their peers and say 'why no...my network's a positive sieve! Thanks for bringing it up!"

The other men on the platform chuckled a little and John nodded, gesturing in Dar's direction. "Yeah, what she said."

Discomfited, the moderator cleared his throat. "Okay, okay, I see your point. But what if..." He paused. "Okay, what if I brought a hacker up here, onto the platform, and he said he could break into any of your networks. What would you say to him?"

The other four looked at each other, and then in unison, they looked at Dar.

"Want a job?" Dar remarked, with a grin.

The entire crowd started laughing.

"Ms. Roberts, it's a serious question." The moderator desperately tried to yank control back.

Dar got up and stuck her hands in the pockets of her skirt. "Of course it is," she replied. "We all pump a significant portion of our collective budgets into hardening our networks." A half tilt of her head. "But to answer your question, no."

"No?"

"No, nothing's ever perfect." Dar shook her head. "You can put machinery and manpower into it until you're blue in the face, but somewhere there's gonna be a hole. There's too many places where it's possible and sometimes out of your control."

John nodded again. "Dar's right," he said, and then paused. "Well, of course, because Dar's always right, and we all know it."

The crowd laughed again. Dar responded with a relatively gracious smile. Her eyes caught a motion at the back of the crowd; the distraction turning out to be Shari having a somewhat animated discussion with Michelle.

They were arguing. Dar's eyebrows hiked, as she caught a gesture in her direction. But Michelle got a firm hold on Shari's arm and started pulling her away.

Hm. Dar's eyes slid to her left, seeing Kerry's head turned in that direction.

"But you know, we really have made some strides in that area...let me go over some of them," John went on.

"Wait a minute," a stocky man in a light gray suit interjected. "Lemme ask...hey, lady."

Dar gazed at him.

"You really hire hackers?" the man asked. "I mean, that's a big story...that ILS hires hackers." He turned and got agreement from those next to him. "As a customer, I don't know how I feel about that."

"You ever been compromised?" Dar asked.

"No...I mean, not that I know of," the man replied.

"Like you'd tell them?" Shari's voice cut through the crowd.

Out of the corner of her eye, Dar saw Kerry slip down from her perch and start through the crowd like a determined miniature cyclone. The romance of the motion appealed to her, and the chuckle it caused brushed the sound of Shari's voice from her ears. "Of course we'd tell them," Dar answered the question in an unruffled tone. "We've never had to."

"You didn't answer my question," the man in gray accused.

"What's your question?" Dar turned the tables on him. "Are you asking if I ever knowingly hired someone who had deliberately broken into someone else's computer systems?"

"Yes."

"Sure," Dar answered.

The other men on the podium were shifting away from her, putting some distance between them as if to disassociate themselves from the very idea.

"But only if they were successful at it," she continued. "I only hire the best. That's why our network..." her eyes went over the room, "has never been compromised."

"Never?" John blurted.

"Never," Dar said, with quiet certainty.

"I thought you said no network was perfect?" the moderator broke in.

"I did," Dar said. "But ours is as perfect as I can make it and it's never been compromised." She folded her arms over her chest. "That's why I've never had to tell a customer they've been hacked. Contractually, and legally, I would definitely have to."

"Okay, so..." The moderator glanced at the restive crowd. "Well, that's quite a claim."

"G'wan. Give it a try." Dar threw the challenge out. "Anyone out there got the guts to take us on?"

She looked over to where Shari had been, but the area was now only a hole in the crowd. Kerry had, ominously, also disappeared. "We get blasted all the time for being expensive stuffed shirts. Well, you get what you pay for and security doesn't come cheap."

"Bet your security manager's not loving you at the moment, " John muttered.

Dar gave him an amused look. "He'd lick his chops at the challenge."

"Okay, folks." The moderator finally decided to wrest control back again. "So this turned out to be a pretty interesting subject after all."

"Very," the man in gray muttered.

"But I don't get it," one woman in the front addressed Dar. "I thought hackers were criminals."

"Depends," Dar said. "They can be, but the truth is we're facing serious attacks from people breaking the law, how responsible would it be of me not to have people who could counter them?"

The crowd was restless. The moderator edged over in front of them. "Okay. So, let's talk about some of the reports we've had lately about Trojans, huh?"

Dar sat down on her stool again and folded her arms. And that, she mused, would teach Eleanor to volunteer her, wouldn't it? She felt eyes on her, and she turned her head, not entirely surprised to find Peter Quest nearby, watching her, a grin on his face.

Now he didn't seem worried about hackers at all. While Dar, on the other hand, was worried about having to bail out a certain green eyed woman she dearly loved.

Time to end the debate.

THERE WERE TIMES, and this was one of them, that Kerry cursed the genetic dice throw that doomed her to a life nearly a foot shorter than her partner. She could see her quarry ahead of her, but as she squeezed through the last line of suited bodies and got into the clear, Shari and Michelle were nowhere to be found.

"Son of a bitch." Kerry stalked toward the booths, half listening to Dar's damning commentary behind her. The security discussion had started off badly and went down from there, and her boss's blithe confirmation that they hired hackers sure wasn't going to make her life any easier, but those were minor details.

Shari going out of her way to attack Dar wasn't. Kerry prowled the aisles, looking for the two women. As she passed her own booth, though, she paused. "Okay, wait a minute." She collected herself. "And what are you going to do when you hunt them down, Kerrison?" she asked "Start a cat fight? Bar room brawl in the trade show? That'll make headlines."

"Ma'am?" One of her techs scurried over, seeing her standing there. "Did you say something?"

Kerry sighed. "Nothing intelligent, no." But her eyes kept sweeping the hall anyway, half hoping she'd spot what she was looking for.

"Hey." Mark appeared. "Dar outed me!" He seemed amazed. "Did you hear that?"

Kerry leaned on the edge of the booth. "I heard it. So did everyone else. I know what I'm going to spend the next two weeks explaining." She sensed the crowd coming back into the display area in back of her. Without turning she knew Dar was heading her way.

It was a really weird feeling. To test it, Kerry casually turned her head just as Dar cleared the booths one aisle over and came into view. She watched a muted look of relief cross her partner's face on seeing her, and she felt a little sheepish as Dar hopped up onto the platform with her. "Hi."

"Hi." Dar glanced around. "You okay?"

Kerry cleared her throat gently. "If you mean, did I flatten anyone recently, no," she muttered under her breath. "Boy, did I feel like it. I think you'd better get me out of here before my hormones land us in court."

"Nah." Dar grinned. "I'm gonna put you in a tank top with the words "My bodyguard" right across your chest." She blew a lock of dark hair out of her eyes. "Okay, I think I botched that pretty big time. Sorry."

"Eh." Kerry indicated Mark, who was studying a console across the booth. "Most of our clients have worked with Mark for years. It's not going to be that big a deal. I'll take care of it." She laid her hand on Dar's shoulder. "By the time I'm done, you'll have started the newest trend in IT hiring."

Eleanor hurried into the booth from the other side, hauling up as she spotted Dar. "Okay, you win!" She held up both hands. "Next time, I'll stick to passing out ILS pens for advertising!"

"Dar!" Jose arrived from the opposite direction, sweating. "Jesu! Could you have warned us you were going to do that? Dios Mio!"

Dar sniffed. "Got us attention," she remarked. "Aren't you the one who's always says any publicity is good?"

They certainly were becoming the center of attention quickly. The booth was surrounded by curious onlookers, as well as customers now clamoring for attention. The man in gray pushed his way forward, heading right for Dar.

"Is this where I take off and let you all clean up my mess?" Dar inquired, with a faint smirk.

Eleanor sighed.

"Just kidding." Dar faced the crowd and held her own hands up. "Okay, folks. Settle down."

"Dar..."

"I've got it," Dar told her quietly. "Keep an eye out for our friends. If you see 'em..."

"Go into my WWF impersonation?" Kerry joked.

Dar turned and regarded her with a puzzled expression. "You going for a panda?"

"Panda?"

"Never mind." Dar turned back to the crowd. "All right. Let's put this in perspective, shall we?" She raised her voice. "How many people here believe police officers always obey traffic laws?"

"What?" the man in gray spluttered. "What does that have to do with anything?"

"Raise your hands." Dar ignored him. "C'mon."

"How can you seriously expect us to trust someone who breaks the law? The man stubbornly kept in her face. "Huh?"

Dar gazed at him. "I'm from Miami," she reminded him with a slight grin. "We elect felons there."

"Dar." Eleanor was getting nervous.

Mark wandered over. "Hey, Mr. T!" he greeted the man in gray. "How's that website, still stable?"

The man frowned. "Um...yes, fine, fine, Mark. Listen, we can discuss that later. Right now I want some answers about this hacker thing."

Mark leaned over the edge of the booth and lowered his voice. "Hey, Mr. T?"

Annoyed, the man glared at him. "I said..."

"I'm the hacker." Mark indicated his own chest. "Only I'm like the number two, if you know what I mean." His thumb inched toward Dar's towering form. "You're pretty safe. Don't sweat it."

The man in gray goggled at him.

"Okay, so let's talk about security." Another man pushed forward. "I don't give a damn who you hire. You say you can't be broken into? My site's been taken offline three times in two months. Tell me how I can stop it."

"Hire us." Dar perched on the corner of the counter, letting her hands rest on her thigh as she settled down in a more comfortable element. Her comment drew a few laughs, and she smiled in response. "Seriously. It's a lot of intensive effort, and a damn substantial budget. You can't ever stop...there's no time where you can take a breath and say we're okay."

"Right." Mark nodded. "Twenty four seven, we're out there checking, rechecking, double checking, coming up with new checks...it never stops."

Kerry eased back and relaxed a little, realizing Dar did, in fact, have the situation very much under control. She leaned back against the booth's center pylon, releasing a silent sigh of relief. So then, of course, she spotted Shari and Michelle at the fringes of the crowd. Her eyes narrowed, but the two seemed content to just stand and listen.

"What a circus." Eleanor leaned on the pylon next to Kerry. "Next time I'm gonna send my assistant. I'm going on a cruise instead."

"Mm."

"Y'know, it's kind of fun to see the old Dar again, though," the older woman mused. "I'm glad she's pointed that way, not this way."

Kerry exhaled. "I'll be glad when the damn doors close tonight and we can get the hell out of here."

Eleanor looked at her, with a puzzled expression. "You not feeling well, Ker? You've been antsy all day."

Had she been? Kerry frowned, thinking about her actions since the morning. "Yeah, well..." She shrugged one shoulder. "Between the weather and our friends over there, my last nerve got Fedexed to Fargo around lunchtime."

Eleanor clapped her on the shoulder, and then she groaned and headed off to join Jose. Kerry watched a moment more, and then she sat down behind one of the consoles and smiled at a customer brave enough to wander past Dar to look over her shoulder. "Hi."

"Hi." The man sat down next to her and looked at the screen. It was currently displaying their top-level view, the huge backbones that made up the core of their network. "That's really impressive."

"Thanks." Kerry smiled at him. "It's a really good design. There's so much redundancy, even when we try to crash it, we can't."

"Bet it cost a pretty penny," the man grinned back.

"It did, but it's already paid for itself," she replied. "Watch this." Kerry typed in a command, taking down one of the core routing centers and removing it from the network. Other than a little greener pulse, the net barely flickered, rerouting around it in a blink of an eye.

"Wow."

Kerry restored the center before her pager started hitting the roof and watched the routes reestablish themselves. "It's flexible and self healing. A pleasure to manage." She glanced past the man, a little surprised to find Peter Quest there, watching her.

"Well, we'll have to look at our budgets," the man said. "It's a tight economy." He patted the desk and wandered off, clearing the way for Quest to approach.

"Hi," the man repeated, holding his hand out. "We met earlier? My name's Peter Quest." He took Kerry's outstretched fingers and clasped them. "People tell me you're the one to talk to about some new business. That true?"

Kerry's ears perked up a little. "It could be," she allowed. "I'm one of the people. What did you have in mind?"

Quest smiled at her again. "Let me ask you something first," he said, leaning on the counter with an elbow. "Are you up for a challenge? Can you put your name on a dotted line, and go head to head for some business...could turn out to be pretty big."

Kerry folded her hands. "What are you asking me?" she queried. "Can I negotiate a contract for ILS? Of course."

"Even if someone else in your company already said no?"

"Well." Kerry sat back. "Maybe. Why don't you tell me what your pitch is, and then we'll talk about it."

Quest nodded, with a satisfied look. "That's all I'm asking for." He leaned forward. "Here's the deal."

DAR CAME OUT of the bathroom, toweling her hair somewhat dry, dressed only in a second towel that was barely decent on her tall frame. She stopped to lean against the door, eyeing the sprawled form on the bed. "Ker?"

"Ungh." Kerry had her arm thrown over her eyes. "Shh. Kerry isn't here. It's just a prune, masquerading as Kerry."

"Uh huh." Dar sat down on the bed next to her, very nearly pulling her towel loose. "That was some downpour. I'm glad we made it back here." She reached over and used the other towel to dry off Kerry's head. "What a pain in the ass long day."

Kerry rolled over and draped her arm over Dar's thigh. "We have to do that again tomorrow, Dar. Augh!" She drummed her feet against the sheets and squiggled into Dar's lap. "Pig farts!"

Not at all displeased by the development, Dar tossed the towel somewhere in the vicinity of the bathroom and concentrated on her armful of cute blond instead. She was relieved herself that the day was over, and she was very much looking forward to the coming hours alone with her partner.

Accordingly, she slid her hand under Kerry's neck to support it as she leaned over and gave her a leisurely kiss, enjoying the simple passion of it. She could taste the last remnants of the lemon soda Kerry had grabbed on their way out of the trade show, and as their tongues gently played against each other, she let out a chuckle.

"What's so funny?" Kerry asked.

"I had fun in the afternoon session," Dar admitted. "I think I got everything back under control."

Kerry tweaked the towel, tugging it free of its tuck and exposing Dar's torso. "Mmhm." She traced a circle around her partner's navel. "I think you did too. Thanks." She felt the muscles under Dar's skin twitch. "I have a feeling you're going to make the news, though...I saw reporters there. With cameras."

"Eurgh." Dar made a face.

Kerry chuckled. "Not that they needed a scandal to take pictures of you...they do that anyway. You could have been explaining subnet masking and you'd still have gotten a crowd." She let her hand fall to the bed and closed her eyes. "Umph."

"Something wrong?" Dar asked.

"Headache."

"Again?" Dar curled her fingers around the back of Kerry's neck and kneaded it gently. "I see my friend Quest found you.. that what gave you this?"

Kerry remained silent, enjoying the massage. Then she exhaled. "He wasn't that bad," she admitted. "He had some interesting things to say."

Dar kept up the motion of her hands. "Ah," she murmured, surprised. "What did he say? Must have been different than what he told me."

Her cheek was resting against Dar's leg, and Kerry let her fingers stroke the skin there before she answered. "I think it was the same offer."

Dar considered that for a little while. "What did you tell him?" she finally asked. "Did you agree to do it?"

Kerry rolled her head to one side and opened her eyes, looking up at Dar with a faintly rueful expression. "Sweetheart, do you honestly

think I would go do something you'd already told me you'd turned
down on the company's behalf?" She reached up to tickle Dar's navel
again. "I was really, really curious as to why you turned him down flat,
though."

"What I don't get is why he asked you," Dar said. "What's his
game?"

"Well...if mom says no." Kerry kidded her. "Just go ask...um...you
know what I mean." She closed her eyes again as Dar's fingers found a
knot at the back of her skull. "He asked me if I had the guts to go over
your head."

"And?"

Kerry opened one eye and regarded her. "What do you think?"

A smile twitched at the corners of Dar's mouth. "I think right now I
trust your judgment better than mine. To be honest, I can't tell you why
the hell I blew him off, Ker. I had no reason for it...no business reason,
anyway."

Kerry's eyebrows lifted.

"Then when I reconsidered...it was because Telegenics was also
bidding, and I wanted to kick their ass. Not because I'd made a good
business choice." Dar exhaled, but looked peaceful. "I think it's time I
vacate that office, my friend. I'm just not into it anymore."

"Dar..."

Dar put her fingers across Kerry's lips. "It's the truth, we both
know it," she said. "I'm not going to walk out, Kerry, but I'm not doing
my job."

Uncertainly, Kerry subsided, confused and disturbed by her
partner's admission. Dar didn't seem upset by it, but she was, and it
was no use pretending she wasn't. "I'm really not happy to hear that,"
she sighed. "Especially because I think you're brilliant at what you do,
and this last year's proved that over and over again."

Dar traced the furrow in Kerry's brow. "Anyway...we can talk about
it when we get home," she said. "So...what did you tell little Peter?"

Kerry rolled onto her back and settled her hands on her stomach.
She recognized the change of subject for what it was, and pondered
whether to let Dar get away with it. Then the ache in her head made
itself felt again, and she decided if Dar didn't want to talk about it right
now, that was okay with her.

Maybe she would think about it some more. It had been a ratty day.
"What did I tell little Peter?" she repeated. "Well, I told him it was an
interesting proposal, it was something we're very experienced at doing,
something we could probably easily handle, and something we'd be
interested in getting involved in."

Dar slipped her hands under Kerry's head and resumed her
massage.

"However," Kerry continued, "I also told him I had nothing but the
highest respect for your judgment, so if he was looking for a champion

to butt heads with you, he picked the wrong blond."

"Mm."

"He seemed to think that was funny."

"Hmm?"

"I think that's when my headache started again." Kerry closed her eyes against the light in the room. "I told him I'd be in touch and booted him out of the booth."

Dar let the silence lengthen after that, as she kept working on Kerry's tense muscles. She watched the skin over her partner's brow smooth out, and her breathing slowed as she relaxed. "You want to do it?" she finally asked in a low voice.

The tiniest hint of a smile appeared on Kerry's lips, and she cracked open one eyelid. "I want us to do it," she replied, huskily.

Hm. "Us as in...you and me, you mean?"

Kerry nodded. "I think it would be good for the company, sure...but to prove I have my head in my workstation just as much as you do, I really just wanted to go there, just the two of us, and whip everyone else's butts."

"Ahhh...ulterior motives." Dar chuckled softly.

"Something like that." Kerry reached behind her and captured Dar's foot. She ran her fingers over the corded tendons and threatened a tickle, feeling the muscles bunch instinctively. "Besides, I'd like to see New Zealand."

Dar let one hand rest on Kerry's stomach. "Ahhhhh." She tapped the edge of her thumb against Kerry's abs. "That brings this whoooollllee thing full circle." With her other hand she lifted something from the nightstand and dropped it onto the bed next to her partner. "To this."

Kerry turned her head and regarded the box. "Ahh." She mimicked Dar. "You know, sweetheart, if you really wanted to know you could have just opened it."

"That's not my name on the label." Dar wriggled into a more comfortable spot and leaned on one elbow, looking expectantly at the package and then at Kerry. "Feeling better?"

How could she not feel better? Kerry wondered, as she rolled over onto her side and reached for the box. She was lying in bed, with her head in Dar's naked lap, looking forward to what was in the box.

Her headache had faded under Dar's touch, and the feeling of pent up tension was being leeched out of her by a combination of being where she was and being able to feel the affection almost pouring out of her companion as the gentle, feather light stroking traveled over her body.

It would be very easy to simply let the world fade away.

But there was her box to open, and dinner to be had, and fireworks to watch from their balcony. So Kerry obediently plucked at the box's wrapping, ripping it apart and freeing the box from its bindings. "There. You have two hands free. Open it."

Dar needed no second invitation. She took hold of the box and pried the top off, peering inside. Then she turned it over and let the contents drop into her hand.

It was a jar, with a white top, and a seemingly hand written label. Dar blinked it. "Double fudge body paint?" She read it aloud. "From New Zealand?"

Kerry affected an innocent look. "They didn't have it at Sawgrass Mills."

Dar bit her lip, then burst out laughing, flipping the jar over in her hand in delight. "Oooohh...housekeeping's gonna be mad at us." She chortled. "Kerry, what made you order this?" Her eyes went to her partner's face. "Getting bored?"

For the first time in a long time, Kerry turned brick red, the color change very evident against her white cotton T-shirt. "No!" She got out, grabbing the jar. "I was just shopping! On the internet!"

"Shopping for..." Dar teased. "Jars? Fudge? Sex toys?"

Kerry cleared her throat loudly. "Did you know they have milk flavored candy there?" She changed the subject. "And hey, look...I've got a canvas all ready to test this stuff on." She tweaked Dar's bare belly. "To be honest, I was looking for some stuff we could take on the boat and the pointing and clicking just got a little...ah..."

"Off course?" Dar grinned. "You and a mouse. Dangerous."

"Trackball. I hate mice." Kerry corrected her. "Dirty balls — not my style." She leaned over and nibbled a bit of Dar's skin. "So what do you say, Dixiecup? Wanna see if I have even one artistic bone in my body tonight?"

Dar set the jar down and picked Kerry up instead, curling her body around her partner's and delivering a passionately serious kiss that coaxed a soft groan from Kerry's guts and set the blond woman's hands wandering over Dar's skin. "Yeah," she breathed into Kerry's ear. "Paint anything you like on me. I won't even check the spelling."

"Spelling?" Kerry snickered, easing her body flat against Dar's. "Baby, I'm not gonna be writing *anything*. You're going to see how us repressed WASPS do finger-painting."

They tumbled together across the bed, laughing as they got tangled in the sheets and ended up almost falling off. Dar clasped her arms around Kerry and held her tight, releasing a deeply satisfied sigh. "To hell with all of them," she said. "Let's go have fun."

"Grrowl."

"I'M IN HEAVEN." Kerry put her bare feet up on the railing next to Dar's as they sat and watched the fireworks. Absently, she reached over and took Dar's hand in hers, as she let her other one rest on a very satisfactorily stuffed belly. "Thank god we don't do this all the time. I can only imagine the amount of gym sweat I'd have to put in to keep up with it."

Dar flexed her toes and leaned closer, pressing her shoulder against Kerry's as a new set of colorful lights exploded in the distance. "Mm." She agreed with both sentiments, though it was hard to focus on the question through the beer they'd shared over dinner and the lassitude the warm air was pressing on her. "That was pretty."

"Uh huh." Kerry rested her head against Dar's upper arm. "Paladar Katherine?"

"Mmm..." Dar peered at her. "What have I done?"

"Nothing. I just like your name." Kerry exhaled contentedly. "So...what's our strategy for tomorrow? There are two big panels in the afternoon...one's on the direction of wireless, the others on outsourcing. I think we should be on both of them, don't you?"

"Oh," Dar mused. "Like I didn't make enough trouble today, you want me to try again tomorrow? Alastair's probably already shredded his desk blotter." She lifted the mug of coffee resting by her left elbow and took a sip from it. "I'm surprised he hasn't called."

"Maybe he hasn't heard," Kerry suggested. "It wasn't that big a deal, Dar. Once you started talking them through it, everyone really relaxed."

"Umph." Dar watched several rockets go up, bursting into red and blue patterns overhead. "Yeah, all right. Sign me up. It's more interesting than wandering around in the hall bullshitting." She squeezed Kerry's fingers. "Besides, I get the feeling one of the pitches Telegenics made is that they're a lot more cutting edge than stodgy old ILS."

"Really?"

A perceptible twinkle appeared in Dar's eyes. "I got an email today from an old acquaintance at one of the accounts that switched. She was passing the time of day," she said. "And, I got a little insider info."

"Ahhh." Kerry rumbled softly. "Do I sense some early reservations?"

"Hedging her bets." A grin appeared. "Shirley Applebaum...she's got a lot of sense, and even though we bumped heads when they first signed with us, she's all right."

"Bumped heads...like you and I did?"

Dar laughed. "Kerrison, no one in my life ever bumped heads with me like you did," she assured her partner. "No, I'd only recently become a regional manager when they came onboard...they were my first account."

"Oh."

"Talk about a learning experience." Dar briefly covered her eyes with one hand. "For a while, I thought they were going to be my last account. But it worked out."

"And she said...?"

Dar rubbed her cheek and rested her chin on her hand. "Just that she'd been talking to her new boss, who's the one who made the contract change, and he's all puffed up about how he's gone with the cutting edge new players on the block instead of the old timers."

"Old timers." Kerry glanced at herself, then at her partner. "I could take offense to that."

Dar chuckled. "Shirley said she'd wait to pass judgment until after her first major problem happens. She's a little skeptical about all the promises."

"Are we really that conservative?" Kerry asked. "The models we use, the pricing structure—that always seemed like good business practice to me."

Dar leaned back and thought about that for a while. "We're not really," she concluded. "Our new net is cutting edge, and most everyone knows that. I think it's that we've been around so long, and we're so big, it's hard to react as fast as a smaller company would. That's probably true."

"Hmm."

"On the other hand, we have very deep resources," Dar went on, in a thoughtful tone. "So once you're under contract to us, if your business changes or you need something done immediately, it's nothing more than a phone call."

"That's true. I've done that for customers a hundred times. I never thought of it that way," Kerry said. "Isn't that something the sales people can use when they go to contract?"

"Tricky."

"Obviously." Kerry admired a sudden burst of color as it spread across the sky. "That really is pretty, but I'm glad I'm not under it. I hate the smell of gunpowder."

They both jumped a little and turned as a knock sounded inside the room, echoing faintly through the sliding glass door. Dar frowned. "Are we expecting anyone?"

"Hell no." Kerry got up and shoved the door open, trading the warm concrete for the rough nubble of the carpet against her bare feet. She pressed her hands against the door and peered through the eyehole, pushing back in annoyance when she recognized Michelle's face on the other side. "Son of a bitch," she muttered. "What do you want at ten o'clock at night?"

For a short moment, she debated with herself, seriously considering ignoring the knock and returning to the balcony. Then with a sigh, she grasped the door hand and turned it, her breeding overcoming her baser inclinations by a whisker. "Yes?"

Michelle gazed back at her, for once dressed down in a shirt and jeans and having left most of her pretensions at home, it seemed. "Hi."

"Hi," Kerry responded, leaning against the jamb but not allowing the door to open past her body width. "What can I do for you?"

"Can we talk?" Michelle asked. "I know it's late, I know it's been a long day, I know you're not pleased to see me here."

Kerry felt a warm stream of air suddenly on the back of her neck, and somehow managed not to jump as Dar's hands settled on her hips. Her partner remained silent, however, leaving the decision up to her. "If you know all that, why push it?" she asked. "Maybe tomorrow's a better idea."

"It probably is. But I'd like to talk to you anyway," their unwelcome visitor stated. "Both of you," she added, a little belatedly.

Kerry's face twitched a little as she was pinched very gently on the behind. Then the warmth behind her disappeared, and she straightened up. "Make it fast." She backed up a step and opened the door. "We've got plans for the rest of this evening."

Michelle raised her eyebrows as she slipped past, giving Kerry's faded T-shirt and bare feet a glance. "Thanks."

Kerry followed her inside. Dar had settled on the couch, her long, bare legs sprawled out across the carpet and her arms spread across the back of the cushions. It left enough space next to her for one other person, provided it was someone Dar liked.

Michelle prudently took the chair across from her, and waited until Kerry sat down within the spread of Dar's reach before she crossed one ankle over her knee and cleared her throat. "Okay, I'll cut to the chase, since we all don't want to be here."

"No." Dar let her arm drop down over Kerry's shoulders. "We want to be here." She turned her head and regarded her partner's profile. "What I can't figure out is why the hell you don't follow your business plan and leave us alone." She glanced back at Michelle, raising her eyebrows in question.

Michelle exhaled. "Because you're part of my business plan," she responded. "Look. I know my infrastructure right down to the nuts and screws just like you do." She looked right at Dar. "I know what the capacity is, and I'm at it. I can't expand anymore."

"And?" Dar shrugged. "I could have told you that. You've promised the same service level to all the accounts you picked up this year. If..." She pointed back at Michelle. "If everything runs perfectly, and no one has any increase in demand, you can provide what you promised."

"Yes."

"But things never do work perfectly," Kerry said.

"Except in your network," Michelle concluded. "So that's why I'm here. I know what ILS must pay you. I also know you've been with them forever, and maybe you're ready for a new set of challenges. I want to hire you."

Kerry looked at Michelle, then she turned and looked at Dar. "I know she's talking about you, not me," she stated, with a half chuckle.

"Actually, I'm not stupid," Michelle contradicted her. "Both of you. I know what conflict of interest is and I hate wasting money."

Holy crap. Kerry kept her mouth shut and waited for Dar's

reaction. She could feel the slow, rhythmic stroking of her partner's fingers against the back of her shoulder and she was close enough to hear Dar's steady breathing.

Dar sniffed reflectively. "You don't have the money."

"To pay you?" Michelle chuckled. "Mm...you do have an ego."

But Dar shook her head. "You don't have the money to put in the infrastructure you'll need to compete, not only with us, but with the rest of the big dogs," she demurred. "I checked your market cap. You're tapped right now."

Their visitor got up and walked around the back of her chair, pacing with short, deliberate steps. "If I can get projections justified, I can get the money. I have backers lined up who are just waiting...watching to see if we can make it over the top. They were very impressed at the progress we've made so far, but now I need to take the next step." She paused and leaned on the back of the seat. "You are the next step. There is no fuzzy logic involved. Every deep pocket I have behind me knows who you are and what you can do."

Dar merely watched her, a faint smile on her face.

"So," Michelle concluded, coming around to the front of the chair again and sitting down. Dressed as she was, she seemed more like them, than the starched figure they'd been dealing with for the last few days. "That's what brings me here. I'm sorry it's been so uncivilized the past two days. My fault. Stupid choices."

Kerry decided to remain quiet. She was in no way tempted by the offer, and she knew despite Michelle's words that she'd been included for reasons that did not wholly encompass her qualifications as an IT executive. However, Dar's words earlier that evening echoed into her mind, and she had to wonder if her partner wasn't at least a little bit flattered and intrigued by the interest.

And in fact, she didn't blame Michelle one bit—far from it. She gave the woman high points for going after a prize she herself valued above all others. In fact, if she'd chosen this approach from the get go, she might indeed have gotten the synergy she'd been hoping for.

However.

"I don't expect any answer," Michelle went on. "I wanted to put the idea out there. We've got the rest of this damn show to get through, and it would make my life a lot easier if we could can the feud now."

"It's not my feud," Dar finally spoke, in a quiet voice.

Michelle watched her face closely, but apparently found nothing there. She lifted a hand and let it fall onto her denim-clad knee.

They were all briefly silent. Then Kerry cleared her throat a little. "Want some coffee?" she offered, indicating the table. "It's pretty good here."

Michelle glanced at it. "No thanks." She half grimaced, half smiled. "I'd never get to sleep. Doesn't it bother you?"

"Not really, no." Kerry shook her head. "Though I generally prefer tea at night." She leaned against Dar unobtrusiveley. "Why don't we agree to behave like professionals for the next few days? I'm sure we can all handle that."

"Mm." Michelle glanced at Dar.

"You didn't get any special treatment," Dar said. "This is how I always act when people get in my face. Have your people stay out of my face, and we'll have a grand old time." She pinned Michelle with a cool gaze. "Your staff has been messing with us since I got here. You made me spend half the night in that damn hall because of your little tricks, and your managers keep harassing my staff. What makes you think any of that makes you or your company even the least bit appealing for someone like me to work for?"

Michelle, surprisingly, didn't counter her accusations. Instead, she ducked her head to one side. "Granted. Like I said, bad choices. I take responsibility for that."

Dar relaxed a little. "All right then," she conceded. "We should have no problems anymore in that case. Stay out of my face and don't antagonize me and I guarantee tomorrow will be a hell of a lot more pleasant than today was. Deal?"

"I think we can manage that."

"I think *you* can manage that," Kerry spoke up. "I think if you really want to get this to happen, send your Rottweiler home."

Michelle sighed. "You're not making it any easier with all this overprotective bullshit, Kerry."

"Tough." Kerry didn't bother to protest the comment. "Did I come over to your booth during your presentation and heckle you?"

Michelle lifted a hand, then let it fall. "We're big girls. We can take it."

"Why should you have to?" Dar asked. "Why not act like professionals like the rest of us?"

Michelle considered that, and then she nodded. "I won't promise you won't be challenged," she said. "But I will do my best to keep it civil."

Kerry exhaled almost soundlessly.

"Civil works," Dar said. "Keep it professional and we should be fine."

"Good." Their visitor put her hands on the chair arms and pushed herself to her feet. "Then I won't take up more of your time. It's late, and it's been a long day." Her eyes fell on the jar, sitting patiently on the table and she blinked, reading the label, then glanced at them, one eyebrow lifting.

Kerry smiled kindly at her. "See you tomorrow." She waggled her fingers.

Michelle walked across the room and let herself out, pulling the door after her with a definite, crisp snick.

Dar drummed her fingers on Kerry's shoulder, then tilted her head back and let out a long chuckle. "Oh, ain't this a tangled web."

"They're going to be assholes tomorrow," Kerry predicted. "You're going to have to lock me in the equipment cabinet or I swear, Dar, I'm going to end up going postal on them."

"Wild thing." Dar ruffled her hair affectionately. "I love that."

"Yeah, well...those two black widows can kiss my butt." Kerry snagged the jar and wrapped her hands in Dar's shirt, tugging her upward. "C'mon, Dixiecup. Hedonism beckons."

Outside the window, the fireworks peaked in silent glory, speckling the room with twinkling lights. They were, however, lost on the occupants.

KERRY GREETED THE emerging sun bathing the balcony with a yawn. The warmth felt good right now after the chill of the hotel room, but she knew it wouldn't be long before it went from soothing to annoying and decided to enjoy it while she could.

So much had happened the day before, she spent a few minutes reviewing it all. Then she looked up as the sliding door opened and Dar emerged onto the balcony.

She took the seat next to Kerry and cradled her coffee cup in her hands, sleepy eyes regarding the view amiably. "Kerrison?"

"Yes?"

"I have chocolate in many places God did not intend," Dar announced. "And you, my salacious little mudpuppy, are going to scrub it off me this morning in that there shower." She toasted Kerry with the coffee. "In fact, I think I still have your name scrawled across my leg."

"No, you don't." Kerry licked her lips. "Trust me."

Dar chuckled, stretching her legs out into the sunshine and tensing her thigh muscles. "Tell you what. How about we get out there before all the munchkins and go in the pool for a while, before we get into our monkey suits? Show doesn't start till ten."

Kerry sucked in a lungful of pine scented, though warm, air. "Yeah. I like that idea." She decided. "Let's do it. Then we can grab a fast breakfast down at that little snack bar thing."

They got up, passing together through the glass door and bumping each other playfully as they maneuvered to the bathroom to grab their swimsuits.

Several minutes later, they had towels in hand and were headed out the door. This early, the hotel was quiet, and they could hear workers beginning to set up in the restaurants as they slipped out the back door and headed for the pool.

It was huge. But they had it pretty much to themselves, save a few tentative sunbathers gathering down at one end and timidly spreading towels out on the comfortable looking lounge chairs. Dar tossed her towel on a vacant one on the far side of the pool and dove in without a second's hesitation.

Kerry took a moment to fold her towel and put it down next to Dar's. She straightened and went to the edge of the pool and dove in.

The water was warmer than she expected, but still refreshing. She surfaced and swam to where Dar was somersaulting lazily in place, enjoying the clear liquid for a change after swimming mostly in seawater for the last few months.

Dar had on her silver gray suit. It had a functional tank neckline, but high cut sides that showed off her long legs. She flipped over onto her stomach and started to swim down the length of the pool, her powerful arms pulling her through the water with apparently effortless ease.

Kerry took off after her, working a little harder to keep up as they swam side by side all the way to the other end of the irregularly shaped pool. Arriving at the wall, they turned, then leaned back and gazed across the water, blinking chlorine out of their eyes.

"Race you?" Kerry grinned.

Dar looked at her knowingly. "How many minutes head start do I have to give you?"

Sticking out her tongue, Kerry kicked off and started swimming as hard and as fast as she could, knowing perfectly well it was a lost cause. She liked swimming, but she'd come late to the sport, since they hadn't had a pool in Michigan and the idea of her going to a public pool would never have been countenanced.

After moving to Florida, and certainly after moving in with Dar, she'd gotten a lot more experience, but she was still working to acquire the skills, whereas her partner... "Dar!" Kerry felt hands pluck impudently at her suit. She stuck her face in the water and opened her eyes, spotting Dar almost right under her, swimming under the surface as fast as she could swim on top of it.

As she watched, slowing her strokes, Dar flipped over and coasted beneath her, releasing a lungful of bubbles that rumbled against Kerry's skin and surfaced around her. Then Dar stroked upward and emerged just in front of her, treading water in circles around Kerry.

"Show off." Kerry splashed her.

"Yeah, sometimes," she agreed, relaxing onto her back and heading off with neat strokes and powerful flutter kicks.

Kerry eased into a breaststroke and followed, starting to grin as she saw Dar angle toward the tall slide. She surged after her, catching up as Dar pushed herself up out of the water and onto the concrete, then turned to offer her a hand up.

"Thank you, ma'am." Kerry latched onto the back of Dar's suit and followed her up the steps to the top of the slide. "I think this is supposed to be for the kids."

"And?" Dar launched herself down the slippery surface. "C'mon, you punk!"

Kerry settled on the slide and shoved herself forward, enjoying the spray of water as she whirled downwards toward the pool. "Better get out of my way, slowpoke!" she yelled in warning, tucking her arms against her sides as she sped up. "Yahhhhhhh!!!"

She dropped out of the slide and plunged into the pool, relaxing her legs as she anticipated hitting the bottom.

Halfway there, she was abruptly intercepted as strong arms wrapped around her and yanked her to a halt. Dar had pushed off the bottom already and they surged back toward the surface, breaking through it into the warm air with a twin yell.

"Me a punk?" Kerry swept an armful of water toward her partner, dousing her thoroughly. "You're a punk, you little..."

"Little?" Dar picked her up and leaned sideways, taking them both underwater. They wrestled around until Kerry managed to wriggle free, then broke out into the open air again. "Rat!" She dove at Dar and grappled with her again, but made the mistake of getting too close and growled as she felt Dar's arms tighten around her with irresistible force.

"Rat, huh?" Dar's low voice tickled her ear.

Kerry tried a wriggle, and then relaxed, realizing she was good and caught. She turned her head to regard her companion, giving her a kiss on her wet nose. "Okay. You're not a rat," she said. "You're a HAMSTER!" She twisted suddenly and got a leg wrapped around Dar's, pulling them both off balance and back under the water.

They finally came back up near the edge of the pool, laughing like kids. Dar ducked backwards and straightened, slicking her hair back as she leaned against the concrete. "Whoo."

Kerry rapidly shook her head, scattering water everywhere before she joined her partner. "That was fun." She glanced around, noting that the pool deck was becoming a little more populated, and several solitary bodies had joined them in the water.

"Yeah, it was," Dar agreed, her eyes drifting across the deck. "Ah. Look who's headed this way."

Kerry actually growled. "If their names start with M or S, this pool's gonna run red I swear it."

Dar snorted, but shook her head. "No. It's our friend Peter, Peter, Cruise Ship eater." She assumed a cool expression as Quest arrived at poolside, hunkering down next to her in his crisp, gray suit. "Morning."

"Good morning, ladies," Quest answered. "Ms. Stuart, did you think about what we discussed yesterday? I have to leave right after the conference today so I don't think we'll get a chance to meet again."

"Gosh, that's a pity," Kerry replied mildly. "Mr. Quest, can I ask you something?"

"Sure." Peter rested his arms on his knees.

"How did you know where to find us?" Kerry reached casually out and took hold of the hem of his pants. "I'm pretty sure we didn't leave a note at the desk."

He hesitated. "Um..."

Dar leaned closer, giving him an icy look. "Answer the lady."

"Or?" Quest rallied, with commendable bravado.

"Or we're going to pull you in the pool and possibly drown you," Kerry smiled kindly at him. "Neither Dar nor I like snoops or weasels."

Quest glanced down at the strong fingers clamped around his pant leg. "No big mystery," he replied. "I paid the bellboys to keep an eye on you." A smirk appeared. "They didn't seem to think it was a tough task."

"Ah, I see," Kerry murmured. "Well, Mr. Quest, aside from the fact that I don't like sneaks, and you have really bad taste in tailors, I really don't think you need a company of our caliber in your little contest."

Quest blinked, obviously not hearing what he'd fully expected to. "But..."

"But?" Kerry replied, releasing his pants.

"You said you could make decisions."

"Um...I just did." The green eyes twinkled a little. "I could repeat it if you want me to. I said..."

"I heard you." Quest frowned. "But damn it, I thought..."

Dar put her hands on the concrete and pressed herself up out of the water. She stood up and glared down at Quest. "You thought Kerry would go against me."

He looked up. "She's ambitious." He shrugged. "Moving up that ladder ain't a piece of cake, even in your company." He stood up and brushed his hands off. "My sources told me it was something she was interested in." His eyes dropped to a slightly boggled Kerry. "My sources said you better watch your back, Roberts."

Kerry put a hand over her mouth, muffling a laugh.

Dar rubbed the bridge of her nose. "Did your sources bother to mention to you that Kerry and I are married?" She paused, watching his face go slack. "To each other?" she clarified, pointing to Kerry and then to herself.

His nostrils flared. "Ah..." An eyebrow twitched. "No, no they didn't."

Dar almost felt sorry for him. "How does it feel to be used?" She reached down and offered Kerry her hand. "Tell you what, Quest. We'll enter your bid. Send me the papers first thing tomorrow morning."

"You will?" He took a step back, watching her warily.

"Yeah." Dar pulled her partner up out of the pool. "And you can tell your source they're lame ass losers."

Quest stood and watched them walk away, his jaw hanging slightly.

"WHAT THE HELL was that?" Kerry threw her towel around her shoulders, lengthening her strides to keep up with Dar's rapid walk. "Hello? Dar?" She snagged her partner by the back of the suit. "Dar!"

Dar slowed, but didn't stop. "Yeah?"

"If I have to put up with you making me look like an idiot, I'd at least like to know why."

Now Dar stopped. She sidestepped into a smaller alcove off the path, which had a sturdy bench in it. "Sit." She took a seat herself, and waited for Kerry to follow suit. "I wasn't trying to make you look like an idiot."

Kerry leaned on her knees. "I know that. I didn't think you did it on purpose, you just reacted to something and I can't figure out what it was or what the hell's going on here."

Dar looked at her. "Didn't you hear him? Didn't you hear him say he'd been told you were looking to stab me in the back?"

"Dar, we've heard that before. Don't you remember?" Kerry put a hand on Dar's knee, seeing the upset in her posture. "I didn't pay any attention... I'm used to people thinking all sorts of things about our relationship."

"I know" Dar sighed, leaning back and stretching her arms out over the back of the bench. "But didn't you find it really coincidental that this guy comes here...to this show... and gets that kind of stuff? You think it came from our people?"

"No."

"Neither do I." Dar bit the words off precisely. "But I'd be willing to bet I know where he got it from."

Kerry slowly let out a breath. "Okay." She also leaned back, feeling first the chill of the water droplets, then the warmth of Dar's skin touch her shoulders. "So...you're thinking it was deliberate? Or...what are you thinking, Dar?"

Dar remained silent, gazing morosely at the green hedge separating them from the path.

Kerry waited patiently, wiping her arms off with her towel. The crickets sounded loud around her, and she jerked her foot as an ant tried to use her as a highway.

"It's something Shari would have said to him."

"Ah."

"That's exactly how she thinks." Dar went on. "That everyone has an angle. Wants something."

"I don't get it." Kerry shook her head slightly. "Yeah, she seems like the kind of person who would say that, but damn it, Dar...what's the point? What's she trying to do?"

"Break us up."

Kerry sneezed.

"My mother always said you sneeze on the truth," Dar remarked wryly.

Kerry turned and faced her, leaning her elbow over Dar's arm. "Are you really serious? You think that's what she was trying to do? Or...I mean, if they're bidding, it makes no sense at all to provoke you...us...into participating."

"No."

Kerry sneezed again. "Pooters." She wiped her face with the towel. "All that chlorine got up my nose." She sighed. "Dar, what the heck's going on then? Let's say you're right. Let's say her motive was trying to break us up. What does that get her?"

Dar studied Kerry's face, watching the sunlight pick up amber glints in the depths of her eyes. "The satisfaction of hurting me?"

blond brows lifted. "You really think that's what she's after?"

"I really think so," Dar replied. "That's why I told him we'd do the bid. It's not that I want it...hell, it's not really even big enough for us to bother with. I just don't want her to get it, and I'm personally willing to make sure that's not going to happen."

Kerry nibbled the inside of her lip. "Hm."

"So. I'm sorry I overrode you." Dar went on. "It was a snap decision. Probably not a good one. Definitely based on something other than business."

"So, what you're saying is that Shari did something to get at you, that goes against her business interests, right? Or...Dar, what if they were trying to force us into the bid — like a showdown."

Dar thought about that for a minute. "Shit, I don't know." She exhaled. "I think she'll do anything to make us look bad, that's true, but I also think she's out to get me. To get us."

"Well." Kerry leaned against her. "Then she's lost already because I'm sure not going to let anything like that happen." She put her arm around Dar's back. "Don't stress it, Dar."

"Sorry I got us into this." Dar rested her elbows on her knees.

"Heh." Kerry chuckled softly. "Well, poop, Dar...I was saying no because I didn't think you wanted anything to do with going up against them. I thought we were going to leave them alone. But if you want to go up in their faces, I'm there with you." She rubbed Dar's shoulder. "My ego will live."

Dar's eyes dropped.

"Of course, we could actually send a bid analysis team, like we would for any other prospective client." Kerry reminded her. "I have people that do that sort of thing, you know."

"I know."

Kerry reached up with a corner of her towel and wiped away the sweat forming on Dar's temple. "That's probably what they're going to do. I don't think Michelle's a qualified engineer, and you said yourself Shari was in marketing."

"True," Dar admitted. "But it's not that way for us." She tilted her head, one brow arching. "We can do this."

"Sure."

"I want to do it." A shrug. "It's new, it's different...I've never been inside that industry before." Dar considered thoughtfully. "I like ships." She pushed a bit of sodden blond hair back off Kerry's forehead. "Maybe you were right. I'm restless. But you don't have to get involved — you've got a lot on your plate back here."

Kerry caught her hand and kissed her fingers. "Where you go, I go," she replied simply.

"Poetic, but you know what I mean." Dar smiled anyway.

"It's development of new business, and implementation of new technologies," Kerry answered blithely. "Both are my job. In fact, it's actually my prerogative to assign an engineer to the project, you know."

"That's true, it is." Dar hauled herself to her feet. "How about we negotiate my services over a corn muffin? I'm hungry."

Kerry got up and followed as Dar started out back onto the path. She caught up and bumped her taller partner's shoulder as they strolled along together. "Hm...can I afford you?" She wondered facetiously. "Maybe I should assign a junior engineer."

"And why would you want anything but the best?" Dar inquired. "I work for Oreos and milk. Can't get much cheaper than that."

"Heh. True." Kerry studied the smooth rock surface they were walking on. "Can I tell you a secret?"

Dar headed for the small café. "Sure."

"Sometimes I'm a little restless too." Kerry nudged Dar to a plastic covered seat, heading herself toward the counter. "My treat, cookie monster. You stay here."

Dar settled into the chair and looped her damp towel around her neck, content to merely watch Kerry as she stepped up to the counter and placed their order. After a moment, she smiled, propping her head up on one fist. "Where I go you go, huh?" she uttered softly. "Y'know, I like the sound of that."

Kerry turned, leaning on the counter as she waited. Her eyes met Dar's, and she grinned.

Dar grinned back.

Today, she decided, she wouldn't wait to see what fate had in store for them. They wanted a show?

She'd give 'em one.

Chapter
Six

KERRY HOPPED UP onto the platform of their booth, waving a greeting to the techs working busily at the consoles. "Morning, guys."

"Hey, Kerry." Mark looked up, then got up and walked over. "Listen, I think the marketing geeks screwed up again. I saw her name listed on another one of those presentations."

"I know." Kerry nodded. "It's okay. I put her on it. Matter of fact, I'm on one too. Anything going on?"

Mark shook his head. "Nope...well, you guys were starring big time on Tech TV, that's all. That's who the cameras were on yesterday. I think they're back." He pointed over her shoulder. "They kept looping that whole thing with Big D holding off the masses at the booth entrance."

"Ah." Kerry put her hands on her hips and regarded the oncoming news crew. "Well, let's see how much good press we can get today." A wry look crossed her face. "Jesus, I never in my life thought I'd hear myself say that."

Kerry started forward, making eye contact with the reporter in the lead. The man grinned, appreciating the attention, and made a beeline for her. "Here we go," she muttered under her breath. "You are the Midwestern Republican WASP face of ILS, Kerrison...now let's let them get a look at the radical gay biker chick considering a tattoo under all of it."

"Hey!" the reporter hailed her. "Can we get a quick interview with you, Ms. Stuart?"

"Absolutely." Green eyes twinkled. "Long as you don't ask me for my hacker card. I left it in my gym bag."

The reporter laughed. So did the crew. Out of the corner of her eye, Kerry spotted Michelle strolling in her direction, and she perched on the edge of the booth, the ILS logo right behind her shoulder giving a great shot to the cameramen.

"Got anything new for us?" the reporter asked first. "ILS doesn't usually come across as razor's edge, but I thought we got a different view yesterday. Want to follow up on that?"

Kerry smiled, crossing her arms. "Yes, I do," she replied. "Let me tell you what we've got planned, but you better duct tape your socks."

A crowd had gathered to listen in, and she saw Michelle on the edge of it, pretending to study a brochure from a nearby booth. "We've gotten a lot of press lately for what everyone thinks is a negative reason," Kerry said. "Let me tell you what the real story is."

Michelle turned and stared, looking her right in the eye.

Kerry's smile broadened, and her gaze turned sea ice cold. You want a fight? You got one.

DAR PROWLED THROUGH the exhibits, aware of and enjoying the attention being directed at her. After the aborted session the previous day, and her grandstanding at their booth, there weren't many in the room who didn't know who she was.

She intended to make sure that number was zero before she left. As she peered critically at a new firewall product, however, her cell phone went off. She pulled it out and glanced at it, recognizing the number immediately. "Sheesh. About time."

Walking over to a small alcove, she answered it. "Morning, Alastair."

"Holy crap, Dar!"

Dar smiled. "I love starting the day out having made you say that," she announced cheerfully. "Better than a cup of café con leche."

Her boss sighed audibly. "I didn't expect to start my morning by seeing you on MSNBC, as the technology headline."

"Was I?" Dar mused. "Didn't even see them there. I thought AP and UPI were giving us a skip this year because technology is 'out'." She glanced casually around, spotting one of their biggest competitors cornering two ILS clients.

"Well, Dar, when you go and announce we hire hackers, and dare anyone to try and hack our network to prove we only hire the best ones..." Alastair replied, in a dry tone. "It's a sound bite no one could resist."

"Got us attention."

The ILS CEO sighed again. "The only thing that offset the 'attention' was the way you handled it. The camera is fascinated by you." He cleared his throat. "With good reason. Nice suit, too."

"Uh huh." Dar leaned against the woven weave wall, feeling it's faint prickliness through the cloth of her jacket. "So let me guess. The board is freaking."

"Surprisingly, no," Alastair answered. "Actually, they asked me to give you a call and say how pleased they were."

Dar pulled the phone away from her ear and studied it with a deeply quizzical expression. Then she knocked it against the wall, making a sharp rapping sound.

"Dar?" Her boss's voice came to her tinnily. "Dar? What's going on?"

"Sorry. I think we've got a crossed line," she replied. "I know I didn't just hear that."

Alastair chuckled. "Well, you know, it surprised me too," he admitted. "But John said he'd gotten a lot of flak lately about how stodgy we are...well, most of us, anyway. He thought this was a damn good boot in the short pants for all those pundits who thought we were mummies in three piece suits."

"Eh." Dar grunted. "Glad they liked it, but it wasn't planned. Damn guy just got my goat."

"Whatever the reason." Her boss shrugged it off. "Something good'll come of it."

Dar watched Peter Quest enter and cross over to their booth, where Kerry was currently holding court. Michelle was there also, and she noted by her posture, not entirely happy. "Kerry's giving an interview right now to TechTV," she commented. "So listen, let me go see if she needs backup. We got invited into a little bid for some new cruise ship IT business."

"What?"

"Yeah. " Dar craned her neck to watch the crowd. "Could end up being a decent sized contract."

"Dar! Why didn't you tell me!"

"Because I just decided to do it. Listen, Alastair...let me get back to you. I've got people looking for me here." Dar studied Kerry's body language anxiously.

"Dar, damn it, talk to me for a minute," her boss shot back. "Kerry's perfectly capable of doing an interview, isn't she?"

The rough bark drew Dar's attention from her lover. She collected herself and re-focused on the phone. "Yes, she is" she replied. "I don't have that many details, Alastair. I was approached by some guy over at American Cruise Ventures who wants to put new tech in all their ships, especially the ones they're bringing over to the States."

"Fabulous!"

Dar sighed. "Yeah, well, we're up against three other companies, including Telegenics."

There was a small silence on the other end of the phone. "Really?"

"Yeah."

Another silence. "Well, we're gonna have to make sure we win this one,"Alastair stated positively. "No taking chances, Dar. I want you to handle this personally."

Dar examined her cell phone again, this time with a bemused look. She poked a button experimentally, then a second, making a small musical interlude.

"Dar?"

"Sorry." Dar put the phone back to her ear reluctantly. "I was checking something. You know, I do have qualified people working for me."

"Dar, this is no time for that. These bastards have been running roughshod all over us. Here's one major chance to stop their momentum. This is too important to let someone else do it," her boss argued. "I want you to handle it. In fact, take Kerry if it'll make you feel better. She's your protégé."

"Alastair?"

"What?"

"Could you arrange for an ice cream machine to be installed in my office?"

"WHAT?"

"Never mind." Dar almost laughed. "I'll take care of it. I've got a vested interest...did you know who the movers and shakers were in Telegenics? I bumped into them here."

"Ahem." Alastair cleared his throat. "Not the day to day folks. They've got some interesting backers. I know they've got deep pockets. Japanese, I believe."

"Michelle Graver, and someone from my past I hate with a passion," Dar informed him. "So yeah, I'll take this one, Alastair. I'll take it and beat them so badly they'll go running off to San Francisco to sell tie-dye shirts and tickets to Alcatraz."

It was, apparently, her boss' turn to be nonplussed. He made a sound something like a cluck, and then cleared his throat.

"Now, can I talk to you later? The person I hate with a passion is about to start bugging my wife."

Another cluck.

"Bye, Alastair."

"Uh...bye, Dar. Talk to you later, huh?"

"Sure." Dar closed the phone and clipped it to her belt. Then she straightened her jacket and headed for the booth.

"WE KNOW WHERE we hold the market lead." Kerry leaned back and crossed her ankles. "Right now, our priority isn't spending time fending off lowball services contract hawkers. We're interested in taking another step forward in providing our backbone customers with the best infrastructure in the world."

"That's bold," the Tech TV reporter remarked. "You guys put a really solid network in place, everyone knows that. But where do you go from there? Only so many bells and whistles you can add before it just becomes more frills customers have to pay for."

"Exactly," Michelle piped up, her lip twitching at the lowball comment.

Kerry met her gaze evenly. "We don't bother with frills." She turned back to the reporter. "What's the next step? The next step is making the network intelligent. Giving it the sentience to be able to react to changing conditions, and flexible enough to respond to the challenge of new bandwidth requirements dynamically."

The man stared at her, and then cocked his head. "You can't do that. The intelligence doesn't exist."

"Not yet," Kerry agreed quietly. "But it will."

"If it's not just empty promises," Shari called out. "Sounds like vaporware to me."

Kerry could have reacted, but she chose not to. She merely gave Shari a brief, dismissive look, and then turned back to one of the men in the front. "Eddie, you know what I'm talking about. You're a pilot location."

Thrust suddenly in the spotlight, her client almost melted into a pocket-protected puddle. Kerry gave him a smile though, and he blinked at the round, staring eye of the camera and managed a nod. "Uh...yeah" he stammered. "It was cool. It was like the pipes knew when the program needed more space, and like...um..." He shrugged. "Gave it to 'em. Real cool."

"Wait...I thought you said it didn't exist yet." The reporter eased closer to her. "Didn't you just say that? She just said that, right?" he asked the audience.

"Right," Michelle drawled. "That's what she said."

Kerry slipped into a nearby console chair and turned the monitor on the desk around so the audience could see it. "It's not in production," she conceded. "But we've prototyped it. Wanna see?"

They were lucky the booth was well built. Kerry suddenly found herself surrounded by curious nerds and a cameraman who seemed more interested in checking out her earlobes than seeing what she was doing on the monitor.

She flexed her fingers, and spared a glance at the part of the crowd unable to fit, giving their rivals a brief, very pleasant, wordlessly wicked smile. "Okay, here's how it works." She tapped out a quick command, fishing in her memory for the codes she'd learned from Dar.

Cryptic codes. Dar never made anything obvious or easy, at least on the back end. She permitted the applications people to put snazzy looking front ends on her stuff, but where it counted, it was all grease on the hands and you better know what you're doing time.

Basic and functional, straightforward yet elegant.

Just like Dar. "Let's say you have this allocated bandwidth..."

"So what, it bursts. Big deal," Shari commented.

"Hey, shut up." One of the men in front turned around. "You don't want to hear this? Take a hike." He glanced at Shari's badge. "Take your petty rivalry and ditch it, sister."

Ah, chivalry. "Thanks." Kerry put a hand on her unlikely champion's arm.

"Don't thank me yet, lady," the man warned her. "If this is all BS, I'll chew you next."

Bet you won't. Kerry felt Dar's presence and knew, if she turned her head, she'd find her partner nearby. "I'm not worried," she told the man. "Now, where was I? Ah. Yes. Bandwidth. Let's use a T1 for example."

Shari started to push forward, but suddenly found herself held back firmly. She turned in annoyance, only to find herself the focus of two chips of icy fury only slightly tinted with blue. "All right, now…"

"If you know what's good for you," Dar spoke in an absolute flat voice. "You'll take the gentlemen's advice."

"Okay, you two. Break it up." Michelle gently eased between them, giving Dar a determined smile. "Time out. We'll continue the discussion later." She took hold of Shari's arm and despite their size difference, maneuvered the larger woman away from their bristling adversary.

"Like she said, it bursts." The loud man shook his head, oblivious to the drama going on behind him. "What's the big deal?"

"The big deal is how it bursts." Kerry released a breath, watching Michelle and Shari leave from her peripheral vision. "It analyzes the traffic flow, and makes decisions on how to route, what to route, and what to prioritize based on the application layer."

"What?" The man snorted. "At a network level? That's impossible to deploy large scale. Sure you can do it for one router…"

"It's not impossible." Kerry shook her head. "Dar's working with the hardware manufacturers to burn the essential code into firmware."

"No way." The man shook his head.

"Guess you'll have to wait and see." Kerry smiled. "But don't wait too long. Your competitors won't."

"Oooh. Nice sound bite," the reporter complimented her. "But…does this really work?"

"It really works." Dar judged that her body had stopped shaking enough for her to move up onto the platform and join Kerry. Her knees were still quivering a little as the adrenaline slowly drained from her bloodstream, and as she came up in back of her partner, she felt sudden warmth as Kerry's hand patted her calf. "Not bad for an old hacker, huh?"

A chuckle went around the crowd. "Can we ask you a few questions about it?" the aggressive man countered, with a visibly higher degree of respect.

"Maybe." Dar let her hands drop on Kerry's shoulder. "But if I answer, I might have to kill ya."

Another chuckle.

So far, Dar decided, so good. Roberts and Stuart several, Michelle and Shari, none.

Let's make sure it stays that way.

MICHELLE FOUND A corner, and put them both in it. "Can I ask what your damn problem is?" She fumed. "Damn it, I'm trying to build something we can use here. "

Shari glared back at her. "It's all bullshit!"she said. "Can't you see what they're trying to do? We spent how many months putting together a campaign, getting new clients, digging a wedge into them. We're going to blow it if we let them steal the spotlight!"

Michelle ran her hands through her hair. "Shari...Shari...you're not seeing straight. Look at them." She turned her companion around and pointed. "How in the hell would you like to remove them from the spotlight?"

"You should have left me alone! If I kept at them..."

"If you kept at them..." Michelle gritted her teeth. "You were going to get your clock cleaned any minute. Didn't you see that look you were getting? You're the one who used to sleep with her. I'd have thought you'd clue into that."

Shari made a disgusted sound. "Psycho."

"Hey." Michelle patted her arm. "It's not psycho to go after someone who's taking potshots at your SO. You were being obnoxious."

"I wasn't."

"You were." The shorter woman exhaled. "So cool it. Go back to the booth and schmooze. Let me deal with those two. At least I can have some sort of conversation with Stuart. Besides...I want to see whatever it is they're developing—that sounds like technology we can't afford to ignore."

Shari glared at the ILS booth, and then she shrugged. "Whatever."

"Stop antagonizing them." Michelle's voice gentled. "You keep pushing them, and they push back. ILS could cover our budget in Robert's lunch money. So let's back off, and see what they're going to do next. Last thing we want is for them to come gunning for us"

"We can handle it."

"Technologically, no we can't," Michelle told her, with a wry twist to her lips. "Our strength is small, personalized niches, and accounts where we can compete with them based on skinny margins. When it comes to the big silicon...baby, we're recycled glass."

"C'mon, this isn't rocket science."

"Shari." Michelle took her by the shoulders. "Listen to me. At the level Dar Roberts works, it is rocket science, and she's a rocket scientist. You may not have caught what Stuart was saying, but I did, and if it's true, they're going to own this market."

Shari studied her. "That hokey bursting stuff?"

"That hokey bursting stuff," Michelle replied. "Did you catch her saying they're working with the hardware vendors to have it put into firmware? That means it's real, and she's patented it, and if it works we're all going to be paying ILS for the privilege of using it."

"Are you kidding me?"

"I'm not kidding you," Michelle said. "It's a big deal. I'm really surprised they're even talking about it here."

Shari drummed her fingers on the table. "Can we steal it? Get a hold of it and look at the...the programming or whatever it is?"

Michelle grimaced.

"Don't grow a conscience on me now." Shari correctly interpreted the expression. "If we can get this thing, if you think it's that big a deal, then we can use it ourselves and compete with them on their own terms."

"I can try to get a look at it," Michelle temporized. "Maybe she'll be willing to brag about it and let me get my eyeballs on it." She exhaled. "Let me see what I can do. At least we don't have to worry about going up against them for Quest's bid. I want that one to be all us."

"I wasn't worried. I wanted them in." Her taller companion stuck her hands in the pockets of her skirt. "I want to keep them off balance," she said seriously. "Dar likes to control what's going on. She doesn't do well when she has to improvise."

Michelle studied the lanky, dark haired form lurking behind Kerry's seated figure. "I don't know about that," she disagreed. "But at any rate, go on back to the booth and let me do my thing. I'm the nerd, and it'll be up to me to find a way to give us enough technology to get a leg up on these guys while you dazzle them with the savings they'll get."

"Mmph. Okay," Shari finally agreed. "I guess I sometimes look at Dar, and I see that grotty kid I actually slept with in the depths of my stupid youth. I can't adjust my focus to believe this is actually a CIO of a major IT services company. I just can't."

Michelle patted her arm again. "Well, I first met her that way, so it's easier for me. And, while you're at it, let's reach out and touch anyone who thinks they can break into ILS's network. Offer a bounty. That's one way to knock the shine off the rep."

"Hm." Shari looked thoughtful. "I'll put the word out to our boys. They like a challenge," she said. "That was a damn stupid thing for her to do."

"That, I agree with you one hundred percent on." Michelle nodded. "G'wan." She gave Shari a push, watching as she reluctantly retreated to their smaller, but snazzy looking booth. She started back toward her target, but stopped when Peter Quest stepped into her path unexpectedly. "Oh, hello."

"Well, Ms. Graver, how are you?" Quest seemed quite pleased with himself. "Ready for a challenge?"

"Absolutely," she assured him. "We're very confident we can put together a package for you that'll knock your socks off."

He chuckled. "You'd better." He turned and indicated the crowd around ILS. "It's going to take a lot of snaz to knock them off. Hope your lean, mean, cost savings machine's up to it." With a grin, he sauntered off, clasping his hands behind his back as he paused to listen to Kerry's smooth, Midwestern voice.

"Shit," Michelle cursed. "I thought he said they'd turned him down. What in hell changed..." She paused to think. "I thought we knocked her back a step yesterday. Damn it."

"Did you say something, ma'am?" A passing usher inquired. "Need directions?"

"I need a tranquilizer. Got any?" she responded. "No, huh?" She watched the usher retreat in confusion. "Damn, damn, damn."

Quest had been so damn sure. Pissed off, in fact, at how he'd been treated and she'd taken quick advantage of that in arranging their position as the prime bidder on his contract.

Gorgeous publicity. Shari had already written the press release on it.

So what had changed? Michelle's eyes narrowed, remembering suddenly Kerry's altered attitude on coming into the hall that morning. In fact, if the blond woman had possessed a ruff she was sure it would have bristled. She drummed her fingers on her thigh.

Something had happened. Michelle didn't mind competition, but she knew this wasn't a stage she wanted to share. "Timing's not right, damn it." She parked herself near the ILS booth and waited for her chance, idly envying Kerry her friendly, open rapport with the crowd.

Kerry was a natural. Personable and good looking, intelligent and engaged, she was the veritable poster child for ILS and since she was also less intimidating than Dar she was the perfect focus for the nearby television cameras.

Damn it.

Kerry finished up her presentation to applause from her audience. Dar lounged behind her like a well-dressed eagle, one hand never far from her partner's back. As though sensing it, Kerry half turned and bumped the taller woman with her shoulder, grinning at her with intimate warmth.

"Dar's having 'Hi, I'm an ILS Hacker' shirts made up," Kerry announced. "I don't think they'll be ready before the show ends though."

"Aww," the Tech TV reporter chuckled. "That was a real hot question yesterday. Did you do that on purpose, Ms. Roberts? You've been accused of being too conservative, you know."

Both of Dar's eyebrows hiked. "Me?" she drawled. "Buddy, I've been called a lot of things by a lot of people...that ain't one of them."

The crowd laughed with her.

"ILS," the reporter restated, with a tolerant smile, "has been accused of being too conservative."

Dar perched on the corner of the desk where Kerry was sitting, letting both powerful hands rest on her knee. "No, I really didn't." Her voice altered, going a touch more serious. "It was something that came out of the discussion we were having. It isn't something I've ever hidden, but on the other hand, it's not something we put in the shareholder's folio every year either. It comes down to having the right skill sets in the right places all the time. Sometimes we do, sometimes we don't, but I would never not hire someone with that skill set only because it might be viewed as radical."

Kerry took a breath, having run out while listening to one of the longest single bits of speech she'd ever heard her partner utter at one time.

"I think most of us view hackers as something bad," the reporter conceded.

"Sometimes they are," Dar agreed. "But the really good ones also have a spirit of discovery, and a hunger for gaining knowledge that in my business, sir, is priceless."

Wow. Kerry blinked. I like that. She cocked her head and looked up at Dar's profile. "You know, you're about the best example of that I've ever seen."

Startled, Dar turned and met her eyes, a hesitant grin tugging at her lips. "Thanks."

The room faded out for a single moment as they gazed at each other.

Then the air conditioning cycled on, and buzzers next to them went off, and another question was shouted at them from the crowd. Dar swiveled back around and answered it after a brief hesitation, leaving Kerry to rest her elbows on the counter to simply watch and listen.

Kerry spotted Michelle near the corner where two walls joined, also watching, but there was no longer any sign of Shari. Kerry gave Michelle a point for good sense in getting her out of the room, because she'd seen Dar's face, as she'd come up behind her heckler.

Oo. She'd been pissed. Shari's obnoxious comments hadn't really bothered Kerry that much—she'd seen much worse in both takeover bids and competing boardrooms. But she found Dar's protective instincts charming in the extreme.

However.

Kerry had certainly felt like pounding their rivals yesterday, but in reality, if Dar had lost her temper, she knew someone could have really gotten hurt.

Probably wouldn't have been Dar.

"So that's really all we have to say for the moment," Dar concluded. "You guys better go pay everyone else some attention."

The television lights went out, and the crowd slowly started to disperse, talking among themselves as Dar eased off the desk and dropped into the chair next to Kerry instead. "Ever tell you how much I hate trade shows?" she uttered under her breath.

"Right back atcha." Kerry smiled pleasantly at the passing throngs. "Boy, will I be glad when five o'clock gets here. Can I interest you in dinner and a beer after that, boss?"

"Mmmmmm." Dar rumbled low in her throat. "I have a taste for Mexican. Want to go pavilion hopping with me at Epcot?"

Kerry found the irritation of the morning slipping away. "If we can have dessert in France, sure," she agreed. "And you buy me that beer in Germany."

Dar leaned back and laced her fingers behind her neck. "You're on, Yankee," she agreed. "I'm gonna send our crew back to the hotel once we shut down. Let someone else clean this crap up—I gave the bar manager over there my credit card to get them all plastered."

"Dar." Kerry covered her eyes. "That's so irresponsible of you."

A shrug. "They're not driving," Dar replied unrepentantly. "They deserve it. They worked their asses off." She paused and leaned over, touching Kerry's arm. "Did you talk to any of them yet about their raises?"

Kerry shook her head slightly. "Didn't think this was the place," she said. "I could pull them out one at a time I guess...might make for a lot more entertaining afternoon for me than it would otherwise."

"Do it," Dar said. "I'll cover this joint."

"Let me get my paperwork." Kerry got up and headed for the locked switch cabinet, where she'd stowed her likewise locked briefcase. "Is there a little room...oh, yeah, I see it. Over there near the entrance."

Dar nodded.

Kerry removed a folder from her case and closed the cabinet back up. Then she stood and went to the first of their techs, sitting at one of the smaller consoles. "John? Can I talk to you for a minute?"

The dark haired man glanced up at her, surprised. "Sure...um..."

"C'mon." Kerry took him by the elbow, and led him out of the booth, giving the rest of the techs now very alertly watching her a smile. "You all are next. Don't worry."

Dar watched the guys, after Kerry walked out of earshot, from the corner of her eyes. They were plainly bewildered, but none of them looked particularly worried.

Now, if it'd been her doing it...

"Hi."

Dar turned to find Michelle on the other side of the divider. Since she was alone, Dar rested her hands on the console and cocked her head in question. "Hi."

Michelle took that as an encouraging sign. "So you're teaching routers to think?"

Dar grinned briefly. "Something like that," she conceded. "It's a project I've been working on for a few months."

"Kerry made it sound pretty impressive. Is it?" Michelle asked, trying for a balance between wary friendliness and challenge. She was pretty sure Dar would only despise fawning.

"We'll see," Dar said. "So far I've gotten a three hundred percent efficiency metric, but it's early days yet."

Michelle blinked. "Are you bullshitting me?"

"No." Dar looked amused. "One of the advantages of working for a stodgy old conservative IT firm is that we've got an R and D budget." She glanced around at the crowd and then looked back at Michelle. "So I hear we're going to be competing over a couple of cruise ships."

Michelle's lips twitched. "I heard you weren't interested in the project. Matter of fact, the principal was calling you all sorts of names for blowing him off."

"Changed my mind." Dar was watching her with those sharp, fathomless pale eyes, so vivid with intelligence they were almost hard to look into. "Should be interesting." She stood up. "Sorry to cut this short, but I'm being waved at." She indicated Jose and Eleanor, who were standing with two men in suits, signaling her.

"No problem." Michelle pushed off from the booth. "Any chance you'd show me how your snazzy router routine works later?"

Dar glanced at her, a cross between mischief and mild irritation on her face. "Can you read assembler?"

Michelle sighed. "No."

"Sorry, then. Guess you're out of luck." Dar stepped down out of the booth and headed for her colleagues, leaving her unwelcome guest to stand there and watch.

Michelle sighed. "Sad thing is, she was probably telling me the truth." She stepped away from the booth and headed back to her own. "So we have to find some other way to scalp that chicken."

"ALL RIGHT, ROBERTS."

Dar tilted her head to one side, making eye contact with the aggressive questioner in gray whom she'd thought had moved on to more interesting things. "Ye...s?" She moderated her usual response.

The man stepped up into the booth and flipped a card at her. Dar picked it up and looked at it, noted the Army insignia then flipped it back to him. "Something I can do for you, Captain Mousser?"

The man turned one of the chairs around and sat on it, folding his arms across the back and studying her with bright, alert eyes. "Yeah. Let's talk. You ever play G.I. Joe as a kid?"

Dar blinked. "What?"

The captain grinned at her. "Wanna get to play with more cool toys than your company could afford in twenty years?"

Oh...Dar groaned inwardly. I've got a bad, bad feeling about this... "No," she said. "I'm happy with the toys I have, thanks."

The Army captain got up and perched on the corner of her console desk. "Hear me out. You might end up interested."

Dar was about to dismiss him, when she thought about how she'd similarly brushed off Quest. "Okay." She settled down to listen. "Pitch me."

KERRY SETTLED BACK in her seat and watched a loaded boat drift by, with two giggling girls in the front and two necking teenagers in the back. She found herself wondering if they were all related, and it reminded her somehow of her much younger years.

They'd never gone to Disney World, but they had gone to a couple of smaller thrill parks up north, usually with some of her father's staff to keep an eye on them. Kerry remembered one such afternoon in the fall, when the crisp air had made everything seem bright and fresh to her. She and Angie had shared a fried dough pastry covered in white powdered sugar, and she'd finally coaxed her sister to come with her on the tall roller coaster.

Angie hadn't enjoyed it at all, she recalled ruefully. She'd ridden the coaster again by herself, but somehow it wasn't the same and by the next year...Kerry dismissed the thought and shook her head, taking a sip of her beer instead.

Dar would go on roller coasters with her, and enjoy them, wouldn't she? "Dar?"

"Yeeeess?"

"How do you feel about thrill rides?"

"Yes," she responded instantly. "They don't have enough of them here."

"Heh." Kerry took another sip of her beer and smirked. "We should try Universal next time. They've got some killer coasters."

"You got it."

Exactly the answer she wanted to hear. Kerry exhaled in satisfaction, casting her eyes around their surroundings with an agreeable smile.

They were inside the Mexican pavilion, where the air was cool and dry, and the lighting a perpetual twilight. It was calm and peaceful, and the scent of Mexican spices filled the air. The restaurant was only half full, and they had a table in the corner with a good view of the 'river' all to themselves.

It was nice. Kerry crossed her denim-covered ankles under the table glad beyond words she was out of her suit and into the jeans and light T-shirt she was currently wearing.

She'd noticed a tendency in herself lately to have less and less affection for the formal business clothing they wore at the office, and at functions like this. Though she never had minded dressing up, and she was self aware enough to acknowledge the vanity of liking how she looked in the neatly tailored fabric, she'd found herself looking forward to shedding them at the end of the day in favor of the softer cottons and denim they both wore at home.

Kerry let her hand rest on her thigh, smoothing her thumb over the faded blue surface with an absent smile.

Across the table from her, similarly attired, Dar was studying the menu with half closed blue eyes. "Hey," she interrupted her companion's ruminations again.

"Mm?" Dar looked past the writing at her. "Are you as glad as I am that's over?"

Kerry grinned wholeheartedly. "You bet, Dixiecup." She lifted her beer, waited for Dar to do the same, and then touched her glass to her partner's. "Here's to a sort of successful trade show."

Dar took a long swallow before she set her mug down. "I think it was successful." She tendered her opinion thoughtfully. "For the company. For us it was one huge pain in the ass."

"Except the dive," Kerry reminded her. "And that first day. That was fun."

"Uh huh."

"And tonight." Kerry reached across the table and fit her fingers around Dar's, giving them a gentle squeeze. "And you know, last night was pretty cool too."

A twinkle grew in Dar's eyes.

"So really, it was the sixteen whatever hours we had to spend in that hall that tanked," Kerry concluded. "And since it's tonight, and I know tonight's gonna be great, to hell with it." She glanced up as their waiter arrived, giving them both a smile. "Hi."

"Buenos noches, Senorita," the boy greeted her cheerfully. "What can I get for you lovely ladies this evening?"

"Two of these, two of these, and one of this." Dar pointed at her menu. "And two more of these in a few minutes." She indicated the beer.

"Got it, thank you." The waiter took the menu and disappeared.

Dar stretched in her chair, then slid down, extending her long legs under the table. She cradled her mug in her hands, sipping her drink slowly as she watched the restaurant fill at a very leisurely pace. Few families, she noted, more couples who seemed to be enjoying the low light and the pavilion's romantic atmosphere.

She tilted her head slightly and let Kerry come into her line of sight, admiring the nice gilded tinge the warm illumination brought to her skin. Her partner's attention was still on the river, so she had a few peaceful moments to simply look at her and enjoy the view.

Kerry must have sensed it, one hand coming up to fiddle with her hair and riffle it back over her ear on the side facing Dar. It was an endearing bit of self-consciousness, and Dar responded to it by dropping her hand beneath the table and finding Kerry's knee to give a light squeeze.

Her partner turned her head and rested her chin on her fist. "Will you ride on the boat with me after dinner?" she asked.

"If we sit in the back seat," Dar drawled. "Sure."

Kerry grinned. "You know, I was just thinking about the last time we were here."

"Mm...that food festival was a blast."

"I had so much fun," Kerry said. "I hadn't had that much fun with anyone for years, Dar. Years." She flexed the fingers of her free hand in front of her, the light catching the ring on her finger. They'd both suddenly found themselves wearing them, after keeping them on neck chains for so long, and neither of them had really discussed why yet.

One morning, for some reason, she'd decided to put her ring on. Later that day, in a meeting with Dar she'd looked up across the conference table and caught the flash of her partner's ring as she moved her papers. Weird. Synergistic in a way she didn't quite understand, but somehow also very comforting.

Maybe they'd find time later to talk about it.

"Years? Me either," Dar replied. "I remember sitting at the Pub looking across the table at you halfway through dinner, and realizing I never wanted to leave that day."

"Really?"

Dar nodded. "Remember when we were talking about IPv6?"

Kerry chuckled. "Yes."

"I think I fell in love with you right then." Dar smiled easily, laughing when she saw the blush creep up Kerry's neck. "No, that's not really true."

"No?"

"No." Dar rested her head against her fist. "I did that when I saw you the very first time, in that old office of yours," she admitted. "There I was, standing in that doorway, just staring at you like I'd just seen my first multi-partitioned disk array."

Kerry wrinkled her nose. "Thanks. I think."

Dar chuckled. "I'd seen a picture of you, but it didn't do you justice."

"You did?" Kerry asked, cocking her head.

"Sure." Dar stifled a yawn. "Mark thought it was necessary to add a full color picture to your personnel file when he gave it to me."

"Oh, he did, did he?" Kerry started laughing. "For what?"

Dar was silent for a minute. "I don't know," she said. "So I could recognize you when I saw you, I guess...or maybe because we both like good looking women?" Her tone was a touch sheepish. "I didn't think to ask at the time, but I kept your folder in my briefcase for a month so I could look at that damn picture."

Kerry blushed a little.

"Damned if I know why it took me so long to figure out I was in love with you." Dar sighed theatrically. "You'd have thought that was a big enough clue along with how tongue-tied I was when we first met."

Kerry indulged in the memory willingly. "I remember that moment," she murmured. "I remember it being such a lousy day...after Robert told me what was going on, and with all those people looking at me...depending on me to protect them." Her lips parted as a sigh trickled out. "And it was a lousy day for me anyway. I'd talked to my parents the night before and they'd put all kinds of pressure on me to get out of Miami."

"Grr."

"Mm." Kerry nodded wryly. "Then the whole office gang went to lunch that day and invited me to go along. I really wanted to, but I stayed there with my carrots instead."

"And met me."

"And met you," Kerry agreed. "No matter how nasty that was, boy...let me tell you, I knew something happened to me the minute I picked my head up and looked into those baby blues. You were the only thing I thought about for the rest of that day." She reached over and tangled her fingers with Dar's again. "My heart jumped every time I saw an email from you come into my inbox."

Dar smiled at her.

Kerry smiled back and they both dissolved into silent laughter. "We're a couple of mooney saps, you know that?"

"Yeah," Dar admitted. "But I don't give a damn."

"Me, either." Kerry straightened up as the waiter returned putting down the appetizers Dar had ordered. She handed over her now empty mug, and settled her napkin on her lap neatly as she surveyed the tasty plate of nachos and other small Mexican treats. "Mm. Looks good."

Dar selected a morsel and nibbled it. "Couple things I forgot to tell you before we left."

Kerry looked up from a piled high nacho, caught halfway into a bite. Her eyebrows did the talking for her, rising up sharply in question.

"Alastair called."

"Ah." Kerry swallowed and wiped her lips with her napkin. "Is he mad?"

Dar shook her head. "No." She toyed with the tortilla in her fingers. "Well, he was, but after I talked to him for a while he chilled out. But...um..."

Uh oh. Kerry could see the fidgets already starting. "What's up?"

Dar set the chip down and leaned back, resting her hands on the chair arms. "I told him about the ship bid," she said, pausing when the waiter returned with two frosty mugs for them. He set the glasses down and gave them both inquiring looks.

"Everything okay here, ladies?"

"Fine, thanks." Kerry almost sat on her hands to prevent herself from shooing him away. She waited for him to leave, and then scooted her chair closer to Dar. "And?"

"He wants me — wants us — to personally do the bid."

Kerry blinked. She looked around at the restaurant, then focused back on her partner's angular face. "Yeeeah...and? That's a problem? We were going to do that anyway."

"Right," Dar agreed. "It's not a problem, but he pretty much told me he expects me to deliver the contract, no matter what."

Kerry sat back and drew one knee up, circling it with her arms as she contemplated the statement. "Okay," she finally said. "And this is news? Dar, he always expects miracles from you." A crease formed across her brow. "You think it's going to be an issue?"

Dar took a sip of her beer. "Not really, no."

Her companion rubbed the bridge of her nose. "Okay, so what's the problem, sweetheart?" she asked in a soft voice. "If that's not the problem, what is?"

"I got recruited." Dar leaned closer and lowered her voice.

"Again? Jesus! I thought we told that guy to back off, and Michelle said..." Kerry straightened indignantly.

"Not by Telegenics."

"Oh."

"By the army."

Kerry's jaw dropped slightly. "The army?" she repeated. "Wait. What? As in...the U.S. Army? They want us to bid for something?"

With an expression that was a mix of consternation and embarrassment, Dar shook her head. "No. They want me." She poked her thumb at her own chest. "As in...enlisting."

"You?"

"Me."

"In the army?" Kerry goggled at her. "Like...boot camp and everything?"

"Uh huh."

Kerry covered her eyes immediately. "Oh, my god." She peeked through her fingers at her partner. "You have got to be kidding me." She watched Dar shake her head solemnly. "What did you tell them? When did this happen, Dar? Where was I? I was with you most of the afternoon. What did they do, follow you into the bathroom or something?"

Dar settled back again, at last allowing a wry chuckle to emerge. After she'd gotten over the shock of the whole damn thing, it had been sort of funny. "I told them no." She exhaled. "But he was pretty insistent. Made me take his card and said he'd be in touch. They've got some kind of project they're seeking high level engineers for."

"Jesus."

"You were talking to the guys," Dar went on. "Maybe I can talk him into an outsource. He talked like it was happening right now, though," she mused.

"Ah." Kerry picked up a chip and examined it, then munched it thoughtfully. She swallowed, washing down her mouthful with a sip of beer as she pondered. "Right now as in the same timing as the ship deal."

Dar nodded.

"So that's the problem." Kerry picked up another chip. "Was he pissed off when you said no?"

A shrug. "Damned if I cared about that...the hell if he thought I'd even consider it."

Kerry leaned over and offered Dar a nacho, smiling a little as her partner took it from her fingers with a delicate grace. "Of course not. Did he really expect you to drop everything...your job, your life...and just join the Army? That's insane, Dar."

"You got that right." Dar licked her lips. "What in the hell would I say to my *father*? He forgave me being a rebel, forgave me being gay, and forgave me becoming a yuppie. " She shuddered. "He'd never forgive me for *that*."

Kerry dissolved into snickers, covering her mouth hastily.

"Chase my butt down and spank me till I sang Dixie," Dar muttered, shaking her head. She leaned back as the waiter returned with a tray, setting down their main courses. "Never hear the end of it, for damn sure."

She watched Kerry drop her face into her hand, her shoulders shaking in silent laughter and after a moment, she relaxed and accepted the absurdity of it all. "What a freaking day."

What a day. Kerry let her laughter run down, and then she picked her mug up and extended it, clinking it against Dar's. "Save it for tomorrow. Whatever happens, we'll just make it work, you and I." She let a smile emerge, looking right into Dar's eyes as she said the last few words. "We can do anything."

"Tonight's for us," Dar agreed quietly.

"For us," Kerry repeated, clinking her glass a third time. "To us."

A strolling guitarist came up behind them, strumming a wordlessly romantic tune as the river took yet another set of lovers anonymously downstream.

KERRY LICKED THE last taste of chocolate off her lips as they strolled around the lake toward the park's entrance. The last firework had gone off overhead, and now the crowds were dispersing, the shops closing up and the park going quiet for the night.

She fit her hand into Dar's as they walked, enjoying the warm comfort as her partner's fingers closed around hers. "Too damn short a trip again."

"Mm." Dar had been humming under her breath. Now she turned her head toward Kerry. "Here, you mean?"

"Uh huh. I want a few more days to play at the water parks, and ride Space Mountain, and go to the Animal Kingdom. There's so much we didn't get to do," Kerry griped mournfully. "We spent too much time being stressed and aggravated by those jerks."

"Well." Dar tipped her head back, regarding the few, thick clouds drifting over the stars. "We've still got tomorrow. We've got the car, and no schedule to stick to," she replied. "I have to get the official bid proposal from Mr. Skunk, but other than that, I'm all yours."

Kerry grinned in pure reaction. "Hmm...that's okay I guess."

"You guess?" Dar laughed.

"I want more," Kerry said. "I want to spend a week with you here just playing."

"Ahhh." Dar released Kerry's hand and draped her arm over the smaller woman's shoulders instead. "That sounds pretty damn good to me, Kerrison. Tell you what. Let's put that on the schedule for a couple months from now."

Kerry pouted.

"Right after Thanksgiving. We'll come up here for two weeks, and do it right." Dar promised. "They'll have the Christmas lights up...it's gorgeous."

"Yeah?" Kerry was willing to be persuaded.

"And not as hot."

Despite the evening's slight breeze and her light clothing, Kerry was sweating like a pig, and she acknowledged that her wise, native Floridian partner might have a point. "Wweeelll..."

"We can make the most of the time we have tomorrow," Dar continued. "We'll leave right from the park as they close...make it home by midnight or so. Okay?"

There was a note in Dar's voice that caught Kerry's ear. "Sure." She curled her arm around Dar's waist. "I was sort of kidding, y'know. I do want to spend time with you here, but I know we've got work to do." Despite the night's warmth, the contact felt good. "I was just teasing."

Dar grunted softly, but didn't answer.

"Christmas time will be really pretty." Kerry fished a little. "Have you been here at that time before?"

A nod.

They rounded the edge of the World Showcase, and started through the passage toward the park entrance before Dar spoke up again. "I'm glad you like it here," she ventured. "I used to think I was being...ahm..." Her shoulders hunched a little in an embarrassed shrug. "Childish for liking it as much as I do."

Kerry leaned against her, depending on Dar's sense of direction to keep them both from heading off into a bush. She'd had three beers, and though she wasn't drunk, there was a layer of pleasant fuzziness between her and the ground. "Shoot." She gestured at the thinning crowd around them. "Half the people here don't have kids as an excuse to be here, Dar. Everyone loves this place."

"Mm. Yeah." Her companion sighed. "I guess you're right."

"Hang on." Kerry steered them both toward a still open wagon. "I need some of that." She pulled Dar to a halt outside the coffee booth and held up two fingers to the attendant. "You want some too, right?"

"Sure." Dar merely draped herself over Kerry, resting her chin on the top of her partner's head. "It's been a long day." Her eyes lifted to study the woman getting their coffee, noting the brief grin she gave the two of them while the cups were filling. "Bet it's a longer day for you, huh?"

"Aren't they all?" the attendant replied wryly. "I think the ones in summer last at least 48 hours." She sprinkled some powdered chocolate on the top of their drinks and set them down. "But, on the other hand, it's not so busy. So..."

"Yeah." Kerry handed over some cash. "It's got its trade offs. Mine included going on Test Track twice." She grinned impishly. "Worth the sweat."

"Yeah, but you're not wearing polyester." The woman grinned back. "But it could be worse—give me cart vending any day over being a character," she said. "My friend just got done being Goofy for the day and he was too tired to even drive home."

"All relative," Dar commented.

"Yeah," the woman agreed. "This job's pretty cool. I get to see people all day, not like my mom. She works in accounting over at the main building. All she sees is cubicle walls." She leaned on the counter. "My partner, on the other hand, is really into being one of the landscaping people. Snip snip."

Partner. Kerry had always liked that term, and remembered the first time Dar had referred to her that way with great fondness.

South Beach. Kerry gazed around her in mild bemusement, watching the crowds saunter past the small table where she and Dar were sitting. They drew looks in return, casually appraising, and she found herself more than a little self-conscious there in the midst of all the trendies and tourists.

Even the always collected Dar seemed a little wary, her pale blue eyes hidden behind silvered shades as she hitched one denim covered knee up and rested an elbow on it, her sleeveless polo exposing her muscular arms to the sun.

Kerry dusted a bit of pigeon down off her neatly pressed cotton short sleeved shirt and sat a little straighter. "You get down here much?" she inquired, still a little shy in their new relationship. "It's sort of fun."

"Eh." Dar fiddled with the spoon resting on her coffee plate. "Not really. It's okay, I guess. I used to hang out nearby, way back when." She gave the passing crowds a cursory glance.

"Used to?"

Dar's face scrunched up a bit. "In my wilder days," she explained. "When I first figured out what side of the street I was walking on."

Kerry rested her chin on her fist. "You mean when you figured out you were gay?"

The dark eyebrows twitched. "Ah, yeah."

"But not now?"

A sigh. "No. I'm not much into the whole gay scene," Dar said. "I keep a pretty low profile."

Was Dar as ambivalent about that as she sounded? Kerry wondered. She watched several more conventional couples go by, holding hands and laughing. It made her think about home, and Brian, and the times they'd gone out together with a group of their friends somewhere.

It was different, when you were gay, wasn't it? In places like South Beach, you could get away with that. But not other places. Kerry felt a little pang of irrational loss as she remembered how normal she'd felt in a restaurant or hanging out in the mall with Brian. If he'd put his arm around her, or they'd held hands, no one looked twice.

If she took Dar's hand, people would look twice, Kerry realized. Better they stay, as Dar had said, low profile. No sense in sticking out.

Ah well. She looked over and studied Dar's face instead, contenting herself with the knowledge that she'd found something very special here, regardless of how the rest of the world looked at it. So what if she never got to throw a bouquet?

"Hey! Dar!"

Kerry looked up to see a man and a woman approaching them. They were nicely dressed, and middle aged, and appeared pleased to see her companion.

"Hello, Marge, Charlie." Dar gestured toward the two empty chairs at their table. "Have a seat."

Kerry watched quietly as they came over and sat down, wondering briefly who they were.

"How are you, Dar? Haven't seen you in years. You haven't changed much," Charlie said, with an easy grin. "Has she, Marge?"

"Not at all," the woman agreed. "That should make you feel good, Charlie, since you taught her in high school."

Oh. Ugh. Teachers. Kerry folded her hands on the table and imagined them meeting some of hers back home.

Yikes. She could picture them all staring at Dar with those disapproving eyes as she introduced her...friend?

Hm. How did you go about introducing your significant other if you were gay? As your girlfriend? Kerry's brow creased. Your lover, and have to die from embarrassment no matter how true it was?

"I'm doing damn fine, for a change," Dar answered. "Kerry, this is Charlie, my high school math teacher, and his wife Marge. Guys, this is Kerry Stuart."

"Hi." Kerry gave them both a polite smile.

"Kerry's my partner," Dar went on without missing a beat. "She's from Michigan."

Partner? Caught by honest surprise, Kerry could only blink for a long moment, looking into the faces of these normal, ordinary middle-aged people and wondering what on earth they were thinking of her.

Of them.

"Michigan, eh?" Charlie chuckled. "Boy, are you a long way from

home. I've got a cousin in Detroit I've been trying to get to move here for twenty years."

"Where in Michigan, Kerry?" Marge asked. "Have you two been together long?"

And then again, Kerry let out the breath she'd been holding, sometimes you find acceptance in the places you least expect it. "No, not very long," she managed to get out. "And, um...Saugatuck, actually, but I..." Without really thinking, she found herself reaching out for, of all things, Dar's hand. "I think I'm a lot more at home here than I ever was there."

Dar's fingers closed over hers and gave them a squeeze, punctuating the statement quite nicely.

Partner. Kerry squeezed back, feeling her doubts dissolve into the late afternoon sunshine. Yeah.

"Ker?" Dar gave her a nudge. "Sleeping already?"

Kerry wound her arm around Dar's waist and bumped her back. "Nope. C'mon, partner." She picked up her coffee and saluted the attendant with it. "Thanks. Have a great night," she added as they turned to continue on their way. "I know I will."

KERRY SETTLED HER sunglasses on her nose against the morning brightness, and then rested her hands on the steering wheel of Dar's Lexus as she waited outside the convention center.

She was glad enough to let Dar go in and handle Quest. After her partner's abrupt about face, she felt a little embarrassed about meeting him again, so she was content to relax in the car and watch the early morning park goers.

They were heading to the Animal Kingdom park, soon as Dar picked up the bid paperwork. Kerry was very much looking forward to it, and she smiled, whistling a little under her breath as she waited.

A family emerged from the nearby restrooms and headed for their car, the parents laden down with backpacks almost overflowing with toys. A little boy and two little girls ran ahead, screaming with delight as they chased each other in circles.

Kerry tried to remember being that small. She could vaguely call up some old flashbacks of her and Angie and Mike playing, but they seemed faded and out of focus.

In the back of the house in Michigan, behind the stately porch and the garden that was meticulously kept by servants, there had been a stretch of green lawn. They had been allowed to play there in the afternoons, but she mostly remembered only the smell of that.

Rich and green. She remembered rolling across the lawn and savoring the scent of the earth, and the newly cropped green, and watching tiny snails scramble away from her curious fingers.

The nanny had chastised her, for getting dirt all over her clothing. Kerry hadn't even understood what she was talking about at the time.

"Well, hello."

Jerked out of her daydreaming, Kerry turned her head to find Michelle there, peering in the window. "Good morning." She rolled the window down and leaned her elbow on it. "On the way out?"

"Waiting for our ride to the airport," Michelle said. "I see you drove up."

"We did," Kerry agreed.

Michelle looked around, and then turned back to her. "I guess you need to get back to start planning your strategy, eh?"

Kerry cocked her head to one side. "For what?"

The red haired woman blinked, her eyebrows lifting. "Mr. Quest's bid? You did know you were part of it, correct?"

"Oh that." Kerry pushed her sunglasses up a little on her nose. "Nah, we're heading for Animal Kingdom. Maybe do some more water parks later, depends on the weather." She rested her head on her fist.

Michelle crossed her arms. "If this is not that big a deal for you, why did you decide to get involved?"

Kerry caught sight of Dar emerging from the center, a folder clasped under one arm. "Dar likes ships." She refused to rise to Michelle's dangling bait. "It's something we're not involved in, sounded interesting...why not?"

"I thought maybe you'd done it to get a head-to-head with us." Michelle gazed at her directly. "Got something to prove?"

Kerry was glad she had her sunglasses on. "Something to prove?" She injected a quizzical tone in her voice. "Michelle, over the last two years I've presided over a couple thousand contract bids that we've won. You must have a pretty inflated ego if you think you're making this a big deal."

"Then I guess you won't mind if we beat you on this one. Because I absolutely intend on it," Michelle said. "Maybe you weren't looking for a head-to-head challenge, but we certainly were."

Kerry tipped her glasses down, revealing her misty green eyes. "Give me a break."

"Sure you don't want to reconsider? Could be embarrassing for you."

The passenger door opened and Dar climbed in, tossing the folder in the back seat and giving Michelle a brief glance. "Let's go. There are goats to pet and tigers to take pictures of." She glanced past Kerry. "Morning."

"That would be no," Kerry answered Michelle's last question. "Excuse us. We've got places to go and characters to see." She rolled the window up as Michelle stepped back, then put the SUV in drive and released the parking brake. "Sheesh."

"Sheesh what?" Dar settled back in the passenger seat, content to let Kerry navigate through the vast grounds to their destination.

"Michelle was fishing." Kerry paused at a stop sign, waiting to turn. "I threw a tin can on her hook." She headed toward the signs pointing the way to the Animal Kingdom. "She seems to think we're in this game because of them."

"We are," Dar responded in a placid tone.

"I know. I wasn't going to give her the satisfaction of knowing that though." Kerry pulled into line at the parking entrance. "Hell with them."

"That's my view." Dar had her sunglasses firmly on her nose. She was dressed in a pair of cotton shorts and a tank top, and had her hair pulled back in a ponytail. "Glad we decided to stick around today."

"Me too." Kerry pulled through and followed the line of cars to a parking spot. She stopped the Lexus and they got out into the warm, muggy air. Kerry settled a ball cap on her head to shade it from the sun and waited for Dar to join her before she started the walk toward the front of the park which could barely be seen through the trees.

Their luggage was stored in the back of the SUV. Now Kerry was triply glad they'd decided to drive, since it gave them so many more options on how to spend their time. No running around, no airports...

"I hear they have a room full of bats," Dar remarked. "I'd like to see that."

Kerry tugged her hat more firmly onto her head. "Lead on." She showed her pass to the gate agent, and was clicked inside. "Into the wilds. Rowr!"

Chapter
Seven

DAR WHISTLED SOFTLY under her breath as she turned onto the causeway and headed toward the office. The early morning sun was pouring through the tinted windows, and she was very glad she'd already put on her sunglasses. "How's your back feeling?" she asked her companion.

"Ugh." Kerry had her eyes closed against the glare. "I wish I didn't have clothes on."

Her partner made a small, snickering noise. "I could go for that," she agreed solemnly. "Told you not to fall asleep before dinner yesterday."

"Yeah, yeah, yeah." Kerry waved a hand at her, wincing as the motion caused a pang from her sunburned shoulders. "It was four o'clock, Dar. Jesus, the sun should have been down by then." She pointed at her companion. "And you could have woken me up, you little rat fink."

"Chitter." Dar made a face, baring her teeth. "I was out doing your shopping, remember?"

"Ermf." Kerry rested her chin on her fist and watched the palm trees go by as Dar skillfully negotiated the morning causeway traffic. "Eh, I had fun anyway," she conceded. "I had a great time at the animal park."

"Me, too." Dar drummed her fingers on the steering wheel lightly. "Damn, I'm tired though," she admitted. "Late night last night."

"Early morning this morning," Kerry countered. "Two hours sleep isn't much to start the day on." She poked Dar in the ribs. "Aren't we getting too old for all nighters?"

Dar turned into their office parking lot, dodging a delivery truck and scooting the Lexus into a spot near the front of the building. "Depends on what we're doing all night." She gave Kerry a saucy grin. "You could have slept on the way home."

Kerry popped the door open and slid out, shrugging carefully into her jacket before she took hold of her briefcase by its handle and shut the door. She pushed her sunglasses higher on her nose as she circled the front of the car and joined Dar for the short walk to the building entrance.

Yeah, she could have slept, she agreed silently, falling in step next to the taller woman. But it had been more fun to force herself to come up with games to keep them both alert for the long, dark drive home in the small hours of the morning.

They'd meant to leave after dinner, but the lure of the parks had gotten the better of them and they'd ended up closing the place and stopping for ice cream on top of it. They had left after midnight, trading their night of fun for going to work mostly without any rest.

But it had been worth it, Kerry decided. So what if she'd need six cups of Cuban coffee to make it through lunch? She'd gotten the quality playtime with Dar she'd craved, enough to hold her for a little while, anyway. "Morning, John," she greeted the security guard at the door.

"Morning, ma'ams," the guard replied courteously. "Have a great day."

"Do our best," Dar muttered, taking her sunglasses off.

The building's air conditioning was welcome as they entered and headed for the elevators. It was early, and the lobby was still quiet as they headed up, alone in the car as they rode to the fourteenth floor. Kerry stifled a yawn as the doors opened and she stood back to let Dar out first.

They walked down the hall in companionable silence, Dar giving her a pat on the side as they reached Kerry's office. "Take it easy today," Dar said. "If you feel like you need a nap, lock the door and tell Mayte to forward your phones to me."

Kerry gave her boss an affectionate look. "Only if you promise to do the same," she answered. "You're the one who drove all night." She slipped inside the outer door to her office and winked at Dar before she disappeared.

"Mmph." Dar regarded the polished wood with a bemused grin, before she continued down the hallway to her own office in the corner. "Morning, Maria," she greeted her assistant, already at work behind her desk.

Maria looked up in mild surprise. "Buenos dias, Dar," she responded. "I did not expect you here today!"

Dar paused on her way to her inner door. "You didn't?" She frowned. "I did say I'd be back after the trade show, didn't I?"

"Si, si," Maria agreed readily. "But I have this notice here that your airplane tickets were canceled. I thought you and Kerrisita were staying for more time." She held up the slip of paper. "I know Kerrisita likes very much the Disney World."

"Oh." Dar relaxed. "Yeah, we got..." Her nostrils flared slightly. "I mean, we decided to drive up instead of flying. We drove back last night." She turned and pushed her door open. "Really late last night."

"Would you like some cafacito, Dar?" Maria called after her knowingly.

"A bucket of it." Dar dropped into her chair. "Maybe if I stick my head in and gargle, I'll last through the sales conference call at ten." She booted the machine under her desk and leaned back waiting for it to come up.

Contrary to her pleas for coffee , she really didn't feel that bad. Dar mused, as she removed a folder from her briefcase and laid it open on her desk. Inside was the bid proposal.

It was a relatively hefty document, and now she opened the first page, creasing it back to hold it open and reviewing the cover page.

Her PC came up and bleated for her attention. Dar pulled her keyboard over and signed in, rattling in her thirty two character password without hesitation. The machine obediently logged in, but Dar drummed her fingers on the desk, recalling the conversations she had at the trade show regarding security.

She punched a button on her phone. After two rings, it answered.

"Computer Center, M...oh, hi boss." Mark's voice came through the phone over the ever present rattling of keys. "What's up? When'd you get back?"

"Couple hours ago," Dar replied. "Tell me again why we don't have biometric security yet?" she asked, opening her mail program and scanning the dark lines as they began to appear.

"Uh..."

"It occurred to me while I was sitting here completely wasted typing in my password that if I got smashed and gave it to someone, I could blow the entire company," Dar said. "Fix it."

"Uh."

"G'bye." Dar hung up the phone and propped her head up on her fist. Most everyone knew she'd been at the trade show, but she had a mailbox full of notes anyway and she clicked on her flagged column to sort them by urgency.

Then she selected all the urgent flagged ones and deleted them. "If you're stupid enough to send an urgent email to someone who has an out of office notification on, you're too stupid for me to answer you." Dar announced to the screen. "Next?" She clicked on the first non-flagged note and opened it, then turned her attention back to the opening page in the bid form.

Scanning the first few lines, she opened her desk drawer and removed the fish food, opening it and pinching out some flakes, then sprinkling them into her fighting fish tank on the far side of the desk. "How are you guys, huh?" She spared the fish a glance as they gobbled their breakfast. "Wonder what it would be like swimming in a tank full of you?"

The red fish blew a bubble at her. Dar gave it an indulgent grin, and then went back to her papers. It wasn't the original fish, of course. She'd gone through two changes of them since that first visit to the pet store when she'd allowed herself to be coerced into giving them a home on her desk. But she'd gotten used to them and now she enjoyed having them there to give her something to look at between tasks.

She'd actually paused to look at a snake the last time they'd been in PetSmart, intrigued by its colors. However, before she could consider adding it to her desktop knick knacks, Kerry had swiftly dragged her outside.

Ah well. Dar glanced up at her screen and deleted the first message, going on to the second one before she continued reading the bid. Maybe she should start small, with a gecko. She pulled her keyboard over and hit reply, glancing at her screen as she typed a response to the mail while she continued to scan the bid contract.

The terms were pretty straightforward. Dar hit send, and then studied the next mail for a second, before simply deleting it. "Nitbrain." She glanced up as the door opened, her nose twitching at the scent of fresh Cuban coffee. "Ah."

Maria brought the small, silver tray over and set it down, then placed the tiny china cup before Dar. She also put down a saucer on the edge of the desk, and balanced a small pot on top of it. "I brought the extra, Dar. They did not have the buckets."

"Thanks." Dar lifted the cup and sipped it. She eyed the tray, which also had a plate full of delicate, flaky pastries on it. "Those for me too?"

"Si, of course." Maria's eyes twinkled. "Did you have a good time, Dar? I saw Kerrisita downstairs and I think that you did."

Now what, Dar wondered, did she mean by that? She rocked back in her chair and sipped her coffee to give herself a moment to consider, studying Maria's face as she did so. Her assistant's expression was open and warm, however. "Sure," Dar answered. "We had a decent show, and Kerry and I got to spend some time out in the parks. How bad could it have been?"

Maria slid the plate of pastries over. "Everyone here was speaking of the interviews about you."

Dar indicated the chair across from her desk. "Were they? I know I kicked some booty that first day," she admitted, with a grin. "But I think it all worked out...did we look okay on TV?"

Her assistant grinned, and removed an envelope from under one arm, extending it toward Dar. "This was from the television program that was on from there. I watched it with my family. We were very proud of you and Kerrisita, Dar. You were wonderful."

Dar set her cup down and stood, reaching over and retrieving the envelope. She opened it and removed an 8 by 10 photo, setting it down on her desk to examine it. "Huh."

It was a shot of their booth, Kerry sitting at the console giving her presentation and caught in the act of looking right at the camera with an appealingly sweet intensity. Dar had been perched behind her, and in the shot, she was also looking right at the lens, her arms folded and her attitude one of intimidating protection. "Don't I look scary," she mused.

"No, Dar, you look very pretty!" Maria objected.

"I was trying to be scary." Dar glanced up from the photo. "There were a couple of people there who weren't friends." She was a little surprised that Maria hadn't heard. "The company who's been moving in on us in the Southeast...Telegenics?"

"Ah." Maria frowned. "I have heard their name, yes."

"It's run by Michelle Graver, and...um..." Dar exhaled, "Shari."

Maria blinked in honest surprise. "No, Dar, not that woman!" she gasped. "I cannot believe it. Is it true? After this long, to have her come back and bother you?" She clasped her hands together. "Never have I disliked a person so as I did that woman."

Maria became her assistant when Dar was promoted to regional manager and chose the woman as her assistant. When Shari came back into Dar's life the first time, Maria had taken the brunt of Shari's caustic comments when she'd discovered who was integrating their account. "Yeah, well." Dar shrugged. "Kerry and I took care of them. But it got ugly a few times."

"Tch."

"Yeah." Dar studied the picture. "She got lucky. I thought Kerry was going to beat her over the head with a chair." She looked up at Maria. "In a way, it almost felt good to see her."

Maria gazed at her. "Because you are happy now," she ventured. "I think that you are."

"Mhmm." Dar nodded. "I am. Damned if it didn't burn her." A rakish grin appeared. "We're competing with them on this." She indicated the folder she was reading. "Something that came up during the show."

"A good thing?"

Dar shrugged. "Could be. Contract's probably worth twenty or thirty million, not a major one for us, but it's a foot in the door of someplace we're not in right now." She flipped through the pages. "Do me a favor? Throw this on the photocopier and send a set up to legal, and one over to Jose's office."

"Si." Maria got up and accepted the folder. "It is good to have you back here, Dar. People were saying this week that things were too...how you say it...too much alike?" she ventured. "That you made things upside down, but that it was a good thing." She gave Dar a smile, and left the office, closing the door behind her.

Dar poured herself another small cup of coffee and took a sip from it. One finger reached out and tapped the photo a few times, and she found herself smiling at the image it presented. "Well." she finally sighed. "I don't know how good a thing it was, but I guess we'll be finding out."

However, remembering how it felt to rise to the challenge was stirring an interest in her she hadn't felt since she'd finished her network project. Doing the second generation of the technology was all right, but Dar hadn't found the same interest in it she had with the original.

Now this, on the other hand, this was brand new.

Dar captured a pastry and popped it into her mouth, chewing it with piratical gusto and blowing a few crumbs onto the surface of her desk.

KERRY FINISHED SCRIBBLING her name for the nth time, running her eyes over the purchase order before she lifted it and tossed it into her outbox. She had her head resting on one hand, and now she straightened up a little, hissing slightly as her shirt pulled over her sunburned back. "Son of a biscuit."

Her phone rang. She checked the display, and then pressed the button readily. "Hey, Col."

"Hey girl," Colleen replied. "You up for lunch?"

Lunch? Kerry glanced at her watch. "Sheesh...didn't realize it was that late. Sure."   She pushed the rest of the paper pile back into her inbox and eased herself to her feet. "Let's go downstairs. I don't really want to put my jacket on to go to the dining room."

"Works for me," Colleen agreed. "Meet you by the elevators?"

"You got it." Kerry hung up and stretched cautiously, then circled her desk and headed for the door. She passed Mayte busy at work, and drummed her fingers on her assistant's desk. "Going for lunch, MT. Hold the fort down."

"That I will for sure," Mayte answered. "Can I take what you finished?"

"Eh." Kerry leaned on her knuckles. "There isn't that much. I signed some of the outstanding PO's, and reviewed that integration report. You're welcome to whatever's there. I'm expecting a call from the LA office about some new circuits, and keep an ear out for Dar. She's in a conference call with the overseas groups."

"Will she need to take hold of you, Ms. Kerry?" Mayte asked.

Kerry's lips twitched slightly at the phrasing. "You never know," she said. "If she needs me, she'll probably SMS me, but she might need some of the statistics I've been working on for the past two weeks. They're on my desk, in the infrastructure folder. Okay?"

Mayte nodded and smiled, giving Kerry a little wave of her fingers as she left the office.

"HEY, COL." KERRY spotted her friend as she exited the elevator, joining her as they walked across the lobby to the cafeteria. "How's it going?"

"Busy." Colleen glanced at her. "You got some sunburn, eh?"

"Mm. Fell asleep in the sun yesterday like a tourist," Kerry admitted. "We were decompressing after the trade show.

Colleen laughed. "Yeah, we saw the film from that, bucko...boy, did you two ever make the news. What got into Dar? She's been so laid back lately, it was a real shocker to see her come out swinging like that."

"Mm." Kerry took a tray and handed one to her companion. She smiled at the attendant, and reviewed her options. "Chef salad, please, and a large iced tea." That taken care of, she turned to Colleen while they waited for their orders. "I think Dar just took the opportunity to get the brand out there. You know?" She half shrugged. "It's what the trade show's for, Col."

"Oh, I know." Colleen took her plate and nudged Kerry forward. "And a great job of it she did. Duks was all over lauding her up and down the hallways, he was."

They walked to a table in the raised level of the café which was mostly empty. By some unwritten convention that level was generally reserved for those members of the upper floors who didn't like to eat in the upstairs dining room. Kerry set her tray down and eased into a chair, resting her elbows on the table top with a grimace.

"You did get burned, huh?" Colleen chuckled.

"Oh, yeah." Kerry took a sip of her iced tea, and reviewed her chef salad. It wasn't something she usually fancied, but the hot weather made the thought of hot food unpleasant, and the salad was a nice mix of greens and protein calculated to keep her alert through the afternoon. "Between that, and not getting any sleep last night, I'm in great shape today."

"Y'know, Kerry, there is such a thing as too much information." Her friend poked a fork at her.

"Hm?"

Colleen snickered at her. "You have no idea what I'm talking about, do you?"

Kerry speared an egg slice and popped it into her mouth. "No." She shook her head. "Anyway, aside from all that, it was a good trip. We may have gotten some leads on some new business."

"Hey, Ker? Can I ask you a question?" The redhead lowered her voice. "About something I heard?"

Yeesh. "Um...sure," Kerry replied. "If I can answer it, I will."

Colleen edged a bit closer. "Someone said one of those new rival companies causing us grief is run by some old flame of Dar's. Is that true?"

Kerry felt a set of conflicting emotions surge through her. On one hand, she'd known Colleen for a long time—longer than she'd known Dar, for that matter. The redhead had been her neighbor in Kendall, and someone she'd spent a lot of time with, time she remembered fondly.

However, she hated gossip. Everyone knew she hated gossip. She didn't want to indulge in gossip with Colleen, but she also didn't want her friend to think she was evading the question.

She put her fork down and leaned on her forearms, pinning Colleen with a direct stare.

"Uh oh." Colleen made a face. "I haven't seen that puss in a while."

Kerry paused, one eyebrow lifting as she allowed herself to be sidetracked. "What puss?"

"That 'I'm gonna tell you what you're gonna die of' puss," her friend replied with a frank grin. "Sorry, Ker. Did I hit a sore spot?"

"Do I have a face like that?" Kerry rested her chin on her hand. "I know Dar does."

"You do. It's cuter, but it's still 'back off,'" Colleen admitted.

Kerry went back to decimating her salad. "Well, yeah. I guess...you know how much I hate BS talk. Especially about her."

"I know. Everyone knows."

"It's true," Kerry said. "Telegenics is run by Michelle Graver, who I told you about." She chewed a moment, and then swallowed. "And her partner is someone called Shari Englewood, who once upon a time Dar was involved with."

"Mm," Colleen grunted. "That kind of thing is always rough. Did you have a hard time with it?"

"Me?" Kerry sounded surprised. "Other than wanting to strangle both of them for harassing Dar? No. Why?" She picked up a carrot and munched it.

Colleen fiddled with her fork. "Well, I mean..." She glanced around, and then shrugged one shoulder. "Doesn't the fact that there was someone before you make a difference to you, Ker? I know it did for me. The last guy I sent packing. We bumped into his former girlfriend at Quiznos, and after that...out the door, boyo!"

Kerry frowned, her eyes shifting to one side as she considered the thought.

Did it matter to her? "Um...no, actually, it doesn't make a difference to me at all, especially since I know Dar's never had a steady, happy, long term relationship before ours," she replied honestly. "Why should the failures bother me any, except for feeling bad for Dar, I mean?"

Her friend leaned back and wiped her lips with her napkin, watching Kerry in silence as she finished her salad. There was little resemblance between the woman she shared a table with now, and the neighbor she'd first met right after Kerry moved to Florida.

Kerry had always been fun to hang with. She was smart, and had a gently sly sense of humor. Generally, she seemed to be enjoying life, despite the problems Colleen knew she was having with her family.

But meeting Dar had changed her profoundly in Colleen's eyes. She remembered very clearly the night Kerry had come home from Disney the first time, so obviously lost in the throes of her first real love she'd worried that her friend would drown from it.

No one, Kerry had once told her, had ever loved her for her. Never. Not until she'd met Dar, and Colleen had been really sort of scared for her at the beginning. She'd been in so deep. "You two are really solid. That's cool," she commented mildly. "Listen, sorry if I stepped into it,

Ker. You know I just care about you."

Kerry's shoulders relaxed under their silk covering. "Yeah, I know," she said. "Boy, we were both ticked off at them big time though. You know what we did?" Her expression turned impish.

"What?"

"You've been to EPCOT, right?" It was Kerry's turn to lower her voice.

"Sure."

"Living Seas? The big aquarium?"

"With the sea cows, sure," Colleen agreed amiably.

"Dar and I went diving in it."

The redhead leaned forward. "On purpose?"

Kerry chuckled, draining her iced tea glass. "Yes, on purpose...it's a program they have. Anyway, we went diving and one of the tank windows is in the restaurant."

"Yeap, I've been there. Nice view." Colleen nodded.

"Yeah well...Shari and Michelle were having dinner, and we scared the living poop out of them and made them spill all over themselves," Kerry told her. "It was hilarious. We were laughing so hard we almost drowned."

Colleen covered her eyes. "Ye gods and little fishes, Kerry. You could have been kicked out of the park for that!"

Her lunch companion grinned. "It was worth it. They were being such jackasses. You know their company actually tried to recruit us?"

"You?"

"Both of us! They had no idea who we were!" Kerry replied. "And then Michelle tried to buy us off. It was such a mess."

"Jesus, Kerry." Colleen's eyes widened. "You think they targeted us deliberately? Because of Dar? Is that why they went after our accounts?"

Kerry made a vague shushing motion with her hand, as several more people joined them. "I don't know...no, I don't think it was that. I think it's how big we are. We're a good target. If anything..." she hesitated. "If anything, I think they're scared of Dar."

"Huh." Her friend exhaled, taking a sip of her drink. "Well, after that show this week, they fair well should be! Besides that, my friend, did you see yourself on television yet? I taped it."

"Eurf." Kerry grimaced.

"C'mon upstairs," Colleen invited her, with a grin. "You didn't see what Dar was doing behind you either, I'm thinking."

"Uh oh." Kerry got up, carrying her tray to the back table. "Tell me she was making faces."

"Weeeeell..."

Kerry groaned again, and followed her out.

"ALL RIGHT, JAVIER." Dar was leaning back in her chair, her feet propped up on her desk. "How much is it gonna cost me?"

"Now, Dar..." The South American sales director laughed. "You know that I have never, never asked for more toys for us down here, have I?"

Dar had her eyes closed as the very late afternoon light tinted her windows. "No."

"Bueno. Now, if we had this capacity available here, in Buenos Aries, I could do very good things with it. I have sold very well the systems you have given me, no?"

"Yes."

"So?"

Dar wiggled her toes, thinking in silence.

"Is it my fault that so many people saw your cable show?" Javier asked, after a pause. "I have had six enquires just today. People are very nervous about security."

"So they want to hire hackers?" Dar asked bemusedly. "What exactly does that say about Brazil, Javier?"

"Tccha."

"I'll review it, see what we have available to put in there," Dar conceded. "We might have an installation I can divert over there, depends on the projections due next week."

The inner door to her office opened, revealing a very tired, very bedraggled looking Kerry. Dar waggled her fingers at her, giving her a wry look when Kerry trudged across the carpet to her desk and sat down on it, draping an arm over Dar's legs.

"Excellent! That is very good news, Dar. I will let my people know." Javier sounded smugly pleased. "So tell me, is every hacker in the world now trying to get in our gates? That was quite a braggadocio you made. I hope it does not come back to haunt you."

Dar leaned over and clicked her mouse, pulling up a monitoring screen and reviewing the results. She studied it briefly. "Eh," she eventually grunted. "Hits are up, but it's nothing overly scary." She turned away from the screen, preferring to gaze at Kerry instead. "We only have the one big website that exposes us, and that's strictly outside the network."

"Really?" Javier murmured.

"Sure. Our entire class A's masked, so the first problem hackers have is finding us. We don't have a lot of things hanging out there. I've got four redundant pipes servicing the website with logic that detects DOS on any link and runs an automatic squelch on the inbound packets," Dar said. "So yeah, they could probably pick at some of the smaller accounts we have, but only the ones where we don't provide the infrastructure. The network itself's pretty locked down."

There was a respectful silence. Then one of the international sales managers cleared her throat. "Lovely. Can we have a side of chips with that, then, Dar?"

Dar chuckled. "I'm glad the show's having some positive spin. I'll try to make sure we don't get backlash if some little nerd creep gets lucky," she conceded. "Anything's possible, but Mark's been working on some new routines that incorporate some of the intelligent logic I'm using for the network upgrade, so we'll see."

Another bit of silence. "Have a pint of Guinness with that one," the same manager piped up. "Never mind the chips."

There was a round of laughter on the phone. Kerry moved her arm and started massaging her partner's bare feet, too tired to really concentrate on what was going on. Of course, the managers on the phone didn't understand one word in ten Dar was saying on the technology side either, but that wasn't really unusual.

"Listen, I'm outta here, folks," Dar said. "I got in from the show very late last night." She reached over and laid a hand on Kerry's thigh, stroking it lightly. "I've got the action items you all asked for—I'll let you know what my decisions are tomorrow."

She let the conference line go after a round of goodbyes and focused her attention on the blond woman sitting on her desk. "You look toasted."

"Get the jam and butter, Sinbad," Kerry admitted. "I want you, a hot cup of tea, a shower, and our waterbed. Can you make that happen, boss?"

Dar removed her legs from the desktop and sat up, reaching down for her shoes. "You bet your crumbs I can, my little Yankee toast," she said. "How about we order in something light from the beach club and go crash?"

Kerry leaned in and collapsed over Dar, draping her arms over her partner's shoulders. "Lead me."

Dar managed to get to her feet, and turned Kerry's sprawl into a full body hug, careful not to squeeze her sunburned shoulders. "C'mon." She picked up her briefcase and nudged Kerry toward the door. "I'm so fried I was about to agree to whatever they asked me on that damn call."

"They'd probably never have realized it." Kerry hooked her fingers inside the waistband of Dar's skirt as she followed her from the office. It was quiet outside. Maria had left a short time before, and the normal sounds of evening were starting to settle over the building. "Euu...they're shampooing the carpet tonight."

Dar's nose wrinkled as the scent of wet, dirty, mildewy carpet wafted down the hallway. "Definitely time to leave." She punched the button for the elevator. "How'd your afternoon meeting go?"

"Ick." Kerry had her eyes closed, and she was leaning against Dar as they waited for the elevator. "I have some wacky problem going on in Vancouver we can't isolate. Two T1's that are supposed to be redundant, but one of them keeps tanking and the other one just sits there dumb and happy like a frog and refuses to pass traffic unless we bounce it."

"Uh huh," Dar mused, guiding her engaging limpet through the doors, and then punching the bottom floor button. "HSRP set right?'

"Duh."

Dar watched the floors count down. "Metrics checked?'

"Baaap. Try again."

"I'm trying to be helpful here, Kerrison."

"I know, but we've checked all that." Kerry yawned. "Three times. I even had the vendor in to verify the configs."

The elevator reached its destination and opened to release them. "Why are you involved in that anyway?" Dar asked suddenly, as they crossed the lobby. "Since when does a VP Ops troubleshoot the WAN links?"

"Since it's been going on for four months and no one's fixed it yet," Kerry replied. "And because they figured if they brought it to me, I'd scratch my head over it for a while then take it to my boss, the CIO who also should not be troubleshooting WAN links, and that was the best chance they had to resolve the problem."

"Hmph."

"It's a compliment, hon," Kerry assured her.

"How ridiculous is it that we need to have the top two technology officers in the company working on a piddling T1 problem?" Dar groused. "C'mon, Kerry. What the hell do we pay people for?"

"I know, it's ridiculous," Kerry agreed. "You know, let me call the vendor again."

They walked out of the building in silence, crossing into the muggy heat of summer.

Kerry was glad to see the Lexus' looming bulk with its promise of comfortable, though overheated leather seats. She put her briefcase in the back and climbed into the passenger side, easing back gingerly as she closed the door. "Ow."

Dar glanced at her. "Aloe time for you," she remarked.

"Yeah." Kerry turned on her side and rested her head against the seat. Her eyes went to the console between them, however, as Dar's cell phone rang. "Want me to get that?"

"Sure." Dar had her hands full starting the car and getting the air conditioner running before they both melted.

"Hello?" Kerry opened the phone and listened. "Oh, yes. Hello, Mr. Quest." She gave Dar a look and received one in response. "No, she's here. Hang on."

Dar took the phone and hit the speaker, then set it down on the console as she put the Lexus in reverse. "Yes?"

"Hello, is that Dar Roberts?"

"Yes," Dar repeated, slightly louder. "You got me in transit, Peter. What can I do for you?" she asked. "I spent some time with your requirements today, but I'm not done reviewing them."

"Yeah, well, the plan's changed," Quest said. "We have to pull out of New Zealand early, so we're going to do the finishing in the States."

"Ah." Dar felt a pang of disappointment. She'd been looking forward to visiting that part of the world. "And?"

"Port of Miami made me an offer. I'm taking four unused passenger piers for two months down there. I figured that would work for you, at least, if not the other two companies bidding."

"Peh." Kerry snorted softly. "We could practically swim there from our house."

"Matter of fact, that's right around the corner from our offices," Dar replied. "Won't those other guys think you're giving us an advantage?"

Quest laughed. "I'm sure they will. But you can handle the heat, or so I've heard." He cleared his throat. "We also moved the timetable up. The two ships'll be at the port in two weeks. Be ready, or don't bother."

He hung up, leaving a distinct echo in the car.

For a few minutes, they drove on in silence. Dar flipped the phone closed and curled her fingers around it, tapping the leather cover with her thumb while Kerry chewed the inside of her lip thoughtfully. Then they both started talking at the same time.

"There's something..."

"Something's not ri..."

"Ahem." Dar coughed slightly as they stopped and fell silent again.

"Hm," Kerry agreed, pursing her lips. "Did you do any background research on these guys?" she asked. "Want me to run our standard client query?"

Dar felt slightly embarrassed. "Yeah." She slowed down to make the turn into the ferry terminal. "I didn't get around to that. I um..." She paused, then scowled as she pulled into a lane. "Shit."

Kerry circled Dar's wrist with her fingers and rubbed the back of her hand.

"Guess my brain was fried, after all," Dar said. "I didn't even think of doing that, Ker."

"Neither did I, until right now. Don't sweat it," Kerry told her. "I'll kick it off from the house while we're waiting for dinner." She saw the muscles in Dar's jaw line relax a little. "Bummer about the trip though."

"Mm." Dar gazed through the windshield. "But it does give us an advantage." Her head turned, and she looked at Kerry. "And I'm going to take every inch of it."

Kerry patted her hand, and smiled. "Our turf," she agreed.

"Our turf," Dar repeated softly, her eyes narrowing. "Yeah."

THERE WAS SUCH a thing, Kerry discovered, as being too tired to even want to eat. She was curled up on the leather couch in the living room, Chino in a ball at her feet. She faded in and out as Dar rambled around the condo.

She wanted to just let go and zonk out. She could already feel that sense of disassociation she often got just before she fell asleep. The only thing that was keeping her from giving into it was the fact that she was listening to Dar talk to herself as they waited for their soup and half sandwiches to be delivered. "Dar," she finally uttered a protest. "Let it go."

The light scuff of bare feet against the marble answered her, coming closer along with the sense of Dar's presence until a warm knee bumped up against her elbow. Instead of opening her eyes, Kerry reached out and wrapped her arm around Dar's leg, tucking her hand back under her arm and issuing a small, contented grunt.

Dar didn't speak. Instead, she claimed the edge of the couch and sat down next to Kerry, pressing against her body and draping an arm over her.

Ah. Delightful. Kerry wrapped her body around her partner's and sighed. One eye cracked open as Dar started rubbing her back with the tips of her fingers. "See? Now isn't this much better than you bitching at yourself?" She nibbled at Dar's thigh.

Dar made a noncommittal sound. "I wasn't really bitching," she protested. "I was just going over the balls I let drop in the last few weeks."

Kerry started biting the inside of her partner's leg, drawing a squawk of protest from her. "Bitch tomorrow," she said. "It's chill time." Her bites became kisses as Dar leaned over and enfolded her in a hug. She moved into a more comfortable position, emitting a happy gurgle as Dar laid her head down on her shoulder.

"If I fall asleep like this, I'm toast," Dar said, with a sigh. "I'm sorry, Ker. I get overtired and my brain goes into spin cycle."

"Yeah, I know."

"Maybe we should have gone for some Frosted Flakes for dinner."

"Maybe," Kerry admitted. "But we didn't, and sure as Sunday drivers, the second we nod off they'll be knocking at the door."

"Mmph"

Kerry peered idly at the large screen television across the room. "Oh look," she said, "an iguana." Her brow creased. "What's it doing with its tongue?"

Dar shifted her chin and licked Kerry's ear, making her sneeze in surprise. "Nothing I couldn't do if I really worked at it."

"Oo."

With another gentle sigh, Dar put her head back down and half closed her eyes, seemingly forgetting her previous self-admonishment. Kerry reached up and fit her hand inside her partner's, pulling it close to her heart, taking the moment of quiet contemplation where she found it.

A brisk knock came at the door. Dar snorted in soft laughter, before she hauled herself to her feet and headed to answer it. Kerry remained where she was, wiggling her toes a little against Chino's fur as she watched Dar admit the beach club's waiter with his tray, giving him a brief grin as he passed her to set it down on the dining room table.

"Gruff." Chino's head popped up as she belatedly sensed an intruder.

"Shh," Kerry admonished her. "It's just Carlos. Be nice, or you won't get a cookie."

The Labrador curled up and put her muzzle down on Kerry's ankle, keeping a brown eagle eye on Carlos as he neatly arranged their dinner on the table.

Dar signed the check and hustled the waiter out, turning and leaning against the door as she regarded Kerry's still curled up form. "Want me to bring it over?"

"Hm." Kerry drummed her fingers on the leather, then she pushed herself upright with a sigh. "If it were anything but soup, I'd say yes." She pulled the first chair on the right side of the table out and sat, waiting for Dar to join her before she started sorting out the food. "So, what do you think that whole change of schedule thing means, Dar? It sure seemed abrupt to me."

Dar looked up from buttering a roll. "Can we talk about fishing?"

Kerry blinked in mild surprise, hesitating in the act of pouring herself a glass of juice. "Um...okay."

Dar shrugged a little. "You told me to drop it, remember?"

That's right, she had. Kerry finished pouring her drink and fell silent, opening up her container of soup and poking at its contents with her spoon. Her eyes burned and she lifted a hand to rub them, ending up resting her head on her hand as she made a half–hearted attempt at eating.

For a few minutes, it was so quiet the sound of the air conditioning cycling off and on was almost startling. Kerry could almost feel it as a physical thing between them and she wondered when it would start to become uncomfortable.

Her eyes burned again, and she rubbed them, setting down her spoon and finding little to interest her in the relatively inoffensive soup as her stomach rebelled at consuming it. "Well, crap." She broke the silence with a small sigh. "This is going nowhere."

The sudden feel of Dar's fingers running through her hair was indescribable. Kerry looked up from her plate to find bloodshot blue eyes looking back at her with gentle weariness.

"To hell with the food," Dar said, getting up and shoving the plate back. She held a hand out to Kerry invitingly. "Let's go to bed."

Kerry abandoned her noodle soup and stood up, taking Dar's hand and following her to the bedroom without any further thought. The room's soothing blue tones made her feel better almost at once, and she stood facing Dar as they set about undressing each other with the beginnings of a smile on her face.

Dar saw it. She unbuckled Kerry's belt with one hand, and laid the palm of the other one on Kerry's cheek, rubbing her cheekbone with the edge of her thumb. Kerry's eyelashes flickered, then she tilted her head up and returned Dar's gaze with one of her own.

It was amazing, that look. Dar wondered if Kerry really knew how much of her feelings showed in it. "Sorry I'm being a cranky curmudgeon," she apologized. "I'm expecting that time of the month tomorrow."

The gentle upturn of Kerry's lips became a genuine smile. "Thought you said you never had PMS."

"You said I never have PMS," Dar corrected. "I said I do, but no one ever notices the difference."

Kerry finished unbuttoning Dar's jeans, sliding them over her hips and letting them fall to the floor. She took a step forward out of the shirt Dar had finished unfastening and put her arms around Dar's waist. "You can be cranky, honey," she muttered. "If you don't mind me being completely wasted and way oversensitive to it."

Dar tossed Kerry's shorts into the corner and turned, easing them both down into the waterbed. She rolled over with Kerry still in her arms so they ended up in the middle, the warm surface enclosing them comfortably as she tugged the blanket up over them.

"Mm." Kerry had her eyes closed. "This feels great."

"Yeah, it does. Damn, I'm glad tomorrow's Saturday."

"Me, too."

They lay there together for a while, this time comfortable in the quiet surrounding them. Kerry began to surrender to the lethargy rolling over her, leaving her with barely enough energy to rhythmically trace the centerline of Dar's belly in time with the slow breathing under her touch.

A soft clank caused her to crack one eye open again. "Dar?"

"Mmhmn?"

"Did you hear that?"

"All I can hear is sheep."

Kerry's other eye opened. "Sheep?"

"Counting themselves to save me the trouble."

Another soft clank sounded clearly from the living room, accompanied by a clatter. "Dar."

Her partner selected the edge of the covers and neatly pulled them over Kerry's ears, patting the tops of them solicitously. "Better?"

Kerry grasped the covers and pulled them down. "No, because it doesn't keep me from wondering what the heck is going on in our living room."

Dar pulled the covers back up. "Kerrison, use logic, wouldja?"

Kerry frowned.

"We left food on the table, and a Labrador in the living room. What do you think is happening?" Dar said. "It's a puppy buffet."

"Ew." Kerry's nose wrinkled. "Dar, she'll get sick." With a groan, she rolled away from the center of the bed and started to climb out, only to be captured and pulled back into a tangle of arms and legs. "Dar!"

"Shh." Dar wrapped her up in the covers and snuggled back down. "Relax. She'll be fine. It's just soup."

Kerry heard distinct sounds of slurping. "She's going to make a mess."

"She's got a tongue, she'll clean it up."

A laugh started to work its way through Kerry's chest. "Honey...c'mon." She tried to untangle herself. "That's fine for my soup, but yours had clams in it. She'll be chewing them for days."

Dar refused to let go. "Chino! What are you doing, you bad girl!" She turned her head and lifted her voice, projecting it into the next room. "Stop that!"

She was rewarded by the clatter of toenails, and shortly thereafter a Labrador jaw was resting on the edge of the waterbed, innocent brown eyes gazing at her adoringly. "Chino. What were you doing?"

Their dog's ears cocked, and she tilted her head to one side in question.

"Very nice." Kerry sprawled over Dar's body and removed a noodle from their pet's black nose. "But you are so busted."

"Gruff." Chino licked her fingers happily, sneezing after a moment and ejecting a piece of clam onto the blankets under Dar's nose.

Dar observed the particle briefly, and then sighed. "Guess we better lock up the chow, huh?"

Kerry started to climb over her. "Stay, I'll go."

"Nu uh." Dar rolled out of bed, taking Kerry with her as she rolled a little too far and lost her balance, ending with them both on the floor. "Gah!"

"Oh, Jesus." Helplessly giggling, Kerry could only lay there, stark naked, as Chino licked her face with enthusiasm. "Chino, stop." She saw Dar grab hold of the waterbed frame and pull herself upright. "Bah...bah, honey, stop!"

Dar sat down on the carpet and took hold of the dog's tail, hauling her backwards. "Chino! Stop that!"

"Groowf!" The Labrador turned her attention to her taller owner.

"Your mommy only likes my tongue licking her," Dar instructed the dog solemnly, shaking one long finger at her. "So you keep that big pink thing inside the teeth, hear me? Or else."

Kerry snorted and rolled over, hiding her face in the curve of her arm.

Dar raked her fingers through her hair, surveying the jumble of bare limbs spread out before her. "This is turning into the kind of story other people tell about you when you're drunk," she mourned. "And I haven't even had a sip of anything."

"Hehehehe."

"Laugh it up, Yankee."

Kerry pushed herself up from the floor and got to her feet, brushing bits of carpet lint off her bare skin. "C'mon." She offered Dar a hand up. "At this rate, it'll take both of us an hour to get the soup in the refrigerator and then maybe...maybe...we can get some sleep."

"Or at least go to bed." Dar released the dog and grabbed Kerry's hand. "Lead on, McGruff."

"Maybe I should get you a beer."

"How about a milkshake?"

"Settle for some chocolate syrup?"

"Hmm."

KERRY LEANED ON the kitchen counter, watching the palm tree fronds outside wilt in the stifling heat as she waited for the water in a nearby pot to boil. The air conditioning puffed gently against her still slightly sore shoulder blades through a layer of soft cotton, and she moved a little to one side to avoid the pressure. She had little ambition otherwise to do much else.

It was nearly noon. They'd just woken up a half hour earlier and, having gotten through coffee and a handful of Advil for Dar's obligingly timely cramps, they had settled in to enjoy a peaceful, lazy Saturday. It felt good to be hanging out here in their own space without work or trade shows to intrude on it.

Kerry turned and surveyed the kitchen, taking in the touches she'd added over time to soften its spartan functionality. A set of imported cooking pots hanging over the stove here, a well oiled, interlaced wood chopping block there...she took pride in her ability to produce edible meals for them, and enjoyed having plenty of tools to do it with.

Also, the stainless steel refrigerator doors were now dotted with colorful magnets, brought back by both of them from various airports they'd either passed through or been stuck in, and the tiled backsplash displayed plates likewise acquired from all over. Kerry especially liked the one nearest the stove, a tacky hunting scene that featured a near perfect replica of their often naughty but much beloved pet, Chino. She ran a finger over it with a smile, then turned to dump a package of pasta into the now boiling water.

"Hey, Ker?" Dar's voice drifted in from the living room.

"In the kitchen," Kerry responded.

"Did I leave that damn folder in there?"

Kerry pushed away from the counter and turned in a circle, studying the available surfaces. "No," she called back. "Thought you stuck it in your briefcase." She wandered out of the kitchen and headed for the corner where they'd both thrown their laptop cases the previous night. "I'll get it."

Caught in the act of getting up from the couch, Dar collapsed back into it and curled up again. "Thanks."

With a tug, Kerry retrieved the somewhat battered folder and crossed the living room, setting it down on the coffee table. She took a seat next to her partner's feet, reaching over to tweak a toe under its pristine white cotton sock covering. "How's the belly?"

Dar narrowed her eyes and growled.

"Hmm...well, if it's any consolation to you, I'm getting that kinda achy feeling myself," Kerry admitted. "Which doesn't really surprise me, because we're usually right on time together."

Dar growled again, but flexed her toes against Kerry's thigh. "Least we're both miserable at once," she conceded. "You think that's what made the past few days even more stressful than they were anyway?"

Hm. Kerry considered the question. She wasn't often bothered by PMS either, though she did have a tendency to be a bit more emotional a few days before. Add that to the stress of dealing with Dar's first girlfriend and Michelle Graver challenging them at every step? "Yeeeah, maybe."

The socked feet flexed against her thigh again, and Kerry gave them a pat before she leaned forward and got to her feet. "Let me go get our lunch."

Dar poked her with a toe as she eased past, and smiled at the pink tongue stuck out in her direction. Then she returned her attention to Quest's requirements, wincing slightly as a cramp twisted her guts. With a soft grunt, she tossed aside the initial document which she'd already gone over, and drew out the set of technical specifications, easing down to put her head on the couch arm as she started to leaf through the pages.

She spotted several big problems straight off. The hulks Quest had gotten his hands on were old as the hills — two of them were steamships, for god's sake, and the rest were retired passenger liners he'd dug out of mothballs somewhere.

That meant, she realized, they had zero infrastructure. Most had been built before computers, and the idiot wanted to outfit them with the latest available technology. "Jesus." Dar clucked under her breath and shook her head. "Jackass wants to put laser video in the Merrimac."

"Did you say something, sweetie?" Kerry called from the kitchen.

"Nah," Dar replied, lifting her head a little as she sniffed spicy pasta sauce in the air. "Just going over this stuff." She went back to reading. Quest wanted a computerized hotel system, a point of sale, connection to the damn Internet, and — Dar had to look twice, voice over IP telephony. "Jesus," she repeated.

"No, just me and some noodles." Kerry appeared at her side, bearing two steaming bowls. She set them down on the coffee table and resumed her perch at Dar's feet. "Parmesan?"

"Uh huh." Dar watched as a small snowstorm of freshly ground cheese settled on the surface of her pasta. "Are those little meatballs in there?"

"Yup." Kerry dusted her own bowl with the cheese. "Last time I made sauce, I froze some." She set the grater down and handed Dar a fork. "So what are you cussing about this time?"

Dar stabbed a forkful of pasta and lifted it toward her mouth, pausing as the utensil came into her close line of focus. She pulled it back a little and peered at the sauce covered bits, then she selected the last one on the fork's tines and pulled it off, holding it up to examine it. "Kerrison?"

"Mm?" Kerry grunted around a mouthful.

"Why am I eating a disk drive?"

Kerry swallowed and wiped her mouth with her napkin. "Ah." She reached over and pushed the bit of pasta toward Dar's mouth. "My guys gave me a thank you basket for helping out at the con. It was full of nerd things, including a bag of nerd pasta shapes. I figured you were the perfect person to share it with."

"Ah." Dar ate the disk drive, and studied the forkful of pc's left to consume. "Feels sorta cannibalistic, but all right." She chewed the mouthful and went back to the report. One finger pointed at a paragraph, and she pushed it toward Kerry as she swallowed.

Kerry edged over on the couch and started reading. Her brow creased. "Dar, am I reading this right — he only wants one set of cables run?"

"Uh huh."

"Does he realize what that's going to cost in equipment?"

"He wants it on a shoestring."

Kerry slowly ate a mouthful of her lunch. She swallowed before she answered. "Dar, you couldn't do that on Paul Bunyan's shoestring."

"Telegenics says they can." Dar replied. "They told Quest fitting it into his budget was a no brainer."

A snort answered the statement. "Obviously whoever told him that didn't bother to use a brain. Dar, you know damn well doing this right's going to cost."

Yes, she knew that. Dar worked her way through her lunch bowl, eyeing the familiar shapes all the while. "Well, let's wait till we see the real deal," she said. "Maybe it's not as bad as the description seems to show."

Kerry tapped the edge of her fork against her lip. "All right. Sounds like it's all we can do," she conceded. "Maybe when we lay the plans out, he'll realize what it is he's asking for. After all, it's his job to try and get everything he can for as little as possible."

"Eh." Dar flipped to the next page. "His timeline's impossible, too." She frowned. "How long did he say it would take those ships to be hauled here?"

"Two weeks," Kerry recalled. "Can they do it by then? Wonder why he had to pull out of New Zealand? Damn, I was looking forward to going there."

Dar set her bowl down. "You know, that's a damn good question." She pulled her laptop over and rolled onto her back, putting the machine down on her stomach and typing on the keyboard. "Did he mention where in New Zealand the ships were located?"

"Auckland." Kerry leaned over and watched the screen with interest. "You think he was lying?"

Dar keyed in a request, and waited, scanning the responses as they flicked across the monitor. "I think outfitting six ships means big bucks for somebody. Now why..." She drummed her fingers on the keys. "Why would 'somebody' throw away those kind of big bucks?"

Kerry rested her elbow on Dar's knee and looked at the list of shipyards now displayed. There were only six, but though she racked her memory, she couldn't recall Quest mentioning any of the names. What had he said? Just that the ships were somewhere in Auckland, being worked on.

Dar called up one of their info-parsing agents and typed the names of the companies into them. "Now." She paused as she got to the intelligent language question field. "How would you tell if a shipyard suddenly lost business?"

"Not stock." Kerry mused, as Dar shook her head. "Layoffs?"

"Too soon."

"Newspaper stories?"

Dar nodded. "Let's see what that gets us." She typed rapidly into the field and hit enter, and then watched the small running dog in the corner dash merrily away. "Okay." She half turned and set the laptop back down on the table. "So maybe that'll answer your question from last night." She put her head back down on the couch arm and picked up the report again.

Kerry extended a fork full of pasta toward her partner. "Maybe," she agreed, smiling as Dar closed her teeth over the offering and removed it. "I'm going to throw the stuff in our overnight bags into the washing machine. Got anything else you need to go in?"

"Thought it was my turn to do that this week." Dar gazed at her. "You did it last week."

"Mm...yes, it was your turn." Kerry put a fingertip on her partner's chin and lifted it slightly. "But it seems some little nerdy gremlin got all my office clothes dry cleaned for me when I wasn't looking. I don't suppose you have any idea how that happened, huh?"

Dar smiled charmingly at her.

"And somehow my car got mysteriously washed and waxed while we were gone. Any ideas?"

The charming smile grew wider.

"Uh huh. I thought so." Kerry leaned over and gave her a kiss. "So I'm going to go grab your dirty clothes from the closet and get those suds going." She pushed off Dar's hip and stood, collecting the dishes from the table before she sauntered off toward the kitchen.

Dar let her hand fall on the forgotten papers, taking a moment to enjoy the simple feeling of warmth inside her left by the look of indulgent affection in Kerry's eyes. It even eased the cramps some, or at least she convinced herself it did as she stretched out, and then curled her body up again into the dark leather.

She took a moment to look around the living room, which for so long had simply been 'the condo' to her. Plain white walls and mostly monochromatic furniture had graced it since she'd moved in, providing her with a pleasant, if unremarkable place to throw her car keys at the day's end, and lay her head down for those long tropical nights.

It had never been her home. But now it was their home, and from the colorful Mexican throw rug over the love seat to the framed photograph of them both on the entertainment center it had become a part of her in a way she never thought it would.

That was why, she acknowledged in silence, she'd gotten so wired being around Shari. It brought back memories of what her life had been like for so long, and had provided a reminder of everything she had to be thankful for now.

She never wanted to take that for granted. She never wanted Kerry to take it for granted either, though she'd never gotten the feeling that her partner felt that way. It was more an impression she got that Kerry considered their relationship a natural part of her life and expected it to remain that way forever.

Kerry had no doubts. Dar didn't have any doubts about Kerry, but the last week had made her wonder if she didn't still have some doubts about herself.

Which, frankly, sucked. She'd thought she'd gotten past that. It was aggravating to say the least, feeling again those tiny darts of insecurity pricking at her.

Dar sighed. Maybe it had been PMS. Certainly today, now that she'd started, the doubts seemed to have vanished completely replaced by a feeling of rock solid stability she'd become used to over the last year.

Kerry strolled across the tile in front of her, heading for the bedroom. "Crocodile Hunter marathon this afternoon...you up for it?"

Dar grinned, releasing a happier sigh. "Sure." She hesitated. "Hey, Ker?"

"Yeeesss?" Kerry paused in the doorway, leaning back into the room.

"Thanks."

"For the laundry?" Kerry laughed. "You forgot the last time I did it I washed your whites with my burgundy sweatshirt and we both ended up pink in inappropriate places."

"I like my pink bra," Dar remarked mildly. "But thanks anyway. I don't really feel like standing over the machine today."

Kerry winked. "I figured. No problem." She disappeared into the bedroom. "It'll be my turn soon enough. You can get me hot chocolate."

Chino wandered over and climbed onto the couch, circling twice before she settled down at Dar's feet, resting her muzzle on Dar's ankle.

"It's a deal," Dar murmured. "Best deal going, matter of fact, right Chino?"

"Gruff."

Chapter
Eight

KERRY HEARD THE soft ding of mail arriving into her inbox. She swiveled around in her chair and rolled her trackball, glancing at the sender and the subject and stifling a curse. "Oh, pooters." She clicked on it anyway and read the text. "Crap, crap, crap."

Finishing, she sat back in her leather chair and frowned at the pc, sitting inoffensively on the center of her office desk. "I can't believe I forgot about the damn party tomorrow night." With a sigh, she hit the intercom button on the phone. "Dar?"

She released the button and waited, but after a minute there was no answer. She pressed the button again. "Dar?"

Still no answer. Kerry got up and circled her desk, emerging from her office on the second floor of the condo and starting down the staircase. She peeked over, but the living room was empty, Dar's laptop sitting mutely on the coffee table spinning its screen saver in lonely silence. "Hm."

She continued down the steps to the lower level, poking her head into Dar's office and finding an equally empty space. "Where are you, hmm?" She turned and realized Chino wasn't around either. "Ah." She headed for the patio, spotting a blond Labrador tail near the two person swing they'd hung out there.

"Hey." Kerry slid the door open and stepped out, grimacing slightly at the contrast between the cool dry air inside and the warm, languid sea breeze outside. "Listen, I fubared."

Dar looked up in surprise from the book she'd been reading. "You?"

"Me." Kerry walked over and joined her on the swing. "I...um...committed us to a party tomorrow night that I completely forgot to tell you about." She studied her bare feet for a moment, before she glanced sideways at her partner. "Fubar."

Dar let the book close over her hand and studied her penitent appearing swingmate. "Hmmm...what kind of party? Don't tell me it's the condo association again."

"No."

"Good. I'd have to whip you with soggy Ramen noodles." The blue eyes twinkled gently. "Let me guess...the church?"

Kerry nodded, watching the expression on Dar's face carefully. "Are you going to kill me?"

"Nah." Dar displayed her book cover. "Conversation there's gotta beat this. I've seen drier material about heuristic switching, but not by much."

Relieved, Kerry rested her head against Dar's shoulder. "Remind me to get you some nice, trashy bodice rippers for your afternoon time outs, honey. You'll go blind reading this stuff." She tapped the book. "But I really am sorry it slipped my mind. I said yes right before we started talking about leaving early for the trade show and...well..."

Dar put her arm around Kerry and pushed against the railing, rocking them both gently in the light breeze. She wasn't that fond of parties, but the church ones were pretty harmless, and she'd taken a liking to a few of the more regular members. "Maybe I'll even stop having cramps by then. Son of a bitch, I got it bad this month."

"Want to go for a walk? Maybe it'll help."

Dar tossed her book down and stood up, taking Kerry's hand as they opened the gate and walked down the steps into the small patio garden with Chino frisking happily at their heels. It was late afternoon, and the breeze from the sea had started to cool off the air a little, bringing the scent of the salt water with it.

They made their way down to the beach and turned to walk along it as the incoming tide chased their steps. Chino found a piece of driftwood and pounced on it, lifting it and returning to her owners with an air of excited triumph.

"Whatcha got?" Dar reached out and took the stick, examining it before she tossed it ahead of them. "Good girl!"

Chino raced after it, living up to her breed as she retrieved the stick and plowed back toward them.

Kerry was content to watch, her hand still tucked into Dar's as they walked along the mostly deserted beachfront. They got a glance or two, but most of the residents knew them and she returned the smiles and half waves of the few still lying on neatly toweled chaise lounges, soaking up the sun.

Dar swerved a little, taking them into the surf up to their calves. Chino bolted into the water, barking as the surf surged back at her.

"Chino, you silly dog," Kerry scolded their pet.

The Labrador bounded over to her and shook herself vigorously, showering both of them with cool sea water. "Gruff!"

"Bah." Dar shielded her face with her free hand. "Chino, you little..."

"Bitch?" Kerry supplied, with a chuckle. "Yes, she is, isn't she? G'wan, Chi...get the stick!" She pointed to the shore. "Get it!"

Chino bounded away to retrieve her prize, leaving her owners to walk out of the surf in peace.

"She's so cute." Kerry sighed. "She gets away with everything, and she knows it," she added. "She has us wrapped right around her little paw."

Dar chuckled softly.

"Walking helping any?"

"No." Dar managed a wry grin. "But the two of you are keeping my mind otherwise occupied, so the end result is all right," she told her partner. "I feel better."

"Mm.. well, that's what your family's for. To make you feel better when you feel crummy." Kerry squeezed her hand around Dar's lightly. "So I'm glad we're doing our job."

Dar didn't answer, but her face lit up visibly at the words, and her step took on an extra swagger as they enjoyed the late afternoon sun. They passed the beach club, exchanging lazy waves with a few people seated outside and continued on along the south side of the island.

It was quieter on this end. They faced the terminal island where the cargo ships loaded up with containers bound for South America and beyond. Dar shaded her eyes and then pointed to one side of the cargo area, a large, open space with several cranes standing slack and waiting for work. "Think that's where he's talking about."

Kerry reviewed the spot. "Dar, it's really twisted that these damn things are going to be almost in view of our bedroom."

Her partner chuckled softly. "Remind me to point that out in a loud voice if we bump into our friends during the process."

They watched a cargo cruiser move stiffly away from the dock, chugging out of the channel toward the cut, shepherded by two hard working tugs.

"I think..." Kerry mused, as they continued their walk, heading around the back side of the island. "I think we should throw a big party. Invite all our competitors over to break the ice, kinda, since we are the...um..hosts...so to speak."

Dar eyed her. "Invite them all to our condo?"

"Uh huh."

"You really mean, invite Shari and Michelle to our condo so they can drool all over it and be jealous of our home life and good taste?"

"Uh huh."

Dar ruffled Kerry's hair with her free hand, feeling around on the crown of her head. "Careful, Yankee, your horns are showing," she teased. "Michelle's got some class. I'm sure they live in a nice place."

Kerry solemnly stuck her tongue out. "Not as nice as ours," she said. "I looked up the address just to prove my excruciatingly thorough WASP upbringing." Her green eyes glinted slightly. "But I was serious, Dar. If we're going to do this, I don't want to spend two weeks being miserable like we were in Orlando. Let's take the high road, and let them be jerks if they want to be."

Dar pondered in silence as they rounded the curve and started up the northern edge of the island, which bordered the cut. Watercraft were moving through the channel, including two daredevil jet ski riders courting disaster as they wove through a stately parade of sailboats. Chino trotted along behind them, and now that the sun was starting a serious tilt toward the horizon a cooling breeze sprang up and made the walk far more pleasant.

"Well, let's see what happens," Dar finally concluded. "After all, they might not come down here. I'm gonna guess most of the bidders will send an engineering team, not executives in silk and pumps."

Kerry accepted the tacit victory with a gentle smile. "Bet you ten bucks they'll be here," she countered. "Because they know you will."

"We will," Dar corrected her. "I think Michelle respects you."

Kerry's face wrinkled up into an expression of distaste. "You know something, I sort of liked her, way back when. I thought she was pretty cool, the way she made that pick the first time, and even after she messed around with those snapshots and came to the office, she seemed pretty straightforward."

"Mm." Dar stepped over a piece of driftwood. Her cramps seemed to be easing after all, and she was finding the walk increasingly enjoyable. "Yeah, I didn't have a problem with her that first time. I wasn't crazy about her sending those photos to Alastair, but I figured she was pretty stung when I blew her off that night at her hotel."

A smile played around Kerry's lips. "The night you came over to my apartment," she murmured. "Ah, yes. I remember that night. I'm surprised I didn't stain that beige carpet green I was so freaking jealous."

Dar looked at her, caught in the middle of continuing her original thought. "You were?"

"Dar." Kerry laughed, rolling her eyes. "Oh, Jesus, please. Tell me you didn't see it written all over my face."

"Um." Dar cleared her throat gently. "Actually, no. I was too busy staring lustfully at the half naked, gorgeous, sweat covered woman on the carpet to notice what color she was."

Kerry looked at her, both eyebrows hiking up. Dar responded with a sexy grin, triggering a now far more rare heated blush that rapidly colored Kerry's face. "Euhr...you do say the nicest things sometimes, honey." Kerry rubbed her cheek with one hand, and then she glanced up. "Really?"

"Really," Dar replied. "It was quite a feeling—after being hit on all night by someone I wasn't attracted to." She tucked Kerry's hand into the crook of her elbow. "Funny how I used to like playing that game. I was in a meeting the other month with a half dozen new reps from that consulting company we integrated...didn't know me, didn't know about us...they started that sniffing around crap and I called a break and went out and put this on." She raised her right hand, displaying her ring. "End of that problem."

Startled to have her unasked question answered in such an unexpected way, Kerry merely stayed silent for a few steps. Then she released a small puff of air, almost a laugh. "So that's why," she mused. "I remember you telling me once how you felt that people formed certain ideas about other people based on whether they had a ring on or not."

Dar nodded. "Yeah," she agreed. "I damn well wanted them to think that about me." She glanced at Kerry's hand tucked in hers, its ring glinting softly in the sunlight, and then she met Kerry's eyes. "Yeah."

"I was wondering," Kerry admitted. "I was getting dressed one morning and I was about to put my necklace on and I stopped just to look at my ring...it's so pretty." She glanced down at their hands. "I decided to put it on my hand instead. Not really sure why, but then I saw you had yours on."

"I thought you did it because I had mine on." Dar cleared her throat.

"No, we just ended up doing it the same day," Kerry said. "Kinda strange, but in a nice way. I'm really not sure at all why I did it."

"Maybe it's an evolution thing," Dar suggested, after a brief hesitation.

"Maybe."

Dar scuffed a rock with her foot. "Anyway. I'm glad we did it."

"Me, too." The smile on Kerry's face left no doubt of her feelings. "You know, Dar, we should do these little walk and talks more often."

A wry chuckle spilled from Dar's lips. "Sure beats cramps." She looked up. "Hey...hey...Chino!!!"

"Oh no." Kerry's eyes widened. "No! C'mere, girl."

Chino spotted a duck and bolted after it, spurring her owners into a mad dash after her, leaving laughter in the air behind them.

"HERE YOU GO." The short, curly haired man behind the makeshift bar handed Kerry a beer. "Careful, it's a little foamy."

"Thanks." Kerry inhaled some of the sharp tasting fizz before it poured over her hand and moved to one side out of the way of the crowd.

The church was mostly full, it's homey interior buzzing with low conversation and the occasional spurt of laughter. Kerry dodged around a few chatting groups and headed for the low couches near the back wall where Dar was lounging inside a circle of people they were more familiar with.

At least the party was casual. Kerry eased past a man in shorts so short she wondered why he really bothered and took the cushion next to her partner on the couch. "What'd I miss?"

"Oh, Lori and I were just filling Dar in on the latest church news, you know," a tall redhead told her. "This and that...we keep trying to lure her into the choir."

Kerry settled against Dar's warm body. "She'd be good at it," she agreed, ignoring the mock glower from a pair of nearby baby blues.

"You should see her singing in the shower. It's amazing."

"I'm sure we'd love to. Invite us over." Lori shot back, with a mischievous grin. "Right, Rachel?"

"Absolutely! Kerry, you little charmer! What a sweetie you are!" Her partner chortled. "When's the viewing?"

Kerry felt Dar start to snicker. "Well, I walked right into that one, didn't I?" she admitted, toasting them all with her beer. "Sorry ladies, I don't share." A reluctant grin appeared. "The view, or anything else." She bumped Dar with her elbow. "And you stop laughing!"

"Ahem." Dar cleared her throat. "Honestly, my work schedule just won't permit me getting involved in anything that regular." She told Rachel, the redhead who was also one of the principals in the choir. "And I don't commit to things I can't guarantee I'll do."

Rachel slouched in the easy chair across from them, swinging one denim covered leg over the arm of it. "Yeah, yeah. But all work no play..." She let the words trail off suggestively. "Workaholics are so uncool these days." She shook her finger at Dar.

An amused glint appeared. "I play," Dar replied in silken voice. "I just save all my playtime for one person." She turned her head and looked at Kerry, catching the quick grin and returning it.

Their attention was drawn by a sudden noise nearby and they all turned to see two women facing off against each other, hands grappling at cotton shirts and faces twisted in anger. "Oh crap." Lori rolled her eyes. "Here we go again." She lifted her voice. "Would you two cut it the hell out and grow up?"

"You keep the hell out of this, bitch!" one of the women yelled back at her.

"Who are you calling bitch, you ugly piece of shit?" Lori got up. "Take your fucking drama out of here, yeah?"

"Lor, sit down." Rachel grabbed her by the back of her jeans and hauled her down into the chair. "Leave them alone."

The short, dark haired woman glowered at the two arguing women, who were now ignoring her, busy with shoving each other around. "Assholes."

"Hey, ladies." David, one of the church workers hurried over. He was a middle-aged man with salt and pepper hair, and a neatly trimmed beard. "C'mon, c'mon now...it's a party! Let's be festive!"

Dar slid her arm around Kerry's shoulders and idly watched the entertainment unfolding before her. The two women were on again, off again partners who always seemed to be arguing about something. Dar suspected they both had some real problems and were using each other to keep their minds off them, but she'd never gotten interested enough in the situation to find out.

That sounded so damn callous, Dar acknowledged, but the two women were nasty to most, unpleasant to the rest, and quite probably deserved each other.

"Kiss my ass, fag," the shorter of the two women snapped at David. "Just leave us alone."

"Hey, c'mon now." David held his hands out. "We don't need to get nasty," he warned. "So calm down, okay?"

"Calm this." The same woman shot him a bird.

Kerry looked at Dar. Dar looked back at Kerry. "Do we want to get involved in this?" Kerry asked.

"Well." Dar set her bottle of YooHoo down. "Either we get involved, or we find a different party. I'm not in the mood to listen to this much pointless cursing." She got up and dusted her faded jeans off, stepping around Lori's chair and heading toward the battleground with a resigned sigh.

Kerry got up and followed, trying not to see the anticipatory grins on the faces of their friends. She caught up to Dar as she reached the outskirts of the disturbance, which had now drawn a small crowd.

The two women were short and heavy set, one with close-cropped hair and the other with long braids threaded with beads. The short haired woman also had an eyebrow ring, and a beautiful tattoo of a parrot on one bare shoulder.

"Okay, people." Dar stopped just short of them, putting her hands on her hips and tilted her head slightly to look down at them. "Do what the man says and take it outside."

David sidled up to her immediately, more than pleased to find a ready ally. Kerry stopped a step behind her partner, folding her arms over her chest and waiting to see what would happen next, satisfied to watch the two other women with a sharp eye.

Not that she was at all worried. Dar could more than take care of herself, of Kerry, of David, and probably of everyone in sight without breaking a sweat. In her red tank top, with her burnished tan and solid muscularity, she had presence that was undeniable.

The shorter of the two women turned to confront Dar. "Did someone ask you to get in our business?" she asked.

"Yes," Dar replied in a calm voice. "You did, by acting like a pair of rutting jackasses. So knock it off."

"Or?" the woman asked, sarcastically. "You gonna beat me up?"

Kerry stepped forward, about to intervene. Dar beat her to it, though, and added a tiny bump to her shoulder.

"No. You'd enjoy it too much. Instead, I'm going to cancel all your credit cards and get your driver's licenses revoked if you don't get the hell out of here and stop being such a pair of pitas," Dar replied. "Scram."

The short woman's eyes narrowed, and she tensed, but after a second she shrugged and turned away. "Whatever. Asshole." She flicked her long nailed fingers as she sauntered off, pushing her way through the crowd as she headed toward the door.

Her partner glared at Dar as well. "You think you're so hot. Why don't you go back to your fancy island and leave the real people alone. We were here a long time before you were."

"Okay," Kerry finally got a word in edgewise. "So let me get this straight. You guys cuss and punch each other and mess up everyone's fun here...and you're mad because we don't like to watch?"

"Stupid asshole."

"Kerry Stuart," Kerry corrected her mildly. "And if you're that much into people watching you, why not join the theatre group? I think they're doing MacBeth this summer...sounds right up your alley." She took a step forward, putting herself between Dar and the other woman. "You know what I think? I think you just like to be the center of attention, so that's why you always act out at these shindigs."

"Oh yeah, sure," the woman replied. "Kiss my ass."

"Never in a million years." Kerry took a swig of her beer. "I have better things to kiss." She heard a faint sound come from Dar, and knew if she turned around she'd see very hiked eyebrows. "So now that the show's over, why not go get a drink and be normal like the rest of us."

"Great idea," David chimed in. "C'mon folks, let's get the music started again. She's right. Show's over." He gave two men next to him a nudge, and then signaled the woman standing near the stereo system to turn it up. "Enough, enough, okay? It's a party. Everyone chill."

Kerry turned and bumped Dar with her head, pushing her back toward the couch. "Gwan, you high falutin' rich chick, you."

Dar chuckled under her breath, allowing herself to be herded back to the couch as the crowd slowly broke up and moved way. They settled back down together, giving Lori and Rachel a twinned roll of the eyes as a few others gathered around, watching them with casual interest. "What's next?" Dar asked. "Unisex twister?"

Lori settled into a half unstuffed chair next to the couch. "You guys are too funny. Like Batman and Robin." She accepted the cup Rachel handed to her after a brief sojourn to the bar. "But those two and their little pod always had a problem with the two of you. I'm not really sure why."

"Our bank balances?" Kerry suggested, with a grimace. "Yeah, like we come in here in silk and pearls, flipping our minks." She glanced down at her somewhat worn aviator pants, with their odd assortment of pockets, and then indicated Dar's faded jeans. "What's up with that?"

Lori shrugged.

"I guess some of them figure..." Rachel hesitated. "You know, we're always raising cash for the place. Maybe they think if you have more, you should just give it over."

Dar snorted. "We donate." She lifted a hand. "They want more, they can come do my job and then they can take what they want. Screw that."

"That's right," Kerry said. "We've never said no when David's called us."

"Hey!" Rachel edged back a little. "I didn't say that's what we thought. I just said maybe that's what they think, you know? I mean, your paycheck's your own, yeah? Like all of ours is." She shrugged. "Some people get really jealous when they see someone who has stuff they don't."

"Give me a break." Dar picked up her YooHoo and took a sip.

Kerry sucked at her beer, a look of wry cynicism crossing her face. "Isn't that the truth. I've had to deal with that since I was in frilly Pampers." She sighed. "But you know what, my family only has money. I earn mine."

Lori perched on the arm of the chair her partner was sitting in. "What exactly do you guys do, anyway?" she asked, tactfully steering the conversation down a different track. "Investment banking?"

Dar settled back and extended her legs out, crossing them at the ankles. "We're nerds," she explained briefly.

"Nerds?" Rachel laughed. "You're kidding me. Really?"

Kerry nodded. "Really. Regular, ordinary, working nerds," she added. "Besides, we do our part here. I'm working with those kids every week, and Dar..." She glanced at her partner, who smiled faintly. "Dar shows up and looks great, and doesn't get mad at me for dragging her in here all the time."

"Heh," Dar responded.

"You could join our community action group," Lori suggested. "We've got a lot of stuff planned for this year...lobbying and all that. Bet you're good at it."

"Bet I'm not," Dar said. "Thanks, but no thanks."

Both women across from them looked uncomfortable at that, Kerry noticed. But it was the truth, and she knew Dar generally refused to sugarcoat her answers. "Honestly, our schedule doesn't permit either of us a lot of slack in doing organized things," Kerry said. "We never know when we might have to travel, or get stuck late taking care of a problem."

"Okay, just a suggestion," Lori said. "I'm getting another beer. Want one?" she asked Rachel.

"Sure."

Lori got up and left. Kerry used the slight pause to finish up her beer, and note that Dar had done the same with her YooHoo. "Want another one?" She indicated the bottle. "Or something stronger?"

Dar fiddled with the bottle, then handed it over. "Nah. I'll stick to this. Thanks."

Kerry eased off the couch and gave her a pat on the knee as she planned a path through the growing crowd toward the bar.

Rachel waited for Kerry to vanish, then turned her attention back to the tall, dark haired woman on the couch. "Nerd, huh?"

Dar plucked at the seam of her denims. "Yeah."

"Uh huh."

"KNOW WHAT I think?" Dar sat back, letting the car's air conditioning cool her off.

Kerry was curled up in the passenger seat, looking tousled and somewhat aggravated. "What?"

"I think we need to find a new church."

"Ungh." Kerry rested her head against the leather seat back. "Tell you what. Give me tomorrow off, and I'll find us a new church. How's that?" She shifted, grimacing at the cramping that had manifested with aching suddenness, giving her an unwelcome, yet welcome excuse to leave the party.

Dar glanced at her in perfect sympathy. "Sweetheart, you can have the day off any time you want," she replied. "I know your area's covered."

Kerry grimaced again. "You know what's not covered?" she asked mournfully. "I forgot to stop and pick up supplies at Walgreen's." Her eyes met Dar's. "And you know I can't handle the kind you use."

Dar put the car into reverse and commenced backing out. "Guess we're going to the drugstore then," she said. "S'all right. I need some stuff too. We're low on Advil..."

"Ahhhh!!!" Kerry squeaked.

"And I need some batteries for my digital," Dar finished. "So put the seat back and relax, and we'll get ourselves taken care of."

Kerry took advantage of the offer, releasing the seat and tilting it back about halfway. She closed her eyes and left the driving to her partner, idly listening to the soft new age music coming from the speakers. "They really were kinda sucky today, huh?" she said. "I wonder why? We never had them act like that before. Did we do something I don't remember?"

Dar was silent for a while, drumming her thumbs on the steering wheel as she made her way through the surface streets toward the drugstore. "I don't know," she finally muttered. "It just pisses me off that they act like we owe them something all the time."

Did they? Kerry pondered the idea. "Well, most churches do assume their memberships will do stuff like bake cookies and put money in the plate, Dar," she conceded. "I know ours did at home. Big time. Not that anyone ever said anything outright, but boy...if you skipped a week, the looks you got."

Dar made a rude noise.

"Well, you know, they have to raise money somehow." Kerry felt herself in the odd position of defending a faith she often was at serious odds with. "They have to keep the place up, and pay the pastor, and do community programs. The money has to come from somewhere."

Dar pulled into the parking lot and parked in front of the drugstore. She set the parking brake, but left the car running. "Yeah, I know." She opened the driver's side door. "It's not that part I mind. They do good stuff, especially for those kids you mess with. It's the

other stuff they expect us to do." She got out. "As if just because we're
gay, we have to be revolutionaries about it. Not my gig."

Kerry watched in bemusement as her partner shut the door gently,
and strode off toward the entrance to the Walgreen's.

DAR WAITED IN line, glancing at the items available for sale on
the nearby racks out of boredom. She had her chosen items, obtained in
quick order, but there was only one clerk working and several people
ahead of her waiting to pay.

C'mon. I've got melting ice cream here. Dar glared evilly at the line
from behind her shades.

The clerk, unfortunately, was busy trying to understand the request
of the first woman in line, who was attempting to obtain a specific type
of cigarette using a language even Dar wasn't familiar with. It was hard
to say at this point which one of them was the more frustrated.

Her eyes fell on a shelf about thigh level, and she examined the
contents, a grudging smile slowly appearing as she reached down and
selected one of the items. After a quick look around, she added it to her
basket, then resumed waiting.

The woman ahead of her let out a deliberately audible sigh.
"Jesus."

The clerk glanced up at her, giving her an apologetic grimace, but
slightly shrugging her shoulders. The foreign woman pulled out a piece
of paper from her purse and unfolded it, showing it to the clerk with a
bit of impatience. "Ma'am, we don't have those."

The woman questioned her in her own language.

"Ma'am, we don't have those," the clerk repeated, with
commendable patience. She pointed at the picture in the paper and
shook her head. The woman shook the paper at her, her voice rising.

"Jesus." The customer in front of Dar repeated. "What an idiot."
With a disgusted look, she tossed her packages onto the counter and
walked away, leaving the store with a slap at the sliding door on her
way out. The man ahead of her did the same, shooting the clerk a bird as
he followed suit.

At the same moment, the foreign woman grabbed back her paper
and shoved it in her purse, storming off and walking quickly through
the door on the heels of the other two.

That left the clerk staring after them, and Dar with no one ahead of
her in line. Not one to look a gift tourist in the mouth, she stepped
forward and began removing her choices from her basket, placing them
down on the register counter.

"Why do people do that?" the clerk wondered, as she picked up the
first item and scanned it. "Move to a place and not know how to
communicate?"

Dar studied her from behind her wraparound shades. "To give

Americans a taste of what it's like to deal with them overseas?" she
suggested mildly.

"Huh?" The girl frowned. "What do you mean?"

"You ever been in another country?" Dar inquired.

"No," the girl replied. "Why would I want to go to another
country?"

"Doesn't matter. How much?" Dar indicated the register. She
watched the total come up, and swiped her ATM card through the
reader, punching in the code with an impatient motion. The machine
hesitated, and then regurgitated her receipt, which she snagged along
with her purchases from the clerk's hands. "Thanks."

"Bye." Now bereft of customers, the clerk waggled her fingers at
Dar. "Have a nice day."

KERRY HAD AMUSED herself by trying to make up stories about
the people she watched coming out of the store while waiting for Dar's
return. The first man who had come out seemed to have gotten
something he wasn't too sure about based on how he kept looking
inside the bag he'd carried out as he walked to his car. She decided it
was a choice between hair growth formula, some feminine products, or
birth control.

She watched him until he got into his car, whereupon he drew
something out of the bag and took a bite of it, skewing her theory.

She hoped.

The next two women who exited were apparently together, talking
non-stop in Spanish as they walked right past the Lexus and got into a
maroon station wagon right next to her. They started their car and
without breaking their stream of discussion, began to pull out.

Kerry's eyes widened as she realized the car's front wheels were
turned sharply to the right, aiming the vehicle right for the passenger
side door inches from her. Reacting instinctively, she leaned over and
slammed her hand on the Lexus' horn, closing her eyes and sprawling
half over Dar's seat as she waited for the crunch and impact.

After a moment's silence, however, she opened her eyes and peered
over her shoulder. The maroon station wagon was gone, and as she
straightened up and looked behind her, she spotted it pulling out into
traffic with a squeal of tires.

A blue Jeep barely missed sideswiping it. Kerry blew her hair out of
her eyes and faced forward again, deciding the women had probably
picked up either legal stimulants or prescription sedatives or maybe a
combination of both.

Another customer stormed by the front of the Lexus, walking with
short, furious steps. She banged into a trashcan on the sidewalk, and
shoved it away from her with a audible curse even through the closed
windows of the Lexus. She gave the can a vicious kick, before she

continued on and around the corner of the store to the other side of the parking lot.

Didn't like her one hour photos? Kerry wondered. She had little time to consider it, because the woman was followed almost immediately by another, equally upset looking, who seemed almost in tears. She walked over to a small four-door car near the entrance and spoke to the man inside it, showing him something she had in her hands.

The man grabbed it and then shoved her backwards with an angry snarl. He pushed the car door open and headed for the door to the drugstore, leaving the woman behind. She looked unhappily at the car for a brief moment, then went around and got into the passenger side, pulling down the sunshade and peering anxiously into the mirror.

Now, what was the story there? Kerry wondered, but not for long because her peripheral vision was filled with an approaching figure that captured her attention fully as she turned her head to watch Dar walk over to her.

Just the sight of that angular face made her smile. Kerry could feel her facial muscles responding, and she watched Dar react and return the grin as she opened the door and slid inside bringing a puff of hot, moist air and the scent of the apricot scrub still lingering on her skin. "That didn't take long. Thanks for getting my stuff."

Dar handed her the bag. "No problem. Careful, there's a jug of..."

"Ice cream in here," Kerry finished, peering inside. "And...what in the..." She removed something from the bag and held it up, letting the plastic bag drop down to the floor between her hiking boots. "Dar, what is this?"

Dar was concentrating on removing the Lexus from the parking lot and keeping the body of the car intact while she did so. "Um...it's a hamster."

Kerry tapped the small, furry foot, and the stuffed animal started to dance to the tune of "Over There..." "It's a dancing hamster," she observed, dancing a little in her seat along with it. "It's a dancing hamster in a sailor suit, Dar."

"Yeah." Her partner peered fiercely through the windshield. "You were calling me a hamster the other day so..."

A giggle worked its way out of Kerry's chest. She set the creature on her lap and tapped its foot again, watching it dance and squiggle in its white outfit and hat. "Is this supposed to be you?"

Dar cleared her throat. "I thought you'd think it was cute."

"Hehehehehehehe." Kerry let out a long, low chortle. "Oh, you're so right, I do." She danced with her new little friend. "Wait till your dad sees it."

Dar turned her head and gave her a look over the tops of her sunglasses.

"I'm going to put this on my desk," Kerry decided.

"At work?" Dar's eyes nearly popped.

Kerry reached over and turned her head back forward, as the light turned green and they were free to proceed across to the causeway home. "Don't be goofy. Of course not at work. At home."

Dar settled back in her seat, relieved. "Yeah, well...I had some time to kill at the register. They were short handed."

"Though it might be a great ice breaker at new client meetings," Kerry mused.

Dar turned to stare at her again, only to find mischievous green eyes waiting in knowing silence. "You're lucky I love you," she mock growled.

Kerry's smile softened and gentled. "Don't I know how lucky I am," she replied. "And I will find us a different church, Dar. I like belonging to something like that. It gives me a sense of community here. But not at the expense of you being uncomfortable with it."

Dar fell silent as she directed the car onto the ferry base. "Does it have to be a church?" she asked as they pulled up to the cones. "Maybe we could join a computer club or something?"

Kerry rested her chin on her fist. "We spend enough time with nerds," she disagreed. "Hey...how about a biker club?"

Dar covered her eyes with one hand.

"Vroom, vroom."

NOW IT WAS Kerry's turn to be a couch potato, and she readily took advantage of it, tucking the light, worn childhood quilt she'd brought back from Michigan around her as she watched the late news. She had a cup of hot blackberry tea on the table nearby, and sufficient quantities of painkillers to render her acceptably comfortable, at least for the moment.

They had paused at the Island Market on the way home and gotten some fish filets, which Dar had insisted on cooking. Much to Kerry's surprise, and also to her partner's she suspected, the relatively simple broiling experiment had turned out very tasty. After that, and some of Dar's newly purchased ice cream, the stresses from the party had finally dissipated.

"Nothing." Dar looked up from her perch sprawled across the love seat. "I don't get it. There's nothing here." She lifted a hand and let it drop, shaking her head at the screen of her laptop. "No mention, no little notes in the paper, nothing in the trades...a major contract falls through, and all you see is news about rugby."

Kerry chuckled softly. "I don't know, sweetie. I think I like those priorities for a change." She took a sip of her tea. "Oh well. We'll find out eventually what the deal is. Once we get to those ships, someone'll talk. They always do, Dar."

"Mmph." Dar was rattling away at her keyboard.

Kerry returned her attention to the big screen television, where an overly earnest reporter was relating the day's news in serious, emphatic tones. The shot cut away to a nighttime scene, with flashing police lights, and after studying it for a minute, she frowned. "Hey, Dar? Look."

"Mm?" Pale blue eyes flicked to her, then to the television. "What am I looking at?"

"Isn't that the Walgreen's? The one we were at today?"

Dar leaned on the love seat arm and peered at the screen. "I don't...hell, they all look alike to me, Kerry. Maybe it is. Why?"

"Shh." Kerry turned the sound up to listen.

"Police are unsure of how the woman got left in the trunk, or who might have done this to her. She was taken to Jackson Memorial Hospital where she's in critical condition." The reporter on the scene drew back, showing a small, four door car parked on the side of the building. It's trunk was hanging open and obviously had been forced. "The car was rented, police say, by an unidentified man they are now looking for."

"Huh," Dar murmured. "Someone locked in a trunk? Lucky they didn't croak in this heat." She shook her head and went back to her laptop screen. "Wonder when it happened?"

"I don't know." Kerry leaned forward. "They can't have found it that long ago. It's a live report. Oh, Dar I'd hate to think that poor woman was in that trunk when we were there!"

Dar looked up again, studying the car. "We weren't on that side of the building," she said. "Car looks a little familiar though, but it's a common rental type. Dime a dozen, Ker."

"Yeah." Something was niggling at Kerry's memory, and she rested her chin on her fist as the news went on to another story. After a few minutes of trying to root it out, however, she gave up and tuned back in to the reporter. "Ah...gonna have rain tomorrow," she chortled softly. "Sure you don't want to spend the day inside with me watching it?"

"Mm." Dar gave her a narrow-eyed look. "Temptress."

Kerry gave her best impression of sultriness, aware that her Pooh T-shirt was probably skewing the impact just a trifle. "Actually, I've got a ton of stuff to do tomorrow. I want to get a hair-cut for starters, and my car's due for service."

"Thought you were going to relax?" Dar reminded her.

"I will," Kerry said. "But I want to get something accomplished too, so I don't feel so guilty thinking of you slaving away in the office stuck in your monkey suit."

"Ahh, and I have to meet with all the international sales directors. They're in tomorrow." Dar reminded her. "So you can really pity me. Maria has a four hour block scheduled in the afternoon."

"Ew."

"Uh huh."

Kerry rolled over on to her back and watched Dar's profile as she worked on her machine. "I could pass on having a day off," she suggested. "You want some backup?"

"Nah." Dar glanced up at her, and grinned. "But thanks for the offer."

"Okay." Kerry wiggled her feet under the cotton covering. "But I'll make sure you've got something great to come home to."

The blue eyes twinkled. "Something other than you? What else do you think I need?"

Kerry sighed happily.

"Besides, you're going to have to run the ball game with Quest," Dar continued dryly. "Don't thank me yet." She went back to her typing, listening to the soft chuckle as Kerry rolled back onto her side and the news switched over to sports.

"Okay." She reviewed her work for the last time, studying the presentation she'd put together for the meeting. "I think that'll work." She set the laptop down on the coffee table and stretched, reaching out to scratch Chino's head.

It was a completely ordinary Sunday night at home. They usually watched whatever was on either the Learning Channel or Discovery, or a movie, then the news before getting together whatever they needed for work the next week and going to bed.

Comfortingly predictable. Dar regarded the shots of football players practicing in the hot sun with a touch of bemusement. "Y'know, they took us to see those guys do that once."

"That?" Kerry pointed. "You mean, summer practice?"

"Yeah," Dar said. "They used to take school kids on different field trips. See the zoo, that sort of thing." A rakish grin appeared. "Summer day, ninety degrees, no water anywhere. We all ran off and raided a McArthur Dairy milk truck that'd stopped to make a delivery. Nearly got tossed in jail."

Kerry started laughing.

"Haven't liked watching those guys play since."

Chapter
Nine

DAR DROPPED HER leather portfolio on her desk before she circled it and sat down, giving her trackball a spin as she settled into her leather chair.

Her mail came up, the screen dark with new messages. She clicked on one, and reviewed it, then sighed and shook her head. "Boy, am I ever an idiot."

After a moment, she hit one of her speed dial buttons and waited for an answer. "Mark?"

"Hey boss." Mark sounded a touch harried.

"You going to kill me?" Dar eyed the phone. "I got the security report."

"Well," Mark sighed. "Our front end web routers are getting pounded. I may have to throw a reserve circuit at it. Freaking hackers."

Dar flipped over to the monitoring screen and reviewed it. She could see the entry points, and the flickers of orange and yellow in their normally green and blue world. "Brute force?"

"Yeah. Pretty lame," Mark said. "Just a lot of volume."

Dar studied the traffic. "Are they trying to hack the site or just DDOS it?" she asked. "We have a sniffer on that outside port?"

Mark rattled a bunch of keys. "Haven't scoped it yet," he admitted. "Gimme a sec."

The attack didn't really affect her internal network. Dar frowned as she studied the stats. They had recorded a rising number of probes at her external interfaces, but those were subtler, and almost hesitant. This seemed like something else.

"They take us offline that's gonna suck, Boss," Mark commented.

Exactly. "I think that's probably what they're trying to do," Dar said. "Bastards." She leaned on her elbows, peering at the screen. "Let's get a scope on it, see if there's a common source or if it's a botnet."

"Will do."

"Call me back." Dar released the phone and sighed. She glanced back at her mail and clicked a second one with a red exclamation point. "Eleanor. Now what?"

She scanned the mail, and then dialed the phone again. Two rings later, Eleanor answered. "What the hell is this mail?" Dar asked. "Who wants to talk to me?"

The Marketing VP sighed. "Apparently CNN's tech reporter picked up the AP feed on the convention. He got wind of this competition between Telegenics and us and wants a story out of it. He's already talked to the Tech TV people that were there."

"Great." Dar leaned back in her chair. "What's his angle?"

"That we're being pushed over by some startup with guts and innovation."

"Nice," Dar grunted.

"He thinks he's got a good yarn, what can I tell you, Dar?" Eleanor said. "Want me to push him over to Kerry? We'd probably get milder sound bites that way."

Dar sighed. "No, I'm not asking Kerry to clean up my mess. Give him my contact info. I'll talk to him." She rubbed her temples.

"Okay," Eleanor said. "Do me a favor though, huh? Try not to get us into more trouble?"

"No promises," Dar answered briefly. "Later." She cut off the phone, and then hit the button again when it buzzed a second later. "Yeah?"

"Okay, got the sniffer on." Mark said. "I'm gonna output to your share okay? I've got a couple of hot potatoes on right now."

"Sure," Dar agreed. "Thanks. I got it." She hung up again, and then glanced up as her intercom buzzed. "Now what?"

"Jefa, I have a customer, Mr. Godson on linea uno. He says he must speak with you urgently."

Godson. Godson...oh. "Okay, put him through," Dar said. "I'll talk to him."

"Si, I will do so." Maria's voice clicked off, then her internal line buzzed.

Dar picked it up. "Hello Stewart."

"Dar, that you? Oh, of course it is," a man's voice answered. "Glad I caught you in. Listen, I've got a big problem I need some help with."

Of course he did. Customers rarely called Dar just to pass the time of day, or compliment her on their service metrics. Godson was the CIO of Betadyne, a very high-powered sales and marketing group that provided fulfillment and call center services for a host of clients.

A big, and influential account. Ergo, why Dar was speaking to him without hesitation. "Sure, Stewart. What can we do for you?"

She spun her trackball again, and studied her mail screen as he started talking, stifling a yawn and wishing the day was moving faster.

"Well, see, Dar, we recently moved to this new application of ours, a real corker," Godson said. "It's fabulous. We love it. It does a hell of a lot more for us than the last thing we were using did, and we can see it's going to really move us ahead in business."

Dar glanced at the phone. "Glad to hear that, Stewart," she remarked. "I didn't know you were moving platforms."

Godson cleared his throat. "Wasn't going to, you know? Change isn't the best route sometimes, but we got a good deal from this company, and our new VP Ops here brought the deal home, said it would revolutionize us."

Uh huh. "Okay, so...what's the problem? Sounds like you're happy with it." Dar leaned her elbow on her desk and rested her head on her hand.

"Well, it's not performing," Godson said. "It's slow as hell, and Meyer, that's my VP, thinks it's the network causing the problem."

Dar turned her head and looked at the phone. "I see."

"Says he's got some people he can bring in to fix everything." Godson sounded a trifle abashed. "You know, consultants or what not. Friends of his, I guess."

"Uh huh."

"But I told him, before we go spending money on that, let's see what you can find out about it." The man cleared his throat. "After all, we've been doing business for a long time, right?"

"We have." Dar now turned her full attention to the phone, turning in her seat and leaning on her elbows, ignoring the screen. "I'm sorry you didn't come to me sooner, Stewart. I didn't know you were having an issue, much less that you considered it to be our fault."

"Now, Dar," Stewart said. "Let's not talk about fault huh? Maybe it's something simple, if you can look at it and see what it is?"

"Absolutely." Dar folded her hands. "I'll look at it right away and let you know."

"Great." Godson sounded relieved. "Looking forward to hearing from you, Dar. Thanks!"

He hung up and left Dar pondering her phone with a dour expression. Then she turned and minimized her mail, calling up her network monitoring program with a shake of her head.

A soft beep made her look up again to see Mark's file transfer completed, the box flashing for her attention.

"Yeah yeah." She shifted in her seat and resisted the urge to open her analyzer program, focusing on Godson's issue instead. "This better the hell not be a capacity problem I missed." Her hand flicked the mouse pointer impatiently. "If it is I'm gonna fire my ass."

KERRY WHISTLED UNDER her breath as she removed a last load of laundry from the washer and tossed it into the dryer. She set the machine and started it running, then took her basketful of already dried clothes and ambled back through the kitchen toward Dar's bedroom, closely followed by an attentive Chino.

She put the basket down on the edge of the waterbed and started sorting its contents out. "You know what, Chino?" she addressed their pet. "Don't tell anyone, but sometimes I actually like doing this stuff."

"Gruff?"

Kerry opened Dar's underwear drawer and began to store neatly folded pairs of underwear inside it. She'd gotten two of them inside when the phone rang, and she reached across the dresser to pick up the portable resting there. "Hello?"

"Hi, is this Ms. Stuart?" a man's voice asked. "This is Bob, from South Beach Lexus."

"Yup, it's me," Kerry agreed. "The buggy ready?"

"Not quite yet, ma'am, we really want to replace the brake pads. You've been kinda tough on 'em."

Kerry frowned at the phone. "I have?"

"Well, they're showing a lot of wear. We can let them go for a while but..."

"No, go ahead, by all means replace them," Kerry interrupted him. "I just didn't think I jammed them that much. Guess I'll have to pay more attention to how I'm driving, huh?"

The man cleared his throat. "Yeah, well, you know, a lot of people have the same problem...must be the traffic down here. Anyway, we'll get them changed, and my guy's gonna deliver the car to you round dinnertime, if that's okay."

"Great," Kerry answered readily. "Sounds perfect. Thanks!" She put the phone down and went back to her folding, inspecting each item for possible holes before she tucked it away. Most of Dar's briefs were plain, and somewhat ordinary, but she did have a selection of whimsical ones, most of which Kerry had purchased for her.

And of course, the red silk ones. Kerry smiled as she put those in the drawer, glancing at herself in the mirror as she finished. A hand lifted and riffled through her newly cut hair, and she gave the results an approving nod, pleased with her day so far.

The phone rang again, and she gave it a look of mild exasperation before she picked up the receiver and answered it. "Hello?"

"Hi," Dar's voice responded. "You're not answering your cell phone."

Kerry sucked in breath. "Oops...sorry. It's upstairs charging," she said. "And I'm downstairs playing with your undies. What's up?"

"Ahh...glad I finally learned my lesson and don't keep you on speaker," Dar chuckled. "Listen, I had to put the afternoon session on delay. Stewart Godson up in New York called, with a brand new project they just threw together. It's maxing their bandwidth out and I have to take a look at it."

"Is that our problem?" Kerry asked.

"Well, he's being told it's our problem," Dar sighed. "Somehow we managed to miss the capacity being pushed there. I've got someone checking the alerter system, but I think we just missed adding an alert for it."

"Ugh." Kerry grimaced. "You're not going to cause me a bottleneck up there, are you? I've got a lot of very touchy accounts up in those parts."

"Would I do that to you?" Dar's voice sounded bemused. "I may have to fly up there and meet with them, though, and I heard from Quest. He's pulling together a meeting of all the bidders at the Intercontinental on Wednesday."

Kerry nodded, even though her partner could not see her. "Well, you said I'd be spearheading that anyway," she remarked. "So forward the info on to me, boss, and I'll take care of it."

"Already done," Dar replied. "Looks like I'll be late. We're just going to start the sales meeting in an hour."

"I'll be waiting for you." There was a momentary silence, bringing a knowing smile to Kerry's face. "Give me a buzz before you leave, okay?"

"I will," Dar answered softly. "See you later."

Kerry put the phone down, her smile still lingering as she picked up her now empty basket and walked back through the living room, her mind busy with planning her strategy for Quest's meeting. A bright flash on the television broke her concentration, however, and she turned to look at the afternoon news blurb. "Oh." She paused, as they seemed to be continuing the news report from the previous night, now showing a picture of the man the police were looking for.

Kerry blinked, and then she simply stared at the picture, matching the somewhat blurry details with a memory from the previous day, from the car across from theirs, in the lazy afternoon sunlight of a summer day.

Was it the same jerk?

She squinted at the picture, which seemed to be from a passport. "Son of a bitch," she whispered. "I think it is."

"SO." THE LOW, powerful voice rolled out over the room. "As you can see, the capacity will remain relatively constant across the board, throughout the international and national grids, but our focus is going to be on refining the bandwidth usage and streamlining demand service."

A grid flashed onto the screen. "The net effect of that project will be for us to be able to add another fifty percent in capacity without increasing the hardware." Dar paused and leaned on the lectern. "Any further questions?"

She let her eyes sweep the room, suspecting the edge in her voice was suppressing the raised hands at last. "All right. Thank you, folks. That's all." Dar stepped back, acknowledging the applause in the room with a curt nod before she shut down the screens and retired the lectern, glad the damn thing was finally over.

Finally.

Dar dropped down into her seat at the head of the presentation table, it's cool leather closing around her as the noise level in the room rose. She picked up her glass of water and drained it, glad of the moisture for her dry, scratchy throat.

The crowd of sales directors was breaking up into clusters, all carrying printed hand-outs of her presentation as they discussed the session. Dar was happy to be left relatively alone, isolated at the front of the room with just enough space between her and the rest of them that even the few eyeing her hadn't gotten up the courage to approach.

Dar assumed a dour glare to reinforce the distance, exhausted from her two hour speech. It had gone over all right, she thought, but that, and the hour of questions after it had frazzled both her patience and her tolerance for occasionally stupid questions.

She did not want to entertain any more of them right now. Though the presentation room was an interior space and she could not see windows from where she was, she knew it was getting dark outside and the long day was nearing its end at last.

Time to go home. It had been a crappy day. On top of her discovering a fault in their monitoring system, the security reports were beginning to pile up on her desk like elephant crap. She was surprised Mark hadn't taken out a contract on her yet.

Jose finished his conversation with another sales director and headed her way. Dar fixed him with her glare, but the Sales VP ignored it and circled the table, taking a seat right next to her. "Good! It was very good, Dar."

"Thanks."

"We have too much people scared out there." Jose went on, resting his silver silk covered elbows on the table. "Everybody was running like chickens. Now, they see we have a plan."

"Uh huh." Dar rested her elbow on the chair arm and propped her head up on it. "We have a plan."

Jose looked at her. "What is wrong with you?"

Dar's eyebrows hiked.

"You are acting like you do not care," Jose said. "These people, what you say to them, that matters how they do their job, Dar."

"I know," she agreed. "I do care. It's just been a damn long day, Jose and I'm tired. It may be exciting to them, but to me, it's a rehash of the same damn speech I've already given the board, given the international board, and given the lot of you down here."

The Sales VP snorted. "You have no attention. It is like my son. He looks at one thing, and then..." Jose snapped his fingers. "It is the old news, and something else he goes to find. You are like that." He pointed at Dar. "Always, you have been like that."

Dar tried to get mad at him, but didn't find it in herself. She ended up shrugging instead. "Yeah. And?"

Jose also shrugged. "Nothing." he said. "I will tell you something however, Dar. Being married is good for you. I say so. My wife, she says so too. She told me she thinks you are not so much a bitch since then."

"Thanks," Dar drawled. "Your being married hasn't made you less of an asshole. How'd she figure that?"

Jose took a breath to answer, a red line creeping up his neck as he lifted his hand to shake a finger at Dar. "What did you say? I am being here so nice to you, and what is this?" His voice rose in outrage, attracting attention from the crowd still chatting around them in the room.

Dar snickered at him. "Miss the old days, Jose?" she inquired, a wry twinkle in her eyes.

"Puta," he growled, slapping his hand on the table. "There is the bitch I remember."

"Oh yeah." Dar leaned forward. "It's in there. It just takes a lot more now to get it to show." She got up and twitched her sleekly tailored jacket straight. "Gentlemen." She gave the now watching salesmen a gracious nod. "Ladies," she added, to the two women directors standing nearby. "Jose," she tacked on just for fun, as she stepped around the table and headed for the door. "Have a good night."

"Wait, Dar!" One of the women directors hustled to catch up to her, the other woman close behind. "Can we steal a moment of your time?"

Dar actually growled at them. "You had three hours of my time."

The women eased out of the conference room with her. "Just a few quick things...while you're walking?"

"Talk fast." Dar headed for the elevator. "Stacy, I've said all I wanted to say for the night in there." She hit the door button and headed into the car almost without a pause as her shoulders just barely cleared the opening. "It's been a long ass day."

The two women followed her hastily inside. "It isn't about the presentation," Stacy Allman said. "We wanted to talk to you about the ship contract." She glanced at the other woman. "Rhonda and I happened to be in the same bar as some old friends of yours, and we got an unintentional earful."

Dar leaned against the wall as the car rose to the fourteenth floor. "Everybody got a damned earful," she said. "I got nothing but the entire time I was up there." She studied the other two women, who could have been twins in their conservative suits and stylish haircuts.

Stacy waited for the doors to open before she answered. "Dar, let us take you out for a drink," she said, as they entered the quiet, half darkened floor. "You need to hear this, and the mausoleum's really not the place, if you catch my drift."

She caught it. Dar headed for her office, holding her outer door open before following the two saleswomen inside. She wasn't especially close friends of either, but they were both relatively old timers and she'd had a somewhat common bond with the few women who had made the climb up the ladder with and around her.

Both were savvy. Stacy was from New York, and Rhonda was from Los Angeles. Even though both women were straight as boards, neither had ever shown the veiled aversion to Dar's lifestyle she'd detected in others in the company. "I don't know, people. Like I said, it's been a long damn day."

"Cmon, Dar." Stacy followed her into her inner office, pausing to look around as Dar continued to her desk and started to pack up her briefcase. "Huh. This place looks a little different."

Dar's head lifted, and she looked around her office in mild confusion, expecting to find the carpet had been replaced in her absence or a different color wall weave installed. But the large space seemed much as she left it, so she glanced at Stacy to see what she was talking about. "What?"

"Listen, Dar, we won't keep you all night." Stacy dropped the subject and took a seat in front of Dar's desk instead. "But I really think you need to hear what we heard. How about the lounge in the Hyatt...give me a half hour, huh?"

Dar considered the question while her peripheral vision tracked Rhonda examining the collection of photos on her wall credenza shelves. "All right," she decided. "Go on. I'll meet you there in ten minutes."

"Cool." Stacy got up. "Ten minutes, in the bar. Good deal, Dar. I think once we finish up, you'll agree it wasn't a waste of either your time or ours."

Dar continued to stuff papers into her briefcase as the two left, only stopping when the door closed. She rested her knuckles on her desk and leaned her weight on them. Finally she grunted and straightened up, slapping one of the speed dial buttons on her phone almost without looking.

The phone only rang once before it was answered. "Hey, sweetie."

Dar's lips twitched. "You know, it could have been someone other than me calling from here," she commented wryly.

"Not on our home number." Kerry replied, a smile evident in her voice. "They'd have called on the cell."

Our home number. The words sent a little tickle down Dar's back even after all this time. "You're right. Shows how long a day it's been." Dar reached up and rubbed her left temple. "I'm done with the sales crap."

"How'd it go?"

"All right, I guess," her partner replied. "But two of the directors caught me afterward. Apparently they've got some BS they overheard from our friends. Want to spill it to me offsite."

Silence. Dar could almost imagine the look of skeptical surprise on Kerry's face. "Yeah, seemed pretty stupid to me, but I've known the two of them for ten years. They're not idiots."

"Sounds pretty bizarre."

"Anyway, I told them I'd meet them over at the Hyatt," Dar said. "Shouldn't take long. I'm sure we already heard most of it last week from the jackasses' mouths." She was aware of a pensive quiet from the phone. "You interested in joining us?"

Kerry chuckled, after a moment's hesitation. "I think you know me too well."

Dar smiled. "Hey, me and two straight women. What a party. Of course I'd invite you." She finished packing up her case. "Especially if you're in those cute overalls you were wearing the other day...that'd shock all the Cubans at the Hyatt happy hour."

Kerry chuckled again, but this time the sound was entirely different. "Oh, the scandals you weave, Madame Roberts. No, you go meet your undercover friends and get the dirt. I'll be here hanging out doing the domestic thing."

Dar's eyebrows lifted. "Domestic thing?"

"Baking cookies."

"Cookies?" Dar's ears perked up. "You're making fresh cookies?"

"The Food Network is dangerous," Kerry asserted. "But if you time it right, you might get some hot from the oven," she teased. "So don't get too dirty."

"They'll be lucky if I sit down," Dar said. "See you in a little bit, Ker."

"Okay—hey, listen. Remember that story from the news last night?" Kerry said. "The car at the drug store?"

"Yeah?" Dar's hand hovered over the button.

"We were there when they were. I saw the guy they're looking for. He was a creep."

It was the last thing she'd expected to hear. "Really?"

"Yeah," Kerry said. "But I'll tell you all about it when you get home. Go scoot and find your snitches."

"Okay. Yeah," Dar replied. "Strange timing, I guess. Be home soon." She released the line and shouldered her briefcase, turning off the desk lamp as she headed for the door.

MIDDLE OF THE summer on a Monday made for a very slow night at the bar. Dar gave the greeter at the door a nod as she entered, sweeping her eyes around the sparsely occupied lounge until she spotted her two colleagues near one of the floor-to-ceiling plate glass windows.

Stacy waved at her. Dar headed in that direction, only to be intercepted by a hovering and obviously bored waiter. She stopped as the man looked inquiringly at her.

"Can I get you something, ma'am? We have chocolate martinis on special tonight."

Much as the thought of a chocolate anything was intriguing to her at the moment, Dar shook her head. "Jamaican coffee, please." She indicated the small group of chairs near the window. "I'll be over there."

"Right away, ma'am."

Dar continued on her way and took one of the seats opposite Stacy and Rhonda. They both had glasses in front of them, with enough half eaten fruit matter to indicate their alcoholic content. "All right. So what's up?"

"Gee, Dar...it's great to see you too." Stacy gave her a wry grin. "Been a while."

Dar crossed her arms. "Half hour, didn't you say?" she asked pointedly. "I didn't come here to be social." She accepted the steaming mug the waiter handed her, and took a cautious sip. The coffee was hot, and pungent with a touch of rum and Tia Maria.

"No, you never really were the social butterfly," Stacy acknowledged. "Though we had some pretty good times back in the old days, out on the road."

"Eh." Dar tilted her head slightly. "I still remember you ending up doing the tango with the chef at that Italian place in New Mexico," she admitted. "They ever stop teasing you about it?"

Rhonda snickered.

"No." Stacy laughed. "They haven't. Trust you to remember that one, too. I think that was the first night I ever saw you drink something other than milk," she added. "Though tough as that damn account was, we were all due it. What a hemorrhoid case that was."

Ah, yes. Dar smiled faintly, and nodded. "Yeah, it was," she agreed.

"Dar, is that the first place you banged heads with that Shari woman? I remember her from that account. You fired her there, didn't you?" Rhonda asked. "That's why she was so familiar when she came into that bar. I remember her pitching a fit in the building as security was throwing her out."

"Yeah." Stacy nodded. "I didn't see her when she came in, but Rho did, and then when she and whatserface..."

"Michelle Graver," Dar supplied evenly.

"Yeah, from Vista, wasn't it?"

"Yeah."

Stacy slowly twirled her straw as she sucked on it. "They sat down, and it wasn't a minute until they were yelling at each other, and the first word I recognized was your name."

Dar grunted. "Yeah, well." She shrugged one shoulder. "Shari and I go a long way back," she said. "So it wasn't the first time we'd met. I had a decision to make and it could have gone either way, but she'd taken the piss out of me one time and I gave her the boot."

"I remember." Rhonda signaled the waiter, and indicated their near empty glasses. "Dar? You up for a second?"

Dar glanced at her cup, which was still half full. "I'm fine."

"So, anyway." Stacy retrieved a tortilla chip from the table and loaded it with salsa. "They didn't know us from Adam's housecat, naturally. They sat at the table behind us, and let me tell you, they lit into each other like nothing."

The waiter returned, putting down two fresh fruity looking drinks. "Anything else I can get you ladies? Some hors d'oeuvres, perhaps?" He picked up the basket of tortillas. "I'll get some fresh chips. Would you like to try one of our combo plates?"

"Sure." Rhonda shooed him away. "Thanks."

Dar slowly sipped her coffee, appreciating the slight burn as the alcohol hit her in the belly. For her, that night in New Mexico had been a great one. The sense of personal vindication had nearly made her giddy. She'd more than welcomed the chance to share a night out with her co-workers, though they'd never known just why their sullen, loner regional tech manager suddenly decided to be social.

She'd had fun. Gotten a little drunk, but not nearly as much as they had, and enjoyed the simple pleasure of sitting back and relaxing after a tough day of work. Even going back to her hotel room alone hadn't bothered her. She remembered spending time on the room's balcony looking out over the New Mexico desert, happy for a change.

Ah. Or she'd thought she'd been happy. Dar felt her cheeks move into a silent grin. Now she knew she'd only been satisfied because over the last couple of years she'd had a much closer acquaintance with happy. "So, they were fighting."

"Like weasels," Stacy agreed. "Graver was pissed off because of some plan of hers that'd gotten screwed up, and I swear, I thought she said she'd offered you a job."

"She did," Dar acknowledged. "Her damn company recruited Kerry and I, matter of fact."

Stacy gaped at her. "Really?"

"Had no clue who we were, but yeah," Dar chuckled. "We were in the show room night before it opened getting our gear set and they thought we were staff geeks."

Rhonda started laughing, covering her mouth hastily. "Oh, my god."

"Wasn't funny then, but I'm laughing now," Dar admitted. "And actually, Graver did offer both of us jobs later on, but I think we all knew that was just a piece of BS."

"That's what she said," Rhonda agreed. "Apparently it was all to keep you from getting involved with that cruise ship deal."

Dar's head cocked to one side. "Eh?"

Stacy nodded. "Yeah, exactly. That's what they were fighting about. Apparently the Shari woman screwed that up by telling someone something about Kerry...that she was after your job?"

Kerry wanted her...oh. "Ah." Dar took a sip of her coffee. "Yeah, actually, that did screw them up," she mused, in a surprised tone. "But why wouldn't Michelle want to get into a pissing match with us? Isn't their whole deal proving they can beat us at our own game?"

Rhonda and Stacy glanced at each other. "Well, that's what we thought too," Rhonda said. "It was pretty screwy. I sort of got the impression Graver was intimidated."

"As well she should be." Stacy lifted her glass in a toast in Dar's direction.

"Jesus." Stacy shook her head. "So anyway, Dar...to get to the point of why we dragged you out here, and didn't just share a cup of coffee in the lunchroom...the Shari woman said she'd gotten back some information on Kerry, and she told Graver they'd been going at everything the wrong way."

Just hearing Kerry's name from Shari's mouth triggered Dar's baser instincts. The evening stopped being amusing, and she leaned forward slightly, her voice dropping noticeably. "Yeah?"

Stacy paused, studying Dar for a moment. "I just realized I've never met our VP of Operations," she commented incongruously. "But I think I want to."

Dar simply waited, her coffee forgotten.

Rhonda leaned forward. "What Shari said was that she had some dope on Kerry, and she told Graver to leave the whole thing to her. She said if she could get to Kerry, then they didn't have anything to worry about on this ship contract."

"Dar?" Stacy uttered, into the quiet that fell. "Do you realize your eyes are actually really shooting off sparks? You're going to set the carpet on fire. Just take it easy, okay?"

With a great deal of effort, Dar forced herself to ease back into the chair. Her heartbeat was a thunder in her ears, and she could feel twitching in her forearms as though her hands wanted to clench into fists. She took a short breath, and released it. "Bitch," she enunciated precisely.

The waiter arrived with a plate of hot tidbits, which he put down, along with a fresh basket of chips. "Here you go, ladies." He turned to Dar. "Are you finished there, ma'am? Would you like another?"

Dar handed him her coffee cup. "Bring me a tall glass of milk, please."

The waiter blinked. "Milk?"

"Milk," Dar repeated. "Cold milk," she clarified, as he turned to go. After he left again, she turned back and steepled her fingers, peering at Stacy and Rhonda with half closed eyes.

"You're really pissed," Stacy murmured. "Wow. I forgot that temper."

"Family trait," Dar finally answered as her heart started to settle down. "But thanks for telling me. Not that I think they've got anything Kerry wouldn't laugh at, but it's good to know."

Rhonda took a mini-taco, and handed it over to Dar, along with a napkin. "That's why we really didn't want to say this in the office, Dar. It's...that woman's got a grudge against you and it's all personal. Even

Graver said so. She said she was obsessed."

Dar mechanically took the taco and examined it, before she took a bite, chewing without tasting it and swallowing it to get it out of her mouth. "Yeah." She took the glass of milk from the attentive waiter and downed a mouthful. "She's something."

"So you think she was BSing?" Stacy asked. "About Kerry?"

Dar waited for her guts to unclench. "Yes," she replied evenly. "Shari always believes she knows the angles on everything. Always has."

"Mm." Rhonda nodded. "Yeah, seemed like it to me. Big mouth, all air."

Stacy took a napkin and a potato puff. "Well, all I can say is I hope we wipe the floor with them. I'm really tired of their sales punks lording it over us every time we meet, telling us all about the latest contract they stole from us." She settled back in her seat. "Especially since they're targeting three of my big ones up for renewal. I'm getting a lot of pressure to cut our costs, Dar."

Dar peered into her milk. "I'm not going to play their game," she said. "I've already said that. No contract gets signed that loses us money. I don't care how many they think they can take."

"We don't have a lot of leverage," Rhonda said, hesitantly. "I mean, I know our service can't be beat, but..."

"But nothing," Dar cut her off quietly. "All it's going to take is one big screw-up they can't cover. So keep your shorts on, and don't panic."

Stacy exhaled. "Well, the trade show helped," she conceded. "I have to admit, Dar, there were six of us in the regional office watching Tech TV, and I hope your ears were burning because we were cheering you on like gangbusters. You go girl."

Dar relaxed a little and leaned back. After the first shock, her mind was now wrapping around and assimilating the information Stacy and Rhonda had given her, and with effort, separating it from the emotional charge.

"Hey, Dar?" Rhonda suddenly leaned forward.

"Yes?" Dar looked up and waited, finishing her milk.

"Sorry if we got you angry."

A half shrug moved the silk over Dar's shoulder. "S'allright."

Stacy swirled her drink in one hand. "You know you totally freaked out most of the sales force when that whole thing with you and Kerry came out. I remember we were at an incentive meeting, and everyone was just stunned."

Dar shrugged again. "Damn slow news day then."

"You have to admit it was a little fantastic," Rhonda offered. "But you know, once everyone got over the shock and worked with her most people were fine with it."

Had it been fantastic? Dar pondered that a moment. Eh. Maybe. "Good thing," she remarked. "Since they didn't really have a choice in the matter."

"What would you have done if Alastair hadn't been cool with it?" Stacy asked curiously.

"Left."

"Just like that?"

Dar snorted. "Yeah. Just like that," she replied. "Now if you ladies don't mind, I'm gonna go home and get out of this monkey suit." She set her glass down and stood up, towering over them in the low lighting. "Thanks for the warning."

"Sure you won't have another, Dar?" Stacy held up her glass. "For old time's sake?"

"No thanks." Dar lifted a hand and waved briefly. "Night."

Stacy watched her disappear, then lifted her glass. "There's a woman who has something she wants to go home to," she chuckled wryly. "Bless her heart."

Rhonda nodded. "Glad we told her," she summed up. "Telegenics won't stand a chance now, the little bastards. She'll take 'em out for sure."

"For sure." Stacy touched her glass to Rhonda's, and they both took a solemn drink. "You think there's anything in that story about Kerry wanting her job?"

Rhonda shrugged. "Wouldn't be the first time, but everyone I talk to says they're a match made in heaven."

"Except Jose. He thinks it was hell." Stacy winked, and they touched glasses again.

KERRY STUDIED HER nicely chilled cookie dough seriously. "What do you think, Chino?" she asked, leaning both hands on the marble counter. "Do you think your mommy would settle for just plain, ordinary cookies?"

"Gruff."

"Mm...no, I don't think so either." Kerry turned and went to one of the drawers, pulling it open and rummaging in it. "You know, I never, ever thought I'd use that old Christmas gift of Aunt Eenie's, Chino, I really didn't. I never saw myself wearing an apron, making batches of cookies for the kiddies."

"Gruff."

Kerry removed what she was looking for and took it back to the counter, opening a baggie and dumping out a pile of thin aluminum. "Hm." Her finger pushed aside several. "Christmas tree, no...Pumpkin...no...four leaf clover...no...ah." She selected one and held it up. "That's the ticket."

Going back to her dough, she positioned the cutter and pressed it down. "So, here I am, Chino...standing in the kitchen, in an apron, making heart shaped cookies." She reviewed her work, removing the heart and placing in on the already buttered baking pan. "And I'm loving every minute of it. What's up with that?"

"Gruff."

"What's up with that?" Kerry repeated, in a much softer voice. "I don't think it's my biological clock ticking, do you Chino?"

Chino whined and lay down, resting her chin on Kerry's foot.

"No, me either." Kerry chuckled. "You know what I think it is? I think I have so much love inside me for your mommy that its always looking for a way to come out. I guess this is one of the ways." She finished arranging her cookies and checked the oven, opening the door and sliding the tray inside. "You think your mommy knows that?"

Something in the look she'd seen in Dar's eyes that morning when they'd woken up together had bothered her. She almost thought she'd imagined it, but the more she thought about it, the more she knew she hadn't. It reminded her of the early days of their relationship when she'd sometimes catch a hint of what could almost be fear lurking in those pale baby blues.

She knew where it came from. Kerry's eyes narrowed a little, as she rolled a ball of cookie dough between her fingers. It had come from that number one whore bitch Shari, whom Kerry would dearly love to punch right in the nose.

"Oh yeah." She let out a half laugh. "That'd look great on Tech TV, Ker. You taking down a rival in a catfight in the middle of the convention floor." Kerry tossed the cookie dough ball at Chino's nose. The Labrador snapped it out of mid air and swallowed it, looking up hopefully for more. "Eh. Probably been the best ratings they'd had all year. No more, you little pig dog."

The dog sighed, warming Kerry's leg. With a smile, Kerry sat down on the floor next to her, and started petting her soft fur. She leaned back against the counter and savored a moment of quiet satisfaction, glad as well that her cramps had finally eased off and gone completely away.

Part of that was due to a new discovery of Dar's. Kerry laid her hand on her belly, feeling the residual heat from a small packet stuck to the outside of her underwear. It was like a portable heating pad, about four inches by two, right where the warmth could do the most good.

Just too cool. Kerry marveled. And it had lasted over twelve hours. "Technology's a fantastic thing, Chi. You hear all those people say how the good old days used to be? Not me. Give me the cutting edge any time." With a stifled yawn, she got up and wandered into the living room, going over to the sliding glass doors to peer out at the moon spattered sea.

Dar would be fine. Kerry leaned against the glass, watching her breath fog it slightly. She only needed a few extra reminders of how much their relationship meant to both of them, and how wrong Shari had been about everything she'd said to Dar years before.

Bitch. Kerry felt her own hands tense. "God, I hate her," she whispered, feeling the passion in the words. "She better stay home this time, Chino. Stay the hell in Orange County and away from Miami if she knows what's good for her."

"Grrr." Chino spotted something outside and let out a low growl.

"What is it, Chi?" Kerry shaded her eyes and looked, but all she could see was the moon reflecting off the sea, and a few palm fronds waving. "Or were you agreeing with me?" She lifted her head as the delicate scent of baking cookies wafted in from the kitchen. "Oo...you smell that, girl? Let's go see how they're doing."

Chino followed her into the kitchen, but two steps inside the dog stopped and turned, frisking back out into the living room.

Kerry just grinned and kept going, peeking inside the stove as she kept one ear cocked for sounds from the other room. She heard the canine yodel of greeting, and only narrowly prevented herself from repeating it. Then she figured what the heck, and did anyway, lifting her voice up in a weird counterpoint to Chino's. "AwwwrrrooooO!!!!!"

"What in the hell is that?" Dar answered, easing into the kitchen with a blond Labrador glued to her knee. "Is there a duck dying in here?" She'd taken her jacket off, and untucked her silk shirt, and now she sidled up behind Kerry and rested her chin on Kerry's shoulder, peering through the tinted glass of the oven.

"Quack." Kerry finished checking the cookie's progress. Then she turned around and faced Dar. Before her partner could step back, she lifted her hands up and gently caught her face, pulling it down to give her a nice, long, heartfelt kiss. "But I bet ducks don't do that."

"Not nearly as well as you do." Dar moved closer and slid her arms around Kerry. "Hi."

Kerry hugged her. "Hey, sweetie. Glad you're here." She felt Dar's chest move suddenly as she inhaled, and tightened her grip instinctively. "Eerrf. Chino and I were just talking about you."

Now Dar's body jerked again, for a different reason as a chuckle emerged. "Oh yeah? What'd she have to say about me?" She rested her forearms on Kerry's shoulders as they parted and looked at each other. "Was she complaining about my CD's again?"

"She was bitching that you were late, and she had to wait to get some cookies." Kerry let her hands rest casually on Dar's hips. "That didn't take long."

"I said a half hour." Dar glanced at the kitchen clock. "So what have you been up to, besides baking?" She reached up and ruffled Kerry's hair. "I like the snips." Her voice warmed with approval. "This looks really cute on you."

"Got my car done, got my hair done, got our laundry done, paid the bills..." Kerry ticked off her accomplishments. "Wrote you a poem," she finished, a trifle shyly, still unsure of her skills in that particular arena. "It's been a good day."

Poem? Dar felt a faint flush of surprised pleasure. Kerry had written some poems she'd shown her, one had even been about her. "What kind of poem?" She didn't recall any that had been written for her, however, and the thought intrigued her.

Distracted her, in fact, from the disturbing revelations in the bar.

Kerry produced a grin. "Well, let's get our cookies and milk, and you can come read it. Decide for yourself what kind of poem it is." She tugged open the oven door and slipped her hand into an oven mitt. She pulled the tray out and set it on wooden holders she'd put out on the counter earlier. "Mm."

Dar peered over her shoulder with deep interest. "Mm, is right." She sniffed delicately. "Are those hearts?"

Kerry nodded, gently easing them free of their baking sheet with a wafer thin spatula and putting them on a wire rack to cool. "Yep, they sure are." She felt Dar's warm breath on her ear and half turned, pressing her cheek against her partner's. "Just wanted to make sure you knew where those little chocolate chips came from."

"Kerry?"

"Mm?"

"It's too warm for it to be my birthday." Dar slid both arms around Kerry's body and simply held her, watching the cookies make their slow progress. "So why does it feel like it?"

Kerry carefully selected one of the smaller specimens and broke it in half, handing a chunk almost dripping with chocolate over her shoulder. "No reason." She took a careful bite, making an approving noise at the taste. "We should let these cool."

"Where's the fun in that?" Dar sucked in air to cool her stinging tongue. "You bring the rack, I'll get a jug of milk. Meet you on the couch."

Kerry was more than glad to oblige. She followed Dar into the living room, nearly tripping over a wildly tail-wagging Chino and settled onto the soft leather of the couch.

Dar dropped off the milk, but kept going toward the bedroom, unbuttoning her shirt as she ducked through the door. "I'm going to take off this damn suit and put on something more comfortable."

"Naked works," Kerry commented, grinning when she heard the dry chuckle from the next room. "I like that suit on you, by the way. I think it really looks good." She selected a channel idly, turning the sound down as Dar returned in a pair of cotton shorts and a tank top. "On second thought, I like that outfit better."

Dar eased onto the couch, laying down on her side and extending her long legs along the leather surface. "Glad you had a better day than I did," she said. "I'm gonna have to go up to New York tomorrow night. That damn project is turning out to be a bigger problem than I thought at first."

"Really?"

Dar sighed. "Yeah, I'm pretty sure it's not bandwidth," she said. "I told Stewart I saw some micro bursting, but the link's not really saturated."

"Least it's not us," Kerry reasoned. "Can you help them figure out what the problem is?"

"Probably," her partner said. "I'd go up there anyway, because their VP has a friend in the business, as they say, and is itching to bring them in to take care of it."

"Ah." Kerry frowned. "That wouldn't make good press if they did. Since you were pretty vocal about our service excellence." She gave Dar a wry look.

"Don't remind me." Dar covered her eyes. "I spent the day kicking my own ass for being such a jerk."

"Aw, honey." Kerry made a face.

"Kerry, I was. Do you know what Mark's having to deal with?" Her partner looked up at her through parted fingers. "That's all we need to have happen after what I said. We slip up, and it'll be all over the news."

Kerry grimaced.

"Not to mention I agreed to give an interview to CNN tomorrow." Dar sighed. "Let's hope I don't do something else stupid."

"C'mere." Kerry patted her thigh, smiling as Dar inched over and settled her head on the spot. "So, just overnight?" She riffled her fingers through the dark, soft hair now spilling over her bare leg. "To New York?"

"Yeah, I'll be back Wednesday, probably late." Dar looked up at her as they both silently acknowledged the change of subject.

Kerry picked up a cookie and broke it in half. "Okay, since I'll be downtown for that meeting, why don't I plan on picking you up at the airport then? We can do D and B's at the Dolphin for dinner."

"Mm." Dar made an agreeable noise, accepting her half of the cookie and taking a bite of it. "Listen. Stacy and Rhonda told me they overheard our two friends fighting in a bar after the trade show."

"They get pictures?"

"No." Dar rolled over and looked up at Kerry, watching the expression shift subtly on her face. "Ker, this wasn't a joke."

"I don't give a damn," Kerry said. "You know what I decided tonight? I decided they, and especially that bitch Shari, had better stay the hell out of my way on this bid."

Dar blinked at her.

"I'm serious. I've had it with them. If they start up with me at that meeting on Wednesday, you'll be coming home to post my bail that night. I swear, Dar. I'm not going to put up with any shit from them anymore."

Dar gazed steadily at her. "Shari thinks she's got something on you that'll make you cave in to them."

Kerry's eyebrows almost hit the popcorn ceiling. "On me?"

"Yeah."

"Me?" Kerry pointed a thumb at herself. "What in the hell do they think they can come up with on me that half the English speaking world hasn't seen for themselves on television or read in the Washington Post? That I'm gay? That I'm Republican? That I'm a budding hedonist? What?"

Dar shrugged. "I dunno, sweetheart. It didn't make a lick of sense to me when I heard it. I think she's just pissing lemonade." She watched Kerry's face, seeing nothing but honest, skeptical bewilderment there.

"My life's an open book." Kerry lifted her hands and let them fall. "What secret could I possibly be keeping? That I wash my hands with lavender soap?"

Dar lifted one of her partner's hands and sniffed it delicately. "Smells more like apple to me."

Kerry tweaked her nose. "I'm going to make some lemonade and shove the pits right up her..." She exhaled. "Oo...Dar, sending me to this meeting may not be a good idea," she said. "I could lose us the bid right up front if they tick me off."

"Don't sweat it, Ker. Just go, listen, and blow them off if they come near you." She took another cookie from the rack and split it, handing Kerry her share.

Kerry ate the cookie slowly. "Are you telling me to ignore them? Leave them alone?"

Dar nodded. "Don't let them get to you."

The pale blond brows contracted. "Paladar, do you find it a little ironic that you are saying that to me? After what we just went through with them? Are you going to take your own advice on that too?"

A shrug.

"I tell you what—I'll blow them off if you will. You stop letting what that whore bitch did to you chew you up inside, and I'll treat them like they were old buddies. Deal?" Kerry heard a sharper tone in her voice than she'd really intended, and saw the flicker in Dar's eyes before her partner looked briefly away. "Because I hate her so much on your behalf, it's the only way I could deal with it, Dar," she added, in a gentler tone.

Dar looked back up. "I don't want you hating people on my behalf."

"Tough."

A sigh. "Got milk?"

Kerry leaned over and gave her a chocolate tainted kiss instead. "Want to hear my poem?" she whispered. "Screw them."

Dar sighed again. She lifted one hand and let it drop in a gesture of resignation. "Poem me, and pass the milk. You're right. Screw 'em."

Kerry's face creased into a happy grin, as she reached over to the table for her writing pad. "You got it, partner. You got it." She leaned over near Dar's ear. "Know what she must have found out about me?"

"What?"

Kerry whispered something, and nearly ended up with cookies all over her chest as Dar convulsed with laughter. She chuckled evilly right along with her partner.

Chapter
Ten

DAR RESTED HER head on her fist, her eyes scanning the reports in front of her. She ran her index finger over the lists of IP addresses, then picked up a yellow highlighter and swiped it over one of them.

Her intercom buzzed. "Yeah?" Dar reached over and punched the acknowledge button. "What's up Maria?"

"Jefa, you have someone with cameras in the security desk downstairs," Maria said. "They have told them you are expecting them?"

Dar checked her watch. "They're early." She sighed. "Okay, have security escort them up to the presentation center. I'll meet them there."

"Si, I will do that," Maria said. "Also, I have your arrangements for your trip this evening, the confirmation is from your hotel, and I have asked for you to be picked up at the airport."'

Dar gazed at the phone. "Thanks, Maria." She smiled. "I appreciate that."

"Of course," her assistant said warmly. "I will arrange for security." She clicked off, leaving Dar to nibble at the inside of her lip for a quiet moment.

Then she pushed herself upright and slid the reports back into their folder, closing it and putting it away inside her top drawer. "Damn it." She leaned back in her chair. "I should really fire my ass for that stunt."

There was a thick pile of printouts in her inbox. She debated, then opened her lower drawer, and picked up the pile, tossing them into the larger space and closing it. Then she got up and went to the closet, removing her suit jacket and slipping into it.

She was straightening the sleeves when she heard the inner door to her office opening, and she turned as Kerry entered, a folder in her hand. "Hey. CNN's here. Want to come watch me make a fool of myself again?"

Kerry came over and took hold of her lapels, tugging them straight and brushing a bit of dust off her partner's shoulder. "Honey, you're never a fool," she disagreed. "But I'd love to watch you charm yet another reporter. Let's boogie."

Dar rested her arms on Kerry's shoulders and leaned forward and rested her forehead against the blond woman's. "We're barely keeping ahead of the attacks on the website. Mark's got a redirect in place, but you're going to have to keep an eye on it."

"Ugh."

"Sorry." Dar exhaled. "I wish I could stay and take care of my own crap, but Godson's high profile. All we need is for him to complain we can't handle his business."

"No problem, hon." Kerry tilted her head and kissed her partner. "I've got your back." She slid her arms around Dar and hugged her. "Wish I could go with you."

Dar silently wished the same thing. "Hey, it's only overnight." She returned the hug, and patted Kerry on the back. "C'mon. I don't want to give the reporters an excuse to try wandering around the building."

She led the way out of her office, giving Maria a brief wave as she passed her admin's desk and emerged into the hallway with Kerry at her heels.

They went to the elevator and rode down a few levels in silence, emerging on the floor that held the big public presentation center they typically used for press functions.

And birthday parties, Kerry recalled, as she opened the door for Dar and waited for her to enter. She'd gotten her promotion to vice president in this very room, and met Alastair there for the first time too.

Now it was full of strangers bearing equipment and cameras, clipboards and strange pieces of gear hung off of every part of them.

One of the women turned as they entered, and headed for Dar. "Ms. Roberts?" She held a hand out. "Christine Banks. I'm the tech news producer."

Dar accepted the offer and gripped the woman's hand, then released it. "Good afternoon," she said, briefly. "Glad you made it through the traffic."

"You aren't kidding," the woman agreed instantly. "Okay, if you'll give us about ten minutes to set up here, we can get started." She indicated a man standing quietly by. "This is our tech reporter, Nelson Argos. He'll be conducting the interview."

"Hello," Dar greeted the man, taking his outstretched hand. "Nice to meet you."

"Likewise," the man said.

Dar half turned. "This is our vice president of operations, Kerry Stuart." She indicated her quietly watching partner. "We'll grab a cup of coffee while you get set up. Feel free to help yourselves if you want."

The cameramen started to unpack their equipment. "Hoss, set up in that corner," Banks directed. "We can shoot back across this way and get the light." She indicated the late afternoon sun coming in the shutters across the western facing window.

Dar went over to the service bar and picked up a stoneware cup in company blue, keeping her back turned to the bustle in the room.

Kerry took a seat on one of the stools near the presentation platform, giving the news people a pleasant smile. The big room was multipurpose, sometimes rows of chairs were put in place, other times tables for executive training, and still other times it could be converted to a small conference center for high level briefings.

That's what it was this time. The floor space was cleared, and the raised presentation area had been set up with a podium and stools, the company logo prominent on the curved wall behind it, lit with unobtrusive built-in lighting.

It was staid, conservative, and expensive with teak wood inlays and high end audiovisual equipment, including the new video conferencing system Kerry had overseen install of a few weeks earlier.

"So." The reporter wandered her way as the rest of the team fiddled with tripods and cameras and lights. "I saw the tape of your presentation at the conference the other day. Nice job."

"Thanks," Kerry responded. "I was glad to have the opportunity to tell our story there."

"Seems like there was more excitement there than anyone expected." The reporter took the stool next to her. "Caught us a little by surprise."

Kerry smiled pleasantly at him. "Technology's like that." She sensed Dar's presence and she turned, to find a steaming cup being held out. "Ah. Thanks." She sniffed the rich scent of cherries and took a sip of the herbal tea.

Dar settled on a third stool and took a sip of her coffee. "Is it true you folks didn't want to attend this year because we bore the hell out of you?"

Argos rubbed his nose, looking a bit abashed. He was medium height, with thick, curly brown hair and freckles. "Well, I wouldn't put it that way," he said. "We just had other things on our plate."

Dar gave him a darkly amused look.

"But you know, I'm not sure your stockholders would have appreciated it if we had been," the reporter said. "A lot more people would have seen that bit about you hiring hackers."

Dar shrugged. "Tempest in a teacup," she said. "No one admits it, but everyone who hires top rank techs knows there's a good chance they've walked both sides at one time or another."

"If no one admits it, why do you?" Argos asked.

"Hey, wait for the camera." Christine protested. "C'mon, people!"

Dar took another sip of her coffee. "I thought you were going to grill me about how I'm panicking about our overwhelming new adversaries, Telegenics," she drawled. "I think hackers are more interesting."

Argos grinned briefly. "Keep talking. I want to see Christine implode."

"People." Christine sighed. "Charles, are you ready?"

"Almost," the cameraman called over.

Dar relaxed a little, lapsing into silence as she drank her coffee, waiting for the set up to be complete.

Kerry felt her phone buzz. She got up and set her cup down, going over to the window before she answered it. "Kerry Stuart."

"Oh, Kerry. Good. It's Eleanor. Listen, we have a problem."

Kerry glanced over her shoulder. "Hang on." She put the phone on hold. "Be right back." She signaled Dar, and eased past the camera crew to duck out the door and move far enough down the hall to find a quiet spot. "Okay, go ahead. Sorry. I was in the presentation center."

"Okay." Christine finished her arranging, and stepped back. "We're ready. Right?"

"Ready," Nelson agreed. He took a seat on the stool next to Dar's, tugging his jacket straight and setting his notes down on his knee out of the camera shot. "You ready, Ms. Roberts?"

"Sure." Dar let her hands rest on her thigh, trying to relax as much as she could under the circumstances.

She wished Kerry would come back.

"Right, let's go," Christine said, briskly. "Nelson, you're on."

The light on the camera lit, and Dar took a breath, letting it out slowly as she felt the tension build in her guts.

Argos cleared his throat. "I'm here today with Dar Roberts, Chief Information Officer for ILS, a Fortune 100 company that provides technology services. Ms. Roberts, thank you for taking some time out to meet with us."

"Anytime," Dar responded amiably.

"One of the big stories at the recent technology conference in Orlando was the budding rivalry between your company and a small startup company..."

"Stop." Dar lifted her hand.

Argos paused, a little startled. "Excuse me?"

"Stop. That's not true," Dar said. "That wasn't a big story there. No one, in fact, even asked me anything about it."

Argos blinked.

"The big stories at the conference were a debate on security and the release of news about some brand new technology involving heuristic advances in networking hardware," Dar continued. "I don't mind talking about whatever you have a mind to talk about, but don't make things up."

Christine's jaw dropped.

Argos was caught very off guard. "I'm sorry, Ms. Roberts," he said. "I was given some information about what happened at that convention, maybe there was a misunderstanding."

"There wasn't any misunderstanding," Dar smiled briefly. "You were pitched a load of BS to get my competitors some good publicity. You should have done your homework."

Argos blinked again. Then he looked off set over at Christine in appeal.

"So." Dar shifted a little. "Want to talk about the conference, or do you want to go through your scripted bit of drama? Your choice."

Argos took a moment to gather his wits. "All right, fair enough." He closed his notepad. "Let's talk about competition, then. From your attitude, I get the impression you don't really think you have any."

Dar nodded. "That's a better question," she said. "Of course we do. We have large competitors like ourselves, and smaller ones like your friends at Telegenics. They're all a concern. No one likes to lose business, least of all me."

"So, does Telegenics have your number? They've taken twenty percent of your renewals this quarter. How much does that count?" Argos went hardball, his expression serious.

"Everyone has our number," his subject answered. "We've been doing this for decades. There isn't a company out there that hasn't studied our methods and found a way to pitch against us. We're not for everyone."

"Something is making your customers turn against you," Argos said. "The contention is that you come with too much overhead. Like this place." He indicated the presentation room. "In this economy, people don't want expensive frills."

Dar cocked her head and glanced around. "I like to think of the difference being between full service and self service," she remarked. "Yes, you can get what we do done with barebones and slim margins."

"And?"

"That doesn't pay for performance and innovation," Dar responded. "I also heard someone say because we're so big, we can't respond as quickly as a smaller company. That's nonsense."

"Really?"

"Think about it," Dar said. "Let's say you're a client, and you suddenly become very successful. You need to open four more branch offices, immediately, to take advantage of your growth cycle."

"Okay," Argo said, in a doubtful tone.

"So who do you think is going to be able to respond faster, giving you connectivity and services? A small company that has to go out and provide them from scratch, or a big company, like us, that can simply make a phone call because we already have built-out infrastructure and services in reserve?"

"But that's an expensive insurance policy."

Dar's eyes twinkled, just a little. "You get what you pay for," she said. "So in answer to your original question — yes. Customers leaving us concerns me. It's something we studied very closely as it was happening, and it was debated around here pretty strongly. But the bottom line is, I wasn't willing to compromise our integrity and reputation in order to retain a handful of services accounts."

"So you're saying their model does work."

"I'm saying in the long run, ours works better. Eventually customers understand their business is worth investing in," Dar countered. "We invest in our service, and in being able to help our clients succeed."

The outer door opened, and Kerry slipped back in, pausing to stand against the back wall. She gave Dar a thumbs up at her last statement.

"Fair enough, Ms. Roberts." Argos let her get the last word in on the subject. "I'm sure we'll all be watching to see what happens next. Perhaps I can revisit this question with you in a few months."

"Anytime," Dar agreed. She wasn't entirely happy with the interview, but wasn't entirely unhappy with it either. She was content to let it end on a somewhat positive note.

"Cut." Catherine waved her hand. "Well." She scratched her head. "I'm not sure where we went with this."

"You're a tough interview." Nelson relaxed back on his stool. "But you're right on one thing, I should have done my homework better." He removed his mic and coiled it up. "I won't make that mistake with you again."

Kerry made her way around all the equipment and ended up at Dar's side. "Sorry I missed it." She rested her hand on Dar's back. "Are you all heading for the airport or staying overnight? I heard there was a big accident on the highway heading to MIA so I thought I'd warn you either way."

"We lucked out," Argos said. "We're staying overnight in South Beach." He got up and handed his gear to a waiting technician. "We weren't sure how long this would take."

"Well, I didn't get so lucky." Dar stood up. "I have a plane to catch, as a matter of fact. So if you folks are done with me, I need to get ready to leave."

"I think we're done, yes." Christine said, with a wry look. "We have some other background things to track down, but I think you covered what we asked." She glanced at Kerry. "Are you up for a go, Ms. Stuart?"

Kerry smiled briefly. "Wish I could, but I have a meeting I can't get out of in about five minutes." She gently nudged Dar toward the door. "My admin will be in here shortly. If you need anything at all, please don't hesitate to ask her."

"Okay, thanks." Christine gave them a brief wave. "We appreciate it."

Dar was glad to hear the door close behind them. "Meeting?" She eyed her partner.

"Yes. I'm meeting you so I can take you to the airport and get you some dinner before you take off." Kerry tucked her hand inside Dar's elbow. "You tell me what I missed, and I'll tell you about the latest disaster."

"Ah."

KERRY SLUNG HER sweat-dampened towel around her neck, and inched her way out of the slim boxing gloves encasing her hands. She was still breathing a little hard from the end of her sparring lesson, and she shook her head with a tiny jerk to clear a few droplets of perspiration out of her eyes.

"Nice moves, Ker." Her sparring partner Rod gave her a light clout on the shoulder as he moved past. "Glad you're back."

'Thanks." Kerry grinned at him. "That was fun."

"Eh." The woman at the locker next to hers gave her a wry look, examining a large purple bruise across the back of one hand. "Mostly fun. How are you, Kerry? We missed you and the Taz last week."

The Taz. Kerry wrinkled her nose at the nickname her partner had picked up from their kickboxing classmates. "We were in Orlando," she explained. "Now, Dar's in New York. She was sorry she was going to miss tonight too. She likes it."

"Well, we like it when you're here to occupy her." The woman grinned at Kerry. "Vacation?"

"Nah. A convention." Kerry stripped off her other glove and tossed it into her gear locker. Her head protector followed it, and the leather belt that protected her mid-section. "Phew...it's hot in here today." She wiped her face off with a corner of her towel, and then grabbed her clothing bag. "I'm going to go shower off. I feel grungier than an old dishrag."

"Hey." Rod poked his head around the door of her locker. "We're doing beer and wings across the street. You up for it?"

Kerry only hesitated an instant before she nodded. "Sure. Cold beer sounds really good right now," she agreed. "See you over there? You too, Sal?"

"Right on," the woman responded readily. "Tom's got his new bike, and he's dying to show it off. But I'm with Kerry — shower first."

"So you can sit in the bar and sweat?" Rod laughed. "You girls are so...so..."

"Girly?" Kerry supplied, with a grin. "If that means we feel good and don't stink, thanks!" She flicked him with her towel and headed for the women's shower room with Sally at her heels. This class was full of new people, and she and Dar had made friends with quite a few of them.

Kerry liked them. They were a mixture of professionals and working class, mostly laid back, with a diverse range of interests including diving and bikes, two of her own current fascinations. The women were into fitness, but not aerobics, and the guys were more relaxed and laid back than the martial artists that tended to populate the more traditional classes.

Cool group. They accepted her and Dar with amiable good nature even after their relationship had become evident and most of them held a healthy respect for Dar's fighting skills. "Ugh." Kerry stripped out of her baggy pants and T-shirt, then stepped under the shower with a feeling of relief.

The water was delightfully lukewarm, and she let it course over her for a minute before she squeezed out a handful of soap from the wall dispenser and scrubbed her skin with it. "So what did we miss last week?" she asked Sally, who had joined her in the next shower cubicle. The spaces were separated by half walls, to give a modicum of privacy.

"John just went over high kicks again," Sally responded. "He was in a bad mood. I think he lost big in that tourney he entered last weekend. You know how he gets."

"Ah." Kerry lathered her hair quickly and rinsed it, feeling one hundred percent better already. Her muscles were a little sore, and she was a little tired from the session, but she'd completed the rounds without taking any hard blows, and was pretty satisfied with herself all in all. "Yeah, he's a little touchy about that, I know. Especially when his buddies show up here to watch the class."

"Uh huh," Sally said. "Rod thinks he picks the wimpiest student he has to spar with when they're here. You notice he *never* picks Taz."

Kerry chuckled wryly. "Well, Dar's not exactly a novice, and he knows it," she explained, rinsing off one last time and grabbing her towel. "She teaches a class at our other gym near work. We're just on break from that right now, and she wanted to learn something new."

"Yeah, me too," Sally admitted frankly, as she joined Kerry in dressing. "I got really tired of spinning. You ever try that?"

"Nuh huh." Kerry pulled on her shorts and buttoned them, then donned a clean T-shirt from her bag. "The idea of riding and riding and riding and getting nowhere just isn't my style." She ran her brush through her hair, settling her newly cut locks into place. "I mean...we run every morning. We could get a treadmill and do it in the condo, in the nice air conditioning, but we don't."

Sally followed her out of the locker room and across the somewhat worn lobby of the boxing club where they had their class. "I kinda see what you mean, but sometimes it's a lot safer to run on the treadmill in here, than on the streets, y'know?"

That was true, Kerry admitted, as they left the club and headed across the street to the small pub already leaking faint sounds of music into the humid air. It wasn't something she and Dar had to worry about, and sometimes she did tend to forget not everyone lived on a private island where that kind of crime just didn't exist.

Rod and three others from the class joined them as they approached, already having claimed a table outside under the ficus tree. The doors to the pub were wide open, as were the windows. The place hadn't had air conditioning any time Kerry had ever been by there.

Outside was cooler, even in the dead of summer. She sat down in one of the worn, wooden chairs and leaned back as the group settled in under the string of tacky colored globe lights hanging from the tree. The place smelled of the distinctive scent of vegetation, of fried food and spices. Kerry considered it just about the most perfect neighborhood dive she'd ever seen. There was even a very worn dartboard nailed to the ficus, and for a quarter you could get three cracked darts to throw at it.

"Hey, honey!" Their regular waitress scooted over on spotting them, stopping in front of Kerry. "Usual?"

Kerry nodded, and stretched her legs out as the rest of the group made their orders. It had just turned dark, and there was just enough breeze to keep the night from being uncomfortable. The waitress had left a moment before the rumbling pop of a motorcycle engine interrupted the night, its roar growing louder as it came closer. "Ah...guess that's Tom."

"You guessed it," Rod agreed, hitching his knee up and slinging one long leg over the chair arm. He was tall and lanky, dark haired and relatively good-looking in an understated kind of way. "Big ol Harley, and damn he wants everyone to know about it."

Kerry snorted and shook her head.

The rider and bike arrived then, the noise precluding any further conversation until Tom turned the engine off and parked the big cycle, displaying it to various noises of appreciation. "Nice, huh?"

"Prettier than you are," Rod called out with a chortle. "Sure you can handle something that rad?"

"Kiss my ass, butthead," Tom replied with a grin. "If you're nice, I might let you touch it." He half turned and glanced back at Kerry. "Whatcha think, Kerry? Sweet, huh?" He indicated the bike, which was a monster in black and chrome with a custom painted gas tank covered in incongruous tropical fish.

"Very," Kerry agreed readily. "I like the soft tail. You didn't opt for a VRSC?"

Tom walked over and sat down next to her, clasping his hands together. "Oh...I think I'm in love with you. A girl who speaks my language." He grinned at her. "You have one?"

"Not quite." Kerry accepted her mug of ice-cold draft beer and sipped it. "We were going for one. Went into the show room, and the guy there told Dar she'd have to buy what he was willing to sell her." She licked her lips and sighed. "One 'kiss my ass' later, we headed over to the Honda dealership and the rest is history. I like my Shadow, though. It fits me."

The group laughed. Tom groaned, and slapped his head. "Kerry...Kerry...Kerry...how could you?" He moaned. "Why didn't you try a different dealership? I got mine in Daytona during bike week. It was like a religious experience."

Kerry took a lazy swallow of her amber colored beer and shrugged one shoulder. "We use it down by the cabin in the keys. If we kept a Harley in the shed, we'd spend half our time writing police reports on it. So, it worked out for us. Maybe my next one'll be a hog."

Tom waggled his eyebrows at her. "Wanna go for a ride after we eat?"

"Sure," Kerry agreed. "As long as you don't have chili again."

The gang laughed again, and Rod threw a corn chip at his buddy. "She gotcha."

"Damn it, I like chili!" Tom whined. "Okay, here, at least get a picture of me with a good looking girl on my bike. I gotta have something to show the guys." He gave Kerry a pleading look. "You mind?"

With a chuckle, Kerry set her beer down and got up, following Tom over to the slick machine and admiring its lines as she hopped up and gingerly settled herself on the back part of the seat. "Hm."

Tom got on in front of her, and did a muscle dude pose, flexing his bicep for Kerry's admiration. Obligingly, she leaned against him and pointed at the muscle, raising her eyebrows for the camera. "Psst," she whispered. "I think Dar's are sexier."

Tom gave her a look over his shoulder. He was blond and football player style buff, and had a crew cut that was almost fifties in its rigor. "Gee, thanks Ker," he muttered. "You really know how to make a guy feel great."

Kerry chuckled, and slid off the bike now that the flashes had stopped. She headed for the table, sidestepping the outstretched feet and reclaiming her chair with a sigh.

"Okay, okay." Tom finally joined them, after he carefully made sure his new bike wasn't going to fall over onto the sidewalk. "This round's on me, since I don't have to start paying on this thing for three months."

Whistles all round greeted his speech.

Kerry relaxed, looking forward to her cheeseburger with a sense of decadent pleasure. She felt sort of bad for Dar stuck in her hotel up in New York, but she was glad to get the chance to decompress after work.

She let her eyes wander as the group chattered about Tom's new bike. The conversation ranged from the latest disaster film premier to the latest storm brewing in the tropic. "So what did you say you're doing tomorrow, Sal?"

"Canoeing." Sally looked quite satisfied. "We're going out to Uleta Park, up in North Dade. You can canoe around there for hours in those waterways. Then we're doing a barbeque at the park. Interested?"

"Mm...wish I could but I have to work tomorrow," Kerry mourned. "That sounds like a blast."

"Call in sick," Sally suggested.

"Can't," Kerry said. "Dar's out of town and I cover for her. But thanks for the invite. Maybe next time? I bet Dar'd like that too."

"You bet," Sally said. "We have a sort of adventurer's club around my complex. We do a lot of stuff like that, hikes in the Everglades, and sailing and all, you guys should hook up with us. There's an online calendar."

"Send it over," Kerry said immediately. "We're looking for

something like that to get involved with, Sal. Thanks!"

Sally looked pleased. "You got it. You guys are fun. I think you'd get along with the rest of my crowd." She sat back. "Cool beans."

Kerry agreed. That would make Dar happy, and that made her happy. The night was looking up so far.

"Here's to my bike!" Tom said, raising his glass and extending it. "And to a bunch of good buddies!" He clinked his mug to theirs. "Just sorry Taz isn't here to see it."

Kerry tilted her mug toward him. "I'll drink to that sentiment. Me too."

Everyone laughed. The waitress returned and set their plates down, waving a finger at the beer steins and raising her eyebrows.

"You bet." Kerry handed hers over. "Let's get this party started."

"LET ME WALK you down to your car, Kerry." Rod hitched his jeans up and followed her away from the dive. "It's kinda late."

"Sure," Kerry amiably agreed, feeling a touch lightheaded.

They started down the sidewalk, and then cut over one street moving closer to the beach. There was a light stream of traffic on the roads, cars rolling along with stereos blaring and people in typically abbreviated clothing.

Kerry stifled a yawn with one hand and gazed casually into the storefronts as they passed. "Good grief. Do people actually buy that clothing?" She pointed at a shirt, which was mostly glitter and spandex.

"Beats me." Rod shook his head. "Especially since that's supposed to be a men's store." He peered at the sequined boots. "Wow."

"Wow," Kerry agreed. "I can't imagine a woman wearing those."

There was a cool breeze coming off the ocean, and Kerry gratefully turned her face into it, reaching back to ruffle her shortened hair and let the air get to her damp neck. It wasn't really that late, a little past nine, and privately she didn't want to rush back to their condo that was sadly lacking Dar's presence.

No offense to Chino, of course.

"Did you park in the public lot?" Rod asked.

"Yeah." Kerry nodded, her eyes drawn to a lurid neon sign. She slowed as they came even with the tattoo shop, looking at the art in the windows and the dimly seen figures inside. "That's some nice art."

"Hell yeah," Rod agreed, stopping to look. "You have any?"

"No." Kerry shook her head with some regret. "In my family, that wasn't something you did if you didn't want to be locked in the attic for twenty years."

"I thought you lived with Dar." Rod pressed his fingertips against the glass. "A good friend of mine works here. He's an artist."

"I do live with Dar." Kerry found her eyes drawn to the designs, some basic and explicit, others fantastic forays into strange art.

"She has a problem with tats? I didn't figure she did. She's pretty cool."

"No, not that family. My birth family." Kerry peered at one of the designs. "Is any of this your friend's work?"

"That stuff." Rod pointed at a phoenix erupting from a bed of flames, and a beautiful Chinese dragon. "That's his." He eyed Kerry. "You want one."

Kerry's lips twitched. "I've thought about it," she admitted.

Rod glanced at the door. "Let's go inside and talk to my friend. At least he can give you an idea of what it costs, and stuff like that. Maybe if you have a design in mind, he can draw it up and show you what it would look like."

It sounded pretty harmless. "Okay." Kerry followed him inside, aware immediately of several things.

One, it smelled clean inside. There was a distinct scent of cleanser in the air along with an almost jarring buzzing noise coming from one of the three dentist style chairs against one mirrored wall.

"Hey dude." The man behind the desk greeted Rod. "You're moving up in the world."

Rod blushed. "Ah...uh, no, uh...this is just a friend of mine. Her name's Kerry. She's in my kickboxing class."

"Uh huh." The man regarded Kerry. "Looking for some art, Kerry?"

Kerry bravely approached the desk, putting her hands on it and giving him a faint smile. "Well, I was thinking about it," she said. "I wanted something sort of personal."

"You mean you don't want a flaming skull with born to die on your bicep?" The artist grinned at her. "Damn."

"Not exactly." Kerry felt her mouth go a little dry. "Let me tell you what I had in mind, and maybe you can suggest something."

The man smiled broadly. "Now that's what I like to hear." He pulled a stool up behind him, and motioned for her to sit down. "Rod, go get a coke." He eyed his friend. "And get one for the lady."

Rod gave him a long-suffering grin. "You want a soda, Kerry?"

"See if they have a milkshake." Kerry felt a nervous clenching in her guts. "I have a feeling I might need it."

He patted her on the shoulder. "You got it. Be right back."

KERRY STUDIED THE piece of paper in front of her, her heart beating a little fast. She was aware of shakiness in her belly, and the air conditioning of the shop seemed a little too cold at the moment.

"Do you like it?"

She traced the outlines of the design with her eyes, all smooth and sinuous. "I do like it. Very much." She looked up at the artist. "I'm just trying to psych myself into doing it."

The artist sat down next to her. They were on the other side of the shop, in a small, almost cozy seating pit with a comfortable couch and two plush chairs. "You know, I hear that a lot."

Kerry laughed faintly. "I'm sure you do," she murmured.

"Take your time," the artist said. "But if you really want to do this don't go home and think it over. You won't do it."

He was right. She could feel it in her heart. If she walked out now, she wouldn't come back. This was one of those 'in the moment' things Dar was always talking to her about.

Did she want to do this, though? Kerry ran her fingertip over the design. She'd been thinking of getting a tattoo for a few months, spurred on maybe by the body art she saw in the gym.

Maybe driven by the need she still had to rebel against her family. The thought of her family's faces if she told them made her lips twitch into a fierce grin. This was something different than everything she shared with Dar, too.

This was just her.

"It is forever," the artist said. "Well, unless you're stupidly rich and love pain. The laser hurts more than the tat itself does. So if the design there isn't something you want on your skin for a long time, give it a pass."

Kerry looked up at him, studying his interesting, angular face. She handed back the piece of paper, and managed a shaky grin. "I want it," she said. "Let's do it."

He didn't seem surprised. He got up and patted her shoulder. "Okay, you sit here and finish your shake, while I get this ready and set my station up." He hesitated. "Did you want to hear the price first?"

"No." Kerry shook her head. "It doesn't matter."

He nodded. "Want to know if it's going to hurt?"

Kerry gave him a wry look. "I assumed it would," she said. "I nick myself shaving and it hurts. Can you stick needles into your body and have it not hurt?"

"It'll hurt," he confirmed. "Especially where you're getting it. But if you get to where you can't take it, just kick me in the kneecap and I'll give you a break. Fair?"

"Fair." Kerry knotted her hands together and took a deep breath as he moved away. "Whooof," she muttered. "Here we go."

DAR TRUDGED INTO her hotel room, tossing her jacket over the nearby chair and kicking out of her formal shoes even before she had the door properly closed. "Know what?" she addressed the empty room. "I'm about ready to go work someplace I can wear jeans every damn day."

She was tired, and aggravated, and here she was near midnight after a very long, stressful day. "Stupid sons of bitches," she cursed, giving her room a glare. "I come all the way up here and the entire pack of jackasses don't have the start of their act together. Pain in my ass, and a waste of my time."

Their client's team had fallen apart trying to answer her questions. Everything she asked was either deferred to their VP Ops who was out of town, or met with an anxious, wide-eyed stare of incomprehension.

Their CIO had been pretty much mortified, and offered to take Dar out to dinner to make up for the chaos. He'd turned out to be a vegetarian.

Dar had forced him into a steakhouse, sending a brief mental apology to her mother as she ordered hers rare and spent a desultory couple of hours making polite conversation about nothing significant at all while a pounding ache in her head slowly grew into what she suspected was the beginning of a migraine.

Aggravated wasn't the word for what she was. Disgusted, hurting, sick to her stomach, and just hellfire damned annoyed didn't even come close either.

With a sigh she started unbuttoning the sleeves on her shirt, slowing as she spotted a basket on top of a small table in the reasonably elegant room. She didn't remember it being there earlier when she'd thrown her luggage into the room before heading for the client, but then the bottle of champagne resting with distinguished chilliness nearby hadn't been either. "Hm. What have we here?"

She glanced at the tag on the champagne. "Forget it, Stewie. You'll be lucky if I leave you an extra set of tin cans tomorrow." Her lip curled slightly at the sight of her erstwhile dining companion's name. "You can keep your damn fake French bubbly."

She tossed the card on to the table and watched it slide off the polished surface and waft toward the carpet with a supremely disinterested shrug.

Now, the basket. Gift from the management? Dar circled the table and cautiously investigated the unexpected offering. The basket was a nice wicker one with a lid. She opened the top and peered inside, a smile appearing on her face when the first thing she saw was a packet of good hot chocolate. "So." She sat down and upturned the basket, spilling out its contents.

Brownies. Cookies. The hot chocolate. Truffles. Dar poked her finger among them and stopped at the last item — a frilly little gauze bag filled with Hersey's kisses. She picked it up and cupped it in her hand, gazing at the silver wrapped treats with eyes that suddenly, unexpectedly, stung.

There was a card attached to the wicker. Dar opened it, already knowing what she'd find inside.

> *Hope you're looking at this as you finish up business early and*
> *are watching the sun set over Manhattan. But I bet you ain't.*
> *Love, Kerry*

"Bet you're right," Dar answered in a husky voice. "Wish to hell you were in that basket."

The quiet of the room settled around her as she sat there, her head resting on one hand and a bag of kisses cradled in the other. Finally she sighed and straightened up, opening the net and retrieving one of the candies. "C'mon, Dar. Get a grip. She can use a vacation from you with all this insecurity crap you've been pulling the last week." With a morose look, she popped a kiss into her mouth and chewed it.

Here, alone in her hotel room, she could lean back and be as depressed as she wanted to.

Her eyes shifted to the table.

But it was hard to do that, when she was practically up to her earlobes in thoughtful presents from her beloved partner whose warm smile seemed to reflect off the packaging scattered over the surface in front of her.

Even if it was midnight, and she had a migraine.

Dar pulled the other chair over and put her feet up on it, leaning back as she consumed more of the kisses. Lacking milk, she reached over and snagged the bottle of champagne, untwisting its top and popping the cork in a smooth motion. She poured herself a glass and took a sip, letting her head rest against the back of the chair as she thought about Kerry.

Slowly, the tension eased from her shoulders. She knew Kerry was trying her hardest to be supportive, she only had to unfold the piece of paper in her wallet and reread yesterday's poem to see that. Chocolate chip cookies, her stuff all taken care of...this...Dar exhaled, acknowledging the deep emotion in her guts the thought triggered.

Kerry cared so much about her. It was almost like she could feel her partner's presence, and if she closed her eyes, she could almost sense a pair of ghostly hands on her shoulders and the faint brush of Kerry's lips on the top of her head.

Tears came again, and Dar rested her head on her hand, letting her fingers slide forward to cover her eyes. "God damn it," she cursed at herself softly. "Would you fucking snap out of this already?"

It was ludicrous. It was frustrating. Dar wanted to slap herself for feeling the way she did, for what she considered such a stupid reason.

For no reason, really. So what if she'd had to tangle with Shari? She'd gotten exactly what she wanted from the trade show, and they'd won, damn it! So what the hell was wrong with her?

I need to kick myself in the ass.

Disgusted, she shoved herself to her feet and went to her window, brushing aside the curtains to lean against the glass and stare out at the city. Behind the thick glass, the sounds were muted, and the garish lights and looming buildings seemed alien beyond their usual to her.

She'd never liked New York. The city seemed big, impersonal, nasty and dirty to her, without any of the exciting energy and pulse she'd heard its residents boast of. The streets were narrow, the buildings were overbearing and in some places dirty, and in the heat of the summer, the place stunk to high heaven.

Exciting? Dar had driven past the financial district earlier, as the cabby proudly pointed out Wall Street to her. Peering down the rows of buildings, it had appeared like nothing more than a huge, impersonal canyon about as picturesque as a bunch of shoeboxes set on end.

The change of subject was helping. Dar took several deep breaths, reassured by the order that seemed to be returning to her thoughts.

She spotted a man walking a dog across the street, and focused on that. He was a street person, she realized, wearing ragged clothing and carrying probably all his possessions on his back. Alongside him a mixed breed shepherd dog trotted, his tail wagging proudly. He had a kerchief around his neck that probably cost as much as the owner's shirt, and as Dar watched them move past and studied the man's lifted head and jaunty step, she decided she deserved nothing but a first class butt kicking rather than chocolate baskets and pretty poems.

"Okay, Paladar," she addressed herself, moving back from the window and starting again to unbutton her sleeves. "That's enough. You're over it. Grow the fuck up."

She slid her shirt off and tossed it over the chair with her jacket. She slipped out of her skirt as she walked to her suitcase, it's top neatly opened. She removed a pair of shorts and a T-shirt, changing into them and breathing in the scent of home as the soft folds settled over her.

"That's better." She took her sundry kit from the overnight bag and went into the bathroom, setting it onto the sink and removing her toothbrush and paste from it. She glanced at the paste and half chuckled, recognizing the flavor. "Grape." She held the paste up. "Thanks, Ker."

Her headache was easing a little, and to further that end, she swallowed a few Advil after she finished brushing her teeth.

Wandering back into the main room she sat down on the bed, flipping the television on more to provide some background noise than anything else. She found CNN and stretched out on the bed, lying down flat and watching the picture sideways.

Some of the CNN anchors, she'd discovered, looked better that way. The news, however, always seemed to be the same thing. Trouble in the Middle East, typhoons in Tokyo, political wrangling in the U.S. Never changed.

Dar checked her watch, hesitantly wondering if it was too late to call home. The thought was only barely articulated when her cell phone, resting on the nightstand, went off with a low, rumbling buzz.

She rolled over a few times to get to the head of the bed, and grabbed the phone, glancing at the caller id as she flipped it open. "Hi."

"Hey, sweetie."

Dar realized as she listened that there was something about Kerry's voice that did something to her when she heard it. It was a visceral reaction—she felt her body relax onto the bed, and the tension across her shoulders eased almost like magic. "Ahhh...Kerrison. Now that's a sound for sore ears."

Kerry laughed. "Did I wake you up?" she said. "I'm sorry if I did. I just got home and I wanted to make sure you got there okay and everything was going fine."

Dar's eyebrows lifted. "You just got home?" she queried.

"Yeah." Kerry sounded a trifle abashed. "We went to the pub after class and talked trash for a few hours. Tom got his new bike." She cleared her throat. "And...I...um...did something I think you're going to kill me for."

Dar blinked, her eyes searching the arched ceiling. "You did?"

"Yeeahhh...but I'd rather tell you about it in person."

"Yeah?"

"Yeah."

Dar's brow furrowed. Kerry didn't sound really worried about it, but... "You know I hate surprises."

A soft, wry chuckle. "Honey, I know that. But humor me. Please?"

The tone reassured her a little. "Okay." Dar sighed. "It's been a bitch of a day. I'm torked," she complained. "I hate New York."

"Wish I was there," Kerry admitted. "Rather than going to that damn meeting tomorrow. At least I have picking you up to look forward to."

It made her smile. "Hey. Thanks for the basket," Dar said. "It was nice to come in to after a lousy night."

"Aww." Kerry chuckled softly. "Glad to hear that. How's the sizing going? Did you straighten out what they need?"

Dar sighed. "No. They weren't ready for me today. I'm going to have to really push tomorrow to get out of here on time. Maybe I should take the morning flight out and forget about it.

"Dar." Kerry cleared her throat gently. "These guys are pretty big. We should take care of them."

"Yeah, I know."

"After that pullout Eleanor told me about, we could use some good news," Kerry said. "That was a big contract."

Dar sighed. "That deal was screwed from the start. I told you those people were never going to sign," she said. "They can say it was pricing but that's BS."

"Well, if they tell everyone we're too pricy does it make a difference?"

Dar sighed again.

"Listen, just do what you can, and then get on the plane. It'll work out," Kerry said. "At least they put you up in a nice place."

Dar glanced around. "Yeah." She shrugged. "It's okay, but it's lacking an amenity."

"Yeah? What's that?"

"You."

A low chuckle came through the phone. "See you tomorrow night, sweetheart. Try to take it easy, huh?"

"You too." Dar smiled. "Night. Love you."

"Love you too. G'night."

Dar folded the phone shut and put it on her chest. Now what, she wondered, could Kerry have done?

That Dar would kill her for?

Dar sighed.

It was going to be a long twenty-four hours.

Chapter Eleven

THE MID-MORNING sun was pouring with liquid fervor across the carpet, it's edge creeping closer and closer to the desk set slightly offset, and at an angle to the door.

Its occupant looked up and studied it, as a puff of dust mingled with the molten light and reflected a dull glitter as the particles drifted toward the floor. "Memo. Get the cleaning crew in here with the vacuum twice a week." Kerry shook her head and scribbled a note. "No wonder I've been sneezing."

A buzz. "Hey, Kerry, I need a favor."

Kerry put her cup down and regarded her phone warily. "Sure, Mark. What is it?" she asked, shifting a little and wincing in mild discomfort. "You're set to come with me to the meeting, right?"

"I sure am, but um..." Mark cleared his throat. "Listen, I had to take one of my bikes into the shop last week and it's ready. Can I catch a ride with you to the meeting, and you drop me off to pick it up after we're done? If I wait till after we get back, they'll be closed."

"Oh, sure," Kerry agreed readily. "No problem. You about ready to leave?"

"Yep," Mark said. "Just putting my gear in the backpack. I've got the scanners and the drawing pad with me, but I gotta tell you, boss, I ain't big D when it comes to this stuff."

"Is anyone?" Kerry smiled, tilting her head and glancing at the picture on her desk.

"Well, you sure you don't want one of the engineers to tag along?"

"Not for this session," Kerry said. "For one thing, it's just an intro. For another, I want someone with me who saw the whole circus in Orlando, and for a third thing, you know the political side of this. An engineer won't."

"Ppphhh...okay," Mark responded. "Meet you downstairs?"

"Ten minutes," Kerry agreed, releasing the line. She went back to her mail, clicking on the next in a succession of minor catastrophes. She sipped her herbal tea while she reviewed the note, shifting her gaze to one side briefly as she tried to recall the location of a resource which had probably been ancient when Dar had joined the company.

"Oh, hell." She picked up her PDA and tapped the screen, typing in a short message. She hit send and waited, twirling the stylus in her fingers until she saw the light of an incoming reply flash. A smile creased her face, and she put the PDA down so she could type something into her pc's message reply, then sent it on its way before she picked her pad back up.

Thanks...what are you doing?

Having a damn boring breakfast. What are you doing?

Kerry grinned. *Getting ready to go to my meeting. I'm taking Mark.*

Good choice. Orange juice sucks here.

"Oh, sure. Drink it there, but not for me, huh?" Kerry scolded.

Are you having grits?

Grits in Manhattan? You want me not to come back?

Oh, never. Kerry's thumb stroked the screen lightly. *Wish you were here right now.*

The reply took a little longer than before. *Me, too.*

Kerry exhaled. "Boy, what is it with us the past few days?" she murmured, sensing the emotion both in herself and in the responses she was getting. *Well, I'll be waiting at the airport tonight, so you better not be late coming back from that crazy apple.*

Ugh. I'll be there, Ker, but if these jackasses don't get their act together, I might have to stay over another night.

"Ugh is right." Kerry frowned. *Ew.*

(frown)

Kerry tapped her stylus against the screen thoughtfully. "Damn." *Let me know, okay? I hope you don't have to stay.*

You'll be the first to know. I am going to dump this bad omelette and go terrorize people. Good luck with the meeting.

Yeah. You too. Talk to you later, Dixiecup.

(grin) Later, Yankee.

The exchange made her feel pleasantly warm and fuzzy inside, though the lingering worry about Dar's state of mind was still there, lurking in the background.

However. Kerry scribbled a brief paragraph onto the screen, reviewed it, and then hit send, waiting expectantly until she saw the reply.

Saucy little wench. Say that again tonight.

"Heh. I will." Kerry put the PDA down and with a final glance at her own monitor, she set her trackball aside and stood up, carefully shrugging on her metallic bronze colored jacket over the gold silk shirt she'd chosen that morning.

It was a bit flashier than she usually preferred, but Kerry hadn't been brought up in a political rat's nest for nothing. She knew how to dress to make an impact, and at this meeting, when she'd be the principal instead of acting as Dar's trusted right hand, she had a bit of a different image to present.

She finished her tea, then slid the strap of her laptop case over her right shoulder and headed for the door, pausing briefly to check her reflection in the small mirror over the credenza.

It was a relatively sophisticated image that looked back at her. The new haircut framed her face a little differently, lengthening it just a touch, she thought. After a fluff of her bangs, she gave her image a grudging nod, then continued out the door. "Okay, Mayte. I'm outta here."

Her assistant looked up from her work. "Oh, Ms. Kerry. You look so pretty today," she exclaimed. "What a nice jacket!'

Not immune to flattery by any means, Kerry paused and grinned, showing off her outfit. "Like it? Dar said I needed something a little snazzier the last time we went shopping so..." She shrugged slightly.

"Did la jefa pick that one out? She has a good taste," Mayte said.

"Yes, she did," Kerry agreed. "And I like to think she does." She winked at Mayte. "I'm going to be offsite all afternoon if anyone's looking for me. I'll be at the Intercontinental at a prospective new business meeting."

"Si." Mayte nodded. "Ms. Mariana called for the employee meeting, and she said she would move it to next week. She is going to be off tomorrow for her birthday."

"Oh, yikes." Kerry's eyes widened. "How did we miss that? Can we get a cake in for Friday? Something big and decorated really crazy?" She made a mental note to remind Dar also, who probably would eschew a card but possibly not something far more bizarre...like the spiny cactus she'd gotten Duks for his last birthday.

"We can do that, sure," Mayte agreed confidently. "I will take care of it, Ms. Kerry. No problem."

With a wave of her fingers, Kerry slipped out the front entrance of her office and headed for the elevators. She felt a little nervous, both from the knowledge that their rivals would be there waiting for her and of the bid process itself.

That, she knew down pat. She'd gone on dozens of new business bids, most as Dar's second, but occasionally as the primary contact when her partner was occupied elsewhere. While her usual job was to come in after the contract had closed and make it all happen, she knew the delicate casting landing the deals took.

Dar was, in the terms of business, a closer. She didn't usually do the initial leg work, she left that to the sales directors and regional managers who worked with the new accounts. Her job was to come in when the money talk got tough and lay down the bottom line of what they'd accept on a contract, and what they wouldn't.

Her word was law, even over the highest sales executives, and everyone knew only Alastair could, or would, overrule her and he never had.

Never.

Kerry was more than aware of that going into any new bid. She felt responsible for doing her job, of course, but she was also very conscious of being Dar's personal and professional representative. She knew people had expectations of her because of that, and she focused intently on living up to or surpassing them.

It was easy for people to think she did what she did because of her relationship with Dar. Kerry eyed the floor counter on the elevator, waiting for it to descend to the ground. People here at ILS no longer thought that — they were well aware of her capabilities.

But she knew she was going into a situation where their relationship was known better than they were, and so...Kerry sighed.

That got old real fast. She hoped she could put Michelle in her place before the whole thing got started so they could stick to business for a change. Maybe she'd get lucky, as Dar had said, and Telegenics would send engineers instead of highly annoying marketing heads whose faces made Kerry want to pick up a sledgehammer.

"Hey, boss," Mark greeted her as the doors opened. He had a nerd backpack slung over one shoulder and was dressed in a more reserved, formal suit than was usual for him. "Ready?"

"Ready." Kerry led the way toward the doors. "Let's go make waves."

DAR SAT BACK in the thick, leather conference room chair and let her eyes travel around the table, just watching as the discussion moved from seat to seat. She rested her elbows on the chair arms and interlaced her fingers, trying the best she knew how not to either fidget or explode.

Clueless. "So what you're telling me," she finally interrupted the conversation. "Is that the developer can't control the resources his program needs to operate."

"Well..." The hitherto absent VP Ops, Jason Meyer, sighed. "Not exactly, but there is a problem with the way the code's written."

"Problem?" Dar's eyebrows lifted. "Given the test I just ran, they've offloaded all their processing to the servers, and it's running everything across your WAN links to minimal clients. That's not a problem, that's a design disaster, Jason."

"But, it's an advantage, Dar," Stewart Godson said. "Every time they make changes, they don't have to alter the client, and it's big bucks to us in savings. They just do what they need to do, and it's taken care of."

Dar exhaled silently. "I'm pretty conversant with the economies of the mainframe based distribution model, Stewart. It's been around longer than I have," she remarked dryly. "And I won't even disagree with it, on a local scale. My support desk often wishes for the old days, when the users just flipped a switch and got a green screen. However," she tapped her thumbs together, "GUI based applications are not meant to be pushed across the wide area network if you expect any kind of reasonable response time."

"Well..."

"Did the vendor do any bandwidth testing?" Dar asked.

Godson shrugged. "He said he did, and that it had an acceptable result."

Dar just looked at him for a long moment. "What did he define as acceptable?" she asked cautiously.

Godson looked at Meyer, who looked out the window. "Ah...there's a language barrier," Stewart admitted. "The developer is German, and he doesn't...um...speak English."

It was like being stuck in some bizarro Dilbert world. Dar rested her chin against her folded hands and found herself at an uncharacteristic loss for words. "Um." She finally exhaled, with a slight shake of her head. "What exactly do you want me to do, here?"

The rest of the room's occupants looked at each other, then focused on Godson. "Well, make it work," he said. "You can, can't you?"

"Sure," Dar replied. "Got a million bucks for infrastructure upgrades?"

Godson actually gasped. "Of course not!"

Dar got up and started pacing, her body's instincts finally getting the better of her. "Okay." She lifted both hands and held them out slightly. "You have a new application, written by a firm over in Germany, which is designed to require four times the amount of bandwidth you currently have provisioned for." She turned and leaned against the table. "So, gentlemen, you have one of three possible choices." One hand lifted and indicated a finger. "You can scrap the application, make the developer fix it so it works right, or pay for expanding your network."

Agitated, Godson got up. "Dar, we can't do any of those. We've already paid for the program...it cost us over 10 million dollars! And it's a good program. It'll raise our productivity ten-fold!"

Dar just looked at him.

"But we don't have a half a million dollars to put new circuits in. That's why we called you. You're our network administrator. Fix it!"

"Your network is based on a usage curve you signed off on," Dar shot back. "We don't have to fix it, Stewart. All we have to do is deliver what you paid for, which is the bandwidth you got right now." She pointed at the CIO.

"Dar, put yourself in my shoes. What would you do?" the man replied, a hint of desperation in his voice.

"Fire myself," Dar told him, bluntly.

The entire room save the two of them was frozen, everyone looking at their hands folded on the big wooden conference table. The morning sunlight entered into the room via a row of small windows near the top of the wall, but the effect was almost like that of a fishbowl.

Dar felt like one of her Siamese fighting fish, in fact. "So..."

"Can't you do anything?" Godson muttered. "You guys are supposed to be the best."

Patience. Dar took three or four breaths before she answered, mindful of the fact that she was, after all, at a client's site. "Okay. I'll fix it. Give me the damn source code," she said. "But I'm warning you, I bill by the hour for programming services and I ain't cheap."

Godson's expression brightened, and he turned to his VP. "Can we do that?"

The VP shook his head. "No sir." He cleared his throat. "We didn't get the source code."

Dar circled the table and sat down again in her seat. She propped her chin up on her fists and stared at the lot of them in patent disgust. "You paid ten million for an application and didn't get the source code?" she asked. "Please tell me you have a guarantee the developer will adapt the program to your specifications."

Godson looked at Meyer.

"I think so," Meyer sighed. "I mean, yes," he amended hastily as Dar started to stand up. "Yes, they'll rewrite whatever we need them to, only...um...they kind of have a little problem understanding what it is we need."

Dar sat back down and leaned back, resuming her brooding posture. "You don't have source code, you can't communicate with your developer, you paid for something that doesn't work on your existing infrastructure and you want me to fix it?"

"Well..." Godson leaned on his elbows. "I mean, who else can we go to, Dar? Really? Okay, so we maybe miscalculated a little, but this project is vital to the company. It has to happen."

Across the table, Meyer lifted his hand to cover his mouth, his eyes taking on a dark glint. "Well, maybe we have other options."

Dar remained quiet for a few minutes, considering her own options. They were as few as Godson's, really. She could walk out and tell them it was their problem not hers, but that meant a disaster for them, and they had a contract up for renewal next year with ILS.

She could force them to pay for new infrastructure, but the thought irked her given the fault really lay not with Godson or his clueless git of a VP Ops, but with the developer who sold them a bill of goods and was now probably laughing his German butt off on the other side of the world. Also, they had a contract up for renewal, and Dar knew if she forced a half million dollars worth of gear down Godson's throat, he'd just take it out of her when they were negotiating in twelve months.

If they re-signed at all. Something like this could cause them not to, no matter how good a deal she cut them.

So.

On the other hand, Dar reasoned, if she could pull this off, and fix Godson's problem, she had his cojones in a blender when it came time for him to sign on the dotted line in those same twelve months. The only problem with that was...

Shit. "Okay," Dar finally said. That meant she had to stay. "Call your developer, and have him put a coder on a plane before close of business today. When he gets here, he's gonna do exactly what I tell him to do, and I'll see if that, plus what I can squeeze out of the pipes, will get your Frankenstein walking."

Godson looked so relieved, Dar suspected he'd need to change his underwear before leaving the room.

"But..." Meyer spoke up, giving Dar a wary look. "His people only speak German."

"I speak German," Dar informed him wryly. "Just don't tell them that, okay? Not until the little bugger gets here and pretends he doesn't know what's going on." She casually took out her PDA and flipped the top open, frowning slightly as she started to scribble on it. After a second, she glanced up to see them all watching her. "Well?"

"Call him." Godson slapped the table, pointing at his VP. "Get that guy here...what's his name, Gunther?"

"Hans." Meyer opened his cell phone. "Okay, I'll get him here. It'll be tomorrow morning, though before he's landed."

"Fine," Dar muttered as she scribbled. "Tell you what. I'll bill THEM for having to teach the bastard how to write a decent application, how's that?"

For the first time, Godson chuckled. "Listen, Dar, I know this was a bitch of a thing to dump on you, but you know we really had no choice. You were the best option we had to salvage this...this..."

"Clusterfuck is the technical term we use." Dar leaned back, calculating the days. If the programmer got here tomorrow, and she was very, very lucky, maybe she'd get the hell out of here by the weekend.

Damn. She didn't want to stay here that long. She wanted to get to the airport, get on a plane, and just...

Her PDA chirped, and she glanced down, to see a hand drawn sad face appear on the screen. Then a second message appeared, and she clicked on it.

I am sitting here in this freaking oatmeal colored hotel conference room having to listen to freaking Michelle Graver go on and on about how wonderful her company is and how they're going to revolutionize Quest's business, and you tell me that??? Augguuhhh!!!!

Dar half listened to Meyer's halting conversation with the programmer as she answered.

Sorry, Ker. More complicated than I thought. I'll talk to you later about it. Might get out of here Friday night.

She sent the message. The PDA beeped almost immediately.

FRIDAY!!!!!!???????????????

"Dar?" Meyer called her name and waited for her to look up. "They can do it. The guy'll be on a flight that gets in here at eight a.m. tomorrow. How's that?"

"Good." Dar nodded, and then went back to her messaging. *I'm not happy about it either. I have to go get a couple spare pairs of clothes, and these*

eugnMelissa Good

bastards are going to cope with them being jeans and T-shirts. She tapped the stylus a few times. *Sorry. Didn't mean to stick you with the crap. Or the crappy jerks.*

"Here's the game plan." Dar looked up after she sent the last message. "We start with laying out the design changes tomorrow morning. I'll give our German friend a framework to start with, and then I'll see what I can do with our existing infrastructure to maximize it. You may end up being a beta site."

"Okay." Godson nodded, a bit nervously. "Do we get a rebate for that?"

Dar stared at him, both eyebrows lifting.

"Just kidding," the CIO smiled weakly.

The PDA beeped. Dar's eyes dropped to it, scanning the message and gaining a faint twinkle as a ghost of a smile crossed her face.

I think Michelle and Shari got my silent mental message because they've been leaving me alone. My turn to lie like a fish is next, and then we're all supposed to have lunch. If I throw chicken Kiev at them, will you fire me so I can fly to NY and be with you instead?

"Dar?"

"Hm?" Dar glanced across the table. "All set?" She realized the room had been watching her, and shrugged, holding up the PDA. "Telling my staff back in Miami not to expect me. I've got a couple of hot irons someone's having to cover." *BRB* She scrawled hastily, hitting send.

"Uh...yeah, we're set," Meyer agreed. "Is there...can we do anything until he gets here? Run some...um...tests, or..."

Dar shook her head. "No." She battled the urge to ignore the room and chat with Kerry instead, finding it disturbingly difficult to keep her concentration on the clients in front of her. "Just tell everyone to relax, that you know it's slower than molasses, but that it's being worked on." She stood up and slipped her PDA into her pocket. "And now, gentlemen, I'm going to make arrangements for the rest of my responsibilities while I'm working on this little problem of yours. I'll see you first thing in the morning."

They hastily scrambled to their feet and started yammering thanks and goodbyes as she strode across the room, heading for the door and the dubious freedom of the Manhattan streets.

Outside, she was hit with a blast of hot air, and all the sounds of a busy city that jarred on her sensitive ears. She ducked between two buildings to escape the worst of the sun and opened her PDA, leaning against the brick building as she started to write. Finishing, she hit send, and then looked around her. "So." She unbuttoned the collar button on her shirt. "What in the hell do you do on a summer day in New York?"

With a sigh, she stepped out onto the sidewalk and began hunting for the proper spot to find a cab. "Guess I'll be finding out." She fixed an oncoming yellow victim with a direct stare, making eye contact with the driver and pulling him over to the curb apparently by the force of her own will. "Shit," she sighed, opening the back door. "Now I won't find out what she did for two whole damn days."

Damn it. The secret nipped at the corners of her conscience as she tried to puzzle out what her partner could have done that she didn't want to tell Dar about over the phone.

Shaved her head maybe? Dar frowned. No, she'd just gotten a haircut.

Maybe she dyed her hair a different color. "Hm." Dar put her PDA away and watched the city roll by. "How bad could that be?"

DAR REVIEWED HER options once she'd changed out of her suit into a pair of shorts and a T-shirt. There was, she had to grudgingly admit, a lot of things to do in New York, but most of them didn't really appeal to her.

Of course, she could stay in her hotel room and catch up on email. She gave her laptop a dour look, leaning over to check the screen. It was dark with new lines, some of them with red exclamation points next to them.

Dar read the first two, then impatiently shoved the laptop away, deciding to postpone the task until later. The sender's idea of urgent didn't jive with hers, and she had other things she needed to be doing. With a grunt, she got up from the bed and went to the small table, grabbing up one of the magazines there and dropping into the chair by the window.

Faintly, the sound of the city came through the glass. Dar turned her head and peered down at the street, but after a brief moment, she lost interest and went back to deciding what to do.

She flipped through the hotel guide restlessly, passing up coach rides in Central Park she'd have jumped at if Kerry was there, and the miles of shopping available to those into that kind of thing. Fancy stores whose advertisements probably cost more than the average family made in a month. Dar's nostrils twitched as she reflected on the fact that despite all her resources, her tastes really hadn't altered to high priced snootiness all that much.

Diamond bracelets? Well...

Dar occasionally enjoyed shopping, but usually only when she and Kerry were out for the day getting stuff they needed, and also mixing it up with lunch, or a trip to the computer store, or something they both found interesting.

They liked a lot of the same things. Dar always found that comforting. At first she'd wondered if Kerry was pretending to like things just because she wanted to make them seem more compatible, but after a while she realized they really did like the same stuff and in the cases when they didn't, she'd learned to read Kerry's facial expressions so accurately she knew in a single twitch of a muscle in her cheek what she was thinking.

That was so nice. Dar exhaled, and went back to her search for amusement. Maybe she could get Kerry a diamond bracelet. Would she like that?

She frowned, imagining Kerry's reaction. Her partner liked pretty things, but she often seemed unimpressed by expensive ones. In fact, the more inconsequential the gift Dar gave her, the more Kerry seemed to cherish it.

Hm.

She needed to do a little shopping for herself, but what she really wanted was some kind of...ah... Dar spread the magazine open and gazed at the advertisement, a quarter page near the back. It featured the picture of an aircraft carrier, and a grin spread across Dar's face as she read the details. "The Intrepid Sea-Air-Space Museum. Yeah. Now that's more my style."

She checked the address. It was on the Hudson River, near midtown, not all that far from her. Walking was an option. Taxies were also an option. Dar considered carefully. Hm. But so was the subway. She drummed her fingers on the magazine, remembering her last sojourn underground.

Chicago, where they'd gotten stuck in the dark under the river. She'd practically run out of the station at the other end, nearly getting herself and Kerry into a lot of trouble.

The clenching in her guts made her angry. "God damn it, not that too." She made her decision and got up, adding her wallet to her back pocket and sticking the room key in there as well. "Maybe I'll ride that damned thing until they throw me off."

Grabbing her sunglasses, Dar marched out of the room and closed the door behind her, heading for the elevator with a grim, determined look on her face.

Dar waited for the elevator to open on the bottom floor of the Hyatt, and then she crossed the lobby and exited the hotel's ornate and stately front door.

Outside, the heat slammed into her, but lacking her wool suit, Dar now shrugged it off as she would have back home. She slipped her sunglasses on and directed her attention to the building adjacent to her hotel. "Grand Central Station. Bet I can catch something there." She headed for the building, trotting up the steps and entering the wide, ornate doors.

Inside, she stopped, drawing to one side and blinking as she took in the vast, cavernous chamber that spread to all sides around her. The scale was immense, but more than that, there was an indefinable sense of history here that even Dar picked up on.

It was also beautiful. "Huh." Dar slowly walked forward, and started down the steps into the main hall. The ceiling curved overhead, painted in a deep blue, and featured the signs of the zodiac. The stone walls seemed freshly scrubbed, their construction solid and imposing.

Slowly, she made her way downstairs, looking around at the status boards listing trains leaving for points outside the city. People walked all around her, intent on getting to their destinations and she was forced to restrict her gawking lest she be bowled over by aggressively marching city residents.

Her PDA went off. Dar stepped to one side and pulled it out of her pocket, glancing down at the screen.

What's the word in Spanish for fornicating pig?

Dar looked around in reflex, clearing her throat before she removed the stylus and considered her answer. *As opposed to a pig that's just standing there eating?*

A man glanced at her as he hurried by, making eye contact as he looked over his sunglasses. Dar gave him a brief smile, then returned her attention to the PDA as it chirped.

Yes.

With a sigh, Dar shook her head. *Hope you aren't getting into that much trouble, sweetheart. Fornicando puerco, but I'm hoping you're not putting that on a Powerpoint slide.*

She only had a moment to wait for the answer.

Oh, yeah. A hundred memorable quotations from the inimitable Dar Roberts, annotated. It's gonna be great!

Dar laughed in pure reflex. *Troublemaker.*

Just venting a little of my frustration with some help from my one and only. The fornicando puerco is finally done. My turn. Later. Love you.

Love you too. Dar leaned against the stair railing and smiled, letting her eyes linger over the words before she sent them and tucked the machine away.

A small kiosk caught her eye and she dodged through the crowd, arriving at the souvenir stand without getting run over. The stand had an old photograph of the station, in black and white, with a striking series of sunbeams pouring through the upper windows.

Kerry would most certainly appreciate it. "I'll take one of these." She selected a poster tube and handed over the money for it to the dour, unlit cigar chomping man behind the desk.

"Sure ya don't want it in a nice frame, lady? Got a great bargain here on this one." He indicated an ornate, gilded monstrosity.

"No thanks," Dar politely refused. "I've got to carry it on the plane. This is easier."

"Whatever. Later. G'bye." The man turned to another customer, leaving Dar standing there with her poster in her hand slightly taken aback by the gruff attitude.

Collecting herself, Dar edged against one of the walls and peered around, finally spotting the entrance to the subway. She approached it, pausing a moment before she started down the steps.

The walls were all bright and cheery, but for every second she was on the stairs, Dar was aware of the fact that she was moving further and further under the ground. Her throat went dry, and she swallowed in reflex as she reached the first platform, and was faced with a number of posted signs laying out the different routes.

Dar stopped in front of a subway map, using the excuse of studying it to allow her heartbeat to settle. She could still see the steps up from where she was, and there was sufficient space around her. "Okay." She exhaled, focusing on the maze of colored lines in front of her. After a moment, her brow creased. "Jesus," she muttered. "I've seen spider webs less complicated than this."

The thought of a taxi suddenly became extremely appealing. Dar glanced over her head at the steel infrastructure, wincing a little as some train nearby rattled past and a gust of cold air blew against her. "What in the hell am I doing?"

Seeing if you have any guts at all left? Her inner voice mocked her.

With a scowl, she turned and walked to one of the token machines, studying it for a minute before she inserted a few bills and retrieved a square of cardboard for her troubles. She looked at it, and then her expression brightened. "Hey. I can prove to Kerry I did this."

Looking around to find her route, Dar started off down a passageway, sidestepping a man playing a flute and two women selling bags of... "Hm." She paused and purchased a bag of churros, taking one out to nibble on as she explored further into the maze.

Her selected route was the Times Square shuttle, since that appeared to let out reasonably close to the Intrepid museum, and more importantly, wasn't that far underground. Dar found the correct platform relatively easily, and leaned against the metal support, waiting for the train to arrive.

Okay, so far, so good. Dar glanced around her, and then she walked down the platform to where a small set of steps seemed to lead downward. She peeked down them, spotting more signs leading to more platforms, leading to different trains, which seemed to run in every direction at many different levels.

The complexity and seeming randomness unexpectedly intrigued her. It was almost as though some kids had taken six or seven of their individual train sets and threw them all together, pouring glue on top and hoping for the best.

Dar turned and surveyed the station she was standing on, taking in the tile mosaics, and the patchwork grid of the ceiling beams that crossed and re-crossed each other. The steel members seemed old, almost ancient, though the station tiles appeared new, and the facility was well kept.

Hm.

The train arrived, in a clatter of wheels and a blast of musky air.

Dar waited until the occupants had exited, and most of the people waiting to enter got in. Then she stepped onto the train, appreciating the chill of the air conditioning as she selected a seat on one side, near the back and settled into it.

The train was about half full. Dar studied her subway map, giving the doors an impatient look every few seconds when they obstinately refused to close. As the train sat there, a few late-comers jumped on. One of them, a tall bronze skinned girl in black denim and leather took the seat next to Dar.

They studied each other for a minute. Then the girl lifted one of her leather boot encased feet and put it on her opposite knee. "Yo," she addressed Dar pleasantly. "You ain't from here, huh?"

Dar's eyebrows cocked slightly. Behind her sunglasses, she glanced down at herself, comparing her appearance to the appearance of the rest of the train's occupants.

Hm. Apparently New Yorkers in downtown Manhattan didn't dress like refugees from a Jimmy Buffet concert. "No," she allowed briefly.

"Yeah." The girl folded her arms over her chest. "That's what I figured. Cause us New Yorkers don't go round half naked like that, y'know?"

Since the train wasn't moving, Dar decided conversation wouldn't hurt, and it would keep her mind off the butterflies in her stomach. "Why not?" she asked. "It's a hundred degrees outside."

"Just cause we don't," the girl responded readily. "I mean, you dress like that, you just asking for guys to come out, and be all like, touching you, and all that jazz. You know?"

Dar tilted her head and let her sunglasses drop down on her nose slightly, making actual eye contact with the women. "No, I don't," she drawled, hearing the touch of molasses enter her tone.

"Yo. You got some really cool eyes. I like that color," the woman complimented her. "They real?"

Dar blinked, her brows arching up. Then she realized what the woman meant. "Yeah." She pushed her sunglasses back up and leaned back. "What's with the train?" She changed the subject to one she figured the woman would know better than she did.

"This?" The woman pointed up over her head. "Oh, I don't know. They do that sometimes. Just make 'em stop, bam. Like that."

Erf. Dar glanced at the still open door. Just then, though, the speakers crackled to life over their heads and a gravelly voice intruded into the train.

There has been a power failure up the line and all the trains are stopped. Do not stand in the doorways. The trains can move at any time. Thank you.

It was like an omen. Dar figured. This was God's way of telling her to get the hell off the damn subway and go take a cab like any other self respecting Floridian would. She started to get up, but as she did, the doors whipped closed, and the train started moving unexpectedly, throwing her back into her seat. "Guess we're leaving now," she commented dryly.

"So." The girl edged nearer. "Where ya from, what's ya name?" She held out a hand. "I'm Scuzzy."

Dar eyed her in alarm. *It's a sixty second ride, Dar. Deal with it.* "Dar. I'm from Miami."

"Cool!" Scuzzy shook her hand firmly. "That's a cool name, and Miami's a cool place," she said.

"Thanks." Dar smiled briefly.

Abruptly, the train slowed and stopped again. Dar glanced outside, and saw nothing but black tunnel walls. Behind her glasses, she closed her eyes and tried not to think about how many tons of granite buildings were perched over her head, pressing down on tunnels she was sure were far too old, based on the ones she'd seen in the station.

"Yo. You like hockey?"

Dar opened one eye. "What?"

"Me and my buds, we're going down to the ice rink and play killer hockey later on, like tonight. You wanna come play? I can see you do somethin' with all them muscles you got."

Dar swore she heard creaking outside.

Subways, she realized, were looking like a bad, bad mistake.

"FUDGE." KERRY GLOWERED at her PDA. "Fudge, fudge, fudge."

"Something wrong, boss?" Mark whispered.

Kerry rocked back in her chair, shedding some of her fidgets. "Ah...Dar's stuck in New York," she sighed. "Maybe until Friday."

The session so far had been nothing more than a recap of the bid request, and then subsequent presentations by the four companies as to how they intended on fulfilling them.

Quest was there along with three of his attendants and four others he'd introduced from his company that were immediately forgettable and seemed more like movie extras than engaged executives.

Mark scribbled a few things on his pad, making a show of paying attention to Michelle Graver's presentation. "Well, she'da been wasted being here. Hell, you're wasted being here. We coulda sent one of the sales interns to do this crap."

"Mm." Kerry had to agree. "It's all a dog-and-pony show." She checked her watch, wishing her turn was over and they at least had the minor entertainment of lunch to look forward to. "Oh well, it's the start off session. I guess it was to be expected. I'm glad Dar's not here."

Totally not true.

"She'd be wigging," Mark muttered wryly.

Totally true.

Actually, Dar would have already left, finding the presentations pointless and the dialog meaningless. She'd probably have been in the taco shop across the road with instructions to call her when something got mildly interesting.

Kerry leaned on her elbow and pictured her partner's restless attitude without any problem at all. Her PDA chirped and she glanced at it, reading Dar's longer, more coherent message absorbedly. "Yeah, yeah, yeah," she groused under her breath. "You're gonna owe me for this, you little southern fried..."

"Uh... Kerry, did you say something?"

Kerry closed her PDA and dragged her attention back to Michelle. "Nope," she sighed. "Isn't it time for lunch, yet?"

Mark looked at his wrist. "It's only eleven o'clock."

"What's your point?" Green eyes studied him from under half lowered lids. "I missed breakfast," Kerry admitted. "I was in a rush this morning because I overslept."

"Forgot the old alarm, huh?"

Kerry managed a wry grin. "My alarm's in Manhattan." She watched Mark's face color a trifle. "You asked."

"Sure did," he agreed ruefully. "TMI, boss. TMI."

"Mm." Kerry listened to the speech with one ear, hopeful she was detecting a sense of closing in Michelle's voice. "Sorry about that. But it's true. Dar's better than any clock I've ever seen, and it's really hard to hit her snooze button." She rested her head on her fist, her eyes traveling slightly as she saw a newcomer enter, walking quietly over to sit by Shari and lean close to talk to her.

Something familiar about the man made her frown, and she nudged Mark's arm slightly. "Who is that guy?"

Mark swiveled in his seat and looked. "Hey...isn't that the guy from Tech TV? The one who was interviewing you and big D?"

Ah. No wonder he looked familiar. "Uh...huh," Kerry mused. "Now, isn't he cozy with the competition. Wonder what's up with that?" The man seemed very friendly with Shari, and as she watched, he took out a pad and a camera, put the camera on the table, and scribbled some notes on the pad. "Ohh...ho. What do you want to bet he's not asking for advice on some DSL routers?"

"So, in sum," Michelle cleared her throat, "we hope to show the kind of value any company looking to outsource their IT solutions has a right to expect." She rested her hands on the lectern. "We hope to open a new era in providing the types of services to all companies that only the largest, richest companies have been able to afford in the past." Her eyes wandered, apparently randomly, to Kerry's and held there for a moment, then moved on.

Kerry deliberately flipped open the top to her PDA and scribbled a note on it, then tapped send.

"Toward that end, I'm sure you'll be delighted to hear, Mr. Quest, we have invited a member of the distinguished technology press to join our bid team and chronicle our progress, and how this challenge evolves into what I'm sure will be a great success for whoever wins it." Michelle went on, smiling easily and giving Shari a knowing look.

"Hm. Somehow I got the impression that Quest dude didn't want this whole thing publicized," Mark muttered under his breath. "He doesn't look real happy."

Kerry observed the forced smile on Quest's face. "No, he doesn't," she agreed, sending a last note on her PDA before she closed it up.

"Thank you for your patience and attention." Michelle surrendered the lectern at last, taking her notes and retreating around the side of it before she headed back to her seat to a smattering of applause.

"Ah. Yes." Peter Quest scratched his cheek, then stood up. "Ah, thank you, Ms. Graver. Now, ah, before we break for lunch, we have one final presentation." He half turned toward Kerry and raised his brows. "Ms...ah, Stuart?"

Kerry stood up and gently pushed her chair in, then walked around to the lectern and rested her elbows on it, leaning forward and waiting until the room's pre-lunch restlessness stilled and she had their attention.

She somehow doubted the scheduling order had been by chance, in any sense.

"Good morning, ladies and gentlemen." She allowed a faint, self-deprecating smile to appear on her face, and took the time to make eye contact with those interested enough to be looking at her. "When I was asked to present a basic infrastructure outline here, I wasn't notified of the three ring circus."

A number of faces twitched, not expecting the gentle attack.

"If I had been, I'd have brought my performing SEAL and dancing hamster to liven this all up." Kerry straightened up, to a sudden, surprised round of laughter. "Unfortunately for you all, I only have an IT infrastructure presentation, so I vote to plow through it at record speed so we can all have lunch, how's that?"

Another round of laughter, and some applause. "You buying?" one of her competitors shouted.

"How about I cook?" Kerry shot back, with an engaging grin. "I'm told I make a killer PB and J."

The crowd loosened up and perked up at the same time, exactly the response Kerry was going for. She waited for the laughter to peter out, and sorted her brief notes.

"Oh, sorry." Michelle half stood, a sour sweet expression on her face. "Did you need the projector? I'm afraid we're pretty connected to it."

"Nah." Kerry removed a small remote from her pocket. "What's the point in being the richest kids on the block, if you don't have the neatest toys?" She pressed a button. "We don't need no stinking projector." She waited for the thin laser wand to emerge from the back of her laptop, and raise up, opening the aperture and shooting a thin blue beam just over her shoulder. Kerry glanced back and adjusted the beam slightly, then triggered her presentation to start. "As I was saying..."

Behind her, a neatly drawn and notated network diagram appeared, starting with a core, and spreading out to the edge devices, all neatly encapsulated inside the outline of a ship.

Kerry turned and peered at it, then swiveled back around to the room. "We have a saying in the IT biz," she said. "Parts is parts." With a laser pointer she indicated first the core, then the remote devices. "Like in any network, best case practices dictate we treat this ship's infrastructure like we would any sound network. The biggest differences we see are the need for solid, absolute redundancy and the need to bolt every darn thing to the floor to keep it from pitching overboard."

"And pay a premium for it," Shari remarked.

"Well, that's true," Kerry agreed cheerfully. "We don't generally give our clients blue light specials." She smiled at Shari. "But I can see the incentive for that for companies with fewer resources than ours and clients who either don't know or don't care about business continuity."

Her finger clicked on the button, and she waited for the screen to paint with Dar's next drawing, an intricate schematic of the primary pieces of equipment she intended to use for the bid. "The design allows for all the functionality Mr. Quest specified. Our complete schematics will be put into his hands for review, and frankly, that's really all I have to say regarding our intentions."

She clicked through two more screens showing some general dimensions of the equipment Dar had chosen, then stopped on the last one, which showed a pretty graphic in several colors that illustrated the interconnected types of communication, which would flow through the system.

"The bottom line, ladies and gentlemen." Kerry made eye contact again, pinning Quest last of all. "Is not who can do this the cheapest and easiest. Anyone can do that."

Shari snorted.

"Economy is a strong motive, Ms. Stuart," Quest reminded her.

Kerry lightly shrugged both shoulders at him. "In the end, Mr. Quest, you're the one who has to stand behind whatever decision you make," she said. "So you have to decide how much you're willing to risk in terms of reliability and protection. Because that's what this is going to come down to."

"B..."

"Parts is parts," Kerry reminded him. "We all use the same equipment. This isn't rocket science. No one's doing anything revolutionary."

"Speak for yourself," Shari spoke up.

"Hey," one of Quest's men stood up and faced her. "You people were allowed to say your piece without getting interrupted. So please be quiet and give others the same courtesy."

Michelle didn't even so much as look at her partner. Shari appeared to consider responding, then she settled for a rare bit of good sense and merely nodded.

Kerry waited, a mildly amused look on her face. "We all know how to do this. Just because it's on a ship doesn't change anything." She looked at Quest. "But you're the one who has to face the rest of your company and your customers if what you buy doesn't hold up. I'll tell you right now, neither I, nor our network architect shops at Wal-Mart."

Quest fiddled with his pencil, clearly uncomfortable. "Yes, well, that's all fine. Are you done?"

Kerry clicked off her projector, and watched it fold neatly back against the spine of her laptop. "Yep, I sure am." She tucked the remote in her pocket and took her notes, which basically consisted of the words 'kiss my ass.' "Let's take a break, shall we?"

Everyone stirred, and started to rise. Kerry circled back around to her seat and pulled her laptop case up onto the chair, opening the top so she could slip her machine inside it's padded bay. The speech had been a trifle more aggressive than she'd planned, but after Michelle's pandering, she knew she had to make a mark and distinguish their plan as something different.

So she had. Kerry was very aware of the eyes on her as she put her gear up, and she carefully and deliberately slid the leather strap into its buckle and fastened it before she looked up. "Okay." She half turned to face Mark. "Ready?"

"Whatever you say, boss," Mark responded, already shouldering his own briefcase. His face showed that he was out of his depth and he knew it. "Lead on."

Kerry only wished she could lead them both right on out of the hotel and down the street to a little sandwich shop Dar favored with little ambiance and great food. Instead, she knew they'd have to suffer through lunch at the hotel, which would likely be robust with carefully shaped lettuce leaves and relatively tasteless.

Ah well.

They all filed out, and she and Mark politely waited as several of the other bidders hurried to follow Michelle and Shari and their reporter guest. After the last had gone on, she fell in step at the end, giving Quest a half nod as he picked up his notepad and prepared to join them.

"You know, Ms. Stuart." Quest kept his voice down as they left the room. "I didn't really appreciate your attitude up there."

Kerry hooked her thumb through her laptop case strap. "Well, you know, Mr. Quest, you asked for competitive bids. I think you got what you asked for." She regarded him briefly. "I'm not here to blow smoke up your tail. I think you know that."

He didn't answer for a few steps as they watched the other bidders cluster around the reporter. "Where's Ms. Roberts?" he asked. "I thought for sure she'd be here for this. She has some very significant competitors here."

Kerry resisted the urge to pull out her PDA. "Dar? She's working with a client of ours who has a major application issue they came to her to solve," she replied. "A strategic partner of ours."

"So that's more important than signing new business?"

A dry chuckle. "If you were the other client, how would you want me to answer that?" Kerry said, as she started down the steps toward the fountain bedecked luncheon restaurant.

Quest was briefly silent. "Well."

"It's not all about getting new business, Mr. Quest," Kerry added, in a mild tone. "If you don't retain your existing customers and help them grow, it's just a shell game."

He looked at her hard. "Are you inferring something, Ms. Stuart?"

Kerry's brows contracted. "Excuse me?"

"Never mind." He glanced around. "I expect you to be competitive. I don't want to be handed an expensive bag of tricks, from anyone here. I have to cut the best deal for my company possible."

"We'll give you the best deal we're capable of," Kerry said. "But we may give you what you need, not what you want."

Quest snorted. "They said you were arrogant. That's why I'm surprised Ms. Robert's isn't here. She's got that down pat."

Kerry felt a growl start deep in her throat. She cleared it just before it became audible. "Dar put time in on the design for your account. Now she's left it in my hands. We're both comfortable with that, I'm sorry if you aren't."

Slightly taken aback, Quest drew in a breath and edged slightly away from her. "Ms. Stuart..."

Kerry pointed suddenly at the reporter. "I thought you said you wanted to keep this quiet, Mr. Quest. How does that impact your plans?"

Quest fell pensively silent. "It was unexpected," he admitted finally, as they reached the bottom of the steps. "But it's all that geek talk. No one I care about will see it or give a damn." He shrugged. "So if you want to spend all your time pissing on each other, Ms. Stuart, and giving them ratings — go for it. I've got more important things to do."

Kerry watched him walk off, glad of the few moments quiet respite before they joined the others. "Know what?" she remarked to her silent companion.

"What?" Mark made a vague clucking noise.

"You know that look Dar gets, the one where she sort of squints, and you think she's going to bite someone?"

"Oh, yeah."

"I'm so understanding that look right now."

Mark sighed. "Man, you guys do this all the time? I don't think I could handle that. These guys suck."

Kerry patted him on the back and had to silently, if ruefully, agree as they reached the group and joined the rest of the nattily suited men and women in sitting down at two large, round tables. "You know what Dar would do?" she whispered behind her hand as they took chairs next to each other.

"Cheeseburger, fries and a shake," Mark whispered back. "Somewhere else."

Kerry took her napkin and popped it open, laying it across her lap with an easy grace as she reviewed the menu card placed on her plate. "Yeah." She exhaled, finding herself directly across from Shari, who took pleasure in smiling fiercely at her. "Or she'd order a pizza." She found herself smiling for a different reason. "Delivered to the table. But we can't, so let's just make the best of it." She lifted her glass and sipped some cold water from it.

It was going to be a very, very long day.

Chapter
Twelve

DAR EMERGED INTO the sunlight once again, after her sixty-second subway ride had drawn itself out to twenty minutes. She had, however, apparently made a friend, since Scuzzy showed no signs of continuing on her way as they exited the subway station together.

Subway station? Dar glanced behind her at one of the many stairwells burping people up out of the ground. More like a nightmare from some science fiction writer's imagination.

The heat had gotten a little worse, or maybe she'd just gotten used to the cooler confines of the underground world.

"So, like, Dar. Where ya goin?" Scuzzy interrupted her thoughts. "Just coming down to see the Square?"

"No. Here." Dar pulled the brochure out of her pocket and displayed it, turning slightly as she tried to orient herself in the busy street. Buildings rose on all sides, and the roads seemed to run together from all directions.

What the hell?

After a moment of blinking, she realized why the place looked so damn familiar. She'd never been here before that she could remember, and now she took a moment to just stand and look around.

Times Square. Dar cocked her head to one side, realizing she'd always considered the place to be more of a stage set than a real city street. Her gaze shifted.

Streets.

She turned her head to look the other way.

Whatever.

The marquees raced across the building fronts just like they did on television, and Dar tilted her head back to look up at the post she'd seen the ball drop from on countless New Years Eves. Then she chuckled and returned her attention to finding her way to the Hudson river.

"You like, into that stuff?" Scuzzy had kept right up with her. "Like, guns?" She handed back the brochure.

Dar stopped and looked at her.

"Hey!" The woman held up both hands. "It's cool! No problem! I'm into that show *Gunsmoke* too, you like that show? It's great!"

"No." Dar figured out what direction to go in and started walking. "My father was in the Navy." She checked the street numbers, and started down one with some confidence. She was mildly surprised when Scuzzy chose to join her, shambling down the sidewalk at her side. She gave the woman a speculative look.

"I figured I'd make sure you got there okay," Scuzzy explained. "Then I'm goin back to get the bus."

Dar stopped walking, forcing the girl to stop as well or else plow into her. She took off her sunglasses and looked her persistent companion up and down, then repeated the exercise on herself. She finally returned her stare to Scuzzy's face, and lifted both eyebrows meaningfully. "Thanks," she drawled. "But I'll get there okay."

Scuzzy studied her for a minute. "You tryin to tell me something?"

With a faint sigh, Dar returned her sunglasses to their perch on her nose and started walking again, shaking her head. A breeze picked up, puffing fitfully between the buildings and bringing the unmistakable scent of water to her. She glanced at the storefronts she was passing, intrigued by the variety of clubs whose identity changed at almost every stride. "Something for everyone, huh?" she remarked, passing a jazz club next to something she imagined catered to the Goth crowd.

"You say something?" Scuzzy peered at her. "Hey, you ever been here to the city?"

"Yeah, I've been here," Dar finally relented, edging over slightly so the woman could walk next to her and not plow into the trees planted incongruously in the center of the sidewalk. "I'm not really fond of it."

"Miami's kinda different, huh?"

Dar looked around her with a wry chuckle. "Like night and day. I wouldn't trade 'em for a million."

"No, huh?" The woman looked around. "Well, y'know, this used to be a really tough neighborhood." She said. "Times Square, man, you didn't want to come down around here. But they fixed it up pretty nice now."

Dar peered at the theatre they were passing, realizing she'd heard its name half her life and never realized where the hell it was. "Bad neighborhood, huh?" she asked with interest.

"Oh, yeah, Absolutely." Scuzzy nodded. "Hookers lined up tits to ass back there, yeah?"

"Yeah?"

"Absolutely!"

It was hard to picture all those people in mink coats coming to see shows stepping around bums and drug dealers. Dar put the idea away for later study, and ducked to one side as a man walking a Dalmatian hurried by. Or maybe it was a Dalmatian walking the man, as the dog seemed far more relaxed than his owner. "You been here when it was?" she asked Scuzzy. "When it was a bad place?"

Scuzzy seemed delighted Dar was warming up to her. "Oh, sure." She made a dismissive gesture. "Me and my bro, we used to come down here all the time back then, cause we'd take the bus out to DC to visit my old man."

"Ah," Dar murmured. "Must have been scary."

"Nah. Just different." Scuzzy peered behind her in the direction of Times Square. "Lotta people usta live over there, y'know? Not no more. I dunno where they went now. The Park, maybe. You gotta have money to live over there now." Her nose wrinkled a bit. "Ritzy."

Dar was struck with an unexpected parallel. "Yeah," she agreed. "That happened down on South Beach, too."

"Yeah?"

"Yeah. It used to be retirement hotels for all these older people. Twenty bucks a week, something like that," Dar said. "Then they put all the money in there and now I think twenty bucks maybe gets you parking for the night. Maybe." Maybe. "Sucks sometimes," Dar admitted. "You pay thirty bucks for a coke and a damn hot dog."

"That's right!" Scuzzy agreed heartily. "You got that right, yeah?" She kicked a rock which rattled ahead of them and rambled through the wrought iron steps that lead down into someone's basement. "So where did them old people go?"

Dar slowed, her head tipping to one side a little as she thought. "I don't know," she finally responded. "But I remember what it felt like when we lived on the Navy base, and they were talking about closing it." A ghost of a memory floated into focus for her. "They wanted to sell the place to build a supermarket."

"Oh, that's cold." Scuzzy patted her on the back. "So you lived with all those navy guys huh? That must have been cool."

"Yeah, it was." Dar shrugged the memories off. "So where are you going on a bus today, Scuzzy?" she asked, as they reached the end of the street and were faced with a four lane road separating them from the piers. To one side, Dar could see the distinctive shape of the Intrepid, and found a smile forming.

"No place," Scuzzy shrugged. "Just get me a ticket and ride somewhere and back. I got laid off last week."

Dar found herself snagged by one of the fits of recklessness that occasionally happened to her. "What do you do?" she asked, turning and leaning against a light pole. "That you got laid off for?"

Taken slightly aback, her erstwhile companion made a nervous motion with her hands. "Oh, you know, just office stuff. I was putting in traffic tickets, callin people. Anything they want me to do, but they got cut sos they had to let me off."

"You worked for the police?" Dar clarified.

"Yeah, kinda." Scuzzy seemed abashed. "So like, that's why I don't like people getting into trouble, you know?" She cleared her throat. "So whadda you do, Dar from Miami? Like what you get paid for?"

"I work with computers." Dar removed her PDA from her pocket and opened the flap. She selected a square of white cardboard, then flipped it over and fished her pen out and scribbled on the back of it for a moment.

"Yeah?" Scuzzy perked right up. "Oh, man, you lucked out. I love computers. I got me a internet mail thing at the library last month and I love going to check that out."

Dar reviewed what she'd written, then held the card up, reverse side forward for Scuzzy to see. "Go there." She indicated the address on the back. "When you get there, give the guard at the desk this." She reversed the card, the ILS logo flashing briefly in the sunlight. "Tell them I said to hire you." She handed the card over.

Scuzzy looked at the card, then looked at Dar. "For real?" she asked, after a long moment. "Like, no shit? If I give them this thing, they're not gonna throw my ass out and call the cops? That's like, Rockefeller Center!"

Dar chuckled. "No." She spent a brief instant of deliciously evil anticipation on just how much twitching she'd cause the company's staid Manhattan office. "They'll take care of you."

Scuzzy looked down at the card again, and turned it over. "Chief Information Officer." She lifted her eyes to Dar's face. "You get good money for that?"

"Yeah," Dar nodded. "But you'll do all right too."

"Yeah?" Now a touch of incredulity entered Scuzzy's tone. "You know somethin? I woke up today and I knew somethin' cool was gonna happen to me." She carefully tucked the card away in the pocket of her shirt and stuck her hand out. "This is all right."

Dar took it and gave it a shake. "See ya." She released Scuzzy's hand and turned as the light changed and gave her the opportunity to cross over to the pier.

"See yah," Scuzzy repeated, waiting until the tall figure had disappeared from sight into the pier's square frontage. "Ain't that a kick in the ass?" She removed the card and looked at it. "I'm gonna go get me a job, so screw you, momma, saying not to talk to nobody on the subway!"

Turning, she sauntered back down the street, heading back toward Times Square.

DAR STOPPED BEFORE she went through the gates into the museum, taking a moment to enjoy the breeze off the water, and the sense that she'd emerged from the close confines of the city at least for a while. She found a bench and sat down on it, retrieving her PDA and opening it up.

To her surprise, a message she hadn't caught was waiting. She tapped on it.

Have I ever told you just how much I love you?

Dar blinked a few times, then rubbed the back of her hand over her eyes impatiently. *Matter of fact, you have. But I never get tired of hearing it.*

She could almost hear the sigh in Kerry's words when she responded.

I'm sitting at a table across from Shari and Michelle, suffering through an endive salad with the prospect of chicken breast over rice pilaf before me.

Ugh. Dar extended her legs into the sun and crossed them. *Well, I'm sitting near the Hudson River, and I just sent a vagabond over to the local office to get a job.*

(laugh) You call me a troublemaker?

Dar smiled in reflex. *Hey, I rode on the subway to get here.*

You did? No fair! I wasn't there to go with you!

The lump in her throat was getting to her. Dar shifted on her bench, then rolled her stylus in her fingers before she answered. *No one was here to see me chicken out!*

But you didn't.

True. *Yeah, specially since the damn thing got stuck three times with me on it. They don't like me.* Dar allowed. *Well, I'm going in to see the Intrepid, then maybe I'll find one of those hot dog stands and get sick to my stomach.*

(chuckle) Have one for me, since I'm suffering here with a raunchy vinaigrette. Hey – get a sailor hat so I can see my life-sized hamster dance.

Oh, god. Dar started laughing, her humor restored. *All right. Take it easy and go grab a burger after the meeting. That's what I do.*

I will. Love you.

Dar felt as warm inside suddenly as she did outside. *Love you too.* She sent the message and stood up, stretching her back out before she headed off toward the aircraft carrier's impressive bulk.

Sailor hat, huh? Dar looked forward to some quality shopping, for more than just her partner. New York, she decided, was potentially looking up after all.

LUNCH WAS AS sour as the vinaigrette. Kerry wiped her lips on her napkin and returned it to its place on her lap. She hadn't even bothered with the chicken, it's dryness evident to her even through the thin, lemony sauce drizzled over it. She stuck to her iced tea instead, and pacified her grumbling stomach with some of the rather benign rolls and butter the table had been graced with.

Long gone were the days, she mused, when she could be satisfied with a handful of carrots and some water. She still liked snacking on them, and had even gotten Dar to eat the little suckers, but they no longer provided a meal for her and neither did this collection of pretentious garden refuse and pseudo free ranging ancient fowl.

Bah. Kerry leaned back and nursed her tea. The small talk at the table was small indeed, and she only half listened to a discussion about an advance release of a new server operating system.

"Hey, Kerry?"

Kerry looked across the table at another of their rivals, though one of the more palatable ones she more or less got on well with. "Hey, Ross?"

"You guys stick to one system? I heard you were a uni-house."

"Nah." Kerry shook her head. "We have a little of everything, depending on the application. We support way too many different companies to stick to one system," she said. "Mainframes, minis, six flavors of Unix, Linux, the full range of Microsoft, some Novell, you name it."

"That must be a support nightmare," Ross Cunningfurth said, with an easy grin.

"Training's the biggest chunk of my budget," Kerry replied. "But it's worth it. We can leverage like crazy. I have six different major support centers that all fall back to each other."

"Six?"

Kerry spread one hand out in a faint shrug. "International."

"Shit." Ross just shook his head with a chuckle.

"Yeah, but how can you even think about giving personal service to your accounts, with that size operation?" Shari's tone was dismissive. "Just a bunch of cookie cutters."

Kerry debated on whether she wanted to engage in the debate. Before she could make a choice, Mark spoke up for almost the first time that afternoon.

"It's not that hard," Mark said. "We got a system that profiles all the different accounts and systems, so whoever answers the phone gets the whole deal in a couple clicks." He shrugged. "What matters is you getting the call to someone who's got the right skill set. That's the trick."

"Exactly," Kerry picked up the thread neatly. "But you guys all know that. It's not rocket science," she added. "We save the rocket science for the solutions teams."

Mark chuckled.

"So, what's the deal with that new system you guys are rolling on?" Ross asked. "Bud here was at the trade show, and he said something like Dar was teaching routers to think?"

Shari laughed in derision. "What a load of BS."

Kerry looked across the table and caught Michelle's eye. The shorter women looked away, then visibly sighed and nudged her partner. Shari gave her an outraged face, but Michelle lowered her chin and stared at her until she subsided.

"Dar's working on a lot of new technology," Kerry went on after the awkward break. "Most of which I can't really go into, but it's fair to say we're being very aggressive in taking the limits out of our new hardware."

"Yeah, I can imagine what you're selling the government with our tax dollars to burn." Shari stared steadily at Kerry. "How many millions was it for the Navy?"

Bitch. Kerry braced her elbow on the arm of her chair and rested her chin against it. "Well..." she finally addressed Shari directly. "Considering that the systems they were running before we went in there were written by Dar when she was fifteen years old, I guess they thought they needed an upgrade."

"Fifteen?" Ross stared at her. "What are you talking about?"

Kerry grinned briefly. "She was trading programming sessions for peanut butter way back then. But the systems held up until they were ready for the next century."

Ross cocked his head. "I didn't know Dar was a programmer. I thought she was all infrastructure and design."

"She has many, many skills." A wicked twinkle entered Kerry's green eyes. "That has been a very successful contract for us. I've enjoyed working on it. It makes me feel good to know we're providing the best to the people who defend our country."

Shari rolled her eyes.

Kerry caught the interested expression on the Tech TV reporter's face as he sat there picking at his chicken. "That's what's given us a leg up on the new project. Dar's helping them write the machine code for it."

"Wow." Ross didn't disguise his reaction. "So we'll all end up licensing her brain cells, huh?"

"Eventually," Kerry agreed. "But you have been all along. She holds I think..." She glanced at Mark.

"Twelve," Mark supplied promptly.

"Twelve patents," Kerry nodded. "That's right. Most of it in behind the scenes firmware advances." She took another sip of her tea, glancing around with a good deal of bland, mock innocence. "Sometimes you really do get what you pay for."

"You'd know," Shari sniped. "Talk about the last century. You're never going to survive in the next one with that old business strategy. Our last six months proves that."

Kerry shrugged. "Time will tell."

"No one wants to deal with you dinosaurs anymore," Shari added. "They want small companies, who can react fast, and not charge an arm and a leg." She looked directly at Kerry. "And you are only as good as your last success. One big screw up in the news, and you don't even have that much."

Kerry looked at the Tech TV reporter, then at her. "Very true."

"Well, if we're done." Quest appeared, his hair disordered as though he'd been running his hands through it. "Let's go get the rest of the meeting started. I've had some things crop up that need tending to."

Kerry gladly got to her feet and shoved her chair in, dropping her napkin on her mostly untouched plate. "Definitely would be my pleasure." She motioned Mark to precede her, and evaded Ross' hastened steps as they headed toward the door.

Outside, she touched Mark's arm briefly. "Go on upstairs. I'm going to take a pit stop." She indicated the restrooms.

"Okay," Mark agreed. "But you are coming back, right?" he asked, with a wry look. "I mean, you want me to call the center and have them broadcast a fake disaster so we can get out of here?"

Kerry narrowed her eyes. "Don't tempt me," she muttered, giving him a bump. "G'wan. Maybe Quest'll give us a break and make this short."

Mark took off toward the steps, and she turned after a moment and headed for the restroom door. She heard steps catching up to her, and felt the odd sensation of her hackles lifting as she imagined them to be Shari.

Her heart started pounding, and she got the same tingles in her guts that she did when they were sparring in kickboxing class, a response to challenge that made her fingers twitch in sudden reaction.

She reached forward and grabbed the door handle, pulling it open only to find not Shari, but Michelle behind her as she half turned to face her pursuer.

Maybe Michelle got the hint. She stepped back quickly and waited, watching Kerry with faintly alarmed eyes. "Sorry."

Kerry glanced past Michelle, and ascertained they were alone. "Where's your traveling jackass?" she asked directly. "Don't you take her with you to critique the toilet paper?"

Michelle sighed, and edged past Kerry through the door she was still holding open. "I'm not going to answer that," she said. "We all have our issues."

"That's not an issue." Kerry followed her inside and headed for a stall. "That's a brain the size of a walnut and an ego the size of the glades." She closed the door with a snick. "And a lack of professionalism that makes you look like an idiot."

Michelle cleared her throat gently. "Gee, Kerry. Tell me how you really feel. Don't hold back."

"Fuck it," Kerry snapped. "You two have been on my last nerve for a week. Grow the hell up, would you?"

Dead silence.

Kerry amused herself by flipping open her PDA and reading some of her saved messages from Dar.

"Well. I see we really did piss you off," Michelle finally said into all that silence. "The real Kerry Stuart emerges." She ran some water in the sink, as the outer walls echoed with a faint announcement. "Look, Shari feels like she's got a right to blow the gilt off of your reputation when she can. It's just business, remember?"

"Shari does it because she's got a hard on for Dar," Kerry replied evenly. "It has nothing to do with business, and we both know it."

Michelle cleared her throat gently. "She does have a personal insight," she remarked. "It's valid."

Kerry emerged, leaning against the stall door to face her adversary. "I have a personal insight too," she reminded Michelle. "Want me to bring out in that meeting how you chased Dar and wanted to get into her skirt? Or how you tried to blackmail her by sending pictures of us to the corporate office? Or how..."

"Okay." Michelle's voice was sharp, and hard. "Let's just relax a minute."

Kerry waited, keeping her eyes fixed on the smaller woman. After a long moment, when neither of them said anything, she stepped forward. "You listen to me," she said, her voice dropping a little. "You want this to be civilized? That's fine with me. I want this to be civilized. I want this to be a tough bid, and the best deal wins. Can we leave all the personal bullshit out of it?"

Michelle shifted and leaned against the wall. "Is that why Dar skipped out? Get too hot for her?"

Kerry rolled her eyes. "Jesus." She threw up her hands. "I give up. Fine. Let it be a bitch fest. Just make sure you know how to duck when I start throwing." She turned and headed for the door, but Michelle edged around her and put her back against it. "You really don't want to get in my way, Michelle."

"Okay–okay–okay." Graver ran her hand through her hair, disordering its fair glossiness. "Listen, just like you have a vested interest, so do I. You may not like the methods, but I respect Shari's skill at marketing, and she's been a big part of the progress we made in the last year."

Kerry put her hand on the door and started to push.

"Yeah, okay—she's got a bug up her about Dar, but I think it's mutual, right?" Michelle persisted. "She's got a beef, and now she's in a position to screw Dar over like Dar screwed her over way back when. It's human."

Kerry stopped pushing. "Michelle," she said quietly. "Did she ever tell you why Dar screwed her over?"

The smaller woman cocked her head slightly. "Did she need a reason?"

"Dar always has a reason." Kerry shoved past her, into the bright chaos of the hotel lobby. "You want this to be nasty?" She turned and regarded Michelle. "I can make it nasty. Dar's just honest and straightforward." She smiled grimly. "I'm a politician's kid. Screw with me at your own risk."

It felt good to turn and just walk away then, sauntering across the lobby well aware of Michelle's eyes on her back. "Bitch, bitch, bitch," she warbled under her breath, as she started up the steps to the second floor conference rooms. "Y'now, there are some days when I wish I'd taken my family's advice and become a teacher." She got to the top of the steps and turned to see Michelle and Shari standing next to the restroom, obviously in a heated discussion. "Heh. But today isn't one of 'em." She tapped the railing, then continued on her way toward the conference room, whose doors were standing wide open.

And as she stepped across the threshold, every single light in the building blinked out, leaving the room, and the rest of the hotel, in total darkness.

"I didn't do it," Mark's voice sounded just behind her. "Honest."

Kerry emerged back into the lobby, which was lit by outside light. "They forget to pay FPL or something?" she commented to Ross, who quickly joined her at the balcony rail. "Nice timing though."

"You got that right," Ross agreed. "I'm not sure what the deal is here, Kerry. What's the game? You never have vendors come in and do a face off."

"Good question," Kerry agreed. "I don't know wha..." She glanced down as her PDA started to go off, then she turned as Mark pulled his phone out. "You getting those too?"

Mark studied his phone. Then he opened it and dialed. He waited, his eyes going a little unfocused, then he hung up only to answer the phone as it rang immediately. "Polenti." He listened, then his eyes went up and fastened on Kerry's. "She's right here."

"Uh oh. That doesn't sound good," Kerry muttered.

Quest came over, leaving the house phone on the wall he'd been talking on. "Well, it appears it's not the hotel's fault," he announced. "Apparently the power is out all over the city." His eyes fell on Kerry. "Some screw up or other."

"Okay," Mark said. "I'll tell her." He shut the phone and clipped it to his belt. "Boss?"

Kerry felt the buzzing against her palm as alerts came one after another. She kept her expression mildly interested though. "So, does that mean your meetings for this afternoon are postponed?" she asked. "We'd like to beat traffic back to our offices if that's the case."

"Well." Quest looked briefly nonplussed. "There's nothing we can do right now. I have a presentation I was going to show, but it will need to be rescheduled. I expect you all to remain available for that." He motioned to his staff and started down the stairs toward the hotel front desk.

"What are we supposed to do?" Shari asked. "Just hang around here in the dark?"

Kerry bit her tongue on the obvious response. "If the AC's off in here, I'd actually go outside if I were you," she offered. "It gets very hot, very fast. Mark, let's head back to our offices. I'm sure we can get some work done in the meantime."

"Gee, thanks Kerry," Ross exhaled. "I was supposed to fly back to Oregon tonight." He started down the stairs. "Damn it."

"See you all later." Kerry motioned for Mark to follow her and they trotted down the steps, getting some distance away from the rest of the crowd before speaking. "Are we in trouble?" she asked.

"Big time screwed," Mark confirmed. "We lost all our links."

"What?" Kerry stopped in mid step, and stared at him.

"Think you better book, poquito boss. They can't even call into or out of the office. Lucky we got our cells."

"Jesus." Kerry fought to keep herself from breaking into a run. "What in the hell happened to the redundant systems?"

"No one can get through to the Telco to find out."

"God damn it."

THERE WAS JUST enough breeze for Dar to be able to sit in comfort, allowing the late afternoon sun to drench her with its oddly pallid light. She had a delightfully intricate tour behind her, two bags of rampantly tourist-flavored purchases next to her, and a bellyful of cherry vanilla ice cream.

Life was good.

The museum had charmed her and she was fairly sure her knick-knack acquisitions were going to charm her family.

Her family. Dar had to stop and take a breath, releasing it slowly as she thought about how full of family her life was now. She'd gotten a sub model and a sweatshirt for her dad, and a space shuttle plus a T-shirt that said 'my husband is in the navy, and all I got was this T-shirt and a pail of seaweed' for her mom, and a bagful of god only knew what for Kerry. Even Chino had gotten a toy.

It was a radical change for her, having so many people to get things for. Dar removed the stuffed squeaky Apollo capsule she was sure Chino would tear apart in no time and examined it, squeezing it gently with her fingers and listening to the wheezy bright sound.

It certainly made shopping a lot more fun though. Dar grinned. She'd gotten herself a few things, but she'd extracted far more enjoyment in picking stuff out for everyone else, especially the bagful of items for her partner.

Silly things. But Dar was certain Kerry would love them, and that a good number of them would find their way into the office to perch in, hopefully, inconspicuous spots near her desk. The hours of exploration had restored her good humor, as had the moments of indulgence in old memories that the smell of brass and diesel had called up to her.

In fact, Dar pulled out her conspicuously silent PDA and opened it, scribbling a little note and sending it on its way. She waited for a short while, but didn't get an answer, and figured Kerry was probably either busy with the meeting, or had fallen asleep at the meeting, but probably was doing just fine.

Dar decided she'd had a long enough rest, and after flexing her calves a few times, she stood up and arranged her shopping bags, then started back down toward the city and away from the docks. Now toward evening, the foot traffic was starting to pick up, and the harried looks of the people on the street were relaxing as the workday was ending.

Well, if she was stuck in New York, at least she'd had the afternoon off. Dar strolled down the sidewalk, pausing as a small bar caught her attention. After a moment's hesitation, she shrugged one shoulder and entered, finding a spot in a quiet area off to one side.

She eased onto one of the high stools and set her bags down by her feet, resting her forearms on the round wooden table as one of the waitresses scooted over to her. "Hi."

"What can I getcha?" the girl asked, putting down a small, square napkin next to Dar's elbow.

Milk? Dar glanced around the place, which oozed a tavern atmosphere she could almost feel coating her skin. Hm. Her eyes fell on the beer tap, and spotted a name she knew Kerry liked. "Ah, I'll take a Killian," she decided. "And a plate of wings."

"No problem." The girl looked approvingly at her. "C'm right up." She headed back toward the bar, leaving Dar to appreciate her surroundings more fully.

Bars generally weren't places she tended to hang out in, at least not by herself. Deferring to Kerry's fondness for good brew, she accompanied her partner into pubs and enjoyed them, but more for the company than for the alcohol.

She didn't mind beer. As long as it was served very cold and didn't have too strong a taste it satisfied her and she'd found it a reasonable thing to drink when she was with others due to its relatively small alcohol content. She'd seen enough people drunk off their asses to know she had no personal desire to emulate them.

Kerry was a cute drunk. She got silly, and publicly snuggly, the sweeter side of her personality coming out. Dar, on the other hand, knew herself to be a surly drunk the few times she'd gone down that road and reasoned she was better off stopping before things got ugly.

She sure didn't want Kerry to have to deal with that. Dar let her chin rest on her fist and sighed.

A television was on above the bar, and she amused herself by watching the basketball game in progress, mildly surprised to find the players female. A news banner ran chattily under the picture, but she steadfastly ignored it until a familiar word caught her attention.

Miami.

Dar leaned forward and focused on the headline, gritting her teeth and squinting slightly to keep the words in focus.

It didn't take long. "Son of a bitch," she uttered with feeling. "Why the hell didn't she call me?" Dar removed her cell phone from its clip on her belt and hit a speed button, waiting for it to connect and then holding it to her ear.

It rang eight times before it was answered, and then the first sound that came down the line was a rattling noise and a seriously Midwestern sounding curse.

"God bless the milkman...yes, hello?" Kerry growled into the phone. By her tone she obviously was at the end of the chain tied to the ribbon tied to the end of her rope.

Dar waited a moment, then exhaled. "I love you."

There was a few heartbeats of silence, then a soft grunt came down the line, and a sound Dar recognized as a body landing in the leather chair in her office.

"Jesus," Kerry exhaled.

"No, just me," Dar responded. "I just saw the headlines on the television. How's it going there?"

"Well," Kerry said. "Entire city has no power."

"Son of a bitch."

"Yeah," her partner exhaled. "On the other hand, every single employee in this building is lighting candles of prayer to your image for having a diesel generator big enough to run the air plants."

"I'm a native. I know better."

Kerry faintly chuckled, then sighed. "Now for the really bad news. I have a headache the size of the Orange Bowl, and Bellsouth blew their backup power to one central office and a spike blew their OC on the other. We have no telecom or data services into the building."

Dar covered her eyes in pure reaction. "Holy shit."

"I was holding off calling you until I was absolutely positive the only thing you could do was pat me on my head," Kerry sighed. "I have every critical thing we've got loaded on the sat links, but..."

"Jesus."

"No. Just me." Another sigh. "The one bright spot in my day was that piece of moose pooter meeting got canceled."

The waitress returned, putting down her beer and giving her a bright smile. "Wings'll be right up. K?"

Dar nodded, picking up the frosty mug of beer and taking a long swallow of it. "Ker..."

"Tell me you're in a bar having a beer, and I might have to fly to New York just so I can bite your butt for that."

Dar almost spit her mouthful of beer out across the table, but she managed somehow to swallow it instead. "Um..." She cleared her throat. "Want me on a plane back there?"

Kerry sighed very audibly. "Yes," she replied in a quiet tone. "There is nothing in the world I want right now more than to have you here right next to me."

Dar checked her watch, then reached for her PDA. "Gimme a minute...let me get the flights..."

"Sweetheart, hold on," Kerry said. "I have so many people pissed off at us down here, do we really need another client ticked off because you walked out?"

"Fuck them." Dar was busy with her flight scheduling.

"Dar."

"In addition to the fact that they all mean jack nothing to me next to you, Kerry, the rest of the company does take precedence over them," Dar replied, reviewing her options. "You should have called me before now."

"Yeah, I know." Kerry's tone now just sounded tired. "But I like to think I can actually do the job you pay me for sometimes."

Dar paused in mid tap. She put her PDA down and concentrated on the phone exclusively. "Kerry, this has nothing to do with your competence. This is outside anyone's scope." She hesitated. "You want me to butt out and let you handle it?"

There was a very long silence after that. Finally, on the heels of the faintest of sniffles, Kerry spoke up. "Professionally? Yes."

Dar winced, the rejection stinging more than she'd anticipated.

"Personally, no," she went on quietly. "So what should I do? Can you give me some advice so I can make some kind of peace with myself?"

Dar released a held breath, and ordered her thoughts, sipping her beer as she pondered the question. "Okay," she said. "I'm assuming the big cluster is our lines being down."

"Yeah."

"I'm assuming you've already browbeaten and bullied everyone in Bellsouth you can get your hands on."

"Mmph...yeah. Problem is, emergency services are priority, and we're not," Kerry said. "Even though we pay them for diversity out the wing wang."

Which was true. "Okay." Dar closed her eyes and thought. "The blown switch is out of our hands, but the other Central Office is just out of power?"

"Yeah."

"Send Mark to Home Depot and have him buy every big generator they've got, then just go in there and hijack the bank we're in and push power through it."

"They're not going to let us do that."

"Don't ask them," Dar said quietly. "Just show up, walk in, don't take no for an answer."

"They're going to think we're nuts."

"Yeah," Dar agreed. "But our customers are going to think we're miracle workers."

A soft rattling of keys came down the line, along with the ghost of another sniffle. "You were right," Kerry said, after the rattling stopped. "I should have called you before now," she admitted. "Damn."

Kerry had been doing everything humanly possible, Dar was sure. They'd been through enough crises together for her to trust her partner's judgment implicitly. But sometimes when Kerry encountered the unlikely and was under a lot of stress, thinking way outside the box wasn't her first instinct.

It was always Dar's first instinct. "It's okay, sweetheart." She tried for a faint joke. "S'why you pay me the big bucks, remember?"

A faint chuckle rewarded her.

"I wouldn't have called anyone either," Dar admitted. "Never have been able to do that. So..."

"Hello pot, kettle here." Kerry sighed wryly. "Wanna get together for some macaroni and cheese?"

Dar relaxed a little, the knots in her guts easing slightly as she felt her heartbeat start to settle and cease its painful pounding inside her skull. "Sounds delicious."

Kerry chuckled a little. "Do me a favor?"

"Anything," Dar responded. "I've got the flights in front of me. Offer's still open."

Kerry was very quiet for a bit, and Dar gave her the space to wrestle with her own conscience. At last, she grunted softly. "Tell you what, partner. If this doesn't work, I'll give you a call with your flight information, okay?"

A compromise. Dar accepted it reluctantly. "You know I'm going to be a mess all night, right?" she found herself saying anyway. "I'll be sweating that call."

"I know," her lover said. "But if it works, I'll take out a full page ad in the Herald and tell everyone what a smart and amazing person I have as my boss."

"That's supposed to make me feel better?"

At last, Kerry laughed, if only briefly. "Or maybe they'll get the power grid back online, Dar. Having the entire city down with no AC is putting more pressure on the powers that be than I ever could."

"Mmph."

"Call you back as soon as I know something," Kerry went on. "Promise."

"Okay." Dar sighed. "Hang in there, Ker."

"Love you."

"Love you too." Dar closed the phone reluctantly, thoughts running through her mind at a furious rate. She looked up as a plate appeared in front of her, meeting the eyes of the waitress.

"Wings?" the girl said.

Wish I had a pair. Dar nodded in response, staring at the crispy golden items before her. With a sigh, she picked one up and turned it in her fingertips, completely uninterested now in everything except for the vanished voice on the other end of her disconnected phone.

Chapter
Thirteen

KERRY FORCED HERSELF not to tense up, concentrating on keeping her hands down at her sides and not balled up into fists. "Listen, Barry, you don't have a choice here." Already in her shirtsleeves in deference to the dank mugginess of the emergency lighting lit office, she resolutely refused to wipe the sweat off her face as she ordered her arguments.

The man she was speaking with, a tall, gangly station manager with a drooping moustache and desperate eyes, slammed his hand on the desk. "Kerry, I can't do it," he repeated, for the nth time.

"You can," Kerry replied inflexibly. "Bottom line is, you have no choice." Her voice already had a slight rasp in it.

"If I let you do it, I have to let everyone. Do you know how many lines go through this building? To the financial district? Jesus, Kerry, do you think you're the only one who's down?"

"We have a contract."

"THEY ALL DO!" Barry yelled, at the top of his voice in frustration. "Woman, you can't understand what you're asking."

What would Dar do? Kerry took a breath. Dar would just yell louder, until the walls shook. But she couldn't do that—it wasn't really her style. "Barry, you have a contract with us to provide diversity. You didn't. Are all those other companies paying you top dollar for that kind of insurance?"

He stared at her.

"We pay you to make sure." Kerry inhaled and upped the volume just a little. "MAKE SURE that we never go down. NEVER. Not 99 percent, not 99.5 percent, not 99.9 percent. 100 percent, Barry. I can't afford any less, and you god damn well know it."

"Yes, I know, but..."

"Barry." Kerry leaned forward. "What is your guarantee worth if all you can tell me is too bad, take a number?"

"You can't just hook this stuff up to a generator," he replied, after a long hesitation. "It just doesn't work like that. You can't fathom the complexity of this stuff, and I..."

Kerry walked right around his desk and grabbed him by the shirtfront, shocking them both. "I can't fathom it? I can't fathom it? Who in the hell do you think you're talking to, the operations vice president of Publix? Jesus Christ, Barry! I've got more complex technology sitting in my living room than you have in this place!"

His eyes widened. "Hey, now listen. Let go of me!"

Kerry did, but she didn't step back. Dar's words were ringing in her head like sea-bells and it was all she could do not to just keep shaking the man until he gave in to her. "Barry, use your head. Get me off your back. Just do it."

"I can't."

"You can," Kerry insisted.

"Kerry, for the sake of god, I can't. It'll be my job!"

Kerry leaned over him, wishing she had Dar's presence. "You will." She nailed him with a look right in the eyes. "Or it'll be your job any way. I swear it."

Would he believe her? Kerry forced herself to hold her gaze steady and cold, offering him no compromise. Her guts were clenching inside, and she only hoped it wasn't showing.

He straightened up and took a breath to answer, only to release it partially as his shoulders slumped. "Kerry, it's not that easy. C'mon now. You can't just plug in one of those things to a damn generator. What if it blows the boards? Then what?"

Ah. Kerry felt the success, like that momentary give in a tug of war when you knew your team was about to break the grunting muddy stalemate, and start to move in the right direction. "Then you hand me a bill," she agreed readily. "I'll take responsibility for the decision."

He leaned forward. "You know how much money you're talking about?"

"Yes, I do." She tilted her head just a little, and gentled her expression. "C'mon, Barry. Get rid of me. You know I have to do it."

Barry relaxed in defeat. "What the hell." He lifted both hands off his chair arms and let them drop. "I'm screwed anyway. I was the dumb bastard who forgot to schedule the maintenance on that freaking backup system."

Kerry felt sweat roll down the back of her neck, and she spared a moment of tired sympathy for him. "Thanks, Barry. Let me get my guys rolling on this." She hesitated. "You got anyone else that's as big a pain in the ass as I am? I can see if we have enough power to share some."

He shook his head after a second. "I wouldn't know where to even start."

"Okay." Kerry turned and headed for the door, already reaching for her cell phone. She keyed the radio button on it. "Mark?"

"Yeah?" a slightly apprehensive voice answered.

"Go," Kerry instructed, now at last wiping the sweat off her face with one hand. "Pull the truck around back. No sense in giving the news people something else to shoot." She looked around for the emergency exit, spotting it on the back of one wall in the gloom. It was hot and very stuffy inside the central office, and eerily empty of workers.

No sense, she had to agree. Why pay for techs to stand around and look at non-functional equipment? With a deep sigh, she hit the door release and opened it, finding some mild relief in the cooler evening air that brushed against her.

Finding a broken piece of punch down block handy, she blocked the door open with it and leaned against the back wall of the building, waiting for Mark and her crew to arrive. She kicked a bit of slate with one toe, glad she'd taken the time to change into jeans and a short sleeved shirt before coming.

Even that was too hot, but anything else risked compromising her ability to project her authority in a serious way, and Kerry wasn't that stupid. She let her eyes close for a minute, the stress of the long day weighing on her heavily.

Then the rumbling of the approaching motor jogged her into straightening up. She brushed off the fatigue and walked to meet Mark as he pulled up close to the building in the rented panel truck, putting the back of the vehicle next to the emergency door.

"Hey, boss." Mark looked as ratty as Kerry felt. He opened the door and jumped out, circling the truck to open the back and let four other techs out into the muggy night air. "Sorry about the ride, guys."

"Shit." One of them rubbed his head. "Oh." He winced, spotting Kerry. "Sorry, ma'am."

"Shit about covers it," Kerry responded. "Okay." She peered into the truck. "Six. Good."

"All they had," Mark explained. "These are the big ones. Most of the small ones were gone already. You know how people are. Lucky we're halfway through the season."

"Right." Kerry studied the machines. "How many to run the one switch inside, Mark?"

"Lemme check." Mark scooted inside the building, pulling out his flashlight as he ducked inside the door. "Holy crap, it's steaming in here!" He poked his head back out. "Hey...I'm not sure we can run those things even if we do juice 'em up. They'll overheat."

Shit. Kerry thumped against the truck, a sense of sick horror coming over her. "Find out what they'll need," she told Mark, to give her a moment to think.

Idiot. Of course they need cooling. She blinked a droplet of sweat from her eyes. Why hadn't she thought of that? Kerry let her head rest against the metal wall. Maybe she'd gotten too used to letting Dar do her thinking for her?

A draft of cool air blew into her face, and she looked inside the truck, sticking her hand into the dark bay. She stepped back and looked at the side, spotting the boast of an air conditioned truck bed. "You got a flashlight?" she asked the tech nearest her.

"Um...sure." The curly-haired tech handed it over.

Kerry turned it on and flashed it over the interior of the truck, spotting the large air conditioning unit near the ceiling. "Okay." She saw Mark emerge. "What's the deal?"

He shrugged. "We can do it with one of these suckers." He indicated the generators. "No problem, but it won't stay up more than ten minutes, boss. I..." He hesitated. "I shoulda thought of that."

"Why? Even they didn't." Kerry exhaled, pointing inside. "At least, they never mentioned it. So maybe they figured we'd figure out a way around that, too."

"Yeah." Mark frowned.

"So we'll have to. Listen." Kerry pushed away from the truck. "Here's the plan. Mark—set these four up and get them going. Figure out what we need to connect them all in series, but use one at a time so we can keep them running longer. When one runs out of gas we switch to the second, but we can't drop any power."

"Uh..."

"When you figure out what you'll need for that, surge boxes or whatever, call me at Home Depot. I'll be there buying air conditioning duct and duct tape so we can run the truck all night and pipe some air in there." She pointed. "Okay? Thanks. Call me."

She turned and headed for her car, knowing she'd left slack jawed employees behind her. Reaching her Lexus, she popped the door locks and hopped inside, starting up the SUV and closing the door as the air conditioning promptly bathed her in a very welcome chill.

Would Mark figure that all out? Kerry wondered. If they didn't find a way to keep things going, it'd be useless. Dropping the lines every couple hours while they refilled the diesel just wasn't going to cut it. "One thing at a time, Ker." She reminded herself, putting the car in gear with a determined expression. "What was that Dar once said? Mouthful at a time and you can eat an entire whale, tail and all?"

She turned the car onto the road carefully, since the signals were out along with everything else. The power outage had been so severe the power company hadn't even been able to project a fix for it. Too much damage had been done to too much of the infrastructure when a freak collapse of a transfer station had sent power back the wrong way up the lines into the grid.

So, she had to come through here. They had to come through. There wasn't any choice—the pressure was building and she'd started getting more and more calls from their clients frustrated with lack of, or slowness of, service to their vital resources.

As if in cosmic synchronicity with that, her cell phone rang. Kerry fumbled it out and flipped it open, keeping her eyes on the road. "Kerry Stuart."

"Kerry, it's Eleanor."

Kerry exhaled silently. "What's up?" she asked. "I'm a little tied up at the moment."

"Yeah, me too," Eleanor replied. "Listen, aside from everyone that comes through here calling Jose every name in the book, I've got that damn CNN reporter here. Someone told him our customers were up in arms."

"Is he aware there's a power outage?" Kerry said, dodging a car stopped in the roadway. "One that isn't ILS's fault?"

"Sure," she said. "But his point is, we made a big deal about service. So now that there's a problem, where's our service? We charge a premium to make sure customers don't go down, so..."

Kerry sighed. "That's exactly the point I just made to our Bellsouth manager here," she said. "We pay a premium to make sure our customers don't go down. But the fact is, they screwed up, and we're down, so now I'm out here headed to Home Depot to find a way to fix it."

Eleanor sighed. "So I guess you can't talk to him?"

"Not right now," Kerry said. "When I get back to the office, I can."

"Okay," Eleanor sounded mollified. "Hope you have a good story for him. Ker. This guy's a skeptic."

"Yeah. Okay," Kerry muttered. "Talk to you later." She hung up the phone, and shook her head. "Jesus."

A clog of traffic at an intersection forced her to stop, and she rested her forearms on her steering wheel as the crowd sorted itself out. A queasy roll of her stomach reminded her she hadn't stopped to have dinner, and though the last thing she felt like doing was eating she knew she was asking for trouble if she didn't.

She already had a stress headache. With a sigh, she let the brake up a little and crept forward, one hand fishing in her utility well until she found a bit of cellophane. Pulling the power bar out, she used her teeth to rip it open, and took a bite without taking her eyes off the road.

It wasn't satisfying, but it was banana nut, and it took the edge off. Kerry chewed at it as she got through the dark intersection, only having to honk four or five times to keep other cars from plowing into her SUV's dark blue sides. "Bah...bah...hey! You jerk! Watch it!"

A Mustang squirted past her in a blare of horns.

Kerry felt her heart hammering in her chest as she got past the intersection, heading toward the nearby hardware store. She got into the parking lot without further incident and headed into the store, regretfully trading the cool leather interior of her car for the heat outside.

The Home Depot was also running on generators, and it was clammy inside. Kerry found it hard to breathe, between the sawdust and the smell of generator oil, but she continued on, glancing down the aisles until she found the central air supply row. She paused in front of the compressed ducting and paused, realizing suddenly she had no idea how much to get.

"Jesus." Kerry slapped herself on the side of the head, unable to believe the stupidity of not measuring the distance first. "I should have had Dar just come back. I can't handle this."

But Dar wasn't there, so after a moment of mentally kicking herself Kerry leaned against the steel shelving and closed her eyes, trying to picture the unfamiliar confines of the telephone building. "Okay." She sighed. "How many Dar's can fit with arms outstretched between the truck and the switch, Kerry. C'mon. Think."

Dar was the easiest thing she could picture, and she knew her partner's outstretched arms were just over six feet across. Mentally, she positioned that tall, lanky frame, imagining her at the truck, then at the door, then inside, then across the aisle and around the corner, just Dar after Dar after Dar, until she was smiling and she had her answer. "Mm...ten Dar's. Lucky me."

With seventy-five feet of ducting to be safe, and four rolls of tape, Kerry loaded up her wagon and then checked her cell phone. It was stubbornly silent, so she pushed the cart over to the electrical section, and started browsing the different devices herself.

What would she need? The urge to call Dar and ask almost overtook her, but Kerry firmly closed her hand away from her cell phone and concentrated on the big boxes lining the shelves. Cables? They had those. Diesel? Mark had stopped for that too. Kerry's eyes roamed over the choices until it fell on a dust-covered box on the bottom shelf labeled GAC Load Control Systems, a lonely looking item, one of its kind.

Crouching down, she tugged the box forward, releasing a cloud of ancient dust that nearly bowled her over. Stifling a sneeze, she peered at the lettering on the box, trying to make the technical terms fit concepts she was already familiar with. "Hm. Load balancing between two or more generators." She let her hands rest on the box. "Well, I guess that's what we're doing." With a grunt, she lifted the item and put it on the cart with the rest, going to the front and hauling the flatbed after in a sweaty, dusty pony-like fashion. She was standing at the counter handing over her credit card when three or four men rushed in, dashing past the entrance and heading for the same aisle she just came out of.

Kerry turned back to the cashier as she was presented with a slip to sign, giving the exhausted looking clerk behind the desk an understanding smile. "Long day."

"Honey, you ain't kidding." The woman handed her card back.

"Damn it, they had one this afternoon." The men came back, obviously frustrated. "Jesus, those damn generators won't do us a lick of good if we can't connect 'em all in series and keep the power up...hey!" He stopped, staring at Kerry's cart. "She got one! She got it!"

Hey! Kerry echoed in mildly amazed silence. I guessed right! Whoa! "That's right. Excuse me, gentlemen." She pocketed her card and started to push her flatbed past them. "Things to do, power to generate, you know how it is."

"Damn! Hey, can we buy that off you? Pay you double for it!" The man in the lead caught up with her. "C'mon, lady...I really need that!"

"No thanks. Sorry. So do I." Kerry steered toward her car with a definite purpose.

"You even know what it is?" the man yelled in frustration.

Kerry stopped, turned and looked at him, one hand on her hip.

"Yeah, yeah, okay." The man waved a hand in disgust at her, shaking his head. "Five minutes too late."

"That's right." Kerry made a shooing motion at him. "Go find another Home Depot. Scoot." A rumble sounded over head, and she glanced up, dismayed to see storm clouds gathering. "Oh, great. Just what I need." She gave the cart a shove and headed for the Lexus. "Maybe I should have gotten a tent."

The thunder rumbled again, as though she was being laughed at.

DAR'S CELL PHONE rang as she entered the hotel lobby, and she found a quiet corner to drop into a leather chair and answer it. "Yeah?"

"Dar!" Alastair's voice belted through the phone. "Good grief, woman! Where are you!"

"New York," Dar answered. "Saving one of our client's asses. Why?"

"Do you know what's going on down in Florida? Dar! We've got half the network down!" Alastair said. "I've got twenty customers on hold on my damn phone screaming their heads off!"

The silent anchors of CNN faced Dar from the bar's big television, the outline of a darkened Miami prominent in the background. "We're page one on CNN. Of course I know what's going on, Alastair," she snapped. "Kerry's handling it."

"What?" her boss almost squealed. "Dar! This is serious!"

"And I'm 2,000 miles away!" Dar yelled back, only in a soft tone, since three men at the bar had turned around to look at her. "What would you like me to do about it? Jesus, calm down!"

"Calm down." Alastair fumed. "I have an international board meeting in two hours, in case you forgot, Dar. One where I have to explain all the calls I've been getting from every big name account we have in the US."

Oops. "No kidding. Me too," Dar replied calmly. "And?"

"Dar."

She could hear the absolute panicked frustration in his tone. "Alastair, it's a power outage. Most of the crits are on the SAT, and Kerry's working on a plan to get more lines up. What is it you expect us to do? Change physics? All the money in the bank ain't gonna cut any slack down there because they can't get the damn hospitals working. Guess what? That's first."

There was a brief silence. "Kerry's working on something?"

"Of course." Dar injected as much impatience into her tone as she could. "I thought we'd gotten past that damned 'I picked her for her looks' thing. What's wrong with you?"

Alastair sighed. "I'm not used to having to rely on anyone but you. That's what's wrong with me."

"Get you something, ma'am?" A waitress came over to her.

Dar hesitated, debating on the answer, covering the microphone with her fingers. Then she half shrugged. "Got a chocolate milkshake handy?"

The woman smiled. "I can find one for ya. Be right back."

"Well." Dar spoke into the phone. "Get used to it."

Alastair paused, taking an audible breath. "What's that supposed to mean?"

What was it supposed to mean? Dar wondered bleakly. "I pay her for a reason," she finally said. "If I didn't think she could handle it, I'd have already headed back."

Her boss sighed. "Yeah, I know," he admitted. "Sorry, Dar. Backhanded compliment, really."

"Yeah," Dar agreed softly. "Look, she'll take care of it. Trust her."

"Since you do, I will," Alastair said. "Just got the jitters, Dar. Been a rough couple of months here. Last thing I need is bad press. What the blazes happened to the backup we're supposed to have down there?"

Dar explained the problem. "So, yeah, it's Bellsouth's issue. They screwed up. Doesn't help us."

"I'll get Ham on it," he stated, his voice now brisk and businesslike. "We can get some cash out of it, anyway. Keep me advised, willya, Dar?"

"I will." Dar promised. "See you on the conference call later."

"With good news," Alastair said.

"With news," Dar clarified. "Or else I'll be on a plane headed south. Guaranteed."

A more contented sigh. "Now I feel better," he replied. "Thanks, Dar. Talk to you soon."

Dar folded the cell phone up and clipped it to her pocket. She slid down in the leather chair, gazing up at the finely plastered ceiling until the waitress sauntered back over with her milkshake. "Thanks."

"Sure you don't want a shot in that?" the woman asked, with a sympathetic grin. "Looks like you could use it."

Dar stared at the glass for a long moment, then her eyes lifted. "No, thanks." She cradled the cold drink between her hands. "Just this for right now." She handed the woman her room key, then signed the resulting check presented to her from the handheld printer. "Appreciate it."

"Anytime, okay?" the woman smiled warmly at her. "Just ask for Angie." She gave Dar a wink, then went on to the next group of older, business suited men seated nearby.

The flirting didn't even register, really. Dar got up and headed for the elevator, hardly aware of the watching eyes.

MARK MET HER as she got out of the Lexus, his face a study in anxious consternation. "Kerry, listen, I tried like a son of bitch to figure out what that electrical stuff was but..."

"No problem. I got it," Kerry said briefly. "I'll need a hand with the stuff in the back. Got the generators set up?"

"Yeah, but..." Mark pointed at the now very overcast sky. "I don't know how good they're gonna be in that."

"No problem." Kerry replied again, with a grim smile. "I brought a tent. Let's go." She turned and headed for the back of the car, popping the hatch and pulling down the rear gate. "You guys, take that ducting and tape out and start stretching it. Need to go from the air unit inside the back of the truck all the way inside the building."

"Yes, ma'am."

"Mark, you get the tent. I'll get this gizmo up and running and connected to the generators. Then we can fire them up and see what we got." Kerry finished briskly. "Any questions? Okay. Let's just do it. I want out of this damned sweatbox."

"You got it, boss." Mark pulled the canopy out and threw it over his shoulder, moving aside to let the two other techs get the ducting gear out. He followed Kerry over to the back door and watched as she dropped to one knee in front of the generators and started tearing the box of her gizmo open. "Whoa. Didn't know you knew the electrical engineering side, boss."

Kerry pulled aside the foam packing and removed the control unit, studying it closely. Four inputs in the back, four in the front, dials, gauges...Jesus. "Yeah, well...you never know when the odd class in college comes home, huh?" She set the unit down and reached inside for the insulated plugs, connecting one end to each generator and the other end to the back of her unit.

Her hands were shaking. Kerry wiped the back of one across her forehead. "Hey, Mark?"

"Yeah?" Mark finished unrolling the tarp and walked over. "Need me?"

"Can you get my backpack from the car?" She fished in her jeans pocket and removed her keys, handing them over. "I need something from it."

"Ma'am...you want this on the floor or..." One of the techs stuck his head out. "It's kinda wonky."

Kerry climbed to her feet and peered inside the building, getting a face full of stale air. "Let me see where the boards are...ah." She stepped over the unrolled ducting and looked at the switch, squatting in damp silence in front of her. "Okay, there's the out-take up there, so the intake has to be back here." She indicated the fan. "So it should pump in right behind that."

"Run it up here?" the tech queried, touching the top of the unit. "It's a hard bend."

Damn it, yes, it was. Kerry looked overhead, taking the flashlight from the tech and examining the drop ceiling. "No, loop some tape over the crossbar, there... see? Then kind of..."

"Cradle it, like this?" The tech wrapped a piece of tape around the duct and held it up. "Like that?"

"Perfect." Kerry gave him a pat on the shoulder. "Just suspend it like that out the door, and then we'll go right to the truck. We got enough duct?"

"Oh yeah." The tech nodded. "Just right."

Kerry managed a smile, before she escaped outside and went back to her work. The sun had long since set, and it was getting dark. She looked up as Mark came over with her pack, and set it down. "Thanks." She dug out another power bar and ripped it open. "How's the tent coming?"

"I'm a lot better at routers," Mark said mournfully, gazing at the poles. "But I think I got it."

Kerry looked up. "You better," She muttered around her mouthful.

"What if we blow that thing up? These generators aren't the greatest," Mark commented, as he got a pole into the corner of the tarp and raised it. "That's some bitching gear in there."

"This thing's got a power massager and anyway if we trash it I'll pay for it." Kerry squinted in the gloom at the directions. She looked up as a warm light bathed her, then gave Mark an appreciative smile. "Thank you."

"No problem." Mark was holding the flashlight in his teeth, and working the tarp with his hands. "You know how many times I hadta do this last time we moved one of the regionals? It sucked!"

Kerry got everything connected. With a slow exhale, she leaned over and pressed the starter on the first generator, holding her breath until the machine caught and came to life in a shockingly loud rumble. A low hum nearly made her jump out of her skin, until she looked down to see the gauges coming obediently to life on her gizmo. "Last one they had." Her voice almost cracked. "Had to fight some guys for it."

Mark peered over her shoulder at the dials, pointing his flash at them. "Wow," he said in a respectful tone. "Man, you know your shit, let me tell you what."

The irony made Kerry smile briefly. "Thanks."

Another bright light suddenly interrupted them, and they looked up to find a television camera pointing its round, inquisitive eye at them followed by a reporter stumbling alongside almost losing his footing on the loose shale.

"Uh oh," Mark muttered. "This ain't' good."

Kerry exhaled as the reporter headed her way. "Wanna be a Vice President for a day?"

"Nuh UH."

"Didn't think so."

"Betcha wish Big D were here."

The sweat in her eyes felt very much like tears. Kerry had to look down for a long moment and wipe the moisture away with her sleeve before she could pick her head back up and face the music.

AT LEAST IT wasn't CNN. Kerry wiped her hands off as she walked over the broken stone and grass, lifting one to shade her eyes from the blaring lights as she recognized one of the local news stations. "Hello."

A woman in her mid-thirties, sweating like a pig, was unwinding a mic cord as she approached. "Okay, hold on, hold on, I'm almost there." She was obviously talking into her own ear. "Give me a minute."

Kerry stopped and hitched her thumbs into her front pockets. She watched the cameraman circle around and take a bead on her, and it gave her a moment to gather her thoughts as the reporter got herself together and made eye contact.

"This is Conchita Gonzalez, of Channel Seven news. We're here at the Bellsouth regional center, where we've been told someone is trying to get something going here in this wasteland of darkness."

She extended the mic. "Can I ask who you are?"

Kerry almost said Martha Stewart. But at the last minute, her better sense prevailed. "Kerry Stuart." She paused, then waited, a mildly inquiring look on her face. "Can I help you with something?"

"What's going on here?" the woman asked, as the camera panned over to the truck. "Are you from the city?"

"No." Kerry shook her head. "We're a private company working on getting our customer's service back." She looked around. "Nothing really interesting going on here."

"Okay." The woman talked to her ear again. "We've been told the emergency services tied through this office are down. Are you helping to restore that?"

"No." Kerry shook her head again.

"Can I ask why not?" The woman focused on her. "We have people who could be in trouble, who could be hurt, or needing help, depending on those services. Shouldn't that be the priority?"

Kerry felt her mouth go dry, as the camera zeroed in on her. "It's not my priority," she said, after a pause. "My priority is doing what I can for my customers. The emergency systems are important, but the people in charge of them are who you should be asking that question."

The woman nodded to herself. "Okay." She said into her ear. "Can you tell us what you're doing?"

It all felt very disconnected. Kerry had the sense that the reporter was only ten percent here with her, and ninety percent in some crazed television news land with people yammering in her head all the time.

"Sure," she said. "We're generating power so that we can bring up

the circuits to our main offices, to restore service to our customers."
The reporter stared at her. "Why aren't you doing that for everyone?"
Kerry stared right back. "Why isn't the city doing that? If it's that important, shouldn't they have backup systems?"
"What?" The woman leaned her head to one side. "They are? Okay. I'm out of here." She looked back at Kerry. "Thanks for your time. I'm not sure what you're doing, but someone should be finding out."
She motioned to the cameraman who flicked a switch on his camera and turned to follow her as she trundled away, her hand pressed to her ear. "What? What? What street is that?"
Kerry put her hands all the way in her pockets and stared after them. "Jesus." She turned and headed back to the crew, pausing when her cell phone rang. She glanced at the caller id, disappointed it wasn't Dar. "Kerry Stuart."
"Hello, Ms. Stuart? This is Nelson Argos."
Oh crap. "Mr. Argos, I don't really have the time to talk right now, I'm in the middle of something."
"Oh, I'm sure you are. I just got off the phone with a couple of your biggest customers and they want to know where that famous bulletproof service is. So do I."
"You can call them back and ask them in five minutes. Until then kiss my ass." Kerry hung up the phone as she got back to the truck, dropping to her knees beside the generators. Her phone rang again, but she ignored it this time, as she braced her hands on the load balancer. "We ready?"
"Just about." Mark had a loop of cable over his arm, and he was feeding it out as he walked toward the open door. "Give me a minute."
Kerry's phone buzzed, then buzzed again. She left it in its holster, as a damp breeze blew in and the first patter of rain dropped on the top of the tent.
"Okay, we're done." One of the techs came out, with a roll of duct tape. "You want to check it out, ma'am?"
"I trust you." Kerry didn't feel like getting up, her stomach in a roiling, churning mess. The phone rang again.
Again.
"Boss, we ready? I'm gonna plug it in!" Mark called back. "Cross your fingers!"
The phone buzzed again. Kerry pulled it off her hip and threw it against the wall. It bounced onto the ground, and sat there rocking, a small puddle growing around it. "GO ON," she called back.
The techs watched her in wide-eyed silence.
Kerry ignored them, focusing on the load gauges as she listened to the phone rattle and buzz, and jump against the pavement. As she watched, the needles quivered, then vibrated, then finally jumped a little, moving from zero up to twenty percent.

"Ms. Stuart, do you want us to fetch your phone?"

"No." Kerry leaned on the balancer, taking a bit of weight off her knees since the broken pavement was cutting into them even through her denim. "C'mon."

"Coming up!" Mark hollered back. "I got blinkies!"

The rain started coming down harder, the mist starting to come in the sides of the tent. The techs rushed to secure them, blocking the rain, as Kerry pushed herself to her feet and made her way inside.

Mark was standing in front of the rack, which was not cool, but not as stifling as it had been. There was a hum in the darkness, and red and green lights reflecting against his profile.

Kerry came up next to him. They watched in silence as the LED's moved from a testing pattern to something else.

"That's traffic," Mark finally said into the quiet.

"Yes, it is," Kerry agreed. "You think it worked?"

Mark opened his phone and watched the display. "We'll know in about a minute."

IT WAS DARK in the hotel room. Dar was lying curled up on her side on the bed, her laptop open in front of her and her cell phone resting near her hand.

But the screensaver whirled unmolested, and the cell screen was dark. Dar merely lay there and watched the hypnotic pattern, waiting through what seemed to be the longest night of her life.

It was very quiet, and after a while she lifted her hand and let it drop on the keyboard, bringing the screen to life and exposing the network map she'd placed there. The lines leading into Miami were still mostly dark, and she felt a moment of intense shame as she hoped they stayed that way.

Not for Kerry's sake. For her own, because if they didn't come up, the phone would ring, soon, and she'd grab her bag and head for the airport and home.

Home.

But as she watched, there was a flicker in the lines, a slow ripple that went from red, to yellow, to green as she blinked and sat up, leaning forward to stare at it. The lights steadied and held, pulsing a healthy color that reflected brightly against the dark background.

She did it. A burst of pride drove aside the gloom, and despite it all, Dar found herself smiling. Unless the power came back but... She checked a gauge. No, the office was still on generator. She released a held breath into a whirlpool of mixed emotions. "Good girl."

The phone rang. Dar looked at the caller id for a long moment before she answered it, cradling the phone next to her ear. "Hey."

A long, long, long sigh. "It worked." Kerry sounded lightheaded with relief. "Oh, my god, Dar. It worked. It worked. We're up."

Shoving aside her own ridiculous disappointment, Dar determined herself to rise to the occasion. "I knew you'd do it," she said. "Tell me how it went."

"Hang on, let me sit down." Kerry was almost out of breath. There was the sound of a car door shutting, then a brief rumble of an engine starting. "Oh god. Sorry. Had to get the AC on in here. I'm dying in this goddamned heat."

Dar closed her eyes and just drank in the voice. "Must be like hell."

"Oh, honey...where do I start." Kerry sighed. "Shit, I have such a headache."

Dar's fingers twitched in pure reflex, a testament to her natural inclination to answer the comment with a gentle knead of Kerry's neck. "You take anything?"

Another sigh. "I want to eat first. Otherwise it gets me sick."

"You haven't had dinner?" Dar checked the clock.

"I didn't have lunch," Kerry admitted. "Just some of my bars. Anyway...they fought me tooth and nail, Dar. No way did they want me to do this, because everyone's up their butts wanting favors and screaming at them."

"I'm sure they were." Dar said. "Where are you now?"

"Outside the central office. Mark and the guys are cleaning up. We're leaving two techs here to keep filling the gas tanks."

Dar opened her PDA and tapped out a message, hitting send quickly. "Good idea."

"Thanks," Kerry said. "We kept running into obstacles, but everything worked out. I got the generators hooked up together, and we were just going to start the power..."

"Hooked them up together?"

"Yeah. I got a gizmo, a thing that let me connect all of them. A load balancer. You know...I mean, you must know because you told me to get a bunch of generators, but I didn't think about how to make them work together and I guess you assumed we'd know so..."

Dar's eyes widened. "Shit." She exhaled. "I didn't even think of that, Ker. I just figured you might need more than one in case our stuff was on more than one switch."

Kerry was silent for a little bit. "Oh," she finally said. "Wow. Well, no...I got this thing to make them all work together, so we didn't have to take the lines down to refill the gas or anything like that."

"Go on."

"So then I had to figure out how to keep the switch cool." Kerry said. "I put some air conditioning duct from the switch out the door to the truck we rented...it had AC in the back."

Dar rested her chin on her fist, a genuine smile appearing on her face. "Uh huh."

Kerry cleared her throat. "So it was going great. Then the reporters showed up." She let out an aggravated breath. "Dar, they treated us like a bunch of squirmy hooligans. Like I was cheating or something to get what I wanted."

"Sweetheart, you were," Dar told her. "But it's okay. It's what you get paid for."

"That's what I told her," Kerry said. "She went away, but I think she's coming back. Anyway, I got it all going, and plugged the switch in, and we all sort of just held our breath."

"And it worked."

"It worked."

"Kerry?"

"Mm?"

"Outstanding job. You went over and above, and I really appreciate that. Well done. Very well done," Dar said, meaning every word.

Kerry exhaled, and there was a soft sound as though she'd let her head rest against the glass window. "Thanks, boss," she replied simply.

They were both quiet for a little while. Then Dar shifted the phone from one ear to the other. "I'm damn proud of you."

A faint sniffle traveled down the cellular link. "Even though it meant you didn't get to come riding to the rescue?" Kerry asked, making a wan joke.

"Yeah."

Kerry made a small sound of contentment, but then she sighed again. "Know something?"

"What?"

"I was just thinking about something you once said to me. About how you felt when you got promoted, that time? And how you just went back home and it was like..."

"It ended up not meaning much, yeah," Dar said. "What brought that up?"

"Uuugh. Because I just was sitting here thinking that after all this, after this crappy, disgusting, horrible day — all I have to go home to is a dark, hot house and an empty bed."

Dar was caught speechless.

"I want a hug," Kerry uttered. "I want you."

Dar swallowed, hearing a note in Kerry's voice she knew meant her partner was very close to tears. "Ker."

A pause. "Sorry," Kerry whispered huskily. "I'm just on overload right now. The stupid guy from CNN called me in the middle of this and I told him off. My phone wouldn't stop ringing."

"I love you," Dar said the only thing she reasonably expected to make her partner feel better. "I wish I was in that car right next to you right now."

Kerry was quiet for a minute, then she exhaled. "I want to be jazzed about what I just did, but you know, Dar...I don't know. I hope it was worth it."

"It was," Dar said, in a positive tone. "I'm sure everyone back at the office is cheering your name right now."

"Hm." Then there was a rustle, and the sound of the car window opening. "Hang on, sweetie." The sound of wind rushed in. "Hey, Mark...oh...oh, yeah, um...that would be great...yeah. Thanks! How...oh, that smells great. Thank you."

Dar smiled faintly at her distorted reflection in the laptop screen. She waited for the sound of the outside to vanish as Kerry rolled up the window again, and heard the rustling of paper bags on the other side of the line.

"Did you have something to do with this, Paladar?" Kerry's voice sounded more normal.

"Me?" Dar inquired. "I'm sitting here in New York. What makes you think I had anything to do with having your dinner delivered?"

A very soft, knowing chuckle answered her. "The fact that my Wendy's spicy chicken sandwich has no lettuce, and extra cheese on it, the frosty is large, and the baked potato has no bacon bits. Mark maybe could guess number two, but the other ones had your little fingerprints alllll over them."

Dar flexed her hand in front of her eyes, studying her fingerprints. Then she let her arm drop to the bed again. "Least I could do," she conceded. "Since I'm not there to do it myself."

"Wish you were." Kerry's voice was muffled as she chewed. "I can admit that now, since this crappy thing is over."

"Wish I was too," Dar echoed softly.

Kerry swallowed, and cleared her throat a little. "Are you okay?" she asked, in a gentle voice. "You sound really down."

Was she? Dar stared at the screen, with its winking green lights. "Yeah, I'm all right," she answered, after a brief pause. "Worried about you all night, that's all."

"Mm."

"Least I have good news for the international board call in half an hour." Dar made an effort to inject some normality into her tone.

"Call? I didn't know you had one," Kerry said.

"Yeah, I forgot too. Alastair reminded me," Dar admitted. "It's on my schedule...woulda binged me anyway. Give me something to do now that the crisis is over."

Kerry seemed to absorb this in silence for a few heartbeats, chewing on her chicken sandwich in a thoughtfulness almost tangible through the phone. "Want some of my frosty?"

Dar chuckled.

"Want me to get on a plane and come to New York?" Kerry asked. "Not for business. Just to keep you company and get my hug?"

"You really have to ask?" Dar responded wistfully. "You know I'd love it. But you've got that damn bid, Ker. This won't take me more than a day or so to straighten out. Then I'll be back and you'll get your hug."

"Mm," Kerry grunted unhappily. "Hell with them," she said. "Oh, crap. I was right. Here come those damn reporters again."

"Ouch."

"You think they'll just stay there filming me if I eat my dinner inside the truck and refuse to open the door?"

Dar smiled. "Worth a try, sweetheart," she said. "Guess I can go order room service now too."

"Bad Dar."

"Bad Kerry," Dar responded promptly. "Two of a kind."

Kerry laughed suddenly, a light, joyful sound that made Dar's tense neck muscles relax in an instant. "Oh, what a compliment that is. Okay, love of my life...let me let you go get dinner, and I'll try not to strangle these reporters. Call you later?"

"Sure," Dar agreed. "I'll let you know what the board had to say about my genius VP Ops."

"Love you."

"Love you too. Later." Dar closed the phone, feeling better than she had all night.

Good enough to make her get up and go to the desk, sitting down and flipping open the room service menu with renewed interest.

Chapter
Fourteen

KERRY TOOK HER time finishing her dinner. She hated wolfing her food, and the cool air and warm leather settled her body down into something approaching comfort. The reporter was hovering outside, and she realized quickly after he'd arrived that it wasn't the local woman she'd first spoken to.

Instead, she recognized the Tech TV reporter who'd been retained by Michelle and Shari and, frankly, Kerry was in a mood to keep him waiting well into the next century if the occasion called for it.

Her techs were sitting in the back of the rental truck munching their own dinners, with a hastily rigged light dangling over their heads plugged into her gizmo along with the power to the telecom gear.

Kerry eased the seat back a notch and propped her knee up against the door, picking up a square of neatly cut potato skin and taking a bite of it. It tasted of sour cream and cheese and love, a little salty and a touch sweet, this fast food manifestation of Dar's care for her.

Totally insignificant in substance, and yet that quiet thoughtfulness meant everything to her. Between that, and the words of praise Dar had showered over her, Kerry found herself well able to push aside the aggravations of the day, and watch the anxious pacing of the Tech TV reporter with a sense of contented amusement.

Near the wall, the generators hummed along, their low thrum audible to her through the closed window. The sun had set, and besides the small pool of light from their bulb, the surrounding areas were eerily dark and quiet now that the rain had tapered off.

It reminded Kerry of the night of the storm, way back when she and Dar had first been getting to know each other.

That scary, magical day. Kerry smiled gently, remembering the moment she'd woken up on Dar's couch, lying there hardly breathing as she felt the soft folds of a blanket settle over her accompanied by Dar's distinctive presence.

Where...Kerry waited for the soft scuff of bare footsteps to move away before she opened her eyes, her fingers reaching out to curl around the feather light covering draped over her. The couch leather had warmed to her body and she let herself indulge in a moment of perfect comfort.

Dar's house. She moved her head a little and looked around again at it. Her ears, though, were focused tightly on the kitchen where she knew

Dar had gone, every sound she detected sending a prickle up and down her spine. After a moment's hesitation, she sat up and ran her hand through her hair, getting up and wrapping the blanket around her as she went toward the source of those sounds.

She stopped short of the kitchen, spotting Dar inside before the taller woman knew she was approaching.

God, she's gorgeous. Kerry's eyes drank in the lanky form in its covering of thin cotton, her body reacting with a surge of sexual energy that almost shocked her.

Almost mortified her.

Almost. "What's going on?" Kerry continued on into the kitchen, reveling silently in the moment when Dar turned and met her eyes and a grin appeared, seeming to acknowledge the boundaries they both were knowingly skirting.

Dar pointed. "Tropical storm. Out of nowhere."

Kerry walked over to stand right next to her, leaning on the counter as she peered first out the window, then up at the television screen. Sure looked nasty...too nasty for cabs to run, maybe? "What does that mean?"

The blue eyes casually met hers and held there, gaining the faintest of twinkles in their depths. "For one thing, it means you're stuck here."

Shucks. Kerry looked out at the pounding surf as Dar made a call, feeling a sense of deep affection for Mother Nature.

"I was right. Ferries are closed down." Dar concluded.

"Guess I should have left when I had the chance..."

The twinkle grew perceptibly.

"I wanted to get the reports done, and only sat down for a minute...sorry." Kerry concluded her apology. "How are you feeling?"

Dar's eyes dropped, and her expression took on a more somber cast. "Fine. Stuff worked great." Her hand lifted and ran through her dark hair. "Listen, I better get candles out."

Candles? "What can I do to help?"

Dar showed her the shutters. It didn't take long, then she was back in the kitchen watching Dar root around in a box full of hurricane supplies.

Including candles. "What else can I do?"

Cloth in her hands. What else could she do? She could change into Dar's clothing. Holy cow. Was this really happening? "Makes sense. Be right back."

Herself in the mirror, in Dar's shirt, in Dar's house. Well, you know something Kerrison? If she's bringing candles, you've got to step up to the plate and do your part. "Bet she could use a home-cooked meal." Kerry whispered to her reflection. "Make it good enough, maybe she'll ask you to come back."

Yeah.

Kerry chuckled softly, shaking her head at her former self with a sense of unreal bemusement. Love had caught her so by surprise, she'd been overwhelmed by it before she even realized what was happening to her. And that had been a wonderful feeling, but she decided she liked the more seasoned, more faceted relationship she had with Dar now.

Though she would always cherish the look on Dar's face when she'd taken over her kitchen for that very first time. If she closed her eyes, she could still see that look in front of her, half amazed and half shy, the briefest glimpse of her soul mate soon to be.

Gorgeous.

Ah well. Kerry dusted off her fingers and neatly wiped her lips with her lurid yellow napkin before tucking it, along with the rest of the wrappings, into her paper bag. She slurped up the last of her frosty and turned the car off, then popped the door and hopped out into the warm muggy night.

The reporter spotted her and headed her way. Kerry debated on ignoring him, then she altered her steps to intercept his path and halted when she met up with him, tilting her head to one side and waiting in silence.

"Ah, Ms. Stuart?" The man readily started the conversation. "We haven't really met but..."

"But you're Telegenics biographer," Kerry supplied. "Something you want from me? I think I said everything I had to say in the meeting this afternoon."

"No, um...well..."

Kerry eyed the camera. "Is that running?"

"No, no." The man shook his head. "No, I wasn't really here to..."

"Watch us succeed?"

The man rocked back on his heels and held both hands up in front of him. "Whoa, take it easy, Ms. Stuart. You've got me all wrong."

Kerry folded her arms across her chest. "Okay." She was in a mood to be mildly benign. "What can I do for you, then?"

"First off, I'm Ben." He stuck his hand out. "And yeah, I know I'm working on that whole ship story and Telegenics being the underdog up and comer. Okay? Okay."

"Okay."

"But you know what?" Ben said. "The real story in that room today, and here tonight is you."

"Me?" Kerry sounded skeptical.

"Yeah," Ben said. "Yesterday, in that meeting, what I got from you was that it was a waste of your time. That's a strange kind of attitude for someone trying to get some new business."

Kerry considered the question. "I did consider it a waste of time. Not necessarily just of mine, but everyone else's also." She paused. "What was the purpose of having us all there? We were just responding to a fairly standard RFP."

The reporter shifted a little. "Well, maybe that's just how the customer likes to do it," he said. "Who knows?"

"Maybe." Kerry watched his face. "But you know, the last time I saw something like that Michelle Graver was involved too. I wonder if she didn't give Quest the idea."

His face twitched, too fast for him to hide it. "I have no idea," he said, after an awkward pause. "But anyway, now here you are, hacking your way into the phone system. What's the story? I heard the local news people say you got this pushed through when there's two hospitals who can't get phones and emergency service is down."

"There is no story," Kerry countered. "I'm just doing my job. Taking care of my customers. You should be asking the county why they aren't doing what I did."

"Maybe you're just smarter than all of them." Ben smiled.

Kerry hiked an eyebrow at him.

Ben studied her, then grinned a little. "Flattery doesn't do you, huh?"

"Buddy...the pond I come from, you wouldn't even register as a goldfish," Kerry told him. "So, if you don't mind — I'm going to close up shop here and go find myself a nice hot shower, and someplace relatively cool to sleep."

Ben laughed. "Oo...now, Ms. Stuart, is that a way to treat the press?"

"No." Kerry's eyes twinkled slyly. "But I don't have anywhere to hide the body here, and it's too hot anyway. So you lucked out."

The reporter laughed. "Okay, I get the message."

"Good. My can of spray paint's in the back of my partner's car. Hate to have to go get one just for you."

Ben laughed harder. "Ms. Stuart, please. When this crazy nuthouse city gets back to normal..."

"You mean it's not?"

"When the power comes on," Ben clarified. "Could you please sit down and let me interview you? I've gotten a really one-sided perspective of the...well, the competition. I'm seeing a different story here than I was led to believe originally."

Hm. "Okay," Kerry agreed. "Sure. If the power's not on tomorrow, the meeting Quest called will be canceled anyway unless he wants to have it in our offices. So...why not?"

It would be a good opportunity to maybe put a screw in Michelle's plan, and turn the tables a little. "Here's my card." She handed over one from her wallet. "Give me a call."

Ben eagerly squirreled away the card. "Boy, that was easier than I thought it would be."

Kerry gave him a wry look. "Good night." She circled around him and went over to the truck, resting one hand on the edge of the deck. "How's it looking, guys?"

"Lot better than it did when we started." The younger of the techs noted. "Ma'am, you rock."

Mark chuckled.

Kerry just grinned. "Well for the record, you all rock too, and not only I think that. Dar wanted me to tell everyone how much she appreciates the effort that was put in here tonight. She's about to go into a board meeting, and you just made her evening a lot more pleasant."

"Wheew." Mark whistled. "Hey, you should get the credit, Kerry. We just did the grunt work."

"It's all a team." Kerry shook her head. "Mark, can you get some people to take turns watching this, and keeping the generators going all night?"

"Already done." Mark rocked up and down on his heels. "I got twelve guys lined up, three guys every four hours. First bunch's due here in like, ten minutes then these guys can beat ass home."

"Good." Kerry looked around into the dark areas surrounding them. "Do we need security?" She lowered her voice. "I can have Matt send some guys over from the office. It's going to be a long night."

"Yeah," Mark agreed. "Good idea."

Kerry stepped away a little and took out her cell phone, glad the ordeal was, for her, almost over. Then another thought occurred to her and she cursed silently, waiting for the line to connect. It did, and she spoke briefly to the security supervisor on duty, then disconnected and called a different number.

"Hey, John? It's Kerry Stuart. How are...ah." Kerry could hear the chaos on the other end. "Ferries not running, huh?" She exhaled, listening to the man's exasperated tone. "Okay, well, thanks." She closed the phone and sighed. "Well, poo."

"What's up, boss?" Mark stuck his head around the corner of the truck. "No security?"

"No, they're on their way over." Kerry sighed. "But I just realized I have no way to get home. Our ferry ramps are shut down. They're getting the one island side on the generator but the one on the causeway end is dead in the water." She paused. "Literally."

"Yow."

"Yeah. Maybe I'll go sleep on the beach...and poor Chino." Kerry frowned. "Rats, rats, rats and fruit bats."

Well, there was always a hotel. Kerry gave the side of the truck a slap. "C'mon, Mark. I'll drop you back by the office for your car. Sorry about the bike."

"Couldn't have given it to me anyway." Mark climbed down out of the back of the vehicle and joined her. "Garage doors won't open."

Hm. Kerry booted a rock out of her way as they headed for the Lexus. Power outages were much, MUCH more fun when Dar was around.

Otherwise, they were just one big pain in the poot.

A FIRE ENGINE woke Dar up. She sat up in a confusion of dark strangeness, streetlights splashing an unfamiliar pattern across the sheets covering her as she spent a moment remembering where she was. The howl of the siren peaked outside, then slowly faded, piercing through the closed windows effortlessly.

Other sounds intruded after it. A chugging rumble, followed by a crash of metal against metal, some garbage truck, maybe. Then the soft, far off sound of a jackhammer.

Another siren, blaring suddenly to life almost under the window, loud and frightening, and much slower to fade.

"Damn." Dar hiked herself up and leaned back against the headboard, raking her fingers through her hair to move it out of her eyes as she waited for her heartbeat to settle back down. The darkness outside reassured her she hadn't overslept her travel alarm, but now that she was wide awake she doubted she could take advantage of the remaining time to fall back asleep.

At least not without Kerry there. Dar reached for the television remote and shifted to a cross-legged position as she flipped the button on to check the news.

Kerry wasn't a break of dawn person, Dar had discovered. Given her own natural preference, her partner preferred to let bright sunlight wake her up, long after Dar normally would be rambling around the condo.

Living together meant they'd had to learn to compromise.

As it turned out, they both enjoyed a morning cuddle, and slowly they'd adjusted their personal body clocks to allow that, plus their runs, plus time to get ready for work without making it to the office too disgracefully late every day.

Sharing a shower helped. Dar grinned slightly. Though occasionally that backfired and threw their schedule off even more when they got the giggles and lost track of time while playing around with each other, indulging in the open sensuality between them.

Natural to them now, but she could remember a time when Kerry had been far shyer, still unsure of herself and far from confident in her attractiveness at the very start of their relationship together.

"A beach party?" Kerry circled one denim-covered knee with both arms and rested her chin on it. "I don't know, Col..." She glanced over at Dar, who was sprawled on the couch in Kerry's apartment, flipping through a Linux magazine. "We're sort of busy..."

Dar looked up. "What kind of beach party?" she asked. "Laying on the sand getting fried, or something that involves volleyball and barbeques?"

Colleen hesitated, a little doubtful of her friend's newest friend. "Ah...more to the second, I'm thinking."

Dar looked at Kerry, raising her eyebrows inquisitively. "You up for it? I can do the beach."

Kerry *was silent for a minute, then she nodded.* "Sure," *she agreed.* "Um...we'll bring the drinks?"

"Great." *Colleen patted the couch arm, then she got up and scooted out the door.* "See you at Crandon, in two hours."

The door closed. Kerry *frowned slightly, then released her knee and straightened.* "Okay, well...I think I have extra towels here."

Dar *got up and walked over to her, settling next to her on the loveseat.* "You didn't sound really stoked about the party."

"Um...no, it's fine. I like the beach," Kerry *said.* "Really." *But there was a furrow in her brow that even* Dar *could clearly discern.* "And the guys here at the complex are really nice." *She got up.* "We've had...um...a few of these sort of parties." *The window seemed to fascinate her, and she walked over to stare out of it, her back toward* Dar.

"Uh huh." Dar *studied her new partner.* "Seems like a nice crowd. A little on the young, yuppie, gym-addicted side, but all right." *She watched* Kerry's *eyes shift briefly across the room to the mirror and her own reflection then back. A thought occurred to her.* "You embarrassed to show off your new girlfriend?"

Kerry *turned all the way around and looked at her, eyes widening perceptibly.* "What?"

Dar *shrugged.*

"N...no!"

"So?"

"So...what?" Kerry *answered hesitantly.*

Dar *felt an uncomfortable sense of awkwardness.* "I got the feeling..." *She saw* Kerry's *hands tense.* "That maybe you didn't want to go there."

"Oh." *The blond woman walked back over and crouched next to* Dar, *resting a hand on her knee.* "Well, no.. it's just that I've never been much of a...um..." *She exhaled.* "You're right. Most of the folks that live here are really buff and into looks and I..."

"Don't want to upstage them?" Dar *inquired mildly.* "Doesn't surprise me. You're a lot nicer than I am."

Kerry *lifted her eyes and stared at* Dar, *caught speechless for several very long moments.* "What?"

"What what?" Dar *responded.*

"What do you mean upstage?" Kerry *added a short, hesitant laugh.* "Maybe you upstage people. I don't." *Her eyes dropped to the carpet and stayed there.* "Maybe I don't want to embarrass you."

It was like a door opening up into a place she'd never seen before. Dar *had to wonder just what* Kerry *saw when she looked at herself in the mirror.*

Well. Dar *certainly knew what she saw when she looked at* Kerry, *and so rather than waste time on words, she slid off the couch and knelt beside* Kerry, *gently capturing her face in both hands and lifting it so their eyes made contact. "Kerry?"*

Those big, green eyes were so trusting. "Yes?"

"Don't be a jackass," Dar said, smiling in reflex at the expression on her lover's face. "You're everything I want in a woman. You care about anyone else's opinion?" The skin under her fingertips warmed as a blush colored Kerry's face, making her pale eyebrows stand out vividly. "Hm?"

Kerry remained frozen in place for the next several heartbeats. Then she hesitantly lifted her hands and let them rest on Dar's waist, leaning forward a little as a look of shy, wondering delight grew in her eyes. "Nu uh."

Dar drew her closer and kissed her. "So let's go to the beach," she whispered in one still pink ear. "And scandalize your neighbors."

Kerry didn't answer. She put her arms around Dar and squeezed her as hard as she could, robbing Dar of breath, but delivering a message as loudly as yelling would have.

Boy. Dar enjoyed a moment of utter giddiness. Being in love sure was a lot more fun this time around.

Yeah, it sure was. Dar rested her chin on her fist. Being in love with Kerry had brought her more joy than she'd ever considered possible, and that, she acknowledged silently, was what was messing her up so badly right now.

What if it all vanished?

Dar knew there were no guarantees in life. She also knew that sometimes, bad things happened, like what had happened to her mother when they were told her father had been lost on a mission. But losing Daddy in that way had been totally different than if he'd just walked out of their lives.

She didn't expect that of Kerry. Her partner had proven to her more times than she could count her dedication to their relationship. But knowing that didn't stop her from being scared anyway, and Dar wasn't really sure what to do about how she felt.

Well. She studied the screen, waiting for any news from home. It would probably pass, if she just chilled out for a while. She'd gotten past it at the very start of their relationship, after all. Her eyes followed the scrolling marquee, and she winced as it reported the power outage still continuing. "Crap."

With a grunt, she rolled over and retrieved her PDA from the nightstand, flipping it open and scanning the screen. Not unexpectedly, there were several notes waiting. She clicked on the first one.

Whine.

Dar, I haven't slept in my car since the night of my high school prom, and it was a heck of a lot cooler in Michigan than it is here. Can I come to New York?

K

Aw. Dar grimaced in sympathy, seeing the after midnight timestamp. She clicked on the second.

I want my Dar.

Is it selfish to want you to be here with me down by South Pointe at 2 a.m.? I am waiting to see if I can catch a ride over home. The HK staff says Chino is okay, but not a happy puppy.

K

Silently, Dar clicked on the third, posted shortly after the 2nd.

Oo. Have I told you lately how much I love your parents? They just rescued me. Sleep tight, sweetheart. I'll catch you in the morning.

K

Dar released a sigh of relief. Not that there was anything she could really do for Kerry, but knowing she was safe and sound in the hands of the two people she trusted more than any other in the world made her feel one hell of a lot better. She tapped the message and set up a reply, then scribed briefly on the screen.

Ker –

Tell mom and dad I say hi, and thanks for taking care of you. Board meeting went fine last night – hope your ears were burning because you were the chief topic of it.

Let me know what's going on with Quest. If the power's still out in the morning, you might want to extend him a gracious invitation to use our conference facilities.

I'm going to go work out. Damn noise around here woke me up. Hope you slept okay – talk to you in the morning.

D

Four a.m.. Dar clicked off the television and regarded the clock. She got up and rummaged through the hotel's directory, flipping the pages until she found the one detailing the properties amenities. A soft snort sounded when she spotted the hours for the gym. "Nine to ten. When the hell during those hours do they expect anyone to be up there?"

So much for that idea. Dar went back over to the bed and sat down. Too early for breakfast, either. With a disgusted sigh, she laid back down and curled up on her side, tucking an arm around her pillow and attempting to relax.

I want my Dar.

Dar closed her eyes and ran the words over and over again in her mind with idle pleasure. Kerry had really done a great job, and after spending all night telling the board that, Dar had even let her own lingering disappointment fade to nothing, trading it for a glow of pride.

As it should be, her conscience reminded her blandly. She doesn't need you hovering over her every second, does she?

Dar exhaled. And she still didn't know what it was that Kerry had done. The thing that Dar wasn't going to like. The thing Kerry would not tell her unless it was in person.

A siren blared again, flashing red through her window.

Dark, sticky webs clung to her, wrapping her tighter and tighter in their embrace as cruel laughter echoed around her.

She struggled, but the more she fought, the worse it got, until she could barely move at all and the heavy, stinking threads were starting to wrap around her face.

She screamed into the wind.

The laughter continued, and worst of all, she was starkly, achingly aware of being totally, utterly alone.

Bereft.

Figures approached her, and she was grabbed by rough hands, helpless and unable to break away or protect herself. She struggled anyway, desperately wrenching herself right and left to keep out of their clutches.

They just laughed all the harder.

But they stopped suddenly, and in all that silence, she heard the thunder of hoof beats.

Kerry jerked awake, heart pounding, her eyes sweeping the darkness as she tried to place herself. A second later, she slumped back onto the compact bed, her eyes blinking at the splattering of moonlight making patterns across the sheets. "Jesus."

At the foot of the bed, Chino raised her head and whined, then curled back up again when Kerry showed no inclination to get up.

The boat rocked under her. Kerry tried to recall the fragments of her nightmare, but the details were swiftly fading, leaving her with only a vague, sick feeling in the pit of her stomach. With a sigh, she pushed the light cover back and got up, circling the bed and making her way out of the small bedroom and into the galley of the Dixieland Yankee.

It was dark outside, but through the main cabin windows, she could see Andy and Ceci's boat resting in the next slip in the moonlight. Kerry took a small bottle of orange juice from the cooler and walked over to the table, slipping behind it and sitting down as she popped open the lid.

Four a.m. Her eyes found the travel clock. "Oh well," she spoke to Chino, as the Labrador appeared from the bedroom. "Two hours is better than nothing, huh, Chi?"

"Growf."

She propped her head up on one hand, hoping the nausea would subside and not force her to lose the few mouthfuls of juice and whatever else was left in her stomach. "Yeah, well...maybe you and I can go for a walk, huh? I don't think I want to go back to sleep right now."

Damn it.

Kerry pulled her PDA over and opened it, seeing the stutter of the message waiting flash. Her face creased into a grin as she saw the sender, and she tapped on the message to view it. After she absorbed the first paragraph, she paused and reread it.

Then she reread it again, as she sipped her orange juice, still grinning. The smile faded a little as she read the second paragraph, then evolved into a faint scowl as she read the third and checked the time stamp. "At four a.m.? Dar!" She clicked over to a new message and scribed a quick note, then sent it.

You still there?

Moments later, the device flashed.

Yeah. Gym's closed. You still up?

Kerry shifted her position, moving to the corner of the small couch and curled up into a ball with the moonlight coming over her shoulder. *Not still. I had a bad dream. It woke me up and gave me a stomach ache.* And a headache, and a pain in her chest. But no sense in freaking Dar out too much.

Where are you?

Funny, how plain text could take on a concerned tone without any embellishment. *On the Dixie. Mom and Dad are parked next to us.* Kerry scribbled.

Wish I was parked next to you.

Kerry felt her chest tighten further. *Wish you were too. I hate waking up from nightmares alone.*

I know.

Her last nightmare, months prior, had scared her so badly she'd woken up in tears, and Dar had insisted on holding her in her arms the rest of the night to allow Kerry to get back to sleep.

Not that she objected. Being in Dar's embrace was very gentle on her soul.

But she hated nightmares. It wasn't anything graphic. In fact, Kerry hadn't even remembered what it had been about minutes after she'd awakened. But the sheer emotional impact of it had shaken her.

Just like the one tonight had, only she didn't have Dar's warm presence to chase the ickies away. But this odd, disconnected conversation was making her feel better. *Glad you're around to talk to, anyway.* She informed her partner. *I feel better already.*

Ker?

Yes?

I'll always be here.

Kerry stared at the words in silence, hearing the echo of them in her mind. *I sure hope so.* She wrote back. *You're the cornerstone of my life.*

The boat rocked softly under her, responding to the wake of an incoming vessel. Kerry tore her eyes from the screen to look outside watching briefly as a huge sailing yacht cruised silently by, heading for the far end of the marina.

She looked back, but the screen was stubbornly silent. *Dar?*

I'm here. You just make me stop breathing sometimes when you write stuff like that.

Kerry smiled gently. *Are we a pair of loons, sitting here at four thirty a.m. writing mushy love notes to each other or what?*

Yeah. (chuckle) But I think I can go back to bed now.

Funny. Kerry stifled a yawn. She'd just been thinking the same exact thing. The shadows from her dream had been chased away, and her stomach ache had eased. *Me, too.* She got up and headed for the bedroom, taking her PDA and her orange juice with her.

Inside the room, the moonlight flooded the bed, and Kerry crawled into its silver embrace. She fluffed up her pillow and settled down, curling onto her side and propping her PDA up where she could keep an eye on it. *I just took you to bed.* She informed her partner.

(laughing) Ultimate nerd-sleeping with palm pilots.

Kerry started chuckling, too. *Would that be your Indian name? Sleeps with Palm Pilots?*

Only if you're changing your name, Palm.

Chino trotted in and jumped on the bed, giving Kerry an indignant look for her wanderlust, and for the bubbling laughter that was shaking the surface they were both laying on.

Thanks, sweetie. I needed the laugh. Kerry finally sent. *Me and Chi are going to try to crash.*

There was a pause before the answer came. *I am too. Glad you tagged me – it was getting to be a long night.*

Kerry let out a small breath, hearing so many levels in what Dar was saying, the written words far more expressive than her spoken ones would have been. For all its plain text, the messaging sometimes brought an intimacy that surprised her. *Yeah. Here too. Sleep good, okay? Wish good dreams at me.*

You bet. Night, Ker. Love you.

Love you too, Dixiecup. Night.

Kerry tucked her stylus away and put her head down, acknowledging the ache in her chest that missed her partner's presence. Though Dar had only been gone a few days, she felt a little anxious about her, sensing the rawness in their communication.

But there was laughter too, she argued silently. Dar was okay, just still a little shaken from their confrontation at the show.

A thought occurred to her. Maybe it was for the best that Dar was in New York, leaving Kerry to handle the ship bid. That kept her away from the source of her upset, and gave her a chance to settle it all out before she came back and got involved.

Yeah. Kerry felt better about things. She would take care of the deal, and take the stress off Dar's shoulders until it was time to get in there and just do it. Her partner was working on an intriguing problem, one she was perfectly suited for. If Dar could focus on that and resolve it, good things would happen.

She was sure of it. All she had to do was hold up her end of the deal, and keep Michelle and Shari focused on *her*. Dar had told her she had complete confidence in her, right? She'd spent a whole meeting tonight bragging about her, right?

So, Stuart, buck up and start living up to your billing. Kerry wriggled into a more comfortable position and closed her eyes. Shari and Michelle were convinced Dar was the key to winning their bid. It was up to her, then, to drop a smelly dead fish into their plans and force them to adapt to her style instead of her partner's.

"I can do that," Kerry whispered as the boat's gentle rock lulled her back toward sleep.

LOVE YOU TOO, *Dixiecup*.

Nicknames. Dar wrinkled her nose at the screen. In the time she'd known Kerry, she'd acquired more nicknames than in the previous thirty years of her life. Dixiecup. Tiger. Taz. She'd always hated people calling her names not her own, but that could have been because her prior monikers were never really that complimentary.

Ah well. Anything Kerry called her was all right, because no matter what the words were, there was always love behind it. So her partner could have called her Cheese Doodle, and she'd have accepted it.

Not that she was going to give Kerry any ideas in that regard, of course.

Dar felt twenty pounds lighter. She pulled the down filled quilt up over her shoulders and spared a glance at the alarm clock, making sure it was set to wake her up in time to get a shower before she had to go meet her German challenge.

She hoped Kerry wouldn't have any more nightmares. "Think good thoughts at her, eh?" Dar closed her eyes and concentrated on that, conjuring up images of some of the great times they'd had together, and focusing on the warmth and joy they shared.

In an instant, her body relaxed and sleep crashed back over her.

KERRY WALKED OUT onto the back deck of the Dixie, leaning her weight on the railing as she regarded the start of what appeared to be a beautiful, if powerless, day. The sun was just rising, and the water took on a luminous sheen as a flock of birds wheeled overhead, looking for breakfast.

"Mm." She inhaled a breath of salt air, then climbed up the ladder to the flying bridge. Sitting down in Dar's usual seat, Kerry carefully set the switches, then turned the ignition for one of the big diesel engines that powered the boat. It rumbled to life immediately, and she adjusted the throttle to idle, letting the engine run to replenish the batteries inside the craft.

After a moment's listening, Kerry nodded in satisfaction and made her way down the ladder to join a frisky Chino waiting at the foot of it.

"Hey, Chi," she greeted their pet. "How about some breakfast, hm? Want to have toast and coffee with me out here?"

"Rowf!"

"Okay, a banana, then." Kerry went back inside and eased into the small galley, setting a teapot on the burner and opening the refrigerator. She'd brought down some staples from the condo last night, and now she selected a cinnamon and raisin English muffin to pop into the toaster.

If Dar had been there, of course, she'd be hearing the tinkling of Frosted Flakes into a nearby bowl, along with the gentle, knowing bump of contact as Dar maneuvered around her in the tiny space. Thinking about that made Kerry smile as she took out two slices of cheese and a small tub of soft butter.

"Ah well." She took one of the mugs from its holder and set up the single cone of coffee over it, looking up as the boat rocked more than the light surf would have caused it to. Then a soft knock came at the door, accompanied by a shadow outside whose height betrayed its identity at once. "C'mon in, dad!"

"Growf!" Chino scrambled for the door as it opened, and Andrew Roberts ducked inside. The Labrador rushed over to him, wiggling in happiness as the tall man crouched to greet her.

"Hey, ya furball," Andy rasped.

Kerry grinned at her father-in-law, who was dressed in his typical pair of shorts and sleeveless blue shirt, and barefoot as Dar would have been. "Morning."

"Howdy there, kumquat." Andy got up and ambled over, joining her at the galley's small counter. "Ah see you're up fore the gulls."

"Mm." Kerry finished her task and turned, opening the refrigerator again. "Want some OJ?" She offered him a container. "You're up early too."

Andy accepted the juice and set it down, opening it with intent, precise motions that were so Dar's image it almost made Kerry chuckle. "Spent a lot of years getting mah butt kicked out of bed at oh dark thirty," the retired sailor admitted. "Long habit."

"Uh huh." Kerry retrieved her now toasted muffin and placed it on a plate, waiting for it to cool before she buttered it. "So, what's Dar's excuse?" she asked. "Because she's better than a rooster, let me tell you. Minute the sun starts coming up, bing bong...she's right there with it."

"Always been like that," Dar's father asserted. "Even as a tot."

Kerry placed a slice of cheese on each half of the muffin. "Can I get you some breakfast, Dad? Since I've now been trained to get up at the crack of dawn, despite my inclination otherwise?" She gave him a knowing grin. "Especially since I'm going to have to beg for a ride back to the other shore?'

Andrew snorted. "You ain't got to beg us for nothing, Kerry. It ain't but a pleasure." He eased into one of the comfortable chairs bolted to the deck. "But I'll take one of them there round things if you got an extra."

Kerry popped another muffin into the toaster and reached behind her for the teapot. She poured some hot water over the coffee grinds. "I haven't looked at the news yet this morning. Any word on power?"

Andy made a sound of disgust. "Fellers ain't got no clue what they're doing."

That thought had also occurred to Kerry quite a number of times the previous day, as a matter of fact. "Well, I won't argue with that. I just..." Her cell phone rang. "Whoops. Scuse me." She picked it up and opened it. "Kerry Stuart."

"Morning, Kerry!" Alastair McLean's voice was certainly a surprise. "How are you?"

Kerry blinked. "Um...fine, sir," she managed to get out. "How are you doing? It's awfully early in Texas, isn't it? Something wrong?" Unconsciously, she ran her fingers through her sleep disordered hair, even though her ultimate boss was a thousand miles away.

"Not at all!" the CEO said. "I just wanted to tell you how much I appreciated your hard work yesterday in getting those circuits up. Brilliant job!"

Kerry made a face, pleased with the praise but a trifle embarrassed at the vehemence. "Well, you know, I had the best teacher," she demurred. "And really, the generator idea wasn't mine. It was Dar's."

Andy sucked at his orange juice, watching her with gently twinkling blue eyes.

"Well now, you know that just figures, doesn't it?" Alastair said. "I'm so glad you two make such a good team."

Kerry's eyebrows jerked up. "Well, I think so," she responded cautiously. "I mean, I'm glad Dar knows when she's tied up helping another client, that I can fill in when something happens and make sure it all comes right."

"Absolutely," he replied. "Well, as I said, great job!"

"Thanks."

There was a slight pause. "Ah, listen, while I have you on the line..."

Ah hah. Kerry leaned against the counter and cupped the phone to her ear as Andy's muffin appeared and she tended to it. "Yes, sir?"

"Oh, Alastair, please. I can't remember the last time Dar called me sir," he said. "If she ever did," he added, in a mildly bemused undertone. "Listen, Kerry...I was talking with Dar last night, and you know...hey, is she feeling okay?"

Kerry's nostrils flared in surprise and her eyes widened. "Ah."

"I mean, you know it's very hard to make that kind of call over the phone, but I've known her for a long time, and you know, she just didn't sound right to me."

Walking around the counter, Kerry handed Andy his muffin as she sat down next to him, trying to decide what to tell Alastair. "Well, I know she was really frustrated with that client," she temporized. "She wanted to be back here by yesterday, but they weren't prepared...now she has to work with their programmer, so yeah, she was sorta pissed."

Andy's eyes fastened on her face and his head cocked faintly to one side.

"That wasn't really..." Alastair hesitated. "But everything's all right otherwise? Her folks okay? You okay?"

It was amazingly personal, and Kerry realized at some level that Alastair's query went beyond business. Her prior dealings with the man had given her the impression he genuinely liked Dar, and she could hear a note of honest concern in his voice now. "Everyone's fine," she replied. "In fact, her dad's here right now." She watched Andrew's brow crease. "I think it's just that we had a tough time at that show, and this whole ship bid is really aggravating."

"Ah," Alastair said. "Telegenics, eh?"

"Yeah," Kerry said. "She also hates New York."

A low chuckle sounded through the phone. "I should have remembered that. Yes, you're right. Well, long as everything's okay, Kerry. Glad to hear it. You know Dar means a lot to me, right?"

"I know. She means a lot to me, too," she said quietly. "Thanks for asking."

"You take it easy today, you hear? Everything's up and hunky dory, and I just got a call from Bantelonics, and they're happy as clams to be up. Wanted me to know it, so I thought I'd call and let you know it," Alastair said, in a brisker tone. "Tell you what...how about I bring lunch in for everyone? I'll have Bea take care of it."

"If you can find someplace whose kitchen has power," Kerry reminded him. "That would be great."

"Ah." A sigh. "Well, everything's just another challenge. You call me if you need anything, all right, Kerry?"

"I will," Kerry promised. "Thanks." She folded the phone up and rested her elbows on her knees, hesitating a second before she turned and met Andrew's eyes. "Well, that was interesting."

"Yeap," Andy agreed slowly, drawing the word out. His grizzled eyebrows twitched. "Something goin on with mah kid?"

Kerry thought hard about what to answer, for a totally different reason than she had with Alastair. "She's okay," she reassured her father-in-law. "We just had to deal with someone who gave her a really hard time way back when, and it shook her up a little." She exhaled. "And I think, honestly...she's a little restless with the company."

"Huh." Andrew took a bite of his muffin. "Someone mess with her?" he asked, deceptively casual.

She loved Andrew. Kerry felt a smile slowly tugging at her lips. He was forthright and honest, a proud man of unbending will whose adoration of his family was so absolute it touched the very soul. So she knew his question was meant to ferret out whether someone had hurt his beloved daughter, and if that was so, well then Andy was apt to see what he could do about it.

There was, she acknowledged, a violence to him that could not be denied. But then, Dar had that same dark thread running through her, though it was far more deeply hidden. "A long time ago," she told Andy. "When Dar was younger...it was someone she got involved with who didn't feel the way she did."

Andrew scowled immediately.

"Yeah, well, I can't understand it either, but anyway, she was pissed off, I was pissed off...it wasn't fun. Then they're part of this bid for the ship contract, so I'm sort of glad Dar's not here. At least from my perspective, I just get mad as hell and want to kick them."

"Huh." The big ex-sailor grunted again. "World's full of jackasses sometimes."

"Sometimes," Kerry agreed. "But then there're people like you, so it all balances out." She rested her hand on Andy's knee. "I guess it's time for me to go take a shower and get to work. At least I got some sleep, thanks to you and mom."

Andy got up and tousled her hair. "Tell you what, kumquat. Ah'll go light me some coals under that there boat, and wake up my pretty lady. You get your gear squared away, and c'mon over when you got a mind to."

Kerry watched him leave, then she stood up and went back to the galley, to take a gulp of her coffee and a bite of her own, now cool, muffin. She leaned on the counter for a moment, acknowledging the fringes of exhaustion still clinging to her from her lack of sleep.

For two cents she'd stay here and sack out. Kerry glanced over at her PDA, which chirped. "But I don't have two cents. So..." She trudged over and retrieved the instrument, glancing at it. A message from Mayte, already in the office.

Miss Kerry, Senor Quest has called, and is wanting to meet with you urgently.

"Kiss my ass." Kerry exhaled, a little knot of worry now twisting in her stomach from her conversation with Alastair. She sent a reply back and put the PDA down, making her way into the tiny head for a hopefully refreshing enough to wake up shower.

She only hoped Dar's day was starting out better than her own.

Chapter
Fifteen

THE CLOCK OUTSIDE the hotel clicked to seven a.m., and as if on cue, the front doors swung open and disgorged a flood of people all heading purposefully out of the air conditioned lobby to somewhere else.

Dar took one look at the traffic in front of her hotel and decided to walk instead. Accordingly, she turned and headed downtown, the early morning sun not yet oppressive as it splashed over her polo shirt and denims.

She'd settled for coffee and a banana for breakfast, after waking a bit later than she'd anticipated and rushing through a shower and dressing in some of the new clothing she'd purchased the previous day.

Shifting her briefcase on her shoulder, she lengthened her strides and picked her path through a slowly increasing stream of humanity, moving quickly to one side as a man walking a goat passed her going the other direction.

Dar kept moving, resisting the urge to turn and see if she'd really seen a hoofed mammal strolling down the sidewalks of Manhattan. After all, she'd seen llamas in San Diego and alligators in Miami. What were a few goats?

The foot traffic was also busy, everyone seeming to want to rush to work early on this Friday morning. Dar relaxed into her walk, though, glad of the opportunity to stretch her muscles out in lieu of a session in the hotel's gym.

She spent the time on the walk deciding how to approach the problem facing her. Her first instinct — to simply run roughshod over the German coder — would probably not get her anything more than a sense of personal satisfaction and a lot of long, screaming arguments.

Not that Dar really objected to long screaming arguments, but the longer the process took, the longer she had to stay here and put up with this noisy, crowded city that conspicuously lacked certain essentials, such as her partner.

And she had decided this morning while peeling her banana, that particular essential was something she intended to regain as soon as humanly possible. That meant she would have to take a different tack with the programmer and gain his cooperation, if she could.

At least she would try. There was always hours of screaming to fall back on. Dar's nose twitched as she caught the scent of strong coffee, and she decided to duck into a nearby shop to take advantage of it, escaping minutes later with a jolt of claustrophobia along with her steaming cup.

Twenty minutes later, she was outside the office building. She entered the revolving door, a flickering grin crossing her face as she caught the expressions of the flannel clad and sweating woman she shared the door pocket with. "Morning."

The woman merely nodded, and continued on her way once they cleared the entrance. Dar adjusted the strap on her briefcase and followed her toward the elevators, which already had a cluster of waiting bodies in front of them despite the relatively early hour.

The thought of getting into one of those elevators surrounded by all of them made Dar's guts churn unexpectedly. With a grimace, she looked around for an alternative path, spotting an out of the way door marked 'Exit' to the left of the elevators.

Dar checked her watch, and found she still had twenty minutes before her eight o'clock appointment. Accordingly, she bypassed the crowd and pushed open the door to the stairwell instead. A flight of concrete steps confronted her, along with a nose-tickling musty scent, but she started up anyway, trotting lightly on the treads to an internal rhythm.

Fifteen stories later, she emerged into a typically painted hallway and made her way between rows of weave cubicles into the conference room she'd commandeered the previous day. It was, as of yet, still empty. She set her briefcase down on the table as she leaned her arms against the wood surface, stretching her back muscles and flexing her legs.

Lousy scenery, she decided, but a nice workout, and no crowds. As she sat down, the outer door opened and Jason Meyer entered, the VP Ops presenting a slightly harried appearance as he spotted her across the room.

"Oh. Good morning, Dar."

"Hi," Dar responded. "Where's our programmer?"

"On his way from the airport," Meyer assured her. "My assistant picked him up." He walked over, fussing with the pen in his hands nervously. "Listen, I'm glad I got a chance to talk to you before he gets here. There's something you better know first."

Dar sighed, and propped her chin up on her fist. "You know something?" she said. "If I had a buck for every time someone said that to me, I'd have retired years ago."

Meyer sat down across from her. "This really isn't funny."

Dar gazed at him dourly. "I have to take my amusement where I find it. What's the problem?"

"I don't think this guy's really going to be able to help you," the man told her. He had sandy hair and now he scrubbed his hand through it, disordering the strands. "I talked to them when we first started up the servers...they know what the problem is. It would just take too much to fix it."

"Too much what?"

"Time. Money," Meyer admitted. "It means they have to rewrite their entire model."

Dar studied his face. The man must have been in his mid-forties. "Then why did you deploy it?" she asked. "If you knew this going in?"

His eyes narrowed slightly. "We're in a very competitive business, Ms. Roberts. This software gives us the edge."

Mild, blue orbs looked back at him. "Not if it doesn't run," she answered. "Know what I think? I think you didn't give a rat's ass about the effect on your infrastructure, because you figured your boss would just ask me to take care of it for you."

Now his look was watchful. "Well, you've got quite a reputation." He deferred the question. "Let's hope you can live up to it. Otherwise, I know a couple of companies who'd love to take your place here."

Ah. Knives were out. Dar allowed a sexy grin to cross her face. "For a fee to you, I'm sure."

"I don't appreciate the inference."

"I don't appreciate the threat," Dar responded. Her ears picked up approaching footsteps. "You made one bad choice already...want to risk a second?"

Meyer got up. "I'm not the one risking anything. You better be careful you don't get in over your head." He turned and walked out, using the back door to the conference room that lead down a short hallway to the executive offices. The door slammed shut behind him, leaving Dar in a momentary peace.

"Well, well." Dar leaned back, letting the fingers of her right hand drum on the table. "Nice to have that out in the open."

Her PDA bleeped. Dar opened it and tapped the waiting message, hoping she still had a few seconds before she was interrupted again.

#%$%$%#$$!!!!!!!!!!

Dar's eyebrows lifted. Cautiously, she tapped reply. *Anything I can do, Ker?*

(sigh) No. I'm okay. I just kicked my desk.

Why? Finally got over the color? Have it painted, babe. Dar joked, though she was a little concerned over the note. Kerry didn't usually assault her furniture without good reason.

I love the color. I just hate Peter Quest. He invited himself and that whole freaking circus here to our office, Dar! He didn't even wait to ask!

Dar frowned. *Jackass.*

Boy, you can say that again. I almost told him to get lost!

Which might have been what he'd been looking for. To see how far he could push them. *Did you make him wait?*

The sense of smoldering frustration was almost tangible in Kerry's answer. *Yeah. I told them they had to wait until after we had our corporate lunch delivered from Houston.*

Dar's eyebrows shot up. *Lunch? Alastair?*

Yeah. Thanks for letting me vent. He called me this morning to say thanks.

No problem. Dar scribbled back, glancing up as she heard the door latch start to work. *Gotta go. Wish me luck.*

Luck? Kerry's answer flashed back. *Honey, you're way too good to need luck. Give them heck for me, okay?*

Okay. Dar hit send as the door opened. She set the PDA down and took a deep breath, resting her elbows on the conference table and settling her posture as a young woman entered, followed by a tall, handsome man in pressed khakis carrying a briefcase not unlike hers.

The woman met Dar's eyes, and smiled briefly. "Okay, well, here we are. Hans, this is Dar Roberts from ILS. Ms. Roberts, this is Hans Erhard, and he's the chief programmer for Etecknics." With that, she stepped back. "Let us know if you need anything," she added, before she turned and left, closing the door behind her with a sharp snick of the latch.

Dar and the newcomer looked each other over in silence. Finally, Dar indicated the seat next to her, and lifted one eyebrow in invitation. The man agreeably walked over, putting his briefcase down and taking the chair, leaning on his elbows almost mimicking her position. "Hallo."

"Hi," Dar responded. "How was your flight?"

He gazed at her in complete incomprehension, just a polite smile on his face.

"Hallo, wie war Ihr Flug?" She amiably repeated the question in German, a little surprised to see the man's eyes light up. She'd been sure after her conversation with Meyer that he'd filled their guest in on their plans. But the reaction so far from Hans was one of a pretty blank slate.

Unexpected. Pleasant, but unexpected.

"It was very good," he answered in German. "Only too long. I am surprised to hear you speak my language, I thought no one on this side of the Atlantic spoke anything but English." One hand extended over the table toward Dar. "And I am especially glad because I have heard so much about you, though I think we will not agree on very much regarding this problem."

Dar took his hand and shook it, pleasantly surprised again by his forthrightness. "Well, you never know," she said. "Why don't we start at the beginning, and see what we can make out of this mess."

Hans inclined his head in agreement. "Yes, yes. But I think we should start with some coffee, since it is almost beer time for me right now. Is there somewhere here we can go?"

Well, this was starting out much better than she'd anticipated. Given the hostility she'd had from Meyer, the pleasant courtesy from Hans was duly appreciated, and she figured taking him out of the office to get some breakfast probably wasn't a bad idea. If she could get his active cooperation, then maybe getting this resolved wouldn't be as much of an uphill battle as she'd been afraid it would be. "Sure." She stood up. "There's a shop across the street. Let's go over there, and you can start by telling me all about this little program of yours."

"With my greatest pleasure." Hans indicated that she precede him. "It is a project that I am very proud of, and never tire talking about, especially talking about it to a very respected colleague who has much to be proud of as well."

Isn't he charming. Dar noted wryly. This might turn out all right. "Ah." She reached the outer door and opened it, stepping back to let him through. "Let's hope we can get both of these perfect products to work together."

Hans chuckled as they walked to the elevator. "I did not claim my software was perfect, however."

"Well, my network is." Dar issued a faintly teasing challenge. "But I'm sure we'll work something out." She watched his profile intently, but he only smiled easily and laughed. Yeah. This might turn out all right after all.

They entered the elevator and waited for the door to shut. Dar managed to catch a glimpse of Meyer as he walked by, his eyes flicking over them, and his face twisting into a scowl as he passed.

"So." She eyed Hans. "How long have you known they've had a problem?"

Hans checked his watch. "They have contacted me, yes, twenty-four hours ago."

"Interesting."

"HOW'S THE TRUCK going?" Kerry paused in the act of making herself some tea, as Mark entered the break room. "Everything seems to be holding for now."

"So far so good," Mark agreed, going over to the soda machine and popping some coins in. "Did you end up getting home last night?"

"I did." Kerry leaned back and sipped her tea. "Pretty late, but Dar's folks gave me a ride over and back again this morning. I spent the night in our boat."

Mark stopped in the middle of opening his coke bottle. "Huh?"

"Air conditioning," Kerry clarified. "It's got batteries, and the tanks were full of diesel to keep them charged."

"Oh, right." Mark nodded. "We had the windows open, but man it sucked. I was glad as hell to get to work this morning and cool off." He perched on the edge of one of the tables. "Did we get any fallout over all that stuff from last night? I didn't see anything on the news."

"Tell you in a few minutes. I have that guy from Tech TV showing up here." Kerry lifted her mug in Mark's direction and headed toward the door. "And a message on my voice mail from CNN."

"Ugh." Mark shook his head as she exited. "You couldn't pay me to do that job."

Kerry got into her seat just as the intercom buzzed. "Yes, Mayte?"

"Miss Kerry, I have Mr. Argos here? He said you were expecting him?"

Kerry's eyes narrowed. She paused a moment and took a breath, then pressed the intercom button. "I wasn't expecting him, Mayte. Please ask security to remove him from the building."

"Si." Mayte bravely stepped up to the plate, and clicked off.

Kerry dialed security, just in case. She waited until someone answered, then cleared her throat. "This is Kerry Stuart. There's an intruder here on the fourteenth floor in my outer office."

"Ma'am, this is Celeste, we just sent two officers up there. Do you want us to call the police?"

It was tempting. Kerry rested her weight on her elbows and bit the inside of her lip, thinking hard. "If he causes a problem, then yes. If he just goes quietly, then no," she decided.

"All right ma'am. We'll take care of it."

Kerry could hear male voices outside, strong and insistent. She got up and circled her desk, heading for the door and reaching it as the sound hit its crescendo. She opened the door, to find two of their security guards braced in front of her, facing off against Argos, while Mayte watched with wide eyes.

She pulled her cell phone off her waistband and dialed security. "Celeste?" She spoke into the phone. "Call the police."

Argos stopped yelling, realizing she was there. "Okay, so now we get somewhere."

"The police are on the way," Kerry said, briefly. "Since you can't cooperate with my security, I'm sure you'll cooperate with them. I would if I were you. I hear the Dade County Jail isn't for the timid."

"You can't call the police," Argos said. "Come on, Ms. Stuart. Give it up and talk to me."

"I've called the police," Kerry responded. "You're trespassing on private property."

"I'm the mainstream press. You can't treat me like that," he argued. "Do you want to make yourself and this company look worse than it already does?"

"Mr. Argos," Kerry addressed him quietly. "If I showed up in the Atlanta headquarters of CNN, and lied to get in, then stormed your secretary's desk, what would you do?"

He paused, and looked at her warily. "I'm only trying to get a story."

"And I'm only trying to run a company." Kerry glanced past him as Celeste and four other security guards showed up, crowding the antechamber. "Thanks Celeste. I'm going to go back to cleaning up after yesterday."

"Ma'am, we've got this." Celeste glared severely at Argos. "Sir, you are going to come with us downstairs. The police are waiting."

Argos ignored her. "You're really not going to talk to me?" he addressed Kerry. "It's in your interests, you know that."

"I know," Kerry agreed. "But I'm not going to give you what you want since you chose to pursue it the way you did. Blame my upbringing. Celeste, please escort him out."

"Son of a bitch."

"Daughter of a bastard, actually." She turned and went back in her office, closing the door with what she hoped was a sound of finality.

"Sir?" Celeste stepped close. "Please come with us."

Argos stuck his hands in his pockets. "You know, I don't really get my bluff called that often. Are the police really downstairs?"

"Yes."

The reporter nodded. "Okay." He meekly took up a place between Celeste and one of the other officers as they turned and made a crowded way out of Mayte's space heading back toward the elevator. "I don't suppose any of you are interested in talking to the press about what it's like to work here?"

Celeste just looked at him.

"All righty then."

KERRY HAD HER hiking boots propped up on her desk, and a Styrofoam plate of Chinese food in her lap as the first rumble of thunder sounded in the distance. She turned her head and observed the gathering clouds, glad she was inside and cool and relatively comfortable.

With a sigh, she went back to her lunch, deftly picking up a mouthful of the spicy, nutty chicken with her chopsticks and getting it into her mouth without dropping saucy bits of rice over the front of her aqua blue polo shirt.

Casual was casual, but going into a meeting with three other companies and a client with a soy sauce stained shirt wasn't something she really wanted to do, and the only extra shirt she had in the office was one of Dar's.

Conspicuously one of Dar's, in fact, a company polo from some show or other with her name on it.

Hm. Kerry pondered a sloppy bit of water chestnut, then regretfully put it safely between her teeth.

A soft knock came at the door. She considered adopting a less casual posture, then shrugged. "C'mon in."

The door opened and Mayte entered, her slim form also encased in casual denim and cotton. She was carrying a sheaf of papers, and a shy grin crossed her face when she spotted her boss half sprawled over her desk. "Miss Kerry, I have the documents you asked for."

"Bring 'em over." Kerry waved her chopsticks at her. "Did you get lunch?"

"Si." Mayte put the papers down in Kerry's inbox. "I have it outside. That was very nice of the big office to do for us."

"Yeah." Kerry selected a piece of chicken and bit into it. "Is the conference room ready? I told Mark to make sure our visitors get active tagged badges so we don't have to worry about them wandering around pressing their ears to the drywall." She glanced up. "Sit." She indicated the chair in front of her desk.

Mayte sat down, raising one hand to push her long, dark hair back behind her ear. "I think everything is ready, yes," she said. "My mother said some not so nice things about some of the people. Is this a bad thing that is happening here, Ms. Kerry?"

"Could you do me a favor?" Kerry asked.

"Of course," Mayte answered instantly.

"Could you please just call me Kerry?" Her boss requested, giving her a hopeful look. "Otherwise I really feel like I'm trapped inside a bad Southern period movie."

Mayte made a face.

"C'mon, it's not that hard is it?" Kerry coaxed.

Her assistant smiled hesitantly. "No, it is not hard at all. I just feel that it disrespects you if I do that. You are my boss."

'Hm." Her boss tapped her chopsticks together lightly. "Why do I think that particular argument might not really hold much water with me?" She inquired, a grave twinkle in her eyes.

Mayte blushed, a deep coral against her tanned skin, but didn't answer.

Hm. Kerry decided to table the discussion for the moment. "Anyway, back to your original question. These people are part of the cruise ship bid that Dar and I have been working on. The man asking for the bid invited himself here to have the meeting, because we're the only ones who have power, apparently. I don't really mind. In fact, Dar suggested I ask them, but I don't like people simply assuming things."

"Si." Mayte had recovered her composure, and now she nodded firmly.

"And yes, we know two of the people who are bidding against us," Kerry added, a trifle reluctantly. "One of them is a former client. The other..." She exhaled. "Knows Dar from way back."

Mayte blinked at her. "You do not like her,"she hazarded a guess.

Transparent as glass. Kerry sighed inwardly. "No," she admitted. "But anyway, I'm hoping this meeting won't be that long. We all presented a bid overview yesterday before the power outage started. I think he wants to put the cards on the table and ask for formal pricing." She scooped up some rice and a bamboo shoot. "And with any luck, I won't have to sleep on the water again tonight."

"Pardon?"

"I slept on the boat," Kerry clarified, taking a sip of her herbal tea. "After I found a way to get out there...I got lucky and Dar's folks found me over on South Pointe." She eyed Mayte. "How did you manage last night?"

"It was very hot," Mayte confessed. "We went outside to the porch, we have screening there, and papa made us hamburgers on the hibachi," she said. "We used candles and we slept outside. It was too hot inside."

Jesus, you're a lucky son of a biscuit, Kerrison. You have no idea. "Wow." Kerry set her lunch down. "Yeah, I remember how hot it gets. Dar and I spent the night in the condo once without power."

Hot and edgy, with the storm raging outside and an even bigger one brewing inside them both. "What a night that was."

"Papa went and got a generator very early today, when I told him what you did for the customers yesterday. He thinks you are very smart," Mayte said. "It is much better for Mama, too. She did not feel well at all."

Kerry's ears pricked up until she swore she felt the hair over them fluffing. "From the heat?" she asked casually.

"I think so," Mayte replied. "She could not wait to come to work today." A shy grin reappeared. "Me, either."

"Well." Kerry put her plate down and pulled her keyboard over. "If those losers don't have the power back on by tonight, I'm authorizing all of you to stay here in the building overnight. I don't want anyone getting sick, especially..." She gave Mayte a direct look. "Your mother."

It took only a moment to type out the message. Kerry reread it a few times, anticipating the problems and objections to it, and then she sent it, remembering to copy Dar visibly. "I know we don't have cots or anything, but we do have showers downstairs," she said. "And you and your mother can take over our offices." She indicated Dar's photo, sitting on the corner of her desk, and then indicated her own chest.

Mayte's eyes widened. "Oh, no, we can find other places..."

"Ah ah ah!" Kerry mock scowled at her until she subsided in meek silence. "It's what Dar would want." She continued in a softer voice. "Your mother means a lot to her, and I know she really appreciates all the support your mom's given her over the years."

"Si, I know..." Mayte admitted. "I remember when Mama came home one time when there was no air conditioning here."

"Ick."

"Si. But she was so upset, because la jefa had stayed here all night, working so hard to get it all fixed, and the next day she heard so many horrible things about her, it made her very angry," Mayte said. "She said it was so unfair."

Kerry shifted her position, crossing her boots and watching her screen fill with answers to her email, some marked with a red exclamation point. "Yeah," she murmured. "But you know what,

Mayte? That was the day Dar and I met."

"Oh! I did not know that!"

A faint smile appeared on Kerry's face. "I don't think she remembers the air conditioning any more than I remember her intending to fire me." She sighed and removed her feet from the desk, sitting up and draining her tea cup. A glance at her watch told her she was running low on time, but she paused to glance at her mail.

Protests. She'd expected that. People objecting to her opening up the offices, thinking more of propriety than of the simple but basic comforts the building could provide.

Then — "Ah." Kerry clicked on one mail at the very end of the list and opened it.

From: Roberts, D.

To: Miami Users All

Cc: Stuart, K.

Damn good idea, Kerry.

D.

Past that mail, the objections petered out, replaced with acknowledgements, brief and conspicuously without exclamation marks. Kerry clicked on the reply button and typed a brief, three word, eight-letter response and sent it back to Dar alone, then got to her feet. "Okay. I'm going to that darn meeting. If anything blows up here, message me."

"I will." Mayte got up as well, and walked with her to the door. "M..." She paused, wrinkling her nose as Kerry cleared her throat. "Kerry, may I ask you something?"

"Sure." Kerry put her hand on the door handle and leaned on it.

"This person who is coming here, who my mother does not like and you do not like...she did something bad to la jefa, is that not so?"

Kerry nodded briefly.

"Mama heard this woman talks bad about Dar, is that true too?" Mayte asked.

Green eyes took on a hint of steel. "Yes."

Mayte nodded solemnly. "La jefa means much to my mother as well. She told me this time, if she hears people saying unkind things about her, she will go get the janitor's broom, and make them fly with it."

Kerry spared a moment to imagine her lover's short, feisty administrative assistant chasing Shari down the hallway with a broom and unexpectedly burst out laughing. She leaned against the door and held her stomach, trying hard to catch her breath as the image played itself out over and over again in her mind.

Mayte blinked at her in alarm. "My Mama is serious!"

"Oh, I know." Kerry slid down the wall and just kept laughing. "But now I gotta figure out how to bug the conference room so she can hear it all and crank the broom up!"

"But..." Mayte sounded very puzzled. "You want her to do this?"

Kerry finally let the laughter run down, and just sat there, one knee raised with her arm resting on it and looked up at her assistant. "Don't worry about it, Mayte." She finally exhaled. "Your mama won't have to do a damn thing."

"No?"

"No." Kerry's voice was quiet and serious now. "Because I'll do it first." She got to her feet and dusted herself off. "Wish me luck." A breath later, she opened the door and went through it, heading for the conference center with a grimly determined air.

THEY HAD TAKEN over the entire conference table by now. Hans had printouts spread out over half of it, and Dar had router and switch dumps littering the other half as she focused on the screen of her laptop. She was leaning on the table and had both legs wrapped around the legs of the chair she was sitting in, rocking back and forth a little as she tapped her mouse pad impatiently. "You're still sending too much data over, Hans."

"It is not!" Hans insisted. "Look, look here." He pushed a paper toward her. "See there? It is only what the program needs. Just that."

Dar pulled the paper over and studied it, one long finger tracing the code. Her brow furrowed, and then she pulled over the next page, her eyes flicking over the lines of text searching for something. "Eh...eh..."

"What?" Hans got up and came around to her side of the table, leaning on the wooden surface and peering over her shoulder. "There is nothing there."

"There." Dar tapped a line of code with the tip of her finger. "Look what you're doing here."

"Nothing!"

"You're sending the whole screen at once."

Hans leaned closer, almost touching Dar's arm as he peered at the paper. "And, so?"

"So it's going as an unbroken string of linked packets and it grabs all the bandwidth," Dar said. "You're sending colors, Hans, as bits. You should be sending only vectors."

He stared at the paper. "Plot it all? Don't be ridiculous!"

"I'm not. You send vectors, it's only four bits, I transmit that as a small packet," Dar argued. "Change it. I'll show you."

Hans took the paper and sat down, frowning. "No. I cannot change it."

"Give me that. I'll change it." Dar held her hand out. "Share your drive out."

"No." Hans refused. "You do not understand, Dar. If this changes, the whole program must change."

Dar looked at him. "That's right."

"I am not changing my whole program. That is not what we agreed to."

"You agreed to make it work for them. That's what it's gonna take," Dar said.

"No, you must change your network, to allow them to work better." Hans shook his head. "I am not at this time going to redo my entire program."

Dar got up, in an almost explosive motion that sent the chair skittering back a few hops. She walked to the window and peered out of it. "Hans, it'll work."

"Pah." Hans pushed a stack of papers out of his way. "It is much easier if you give them more room."

"They have to pay for it."

Hans shrugged. "The world turns around on such things."

Dar turned and leaned against the window. "Hans, cut the dirt. They contracted you for a working program. You gave them a big, smelly white elephant."

"In no way!" he shot back, slapping his hand on the table. "This system works as designed! As designed! I will not change it!"

"You will." Dar crossed the space between them and braced her arms on the table, leaning toward him. "Because I'm not going to ask my clients to pay more for bad programming."

"You cannot say that!" Hans warned. "There is no way that I will..."

Dar moved suddenly, leaning much closer and lowering her voice. "Yes, you will," she growled. "So get it into your head right now you're going to make those changes. Do it, or I'll call in their legal department and we can start drafting up a breach of contract filing."

"You would not dare."

"Sure I would," Dar rasped. "So you'll sit there, and make that change." She pointed a finger at him. "Because you know damn well I'm right."

"You are not!"

"I AM." Dar's voice built up to an impressive bark.

Hans glowered at her. Dar kept her eyes locked on his, refusing to let up. He shoved back from the table and threw his pencil down, then walked out of the room, slamming the door behind him.

Dar straightened up with a reflective sniff, and resumed her seat. "Hm." She crossed her ankles. "Forgotten how much I really like doing that." She looked up as the door opened again, ready to resume her argument but put it on hold as Meyer walked in instead. "Hi."

He gave her a slight nod. "Not going well, I see."

Dar blinked mildly at him. "I think it's going great." She checked her watch. "Only took me four hours to figure out what the problem is. With any luck, I'll be able to get him to fix it in less than a decade."

Meyer rested his hands on the back of one tall chair and regarded her. "If you get the chance. I don't think you will. I think you upset our friend Hans so much he's leaving." He smiled grimly at her. "So I guess your great discovery is a bust."

Dar leaned back and laced her fingers behind her head. "Unfortunately for you, I think he's got more integrity than that," she remarked. "Not that you'd recognize it if you saw it."

"Just who the hell do you think you are?" he asked, angrily. "You think you can come in here and mouth off like that to me? I'm your customer!"

The door opened again, and this time Stewart Godson walked in. "Well, hello you two." He smiled, apparently oblivious to the dark thunderclouds hovering over the conference table. "How are things going? Made any progress? I see you've got a lot of paperwork here."

"Excuse me, sir," Meyer murmured, dodging past his boss and leaving the room.

Godson peered after him, then he turned and looked at Dar. "Did I interrupt something? I knew you two would get along if you just got to know each other a little bit. He's not a bad sort, Dar."

"He's a scheming skunk who wants your job and has the skill set of a pickle," Dar replied, with a light drawl. "Watch out for him, Stewart. He'll sink you."

"Oh, c'mon Dar." Godson took the seat next to her. "You always think the worst of everyone, don't you? He's all right. He's done some great work for us, and not only on this project."

Dar wondered if her counterpart was really that oblivious. Finally she just shook her head. "Whatever," she said. "All right, here's the deal, Stewart." She sat up and pushed the piece of paper over. "I found the problem."

"Did you? Excellent!" Godson was delighted.

"Yeah. Only Hans is giving me heartburn about fixing it," Dar said. "So I don't know how far we're gonna get," she admitted. "Especially if your boy Meyer gets to him, since he's got a reason to keep him stubborn."

"What? Oh, really now, Dar. Let's stop this talk." Godson frowned. "He's a valuable employee, and I don't appreciate you tearing him down like that," he said. "You wouldn't talk like that about your next in line, would you?"

Dar folded her hands on the table, and took a breath. "No," she replied evenly.

"Well, there then."

"I wouldn't talk like that about Kerry because she's the very best at what she does," Dar went on. "And because she's proven herself to be a person of high skill and integrity. Can you say that about Meyer?"

Godson frowned.

"Do you trust him?"

"Well, I..."

Dar got up and roamed around the room. "Stewart, you're my customer." She stopped and gazed out the window again, blinking as she spotted Hans on the street below. He was pacing up and down, frustration evident in every line of his body. She exhaled, reluctantly censoring her words. "I don't want to upset you. I just call them as I see them, sometimes."

She watched his reflection in the window, his face folding into a pensive expression. Well, good. Maybe he'd think about it a little. In the meantime, that left her with her own problem down there on the street. What if she couldn't talk Hans into it?

"Oh, I know that, Dar," Godson finally answered. "Listen, I'm the one who asked you to come here, remember? If I didn't respect your opinion, would I have done that?"

Dar felt a moment of almost dizzying doubt. What then? What if the programmer refused, and really did walk out?

"Dar?"

"Yeah." Dar swallowed before she turned back around. "Sorry. Just thinking." She returned to the table and sat back down. What would she do? Her eyes fell on Hans laptop, left invitingly close to hers. Could she take the code and, if he refused, do it herself?

Godson clasped his hands together. "Well, look, Dar. Why not let me take you and Jason and Hans out to dinner tonight, hm? We could go down to the Italian place on the corner. How about it? You guys will be ready for a break by then, right?"

Would that be ethical? "Stewart, mind letting me look at the contract you have with these people?" Dar asked. "Just want to see what leverage we have."

He shrugged. "Well, sure, Dar...sure. Let me get legal to bring you up a copy. "

"Thanks." She nibbled the inside of her lip. "Let's hold on dinner until we know how far we're gonna get today."

"Fair enough." Godson stood up. "I'll leave you to it then. Seems like you and Hans are getting nice and chummy!"

Okay. Dar finally decided. He's just an idiot. "Not really how I'd put it but..."

"Oh, sure, I saw you two."

The door slammed open, smacking against the wall and making a resounding crack. Hans strode in, brushing past Godson and slamming his hands on the table in front of Dar. "This is what my decision is." he barked in German. "And if you do not like it, then it is just too bad!"

Godson's eyes turned to saucers. "Hey!..ah..."

Dar leaned forward, and rested her chin on her fist. Her eyes narrowed a little, and she allowed a rakish grin to appear. "Talk," she replied. "Or walk."

Hans grabbed the paper they'd been discussing and shook it at her.

"I will make one, ONE change in this. In only this one module, and then you will show me this big difference it will make. I will see it with my own eyes how this is the big problem you claim."

Ahh. Gotcha. "All right," Dar agreed. "One change."

"And if it does not make anything better? Then?" Hans demanded. "What will you do? Because I will make no further changes."

Was she confident in her own analysis? Dar felt uncharacteristically unsure.

"Well?" Hans barked.

Stewart Godson was looking from one of them to the other, his eyes wide and his jaw hanging. "Ah..." he stammered. "Now, everyone relax, okay?"

Dar exhaled. "If I'm wrong, I'll give him the bandwidth," she said, in an even tone. "On me. How's that?"

Hans drew back and studied her. Then he grunted eloquently. "Good." He held his hand out to her. "We have a deal."

Dar accepted his grip, and released it. She sat back as Hans flopped into his chair, almost pushing Stewart out of his way as he pulled his laptop over and started pecking at the keys with long, agile fingers. After a second, she looked up. "Rain check on dinner, Stewart?" she suggested, in English.

"Uh...well, yes." Godson lifted a hand and started to back away. "Glad you two...uh... got things settled. Listen, if you need anything, just give me a call, okay?"

"Sure."

Godson left. Silence settled over the conference room again, punctuated by Hans' typing, and low, under his breath German muttering. Outside, faint sounds of the city filtered through the thick glass, but they were mostly obscured by the air conditioning cycling on.

Dar slowly let out a held breath, and picked up her PDA. She flipped it open and tapped a new message into being.

Ker?

A few seconds later, the message light stuttered.

Hey! How's it going?

Very good question. *All right. Think I found something. How's it going there?* She answered, then waited for a reply that seemed to take a while to come back.

Could be better. I just bumped into Michelle in the bathroom.

Dar winced. *You didn't drown her, did you?* This time the answer came back much faster.

I wish. I just want the day to be over. I'm trashed. Any idea when you'll be home?

Dar could sense the wistfulness in the words, subtly reassuring. *I'll know better tonight. Cross your fingers.*

(smile) Everything I have is crossed. I miss you.

Dar glanced furtively at Hans, but he was oblivious to her, his attention focused completely on his laptop screen with an intensity she recognized. She went back to her scribbling. *Same here. Call me when the meeting's over, okay?*

You got it. Love you.

Love you too. Dar folded the cover over the PDA and chewed on the back end of the stylus absently. Hans was working hard, but she found herself suddenly wondering to her own shock, if she shouldn't just open the pipes and have it over and done with.

What was going home worth?

Dar bit down on the stylus, lost in thought.

KERRY PAUSED FOR a moment outside the conference room to gather her composure. Consciously, she relaxed her shoulders and straightened her spine, and then she worked the latch on the door and pushed it open.

Inside, ten people were already circling uneasily around the big oak conference table. They were dressed in typical business attire, the worse for wear given the heat outside, and they all looked up as Kerry entered and crossed to the table.

"Afternoon," Kerry greeted them briefly. She laid her leather portfolio and her PDA down by the chair at the head of the table and walked over to the well stocked sideboard to get herself a glass of iced tea. Even with her back turned, she could sense eyes on her, but she took her time pouring her drink, mixing a spoonful of honey into the glass before she returned to the place she'd chosen.

Her conference room, her chair. Kerry sat down and leaned on the chair arm, sipping her tea as she regarded the room. "Mr. Quest? Are we ready to start? I've got a full afternoon scheduled besides this." Of course, if Dar had been there, it would have been her chair. It was the one she always used in this room and if Kerry concentrated hard enough, she could almost convince herself she caught a hint of Dar's usual perfume lingering on the leather.

Looking like he smelled cabbage, Quest walked stiffly over to the other end of the table and sat down in the seat facing Kerry. "Thank you for allowing us to use your conference space, Ms. Stuart. I'm sure we all appreciate being out of the heat and sitting somewhere comfortable." He looked at the rest of the room's occupants. "Would you all like to take a seat? I don't really want to waste..." His eyes flicked to Kerry's briefly. "Anyone's time."

"Fine," Michelle replied for all of them. She took a seat mid-way down the table, and Shari settled in next to her. They were both in smart, well-cut business suits, and despite the heat Michelle at least, had managed to retain her air of crisp professionalism.

The Tech TV reporter, Kerry noted, was nowhere to be seen.

The representatives from the two other companies remaining in the bidding sat down across from them in the center, and Quest's two attendants joined him at the far end. Kerry took the opportunity to lean back in her chair and hike one denim covered knee up to rest against the table edge.

Shockingly unprofessional. She took a sip of her tea. But then, so was her techno-nerd polo shirt whose sleeves were rolled up two turns to reveal her biceps. "I'm glad you felt comfortable enough to ask me to host this for you," Kerry said. "It's been a tough couple days for all of us, I'm sure."

"Say that again," the man immediately to her right sighed.

Rickenback, his name was, Kerry remembered. His company was one of ILS's bigger competitors, while the man next to him, John Sellars, was from a small outsourcing firm in the Midwest. Both had engineers with them, and both were male. It made an interesting counterpoint to both the Telegenics team, and their own.

Half men, half women. Kerry wondered if Quest had deliberately picked it that way. He seemed odd and disconnected enough to have. "Tom, did you say your hotel didn't have power?"

"Yeah," Rickenback agreed. "Let me tell you, Kerry, you may like this swamp pit, but you can keep it." He gave her a wry look. "How in the hell do you deal with this heat all the time?"

"We stay inside." Kerry waited for the chuckles to fade. "Drink a lot of this." She held up her iced tea.

"And don't wear much clothing," Shari snarked.

Kerry ignored her. "Well, Mr. Quest? The floor is yours. If you need anything in the way of presentation material, let me know." There was no point in antagonizing him any further, was there? "We're all ears."

Quest hesitated, and then gave her a gracious nod before he got up and walked a little to one side, turning to face them. "Thank you all for coming out here," he said. "I realize it was short notice, and I realize we've all had some personal challenges the past day or so. However, I have a project to get started, and I don't have time to waste on waiting for things to smooth over." He cleared his throat. "So."

They all leaned forward toward him, except for Kerry. She remained relaxed in her chair, slowly sucking on her iced tea. The taste of raspberries and honey filled her mouth, and she let her peripheral vision take in the rest of the table as they waited for Quest to fill them in.

"I've heard a lot of talk the last two days," Quest said. "I've heard proposals, and concepts, and mostly I've heard bullshit."

Kerry's eyebrow quirked, along with the corners of her lips.

"All I've heard is promises and hot air. All of you think you can do the job I need to get done. But all I've seen is paper and smoke," Quest went on.

"Excuse me," Shari started speaking. "What did you expect us to do, bring the technology with us and put it on your desk?"

It was, Kerry acknowledged, a surprisingly reasonable question. "Mr. Quest, you got proposals because that's what you asked for." She threw her own comment in. "Are you looking for a demonstration of the technology?"

"Yeah," Tom Rickenback spoke up. "You called us down here to respond to your request for technical specifications. What exactly did you expect?"

Quest waited them out. He paced near the wall, past the sedately framed international certification certificates. "This is what I expect." He turned and put his hands on his hips, brushing aside the khaki folds of his jacket. "I want to see you deliver. I have four ships I need to fit out for business in less than three months. I want each one of you to take one ship, and put your money where your mouths are."

What? Kerry put her glass down.

"Whoever does the best job for the best price, gets the rest of our fleet." Quest folded his arms across his chest. "Twelve ships."

There was a conspicuous silence after he finished talking. The occupants of the table all looked at each other. Kerry finally broke the tension with a slight chuckle. "Okay, let me get this straight," she said. "You basically want to get your four ships equipped for free, so you figure by tempting us with a contract you'll get that to happen, because all of us are more than capable of putting a network just about anywhere."

It even got a smirk out of Shari, she noticed. Michelle licked the tip of her index finger and made an unobtrusive swipe in the air, before she settled back in her seat and folded her own arms.

Quest shrugged. "You can look at it that way, if you like. But the offer is real, and it's here on paper. So." He walked over and removed four reams from his briefcase and slapped them down on the table. "Put up, or shut up, as they say. Either you're in and interested, or you can take off now, and if you're lucky get a flight out of this place."

His assistant got up and lifted the papers, walking around to distribute them. He handed Kerry hers last, stopping a little short and forcing her to extend her arm for it. "Sorry," he apologized, handing it over. "Here you go."

Quest waited until they all had their copies. Then he closed his briefcase with a snick and picked it up. "I'll be at the Intercontinental," he stated. "Present yourselves with your signed copies there tomorrow if you intend on participating."

His eyes scanned the room. "We expect to be taken seriously. If you can't give us evidence of that, we reserve the right to reject your bid."

"So, you're saying no balloons tied to the paperwork?" Michelle asked in a dry tone.

He signaled to his assistants. "Thank you again, Ms. Stuart, for the use of your facilities. I'm sure everyone was a lot more comfortable here than they would have been at the hotel's conference hall. There's no AC there."

"My pleasure," Kerry murmured.

"Can't believe you haven't fixed that problem yet," Shari commented. "Must be almost as frustrating as living with Dar."

Instead of blushing, Kerry felt the odd sensation of a cold chill flushing through her body instead. She barely recognized the churning fury in time to take a strong hold of it, hearing the soft creak of leather as her frame reacted instinctively and tensed up.

She kept her eyes on the contract, forcing her hand to move and flip the first page over. After running her eyes over the first paragraph three times without reading it, she finally looked up, giving Shari a bland look. "You want me to snap my fingers and have the power come back on? Sure." Kerry obligingly lifted her free hand and snapped her fingers. "Since you think everything we do requires no effort."

The lights flickered suddenly in the room, and everyone looked up, startled. Kerry straightened a little, cocking her head as she heard a low thrum, then a series of snaps, before the lights brightened again and steadied.

"What the hell was that?" Tom asked. "You forget to pay the diesel bill, Kerry?"

Kerry scratched her jaw in bemusement. "Not exactly," she said. "That was our generator kicking off. We're back on city power," she admitted. "So I guess you can go back to your hotels and get comfortable with Mr. Quest's reading matter."

Quest tilted his head in her direction. "I'm looking forward to seeing you all tomorrow." He started to turn, then paused and met Kerry's gaze. "Thanks for fixing that little problem, Ms. Stuart. Good to see you living up to your reputation." He left the room, with his assistants trailing him as the rest of the people shuffled and started moving.

"Well." Tom eyed the contract. "Got a fax machine I can borrow, Kerry? Now that you fixed the power?" He managed a slight grin. "I don't mind stealing paper and a phone call from you since you'll have the home field advantage down here."

Kerry pressed the radio button on her cell phone. "Mayte?"

A moment later, her assistant answered. "Si?"

"Can you come down to the conference room please? I need something taken down to legal, and there are some people here who need to use the fax machine around the corner." Kerry put the document down, and rested her hands on the table.

"Yeah, he's right," Shari spoke up again. "We should get an advantage written in to make up for the bid being held down here. We have to get everything shipped in."

Kerry remained silent, her eyes dropping to her PDA as she opened it and started to scribe.

John Sellars spoke up, his voice quiet and gentle. "Good call on him getting those ships done, Kerry," he said. "Pretty slick, if you ask me.

He knows he'll get all the bells and whistles, and we'll be fighting each other to cut costs."

"Agreed. He's a player," Shari commented. "But then, so are we all."

"Mm." Kerry looked up from her screen as the door opened and her assistant entered. Mayte walked around the table and came to Kerry's side, keeping her eyes strictly on her boss. "Thanks Mayte." She held out the contract. "Can you tell them I need this reviewed for execution tomorrow? And show these gentlemen to the fax machine?"

"Of course." Mayte gave Kerry a smile. "Did you know we have the power on now? Everyone is cheering, except there were some people who I think really wanted to be sleeping in our office."

"Best news I had all day." Kerry returned the smile. "Tom? You wanted to send a fax? Anyone else?"

"We make our own decisions," Shari assured her. "We don't need our asses covered by our lawyers."

Tom stood up and hefted his bag. "Then you're a bigger idiot than you sound like," he told her briskly. "As well as being one of the biggest boors I've run across in a decade. Ma'am? After you." He courteously indicated Mayte precede him. "Gentlemen...ladies..." His eyes went to Shari. "Whatever. Have a great day."

He left with his associate. John Sellars and his assistant scuttled after him. "We'll take you up on that fax, Kerry, thanks." He gave her a half wave as they disappeared through the door.

That left Kerry with Michelle and Shari, a condition she had no intention of continuing. Accordingly, she picked up her cup. "Excuse me."

Michelle half stood. "Kerry, wait."

Her polite upbringing was sometimes very unfortunate. Kerry paused and waited, one eyebrow cocked in a reasonable imitation of her partner's attitude.

"Can we take you to dinner?"

Kerry almost laughed. "You're kidding, right?" she finally answered. "Come on, people. It's been a tough couple days. You think I'm into sitting and listening to bullshit all night?"

Shari snorted. "You just can't take it." She waved a hand. "None of you people have a sense of humor."

"I have a sense of humor," Kerry replied. "Jerks being rude don't qualify as funny in my world. Sorry about that."

"Well, if you..."

Michelle stood all the way up. "Shari, would you please shut the hell up," she said. "You're not making this situation any easier on any of us."

Shari's eyes narrowed, but she closed her mouth with a click of her teeth.

"Thank you." Michelle turned back to Kerry. "How about it?"

Kerry turned to leave. "Sorry. I'd rather have dinner with my dog."

"Kerry. C'mon." Michelle moved forward and intercepted her on the way to the door. "We're going to have to deal with each other for this whole damn project. Let's not start it off this way."

Kerry stared at her, then pointedly at Shari, then back at Michelle.

"Besides, we've got something you might want to hear." Michelle tilted her head to one side in acknowledgment. "You pick the place. I know this has been a battle so far, but I promise you won't regret listening to what we have to say."

On the verge of saying no, Kerry paused, remembering what Dar had said about Shari's plans. Maybe she could get her to put her cards on the table now, and have it be over and done with, before her partner even got home. "Okay," she decided. "My choice, huh?"

"Anywhere you want to go," Michelle assured her. "How bad could it be?"

Kerry smiled. "It's a favorite spot of mine. Out on the beach. I'm sure you'll enjoy it."

Chapter
Sixteen

DAR BUMPED THE door open with her elbow and proceeded inside. Hans was still hunched over his laptop cursing in German, and the sun was slanting inside the tinted windows to a far more radical degree. She set one cup down next to the programmer and went back to her own seat, settling into it and leaning back. "How's it going?"

"Like crap. Do you know how much I have to change in this to do your foolish test?"

Dar sipped her cappuccino. "Want me to take a look at it?"

"No."

Programmers. Dar cheerfully acknowledged her own species. "Yeah, I'd give you the same answer," she admitted. "Keep your paws out of my code."

Hans glanced up at her briefly, then went back to his screen. "Do you program?"

"I used to," Dar admitted. "Before I went into design and engineering. I still mess with it a little bit sometimes."

"Hmph."

Dar pulled out her PDA and opened it, seeing the stuttering light. She tapped on Kerry's message.

Hi sweetie.

Quest just chucked up strained peas on the conference table. He wants all of us to do one of his old ships and whoever comes in best value wins his fleet contract. I complimented him on getting his ships done for free, but I'm sending the contract down to legal now. Is it worth doing?

K

Oh, ps – I snapped my fingers and the power came on. I think your geek genes are leaking into me.

Dar snickered. "Oh, that's rich." She shook her head. "Slimy bastard."

"Eh?" Hans glanced at her again.

"Another company." Dar started scribing. "My partner's handling it."

Ker –

My geek what? Glad the power's on. Least I know you'll be comfortable tonight while I sit here babysitting a cranky programmer – must be paybacks.

Quest is a slick operator. I wish I could tell you to drop it, but with the coverage Telegenics has started, we'd look like crap if we gave up now. They'll say we're afraid of them. So we'll suck it up and participate unless you find something in the contract you don't like.

Dar hesitated, and then continued.

I think I found the problem up here. This guy's trying to fix it, and then we'll test. If it's what I think it is, he'll have to rewrite half the program code. He's pissed off. I half want to open the pipes even if it's not the problem. I want to go home.

D

She hit send, and then waited a little. However her PDA remained silent and she set it down on her leg, reasoning that Kerry might be busy. Bored, she pulled her laptop over and set it on her knees, minimizing the network sessions she had open and clicking to her personal storage icon instead.

She had several folders there, but she opened her favorite one, which had pictures of Kerry, her family, and scenes of home in it. They were set in date order, and she occasionally amused herself by just letting her eyes linger over this visible record of their relationship.

One of the ones she liked the best was the one that had caused Kerry the most problems when she went home that first thanksgiving. It was of the two of them, sitting on the couch together. Kerry had one leg slung over hers and they were leaning against each other, grinning at Colleen's camera.

She shifted her eyes to a picture of the two of them dressed for her high school reunion. She was standing behind Kerry in this one, her arms wrapped around her partner's bare middle. The sight of Kerry's mildly embarrassed expression at her skimpy gear always brought a smile to her face. But she looked adorable in her leather bikini, and Dar was always trying to find an excuse to have her wear it since then.

Maybe next Halloween.

She went on to a picture taken by her mother of the two of them relaxing on the offshore island during one of their picnics. Kerry was curled up on her side, asleep in Dar's lap. They were both covered in sand and blown by the wind and the sea, and were totally zonked, but Dar liked the picture mainly for the smile of pure joy plainly visible on Kerry's face.

It was amazing to her to know she'd put that look there. Or the look in the next picture, a single picture of Kerry that she'd taken on the boat, just at sunset after they'd come up from diving and were resting before going in for dinner. With reddish gold light surrounding her, Kerry gazed not into the lens, but into Dar's eyes past it, a warm and gentle love fairly glowing from her.

Dar exhaled softly.

"Fizzing crap," Hans cursed. "All right. Are you ready to do this test?"

Dar flexed her fingers and maximized the network session, logging into her local routers and keying up the monitor. She set several parameters, and then reviewed the results. "Okay." She rattled more keys. "Let me...that's a test database you're using, right?"

"Of course."

"Okay...let me give you a subinterface...hang on." Dar quickly set up the port. "Change your default gateway to the .2."

Hans muttered something under his breath, but set to work on his computer anyway. "It is done."

Dar set up a graph of the existing port, and her new one, and arranged them side by side. "Okay, start up your database...wait. You got someone on the other side who can hit it?'

Hans paused in mid key, then he looked up at Dar.

Dar didn't even wait for him to speak. She leaned over and picked up the phone, hitting some buttons. "Stewart? We need someone at a remote site to work with us. They'll have to have enough brain cells to change their application database source."

"Ah..." Godson's voice trickled through the speakerphone. "I think I can find someone for that...give me a few minutes, Dar. Okay?"

"Okay," Dar agreed, and hung up. She drummed her fingers on her keyboard, then retrieved the PDA that had slipped off her lap and opened it when it started flashing.

Ah. Note from Kerry. Dar tapped on it.

Hey Dardar.

Honey, no one wants you home more than me – but don't tank the Northeast, please? I'll come up and keep you company if it doesn't work. We can find some little Italian place and get drunk on Chianti and cheesecake.

Dar scowled.

Michelle and Shari want to take me out to dinner. I get to pick where. I'm going to take them to the place we go after kickboxing, and not give them a chance to change out of their suits. Think they'll refuse to talk to me after that?

Hope so.

Love you, K.

The scowl edged into a reluctant grin, which then faded out to a pensive stillness. She spent a moment thinking about Kerry spending the evening with Michelle and Shari, dive or no dive, and unexpectedly felt her blood start to boil.

The phone rang next to her elbow, and she had to tear herself back from a descent into furious jealously to answer it. "Yes?" Her voice came out a growl.

"Ah...Dar?"

Dar cleared her throat. "Yes?" she repeated, in a more reasonable tone.

"I've got someone from Tucson who'll work with you...ah, is that okay?" Godson said, a trifle hesitantly. "I've got her on the line, I can conference her in."

Focus. Dar felt the muscles in her thighs twitch, a leaking of the nervous energy that suddenly filled her. "That's fine. Thanks." She heard a click, then background noise came on the line. "Hello?"

"Um...hello?" A voice came through timidly. "This is Angie. Did you need me to do something?"

Dar had an overwhelming urge to hang up and walk out. Go somewhere private and give Kerry a call and tell her...

Tell her what? That you don't trust her? Dar took in a slightly ragged breath. "Ah, yeah." she answered Angie. "We need you to open up your booking engine, but we need you to make some changes in the setup first. You know where that is?"

"Yes." The woman's voice became blessedly confident. "I sure do. What do you need me to change?"

Dar looked at Hans. "Settings?" she asked in German. "For the database?"

He gruffly gave them to her. Dar repeated them in English for Angie's benefit. While the girl in Tucson was making the changes, Dar half decided she was going to force the ports to show what she needed them to show, and the hell with it.

Get on a plane home, tonight. If she was coming in, Kerry would surely toss up the dinner and come get her, right?

Of course. Dar stared at the screen, unable to suppress the churning emotion.

"Okay, I'm done. Want me to open the program now?" Angie asked.

I don't care. Dar forced her attention to the screen. *I swear I don't care. I don't give a shit about any of this.* "Go ahead." She looked up as Hans got up and came to peer over her shoulder at the monitor. On it, she had the production port, which was saturated and blinking red, and the test port, a benign green.

"Now we will see that I am right," Hans stated calmly. "I am sure of it."

I don't care. But Dar called up the router config anyway, making sure the buffers were set to take advantage of the changes, and her priority lists were in place. She watched as the new port showed activity, the traffic statistics building as Angie started it up.

All mechanical. She was hardly aware of what her fingertips were doing.

"Hey!" Angie's voice erupted through the phone.

The port stayed a placid green. Dar exhaled, her vindication meaningless at the moment.

"That was really fast!" the girl from Tucson blurted, in an amazed tone. "What the heck did you do?"

"Shit." Hans turned and walked away, taking a stack of printouts and throwing them against the wall with shocking violence. He got to the door and yanked it open, slamming it behind with such force the certificates hanging on the wall jumped and crashed to the floor.

"Hello?" Angie repeated. "Are you there?"

"Sorry." Dar laid her fingers on the keyboard, noticing now that they were shaking. "I'm here," she answered briefly. "We made some changes. Guess you can see the difference."

"Wow! I sure can!" Angie sounded very enthusiastic. "It used to take me twenty seconds to move from page one to page two on this database, and now I just clicked it, and it was right there! Fantastic!"

Dar measured the traffic. It had made a difference, no doubt. However, it was only one session, and she realized under full load, it would need more than that. It was a perfect opportunity for her to try out her new intelligent algorithms.

Damn it. But that meant she had to stay here. Just the thought made her want to scream in outrage.

"Are you going to do that with the real system?" Angie sounded excited. "Like, now?"

Dar's cell phone rang. "Hold on." She pressed the hold button and unclipped her cell, flipping it open and putting it to her ear without looking at the caller id. "Hello?"

"Hey, sweetie."

The angry, buzzing bees in her head settled suddenly. "Hi," Dar replied. "What's up?"

"Did you get my note?"

Dar settled back in her seat, pushing her laptop back and out of her view. "Yeah."

"Mm." Kerry's voice dropped a note. "You sound pissed. What's wrong? Didn't your idea work out?"

She'd only said three words. Could Kerry really tell how she felt based on that? Dar exhaled a little. "Matter of fact, it did," she admitted. "But goddamn it, to make it work in production, I need to throw my beta program in this fucking router after that goddamn programmer fixes the whole fucking thing."

Kerry was silent for a moment. "And...that means you can't come home," she ventured. "Is that what I'm hearing?"

"Fuck."

"Sweetheart."

Dar sighed heavily. "Sorry," she muttered. "I'm just so damn frustrated. I don't want to be here," she admitted. "That bastard Meyer...I think he set us up for this."

"Really?"

"He told me they knew it was a problem from the start. No one wanted to admit it because it would take too long to fix." Dar lowered her voice, even though she was alone in the room. "I think he figured to have Godson squeeze us for a bigger pipe as part of the new contract."

"Wow," Kerry murmured. "Would that fix the problem?"

"Actually, no." Dar exhaled. "I had the programmer here make one fix, and we tested it, and it flew. He's torked. I don't know if he's even going to come back and I..." She stopped talking. "Damn it I just want to kick something."

The frustration was achingly evident. "How about I ask Col to stay at the house and I hop up there?" Kerry asked. "Tell you what, I'll make the reservations. What hotel are you in again? The Hyatt, right?"

Strange, but all of a sudden, the bid and everything else she had to do went rolling into the bit bucket, overshadowed by the overwhelming need to respond to that note in Dar's voice.

"And miss dinner with Michelle and Shari?" Dar asked.

Kerry laughed. "Oh, would I love to not only get them down to the burger shack, but stand their obnoxious pig fart butts up in the bargain. Maybe I'll even call the guys and have them come harass the two of them."

Dar picked at the seam along the inside of her knee. "Rather have you here than out with them, that's for sure," she finally said. "But I can't ask you to."

"Why not?" Kerry cut her off. "Do you know how many times you've dropped everything and gotten on a plane for me?" she said. "Jesus, Dar. Give me a break!"

Dar chewed the inside of her lip. She was saved from answering by the door slamming back open, as Hans reappeared and stomped across the carpet toward the table. "Hang on," she told Kerry quietly. "You finished sulking yet?" she asked Hans in German. "Because frankly, I hate sore losers, and I'd really like you to grow the hell up and just do your damn job."

"Oo...that sounds nasty," Kerry whispered into her ear. "I have no idea what you're saying, but that language sounded like you're cursing."

"I am," Dar replied in English to her. "Well?" she barked at Hans.

Fuming, he sat down across from her and let his arms drop into his lap. His pale eyes smoldered as he met her gaze, his frustration written clearly across his face. "Damn you," he finally said. "I would like to smack you right across the face."

Dar leaned forward slightly, her own inner turmoil rising back to the surface. "Ohh...please try it," she growled out in English. "I am so in the mood to kick someone's ass."

"Okay. One flight to New York, coming right up," Kerry said, briskly. "See you in a few hours, sweetie. Keep the sheets warm for me, will you?"

Dar jerked her attention back. "Kerry, you don't have to..."

"Too late. It's done." Kerry cut her off again. "You're stuck with me. Gotta go pack. Talk to you later, okay?"

"B..."

"Love you." Kerry's smile made it easily through the cellular connection. "Call me when you're finished yelling. I'll be on the way home."

"You must think much of yourself," Hans said. "But I do not hit ladies."

Torn between two conversations, Dar decided to abandon one of them. She half turned and focused on her cell phone. "Kerry..."

"Yeess?" her partner's voice warbled back at her. "Please don't tell me not to come there, Dar. I really want to," she added gently. "I miss you so much."

The words died on her lips. Dar swallowed, and felt a smile tugging at her lips instead. "See you soon," she got out. "Thanks."

"Okay. Love you. My flight's at eight...so have the hot chocolate waiting, huh?"

"I will," Dar promised. "Bye."She closed the phone and held it a minute, then she sat up and turned the chair around to face Hans.

They looked at each other for a long moment. Then Dar exhaled. "Listen," she said. "I don't like being wrong either," she said in German. "Can we please just get it done?"

Hans leaned forward. "If," he pointed one long finger at her, "you buy me an expensive dinner, I will consider it."

Her heart was settling back into its normal rhythm, and her body was relaxing again, under a wave of lethargy that followed the easing emotion. "Sure," Dar agreed. "Buy you a whole damn side of beef if you want. Let's go." She stood up, surprised when her knees shook under her. "We can start with a beer."

"Ah." Hans shut down his laptop. "Now we are again speaking the same language. It will also help me drown my ego. Let us go, indeed."

Dar found herself smiling, through a sense of vague embarrassment. She felt very mixed up, and somewhat off balance, but all in all, she didn't really care.

Kerry was flying to New York.

That's what mattered.

KERRY LEANED BACK in her chair and studied the hiking boots she once again had planted on her desk. She knew she had to get moving home shortly, but she took a moment to bask in the sense of pure happiness she felt knowing how her night was going to end.

She had no idea what was going on with her partner. But she knew stress when she heard it, and caution went out the window. Besides, Dar had, in fact, dropped the world several times on her behalf and paybacks in this case were certainly justified.

Now. Kerry folded her hands over her stomach and reviewed her altered agenda. She had to go home, of course, and pack. Colleen had already responded to her email and agreed to come over and sit with Chino, and she'd double checked her inbox to make sure all the creepies were chased out of it.

Not that it would have mattered if they hadn't been. Kerry eyed her ceiling thoughtfully. Her head turned as her door opened, and Mayte stuck her head inside. "Hey, Mayte. C'mon in."

"Kerry." Mayte almost trotted across the floor over to her desk. "They said at Legal they are working on the documents I brought them. They will try to work quickly, but it is much to review."

"Good," Kerry said. "Since I won't be here tomorrow anyway." A grin appeared. "So Mr. Quest will get his executed copy next week and the hell with it." She felt a sense of relief. "If he doesn't want us to bid, then he doesn't."

"No?" Mayte watched her face closely. "Are you going to New York, maybe? I think you are."

"How can you tell?" Kerry inquired, feeling the skin around her eyes crinkle up as her grin grew broader. "Yeah, I am. Tonight, as a matter of fact," she added. "So, since I've got to get out of here and go pack, I declare the office closed. Go home."

"Really?"

"Yep." Kerry got up and closed her laptop case. "Power's on, crisis is over, and I've got a plane to catch."

"You are happy," Mayte said, shyly.

Kerry lifted her eyes from her case. "Does it show?" she asked in a wry tone.

"Oh yes."

"Well, I am." Kerry finished latching the leather catch and hoisted the bag to her shoulder. "Dar's having some problems with that programmer up there, so I'm going to go up and give her some moral support," she explained. "Or that's what my official story is. The truth is, I just miss her and I want to go up there."

"That is so sweet," Mayte said. "La jefa must miss you too."

"Mm." Kerry started for the door. "I know it sounds a little crazy, since she's only been gone a few days, but..."

"No, not crazy." Mayte opened the door for her. "It is beautiful."

Kerry walked to the outer entrance and paused, leaning a hand on the wall and turning to face Mayte. "You know, it is," she said. "People say all sorts of things about being in love, but you almost never hear anyone say how beautiful it is when it happens to you." With a faint shake of her head, she turned and left, heading for the elevator.

Mayte went to her desk and perched on the edge, jumping a little as her mother joined her unexpectedly from Dar's office. "Oh, Mama!"

"It is me, yes. At last they have stopped calling for Dar's office with the power and I will have some peace," Maria said. "Where is Kerrista going? Home I am hoping? She did not get much rest yesterday."

"No, Mama." Mayte solemnly shook her head. "She is going to New York."

"Ahhhh!" Maria smiled broadly. "It is about time! I was worried about poor Dar up there in that nasty place all by herself. I am glad Kerrisita is going to be with her."

"Si," Mayte agreed. "But Mama, I think Kerry forgot something before she left. She was supposed to go with those women to a dinner, and she did not tell them she was going away."

"Tcha." Maria folded her hands. "Is this those two perras?"

"Mama!" The younger woman affected to be shocked. "What would Papa say?"

Her mother expressed a sound very much like a sneeze. "I do not like those women, Mayte. They cause bad problems for us, and they were not nice to Kerrisita and Dar. I am glad there will be no nice dinner with them. They do not deserve it."

Mayte merely blinked, giving the solemn pronouncement it's just due.

Maria folded her arms over her chest. "Where was Kerrisita taking them?" she asked, almost as an afterthought.

"Tail of the Pig," her daughter supplied promptly.

"Como?"

"Si." Mayte shrugged. "That is what Kerry said."

Maria frowned. "I have not heard of this one. Have you?"

For an answer, Mayte circled her desk and sat down at her computer, accessing her screen with efficient fingers. "No, Mama, but I am sure we can find it on the Internet. There is everything on the Internet."

Obligingly, her mother followed her around and peered over her shoulder. After a moment, they both straightened right up. "Dios Mio," Maria spluttered. "I do not think Kerrisita is going to THAT place, Mayte. She is very the open minded, but...what are those two men doing?'

Mayte hastily clicked off it. "I think that is the wrong one, Mama." She continued hunting. "Here is one...oh." She frowned. "That does not look nice at all, but it is not too far from here."

Maria looked at the address. "That is near the place where they have their hatboxing lessons."

"Kickboxing, Mama," Mayte murmured. "Do you think Kerry was going there? The other women were dressed so nice."

Maria chuckled. "Come, Mayte. I have not yet had lunch. It is time for us to go get the burgers." She headed for the hallway at a purposeful trot.

"But Mama..."

"Vamanos!"

Mayte hurriedly locked her screen and grabbed her backpack, hoping Mama wasn't going to cause too much trouble. "I am too young to be arrested, I hope," she lamented, flipping off the office light as she headed for the elevator.

KERRY WHISTLED SOFTLY under her breath as she punched her door code in, and pushed the condo door open. "Hey Chi!" She eased inside. "How are you, sweetie?" She reached down to give her pet a hug. "Chi, you're going to be very upset with me, because I've got to leave tonight but I promise you when I come back, I'll have your mommy with me. How's that?"

"Growf!" Chino whirled around in a circle, her ears flying.

"That's how I feel too." Kerry confided, dropping her briefcase and jumping around in a circle herself. "Whoo!" She hopped up and down along with Chino, dancing across the floor with her. "Yeah baby. I'm gonna go get your mommy. You like that?"

"Groouf!" Chino bucked around Kerry and retrieved a stuffed toy, presenting it gleefully to her.

"Gimme that cow." Kerry grabbed the toy and cocked her arm, waiting until Chino scrambled over near the dining room table before she let it fly, clapping when the dog caught it in mid-air. "Good girl! Good catch!" She chuckled, continuing on past the Labrador and opening the back door for her. "Go on." She waited for Chino to go outside, then she leaned against the kitchen counter, glad the condo had already cooled down.

It felt very nice to be comfortable, and not sweaty. Kerry opened the refrigerator and took out a bottle of tea, popping the top and taking a sip of it. Inside the box, containers of dry ice thoughtfully provided by the island staff had kept the contents acceptably chilled through the power outage They'd even left a covered plate of fruit, which she removed and uncovered, attracted by the big strawberry in the center.

"Mm." Kerry glanced at the clock. It was only five thirty, and her flight was at eight. Still plenty of time. She figured to leave for the airport at six thirty. With only her overnight bag getting on the plane shouldn't be a problem. "Okay." She waited for Chino to come back in, then headed for the bedroom.

Chino accompanied her, but when she saw Kerry take out the leather overnighter, she gave her owner a pitiful look and went to go lay down on her bed. "Aww." Kerry put the bag on the waterbed. "You know what this is, don't you?"

Chino whined.

"Now, I told you I'd be bringing your mommy back. Don't I get points for that?" Kerry unzipped the bag and retrieved her traveling sundry kit, tucking it into one side. "Wish I could put you in here too, Chi...I bet mommy Dar would like to see you, huh??"

"Growf."

Kerry chuckled as she put three pairs of jeans into the bag, neatly folded, and added a few T-shirts and one long sleeve silk that refused to wrinkle just in case she needed something a little jazzy. A pair of leather flats along with it, then some socks and a handful of underwear. "There." She put her hands on her hips and reviewed her choices. "I think that'll do...unless Dar decides to take me to a Broadway show."

The thought rambled around in her head, bumping into her other random thoughts. Hm. Kerry wondered if Dar would like to go see a show...maybe she could find something really cool and entertaining to keep her restless partner occupied for a few hours. "And if we do..." She observed thoughtfully. "and it requires spiffy duds, well then, we'll go buy 'em." She snapped the catch on the bag handle. "Right, Chi?"

"Whine."

Kerry walked over and crouched down next to the dog bed. "Aw, c'mon, Chino...it's only a few days. Your mommy needs me." She stroked the Lab's soft head. "You know how important mommy Dar is to me, right?"

Chino wagged her tail.

"You know how much I love mommy Dar, right?" Kerry added, in a soft voice. "I can't wait till I get there, Chi. I can't wait till I see her, and I can give her a great big hug." She leaned over and hugged the dog. "Just like that, and I'll give her one for you too, okay?"

"Grrr."

"You know what? I think we might have a good time in New York. Maybe we can go to Central Park, and take a carriage ride." Kerry straightened a little. "I'd like that."

Stifling a yawn, she got up and headed back into the living room. Figuring the chances of being fed on an eight p.m. flight were slim and none, she decided to see what she could toss together for a quick dinner before she left. "C'mon, Chi...come get food."

She gave the dog a bowl of mixed kibble with some shredded chicken and got herself a cup of yogurt, a banana, some peanut butter, and the rest of her iced tea. "Mm." She surveyed her banquet. "But what I'm getting for dessert is worth it."

Cheerfully, she took the items into the living room and settled on the couch, flipping the television on to the news as she put her feet up and popped the top off her yogurt.

Now, at last, she listened as the power outage and it's restoration was explained. "Holy cow," she muttered around a mouthful of vanilla yogurt. "Look at that thing." A helicopter view of the Turkey Point nuclear plant showed the transformer building that had disintegrated, sending surges in all directions and causing the problem in the first place.

They'd been lucky. Only the transformer building had been affected by the explosion, as yet of unknown origin. Nothing had touched the nuclear part of the facility, but to say the authorities were nervous would be the biggest understatement of the fiscal year.

It was scary to think of what might have happened otherwise. Kerry felt a chill go down the back of her neck. "Tell you what, Chi," she murmured to the Labrador, who had finished her dinner and was now hopping on the couch to curl up next to Kerry. "I know where I'd like to be if the world blows up."

"Growf?"

"Mm." Kerry removed the cell phone from her belt and speed dialed, tossing her head to move her hair out of the way before she pressed the phone to her ear. "Hey, sweetie."

"Hey." Dar's voice sounded a half ton lighter than it had. "What's up? You leaving?"

"Just about. I'm having a banana first," Kerry told her. "Just wanted to know if you needed anything from here."

"You."

Kerry grinned at the ceiling. "Besides that," she said. "More undies? Shirts? Anything? I got a little room in my bag."

"Just you."

Kerry wriggled on the couch. "Okay. I'm heading out to the airport. See you in a few hours."

"I'll be there," Dar promised. "Hey...what'd you tell the terrible twosome?"

"Nothing."

"Nothing?" A laugh. "You stood them up? Really?"

"Sure did," Kerry agreed. "Fuck 'em. Hope they get run over by the guys on their bikes, and end up head over keister in Snake Creek canal."

"Kerrison." Dar laughed. "You little demon."

"Yeah." Kerry said. "Wait till you see my horns. You at dinner?"

"Yeah."

"See you in a few, hon."

Dar chuckled again. "Will do. See you later."

Kerry folded her phone and hauled herself off the couch, grabbing her banana as she headed for the bedroom. "Little demon," she repeated to herself, with a slight laugh. "Yeah, what a rebel I'm turning out to be. Dar, you don't know the half of it."

The sun twinkled placidly on her bag as she grabbed the handles and headed on out.

THEY'D FOUND THEIR way down to Mulberry Street, and into what was, for Manhattan, a relatively spacious and great smelling Italian restaurant by the time the sun was going down.

Dar settled into a seat near the window, eyeing the colorfully decorated walls with a bemused expression. "My partner would love this place."

Hans flipped the menu over and then tossed it aside. "I will take your word for it. Do they have something with fish here?"

Dar investigated. "Yes. Grilled salmon or snapper francese," she reported. "What's your poison?"

"If I were French, that would be an excellent joke," he replied. "I will have the snapper, and if they can please give me the noodles with just some olive oil. I do not like tomatoes."

Dar leaned back and extended her legs, crossing them at the ankles under the table. She didn't mind the restaurant, but already her body was twitching with impatience, willing the minutes to go by faster. "You still mad at me?" she inquired.

"Yes," Hans said. "You have made me too much work."

Dar merely grinned and played with her fork.

"Why could you not have said this when this program was being written?"

"I wasn't asked."

Hans made a face. "This client, yes? He is not so bright." He grumbled.

The waiter breezed by and simply looked at Dar with a raised eyebrow. "*Bier?*" Dar guessed, getting a nod from Hans. "Two of whatever import you have on tap, the appetizer sampler, one snapper with no sauce on the pasta, one veal the same way, and a side of olive oil."

"Awright," the waiter grunted, putting down a basket of bread and walking off.

"Very nice." Hans chuckled wryly. "It is so wonderful to be here in the friendly United States."

"This is Manhattan," Dar advised him. "You're lucky he didn't throw the bread at you." She took a piece and nibbled it. "Godson's all right. He's no technical genius, but he's pretty good on the financial side. I thought it was his VP who pushed the project through."

"Meyer?" Hans frowned. "He came late to the table on it. I think he has not been here that long." He selected a bread stick and broke it in half, placing one half on the table and chewing the other. "He does not care for you."

Dar shrugged. "He's at the end of a very long line." She watched the waiter as he returned and put down two frosty looking mugs, dribbling foam down their sides and onto the table. "Thanks."

"No problem." The waiter turned and left again.

"He's got his own agenda." Dar continued, taking a sip of her beer. "He's got an interest in a competitor of mine. Wanted to bring them in to save the day."

"Pah." Hans snorted. "Yes, I thought he was something like a player." He chewed his breadstick thoughtfully. "It could be he knew this was a problem, and did not want to change it. However, he does not understand technical matters which did indeed surprise me."

Dar tilted her head. "You mean he didn't understand programming?"

Hans waggled his index finger. "He does not understand technology in the least," he said. "He says...how do you say it here, he uses buzz words?"

"Huh."

"But if you question him closely, as I did, he has no understanding. I used this to my advantage, I do admit. I learned I could tell him anything and he would go along," Hans went on, in a mild tone. "His background, maybe, was business, not computers?"

"Mm. Could be," Dar agreed. "He kept telling me that we would have to take care of the problem ourselves. He didn't think you would cooperate."

"Me? I am a businessman," Hans objected. "I keep to my contract, and the contract says yes, we will make this program work. I do not have to like it, and I do not have to be pleased with having to do so much work, but I am a fair man." He took a gulp of beer and set the mug down. "If he says anything else, it is not true."

Dar nodded slightly. "I don't think he counted on me speaking German."

"Well, I did not either," Hans chuckled abruptly. "To be honest. I have used this to my advantage in this situation many times as well. It is easier to just accept what is given, and not have to struggle to communicate." He leaned back. "But, when I arrived, and we spoke, I rearranged my plans, and so here we are."

"Here we are," Dar agreed. "And, for the record, I really didn't want to make you change your whole damn program."

"I am not," Hans replied in an unruffled tone. "I have sent the damn thing back in pieces to Germany, and six young healthy boys are right now sweating over changing it while I sit here having reasonably good beer and horrible service in the good old US."

Dar started laughing. "You fraud."

"I am not." He maintained a dignified air.

Dar's cell phone rang, interrupting their debate. She pulled it out and opened it. "Yeah?"

"Well, hello Dar!" Alastair answered. "How are things? Sounds busy there!"

"I'm in an Italian restaurant," she answered dryly. "So yeah, it is. Things are all right. We found the problem."

"Did you? Great!" her boss said. "Not that I'm surprised. Listen, something's come up."

Damn. "Yeah?" Dar responded warily.

"Don't worry, it's not a disaster," Alastair chuckled. "Matter of fact, it's good news for a change. Bob Alexander just gave me a call. He's my opposite number for Allied Cruising."

"Ah."

"He's been watching the action around our little bid war. He's interested."

"In?" Dar inquired. "He wants to buy out those little stinkers, and put me out of my misery with the whole damn thing?"

The CEO snorted. "Nothing that simple. He's been thinking about upgrading his fleet. Eighty-seven ships. He says he's going to look hard at going with whoever wins the little one."

Dar blinked. "Holy crap."

"Uh huh," Alastair agreed smugly. "So those peanuts could turn into gold leaf peanut butter, lady. I knew the big boys were keeping an eye on this whole little circus, but Alexander sounds serious."

"That's a big contract," Dar uttered. "Jesus, Alastair, that's..."

"This quarter's catch up. Yep," he agreed. "And you know what? He called me because he thinks we've got a good chance to nail it. So do me a favor, huh? Nail it?"

As if it were that easy. Dar exhaled. "He just put the proposal out. It's down in legal being reviewed. He wants each company to do one ship. Whichever comes out best value wins."

"Yeap, Ham called me," Alastair said. "After he finished calling Quest a skunk, and an ape, and a skunk ape, he cleared it. I had him send it back on down to Kerry's office."

"Okay." Dar gathered her wits. "We'll talk about it tonight then. She's on her way here."

Alastair made a small sound of surprise. "Is she? Thought you said you had everything squared away there...more problems?"

"No," Dar said. "I mean, we've got the problem here isolated, but it'll take some work to fix it, but no. She's just coming up to keep me company." She knew the words sounded a trifle odd, but Alastair didn't even miss a beat.

"Good for her. You two take in a show or something, willya? Hey! Wait a minute...Bea! Bea!"

Dar pulled the phone away a little giving Hans a mildly apologetic look as the waiter returned with their appetizer platter and set it down on the table, along with some small plates.

"Business is business." Hans half shrugged, taking a mozzarella triangle and putting it onto a plate for himself. "It is nice for me, yes? I left my cellular phone in Germany."

Dar picked up a deep fried stick of something or other and took a cautious bite. She could hear the faint sound of the main office soothing music in her ear, and made a mental note to have someone hack into the phone switch and change it. After a minute, she checked her watch, wondering if Kerry was at the airport already, and if everything was all right with her flight, and if it was on time, and...

"Dar!" Alastair picked up the line. "Listen, I have in my hot little hands a pair of tickets to Radio City Music Hall. Can I send 'em up to you?"

Radio City Music Hall? Dar stared quizzically at the phone, ready to refuse. Then she paused. *Well, redneck, maybe Kerry would like to go there, you think?* "Ah...sure," she replied. "Sure, Alastair. I'd love that."

"Great!" Her boss fairly chortled. "Bea's sending them now."

"Hi Dar!" Bea's voice filtered through. "Have a great time!"

"Thanks," Dar responded.

"Well, I'll let you get back to dinner, Dar. Talk to you later," Alastair said. "Say hi to Kerry for me."

"Okay." Dar listened to the click as the phone hung up. "I'll do that." She folded the cell up and clipped it back onto her belt. "I'll certainly do that."

"Everything well?" Hans inquired.

Dar picked up her beer and took a healthy swallow. "Yeah," she said. "Pretty much, and the rest will be good in a few hours."

"When this partner of yours gets here?" Hans hazarded.

Dar nodded.

"Hm. I see." The programmer helped himself to another appetizer. "I am much looking forward to meeting this partner of yours. I think my horizons will be very broadened."

Dar checked her watch again, and drummed her heels on the linoleum floor.

Night was getting longer every damn minute.

KERRY FLIPPED THROUGH her magazine for the second time, glancing up as the flight attendant stopped at her side. "Hi."

"Hi. Can I get you anything? Another drink?" the man asked, with a smile.

"Faster airplane," Kerry requested seriously. "Can you ask the pilot to speed it up a little?"

The flight attendant chuckled. "It won't be that long now. It's just a three hour flight."

"This plane's call sign isn't 'Minnow' is it?" Kerry joked. "I'll have another orange juice, sure." She handed back her glass, then leaned back as the attendant strolled up the mostly empty first class cabin toward the service area.

Three hours really wasn't long. But she'd been at the airport for an hour that had seemed like forever. Now she just wanted the ride to end. She wondered if Dar would be at the airport to meet her, since her statement about being around wasn't really specific, and there really wasn't any need for her to ride all the way out to meet the plane, was there?

No, not really. Kerry hitched her foot up over her knee and smoothed the denim fabric over it with her fingers. No real reason, but she hoped Dar was there anyway. Airports were noisy, depressing places and she really, really wanted to see that tall, lanky frame and those pretty blue eyes waiting for her when she cleared the gangway.

Selfish?

Yeah, maybe. Kerry accepted the new glass of juice and sipped at it. She'd had enough time for a beer and some appetizers at the Chili's to Go in the airport, but the selection on the plane wasn't enough to entice her further.

Ah. Kerry paused, waiting. The ghost of a pressure she'd thought she'd felt on her ears returned, and increased slightly. They were going down. She only barely resisted the urge to hop up and down in her seat to make the plane drop faster.

"Jesus, Kerry," she muttered to herself. "What is up with you? Dar's only been gone a couple days. You'd think you'd been away from her for six weeks." She wasted a little time trying to imagine that, being gone for six weeks from her partner, and immediately switched to thinking about something else just from the sheer discomfort of it.

And wasn't that strange? Two married people should be able to be separate from each other without going crazy, shouldn't they?

Kerry welcomed the popping in her ears like an old friend. Okay, so she was strange. She was strange, and weird, and through all of it she wanted to be down on the ground and walking out that ramp and falling into those arms.

Because Dar would be there.

For sure.

DAR LEANED AGAINST the window, peering out into the taxiway area with enough intensity to hopefully force a large Boeing airplane into existence without further delay. Her breath fogged the glass and she backed off, wiping the moisture off with impatient fingers.

A small cart scooted across the concrete, and she leaned back in, watching it alertly as it parked itself under the jet way connected to the gate she was standing in. A man got out, and he pulled from the back of his belt a pair of reflective wands.

Ah. Good sign. Dar smiled happily. Her attention was caught by her reflection in the glass and she drew back, blinking at the brilliant blue eyes sparkling back at her. "Look like a kid at Christmas," she accused herself. "C'mon, knock it off."

A soft whine heard in the darkness drew her attention and she peered out again as a number of other little buggies drew up near the jet way. Her undignified glee embarrassed her. What would Kerry think? They'd only been apart for a few days, and now...

Jesus. Dar forced herself to pull back as she spotted the nose of a large white aircraft meandering in. She walked back around in front of the gate agent's pedestal and took a seat in the front row of chairs, folding her hands over one knee and affecting an air of unconcern.

The agents paid her little attention, being busy with paperwork. One turned and opened the jet way door, propping it wide with a metal stop before going back to checking something against his computer.

Dar watched the nose of the plane bounce to a halt, and heard the whine of the jet engines as the jet way moved out to meet it. Unaccountably, her heart started to pound, and she took several deep breaths to calm it without much success.

What if Kerry wasn't on the plane?

The thought suddenly struck her, bringing a sense of shock that made the room fade out just a little. "Don't be stupid," she muttered aloud. "Of course she's there, or she'd have called me." Dar firmly crossed her arms over her chest and refused to look at the cell phone clipped to her belt. Instead, she fixed her eyes on the opening in the jet way.

Of course Kerry was there. Probably right in front, taking her bags down from the overhead, and trying politely not to get in anyone's way.

Twitching her jeans straight, and running her hand through her hair as she took an impatient breath, waiting to get out.

Dar could almost see her if she closed her eyes, edging past the seats and heading for the door, head a little down.

She opened her eyes and stared at the empty opening, sensing motion approaching.

Hearing the scuff of soft soled shoes on the carpet, in a gentle rhythm she recognized, moments before the opening was filled with Kerry's familiar sturdy form, her head already moving around as her eyes searched the space before her.

"LET ME OFF this darn plane." Kerry suppressed the urge to give the flight attendant a poke, and adjusted the shoulder strap on her carry-on instead. They'd finally taxied up to the gate, and it seemed like forever to her before they moved the gangplank in and started to open the door.

She was in front. Usually, she patiently waited her turn, and let everyone else go before her, but not tonight. She'd scooted up past the two other flyers in first class and claimed a spot near the exit, watching impatiently as the attendant worked the door lock and pushed the big door open.

Bounce bounce. Kerry waited for the man to move back, then headed for the opening without hesitation. She'd been watching out her window as they'd pulled up, and she'd sworn she'd seen Dar standing there waiting.

Just a brief glimpse, but that had been enough for her to recognize that tall figure, hands pressed firmly against the glass, watching out for Kerry's arrival.

"Thanks! Have a great time in New York," the flight attendant told her, as she whisked on by.

"Oh, I will," Kerry promised, heading up the slanting ramp toward the terminal. It was musty smelling and rank inside, and she grimaced as she passed a dark spot in the carpet that stank to high heaven.

Hadn't Dar said the city smelled? Well, here she was, and boy, did it. Kerry saw light at the end of the tunnel and came around the last bend in the jet way, clearing the threshold and looking around her.

Her eyes locked with pale blue ones at once. Dar was sitting not ten feet from the entrance, and Kerry let out a whoop as she bolted across the floor, dropping her bag and throwing her arms around her partner as Dar stood and took a step forward.

"Eeeeyow!!" Kerry let out a soft yodel. "Am I glad to see you!" She buried her face into Dar's chest and wiggled.

Dar wrapped her arms around Kerry and lifted her off her feet, holding her tight without answering. The warmth of her body felt almost shocking, and before she knew it Kerry had a snug hold around her neck and was leaning up to kiss her.

Spectacle at the airport. Ah well. Worse they could do is toss them out and they were going anyway. Dar shrugged off the concern and responded, brushing her lips lightly across Kerry's before she made a longer, sweeter contact.

It felt familiar and wonderful, and the tension coiled inside her body relaxed as if by magic as Kerry pulled her head back a little and looked up into Dar's eyes again.

"Hey, sweetie." Kerry gazed at her with unmistakable adoration. "Are you ever a sight for sore eyes."

Dar grinned like an idiot. "Hey." She cleared her throat slightly. "Want to move out of the way of those folks?" She picked up Kerry's bag and shouldered it.

"Sure." Kerry wrapped her arm around Dar's waist as they moved down the aisle of seats, and away from the gate. She caught a look of disgust from one woman. "Something wrong?" she asked politely.

"Disgusting," the woman answered, drawing away.

"Thank you," Kerry replied graciously. "Have a great night. I know I will." She gave Dar a squeeze, and grinned unrepentantly as the woman hurried past and left them behind. "What a creep!"

"Her loss." Dar circled Kerry's shoulders with one arm and rested her cheek against her partner's soft, fair hair briefly. "How was the flight?"

"Took forever," Kerry admitted. "I just wanted to get here. It was okay, I guess." She craned her head. "Oh, I like those. Are they new?" She plucked at the waistband of Dar's jeans. "Very sexy."

"Mmhm." Dar felt herself relaxing further at the casual banter. "Thanks...you hungry? We can stop for something..."

Kerry looked around. "Not in here, honey. I've seen scrungier airports, but not by much," she remarked. "Can we get something at the hotel? I've got a headache Bayer would pay for."

"You got it." Dar shifted her arm, switching the casual drape for a light grip on the back of Kerry's neck. She kneaded the tenseness there as they walked, producing a half grin at the little sounds of contentment it drew from her partner. "Long day?"

"Ungh," she exhaled. "Long couple of days, and with as little sleep as I got last night, I'm raisin toast."

"With cream cheese?" Dar nibbled her hair a little. "Glad you're here," she whispered, seeing the shift of muscle under skin as Kerry smiled.

"I'm glad I'm here too." Kerry leaned against her as they walked through the door to the outside, and were greeted with a sultry New York night. "Hm. Almost as muggy as home, but with much nastier scenery." She wrinkled her nose. "We taking a taxi?"

Dar spotted an alternative, a long, plush looking town car with a diffident looking driver leaning against the side. "Got a better idea." She steered Kerry toward the car. "You go to Manhattan?" she asked the driver.

The man looked at them, head cocked to one side. "Do I go to Manhattan? Whaddaya think, this thing look like a tour bus? Sure I go to Manhattan. Where ya goin?"

"East side Hyatt." Dar felt slightly sheepish. "Sorry, it's late."

"You got it." The man opened the door with a flourish, and removed Kerry's bag from Dar's shoulder. "Gwan, get in there. I got better places to be than LaGuardia, that's for damn sure."

Kerry scooted in first, and waited for Dar to join her and shut the door before she edged back across the seat and snuggled against her partner with a contented sigh. There was a faint scent of oregano and garlic clinging to Dar's T-shirt, along with the touch of spice that was their mutual body wash. "You smell good," she commented, resting her head against Dar's shoulder. "Damn, I missed you. I thought I was going nuts. You've only been here a couple days, but I feel like it's been forever."

Dar was startled to have her own feelings articulated so precisely. "Yeah," she uttered. "Just real stressful days, I guess."

"Mm." Kerry rubbed her thumb lightly over Dar's belly. "You know, they really were. So much crap, and that damn power outage. Jesus."

Dar watched the lights of the city flash by, the driver surprisingly silent up front. It was amazing how much friendlier New York looked from inside the car with its present occupant wrapped around her. "Well, it's over," she said. "And who knows? Maybe we can have a little fun here."

"I'm having fun now." Kerry closed her eyes. "Dar?"

"Yeah?"

"We're a little nuts, y'know."

"Yeah, I know."

"Do you care?"

"Hell no," Dar said. "Do you?"

Kerry drew in a lungful of air infused with cotton, spice and love. "Oh no," she whispered, a smile pulling at the muscles of her face. "I'll take crazy any day."

They both fell silent, the restrained classical music becoming audible for the first time as the car raced toward a tunnel and the skyline of Manhattan spread out before them.

KERRY FINISHED ADDING her bathroom doodads to the sink shelf as she listened to Dar ordering them something from room service. The hotel room was big and very nice, but she could really have cared less as long as it had Dar in it, a shower, and someplace for them to sleep.

Even the second thing wasn't really a requirement, if she was honest.

With a smile, Kerry ducked back into the main room, pausing to lean in the door way and watch Dar as she paced idly back and forth in front of the desk.

"Thanks." Dar put the phone down and turned. "Twenty minutes. Did you get Advil?"

Kerry held up the small bottle she'd taken from Dar's kit. She uncapped it and removed a couple of the brownish pills, crossing to the pitcher of water sitting on the side table and pouring herself a half glassful. "That's a nice looking bed there, Paladar."

"Mm." Dar came over to her. "Too big for one person, though," she said. "Had a tough time getting to sleep in it," she admitted.

"Guess we've got the solution to that problem." Kerry swallowed her pills, dropping her head forward as Dar's hands gently kneaded her neck. It felt incredibly good, and not just from the warmth. "Know what?"

"What?" Dar's breath tickled the edge of her ear.

"My life suddenly got really good again." Kerry's tone was quietly serious.

Dar leaned against Kerry's back. "Mine too," she replied. "I missed you."

"I felt really lousy when I woke up this morning," Kerry mused. "I'm glad I'm here."

"So am I." Dar sounded just as serious. "So." She wanted to get this out of the way first, to untie that one knot of uncertainty deep in her guts so she could deal with whatever it was, and get past it. "Kerry."

"So, Kerry what?" her partner asked curiously.

"So. What is this thing you did that I'm going to kill you for?" Dar got the words out in a stolid rush, chasing the last one out of her mouth and clamping her jaws down after it.

Kerry turned, letting her hands rest on Dar's hips as she looked up. "Huh?" she queried. "What did I do now?"

A wrinkle appeared in the skin above Dar's eyes. "Ah...you...said you...the other day?"

"The other day." Kerry's gaze slid to one side, as she thought. Abruptly her expression cleared, then took on an immediate look of embarrassed chagrin. "Oh." She lifted a hand and half covered her eyes. "Yeah, that."

"That," Dar repeated, reassured. If Kerry had forgotten all about the damn thing, how bad could it have been? "Which is...what?" she asked, a touch hesitant.

Kerry had completely forgotten 'that', and now she felt like an idiot. With a sigh, she took Dar's hand and led her over to the bed, sitting down and waiting for her partner to take a seat next to her. "You really are going to think I'm a nut."

Dar's eyes fastened on her partner's expressive face intently. "I am?"

"Yeah." Kerry rubbed her nose. "I think you are."

Dar waited, but nothing more seemed forthcoming. "Well." She cleared her throat gently. "Why don't you give me a try and see? I mean..." She examined her partner. "You don't usually do nutty things."

Kerry took a deep breath, and looked Dar squarely in the eye. "I did this time," she admitted. "I...um..." She took another breath. "I got a tattoo."

Dar's face remained very still for a long, long moment. Then she blinked several times. "You did?"

Watching her face anxiously, Kerry nodded. "Yep, I did." She didn't see the little signals she'd learned were disapproval from her partner, and it gave her the courage to continue on. "You know I've been sorta thinking about it..."

"I know," Dar finally managed to get a few words out of her shocked throat. "You said a few times, but I um...a tattoo?"

"A tattoo," Kerry confirmed, peeking sheepishly up through her bangs. "It was a spur of the moment thing."

"Wow."

"Anyway, after that night with the gang, I was talking to one of the guys about it and he said his friend was a great tattoo artist, so..." Kerry grimaced a bit, half shrugging one shoulder. "So I went to talk to him and I saw his stuff."

"Nice?" Dar asked.

"Gorgeous," Kerry admitted. "We got to talking, and I told him what my ideas were and he drew this thing and..." She let the words trail off, sneaking another look at Dar's face. The pale blue eyes were focused on her face, a look of mild intrigue mixed with curiosity in them.

Not disgust. Not disapproval. Kerry felt a little better. "I guess I decided to do it before I thought about it and chickened out."

Dar absorbed this. Of all the possible things Kerry could have thought she was going to kill her for, this was by far the least of anything she could have imagined. Why would Kerry have thought she'd be upset anyway? "Ker, it's your body," she said. "You could paint it orange and I'd be fine with it."

Kerry didn't respond to that for a moment. She took Dar's hands in hers and squeezed them, her eyes fastened on their tangled fingers. "I just thought it was a pretty radical thing for me to do."

"Nah," Dar disagreed. "If you'd gotten your face pierced, I might have freaked out. But tattoos...hell, I wanted one when I was a punk. Why not?" She watched a smile appear on Kerry's face. "So...um..." The green eyes lifted to hers. "You going to let me see it?"

Kerry nodded. "Absolutely."

"Where'd you get it??"

Slowly, Kerry released one hand and lifted it, tapping her chest lightly.

Dar winced. "That must have hurt."

"Eh." Kerry exhaled, responding to a gentle pressure on her shoulder and lying down on her back on the bed. "This is where I'm supposed to carry on the grand tradition and prove my primal womanhood by telling you it didn't"

"Ah." Dar brushed Kerry's hand aside and unbuttoned her shirt, reclining next to her as she started to pull the fabric back.

"But it's not true." She forced herself to relax, letting her arm fall to the bed and focusing on Dar's face as that warm touch brushed across the skin under her shirt. "It hurt like hell, and I betrayed tough chicks everywhere by screaming like a weasel when he did it."

Dar chuckled softly, finishing her unbuttoning and pulling aside the left side of Kerry's shirt, exposing her shoulder and chest. A flash of color met her eyes, and she leaned closer staring at this new and very different thing with intense curiosity.

Kerry held her breath.

"Wow," Dar murmured. "It's...beautiful." She edged a bit closer. "Is that a rope or..."

"No, it's a...um...it's a snake," Kerry uttered softly. "You know, it's that Celtic thing, the one with its tail in its mouth?" She hesitated just an instant. "The one that means eternity?"

"Oh...yeah!" Dar now found the pattern. Each scale of the snake's body had been outlined and done in a different color, and the effect was truly striking. The snake was winding itself in and out of a darker pattern and Dar had to stare at it for several seconds before her mind resolved what the pattern was.

It was her name. Dar put the word 'eternity' and those letters together and slowly lifted her head to stare into Kerry's eyes.

After a moment of utter silence, Kerry managed a smile. "No offense, sweetheart, but I'm really glad you shortened it. I don't think I could have handled the long version of your name."

It was stunning. Dar felt short of breath. It was overwhelming. She blinked and felt the surprising sting of tears. Her head jerked a little, and the droplets scattered over Kerry's bare skin, trembling as Kerry drew in a shaky breath.

With a little sigh, Dar just buried her face into Kerry's belly, giving her mind a little space to absorb this most explicit of messages.

Well, I don't think she's mad. Kerry reached up and ran her fingers through the dark hair draping over her middle, scratching Dar's scalp with her fingertips.

In truth, she'd forgotten completely about her anxiety over the damn thing, too, and the sudden stress after the long day was leaving her feeling totally wasted. But it had gone off rather better than she'd expected, so maybe not preparing for it was the way to go.

Anyway. "I know you know how I feel about you," Kerry ventured. "So it's not a big shocker, but..." She felt Dar exhale against her skin. "Now I want to find an excuse to wear a strapless gown so everyone can see it."

Dar's body twitched as a tiny chuckle emerged.

Kerry stroked Dar's hair gently, loving the feel of it against her skin. The pain, she decided now, had indeed been worth it, and her last doubt drifted away as Dar turned her head finally and their eyes met, and she saw the wonder and the tears there.

Definitely worth it.

Chapter
Seventeen

DAR WOKE MERE seconds before the alarm went off and hastily silenced it before it could rattle its way across the nightstand. It was just dawn, and she spent a moment catching her breath from her abrupt wakening before she settled back down and resumed her position snuggling with Kerry.

A roll of thunder boomed overhead, and a quick look verified the lash of rain across the hotel room window. Dar regarded the storm peacefully, however, since she was in a place right now that no weather could touch, regardless of the severity.

She didn't even care that she was in New York. Dar tilted her head and studied Kerry's profile, trying to remember when they'd fallen asleep last night. The last thing she could clearly recall was sharing a fudge brownie as they lay together watching the news, then...

Then she woke up, a minute ago, crashed in the middle of the big bed with Kerry wrapped around her in her usual way, with her head pillowed on Dar's shoulder and one arm draped over her as though she was nothing but a big, animated body pillow.

Just how Dar liked it.

Curled up as she was, her new adornment wasn't visible, but Dar found herself thinking about it anyway. Though still a bit red and not quite healed, she could see the tattoo was, in all truth, a beautiful design. The man who had done it was no question an artist.

Dar was flat on her back flabbergasted over it. The thought and emotion behind the tattoo filled her with such a sense of awe, and surprisingly, excitement. She found her breathing speeding up again just thinking about it.

My name. Dar gazed up at the dark ceiling. She put my name on her body. Holy crap. She had never looked for that kind of commitment from Kerry. The rings and the ceremony they'd shared had seemed enough, hadn't they?

She blinked. Maybe Kerry had felt she needed to take that one step farther. Maybe she'd...maybe she'd sensed how her partner had been feeling these last couple of weeks and this was her way of saying Dar was stuck with her.

In a forever kind of way. Graphically.

Wow. She was totally thrilled by Kerry's decision to decorate her body with this particular symbol and now she was halfway wondering...

Well, should she do it too?

Hm. Dar hadn't seriously thought about tattoos since she'd been in high school. Then she'd wanted...what was it again? Oh, right. A dagger across her right bicep. She turned her head and regarded the spot introspectively. What could she put there or anywhere that would match what Kerry had come up with?

A picture of Kerry, maybe? Dar felt a tiny snort emerge as she imagined herself taking off her jacket in a high level meeting and revealing *that* with her usual short sleeve silk shirt to the world if she had it done on her arm. As valued as she knew she was to the company, Dar conceded that would cross the line for even the most liberal of the board, and though she really didn't care what they thought about her, it also would probably embarrass Kerry.

Okay, so not a picture of her. Then what? Or...maybe she could put the picture somewhere else most people wouldn't see...

Kerry stirred, and Dar decided to put off her thoughts until later. She tilted her head to watch her partner as Kerry's eyes slowly blinked open and she took in her surroundings, a smile appearing on her face. "Morning."

"Uh huh." Kerry gave her a squeeze. "Boy, did I sleep like a rock," she admitted. "I don't think I moved since I crashed last night."

"Me either." Dar ran her fingers lightly through Kerry's sleep mussed hair, sorting the pale locks into their proper sides. "Did you look outside?"

Kerry lifted her head and peeked. "Eew." She resumed her prior position. "Perfect day to stay in bed. Unfortunately, we're not home to do it."

"Mmph." Dar laid her hand on Kerry's back, then started rubbing it, muffling a grin as her partner started to produce small purring noises. "Hey, Ker?"

"Uh?"

"I really love your tattoo."

Kerry rested her chin on Dar's breastbone, her green eyes sparkling happily. "You do? Really?"

"Yeah."

"Good." Kerry rolled over, stretching and arching her back before she peered at her new adornment. "I really was excited about doing it, but then when I got home, and saw it in the mirror...it was just scary."

"Scary?" Dar traced the outline of the design with her fingertip.

"Yeah. Like, oh my god, how could I have done this?" Kerry laid a hand on her stomach and gazed up at the ceiling. "I was worried about what you'd think, and if I should have talked to you about it first."

Dar sat up in bed and gracefully half turned, extracting herself from the covers and settling cross-legged in the same motion. She rested her elbows on her knees and regarded Kerry seriously.

"I mean...I knew you wouldn't hate it, at least I think I knew that, but..." Kerry put her hand on Dar's knee. "I thought about how I'd feel if you just came home with one and hadn't talked to me, and I didn't like how I felt about that."

"Ah." Dar's expression moderated to a more thoughtful one.

"Would you have talked to me first?" Kerry asked, curiously.

Dar rested her chin on her fist. "Not if I wanted it to be a surprise," she said. "And believe me, you putting my name on your chest was definitely a surprise."

"Hm. Hadn't thought if it that way."

"Anyway." Dar leaned over and kissed the spot gently. "I love it." She moved up and kissed Kerry's lips next. "I love you." She paused, nose to nose with her partner. "You think you could wear a strapless gown to Radio City Music Hall?"

The green eyes widened and brightened. "When?"

"Good question." Dar chuckled. "I'll know when the FedEx envelope gets here. Alastair's sending us a pair of tickets he happened to have around," she said. "Tonight maybe, or tomorrow...you interested? I have no clue what's showing there...guess we'd better check that first."

Kerry sat up next to her. "Sure," she agreed, with a grin. "So what's on the agenda besides that today, boss?"

Dar studied the thick, white covers. "Guess I'll call Hans...see if his six sturdy young Germans got anywhere with that code. If he did, I'm going to have to hold up my end of the deal and figure out how to get those damn algorithms working."

"The beta ones?" Kerry asked, in surprise. "I thought you said the problem was on his end?"

Dar got up off the bed and paced over to the window, gazing out at the rain.

Kerry waited, hearing a screeching of tires on the street below and amusing herself with wondering if a naked woman standing at the hotel window had anything to do with it. The dull gray light outside outlined Dar's body, so Kerry enjoyed the view, admiring the long, graceful lines of her partner's torso.

Finally, Dar turned back around, and leaned against the window sill. "It is his problem," she said. "But even if he fixes it, that won't be enough. We'll have to do the rest."

Kerry leaned back on her elbows, extending her legs out and crossing them at the ankles. "Honey, you do realize you're mooning Manhattan, right?"

Dar's head inclined slightly and her brows creased. "What?"

"C'mere." Kerry crooked a finger at her. "Before someone takes a picture of you through that window and you end up on the NY Times front page."

Dar turned around, stared at the window, and then sheepishly retreated back toward the bed. She climbed across the covers and collapsed onto her side next to Kerry. "Sorry. Wasn't thinking." Her voice sounded disgusted. "Story of my life lately, it seems."

Kerry nudged her with her knee. "What's that supposed to mean? You haven't been noticeably less brilliant than usual any time in the near past that I know of." She consciously lightened her tone. "Have you? Did I miss something?"

Dar shrugged. "No. I've just felt out of it lately," she admitted. "Anyway, you want to have breakfast here, or go downstairs? It's not a bad little place." She changed the subject, one hand plucking idly at the covers.

"I'd rather stay here." Kerry reached out and took Dar's hand in hers. "Spend some time with you just hanging out, if I've got a choice. If you don't have to go meet that guy, I mean."

Dar appeared pleased with the answer. "Sounds great to me," she nodded. "I'll give Hans a call, you order?" She leaned over and snagged the menu, handing it to Kerry. "Then maybe we can check out that music hall. Not sure what got into Alastair on that one."

Kerry opened the menu and let her hand rest on a page of it. "He's a little worried about you," she told her partner quietly.

Alert blue eyes found hers suddenly. "Me?"

"He thought you sounded a little off the other day," Kerry explained. "He mentioned it to me when he called."

Dar frowned. "What did you tell him?"

"Not much," she said, slowly. "Just that the trade show had been stressful, and the cruise bid was a bitch. You know. The truth."

"But not all the truth." Dar sighed, lowering herself back down and putting her chin on her wrists.

Kerry put a hand out and ruffled Dar's dark hair. "Honey, I wasn't going to go into your personal history with him. It's none of his business."

"Mmph."

"Even though I kind of get the feeling he really, really does like you as a person," Kerry went on. "And he does care about you."

Dar peeked up at her. "I know he does." She sighed. "I didn't realize I was coming off as something he needed to worry about." She extended her hand and cupped Kerry's knee, stroking the skin over it with her thumb. "It's frustrating. I just want to kick myself."

The fact that Dar was talking about it reassured Kerry immensely. "Well, that's why I'm here. To give you an ear, to give you a hug, or just to give you someone to have dinner with," she said. "Whatever you need, I'm here."

Dar studied Kerry's kneecap pensively. "I'm not used to being needy."

"I know. It's usually the other way around, and you've always been there for me when I've needed you. So, think of this as a minor payback." Kerry coaxed her, encouraged when Dar inched closer and curled her hand around Kerry's calf. She responded by leaning forward and sliding her hands up Dar's arms, kneading the thick muscles there with small, gentle motions. "You're in good hands, aren't you?"

Dar's shoulders relaxed and she cocked her head slightly. "The best," she relented, giving in and squirming closer. "All right. But if I tell you to kick me in the ass, you better do it. Don't pat me on the head."

Kerry leaned over and kissed her. "You got it," she promised. "Now, since you've entrusted me with the breakfast order, can I ask if you're in the mood for sweet or salty?"

"Sweet." Dar exhaled contentedly. "They have pretty good waffles."

"Mm...would that be the strawberry covered Belgian ones, or the banana?" Kerry scratched the back of Dar's neck with her fingertips and watched her close her eyes in reaction. "Can I ask you something else?"

"Uh huh."

"What's in that bag over there?"

"What bag?"

"The one with the sailor hat sticking out on top."

One blue eye popped open and regarded her.

RAIN OR NO RAIN, it was a gorgeous day. Dar finished rinsing the soap off her body and stepped out of the shower, bumping the translucent door closed behind her as she picked up a towel and headed for the sink.

A very wet and disheveled figure looked back at her from the mirror, but she smiled at it as she dried her arms, one ear cocked to listen to the soft humming coming from the other room. Having Kerry around was really making a difference, she realized. She was a lot more relaxed, and the thought of dickering with Hans over his application was now amusing her more than rubbing her temper raw.

The thought of introducing Hans to Kerry was also amusing her, though she wasn't sure her partner would appreciate being in a room where the other occupants were speaking a language she didn't know. "Ah." Dar addressed her reflection. "What the heck, she lives in Miami. She's used to it."

"Dar?" Kerry's voice drifted in. "You say something?"

Dar chuckled softly. "Nah—just talking to myself. Be out in a minute."

"Well you better...it's getting pretty boring out here."

"Uh oh." Dar toweled her hair dry as she walked out of the steamy bathroom, not immediately spotting her target. "Ker?" She looked around, finding her blond partner in just her own towel standing near the desk leaning over her laptop. "Problem?"

"Eh?" Kerry turned her head. "No, no...I was just picking up my office mail." She perched on a corner of the desk. "What time do we have to meet at the client's, eleven, right?"

"Right." Dar draped the towel over her shoulders. "Anything interesting?"

Kerry skimmed over her mail. "Nah, nah, nah...whoa." She leaned closer and clicked on one mail, her eyes tracking over the text. Abruptly she straightened. "Holy cow!"

"What?" Dar put her chin on Kerry's shoulder and peered at the screen. After a second, she put her hand on the desk and let out a snort. "Am I reading that right?" her voice rose incredulously.

Kerry slid off the desk and sat down in the chair. "Oh, boy, I hope not," she muttered. "Oh my gosh, what on earth went on there last night?"

"Only one way to find out." Dar pulled her cell phone over and dialed the office number. It rang, then was answered. "Morning, Maria."

A perceptible hesitation. "Oh, good morning, Dar. And how are you this morning?" Maria answered. "Did Kerrisita make it there all right?"

"Just fine, thanks." Kerry answered for herself as Dar set the phone on speaker.

"That is wonderful," Maria stated. "I am so glad."

"And I was doing really great until I opened up my mail just now," Kerry added. "Does Dar have one of these in hers too?"

Maria sighed. "Si," she said. "It was not exactly so as they said it, but..."

"Maria, what the hell happened?" Dar interjected. "That damn email from Mariana said you assaulted someone?"

"Jesus," Kerry muttered, covering her eyes with one hand.

"Jefa, it was not so," Maria protested. "I did not hurt anyone! It was just that Mayte told me about those two women who were being so mean to you and Kerrisita, and how they were going to be at this restaurant to wait for Kerrisita, and so we went there to tell them she would not be coming."

"Uh huh," Dar grunted encouragingly. "And?"

"And that is all! We did not mean to cause such problems!" her assistant stated. "Here we were doing something so nice, and they were so mean to us as well. They are bad people, Dar."

"Okay." Kerry leaned against Dar's shoulder. "But um...what's all this about charges, if all you did was tell them I stood them up?"

Maria cleared her throat delicately.

"Not that I don't appreciate the thoughtfulness, Maria, honest, I do..." Kerry went on. "But they could have stagnated there all night for all I care. I wouldn't have asked you to go out of your way to tell them anything."

"Oh, si, Kerrisita, I know that," Maria said. "It is just Mayte and I thought we would do this on our way home, since we had to go that way a little anyhow."

"Maria." Dar took the reins back. "Charges?"

"Jefa, they were very nasty to us. I went to them and told them about Kerrisita's trip, and they started saying such nasty things!" Maria replied in protest. "I could not get them to stop! All of the people in that little place were coming to find out what the matter was and so I thought these women would not like to be such a spectacle, so I would do something to keep them from being so loud."

Dar and Kerry looked at each other. "Like...what?" Kerry ventured.

"I gave them something into their hands to take and make them stop what they were saying," Maria said, almost audibly squaring her shoulders. "I took the plates of the dinner they had, and put them in their faces!"

"Oh, Jesus," Kerry whispered.

Dar stared at the cell phone, momentarily speechless herself. "Ah."

"And it was so hot, the things there, that Mayte was so courteous and kind to them she put the glasses of beer over their heads to cool them off."

Dar wandered off toward the window, shaking her head as she covered her eyes with one hand. "Anyone get pictures?"

"Jefa?" Maria queried.

"Dar was just wondering if anyone got...ah...hurt, Maria. Are you okay? Is Mayte all right?" Kerry asked.

"Oh, si." Maria sounded a little less stressed. "We are fine, si. My husband, he was very shocked to hear about what his senora and senorita did, but we went very fast home after that, Kerrisita. Yes, we are fine."

"Well, good. Good." Kerry pondered what to say next. "Now, ah...it's not that we don't appreciate what you did, ah...but you know..."

"Kerrisita, we could not stay there and listen to those women. They were being so nasty about you, especially," Maria said. "They were saying such horrible things about you! Terrible! I could not stand to listen to them."

"Well, I know, but..."

"Hey, Maria." Dar swooped in from the right and very gently clapped her hand over Kerry's mouth. "You remember Elena?"

"Dar!" Kerry nipped at her partner's palm.

A moment's silence. "Si! Si, yes I do, Dar. Yes," Maria said. "Another very nasty person."

"Did Kerry ever tell you about us meeting her at dinner once?" Dar asked.

"Noo...I do not think so."

Dar released Kerry, who folded her arms over her chest and smirked, ducking her head in acknowledgement. "Remind her to tell you about that when she gets back, huh?" She slid one arm around

Kerry's waist and tugged her closer. "Anyway, don't worry about it. I'll take care of Mariana, and tell her to get legal to get this whole pile of bullshit thrown out."

"Si, Dar. Thank you." Maria's voice warmed several notches. "We did not mean to cause you trouble."

"You didn't," Dar stated firmly. "Especially if they were talking trash about Kerry. They're goddamn lucky it was you and not me that was there, because if I'd been there, they'd have gotten a lot more than...what did they have, anyway?"

"The chili, jefa."

Kerry slowly dissolved into silent giggles, sagging against Dar's body and hiding her face in Dar's shoulder.

Dar cleared her throat. "Yeah, well...waste of beans in my view," she drawled. "Anyway, Maria, thanks. Don't worry about the charges. It's all crap."

"Si. That is what the man who came to speak with us this morning also said," Maria agreed. "It is just so aggravating, no?"

"Yeah," Dar said. "Sorry you had to get involved."

"I am not," her assistant said surprisingly. "Dar, I have been watching you put your head out for other people for so many years now, and it is good to be standing up for you if I can do that."

Dar stared at the phone in silence for several heartbeats.

"Me, too," Mayte's voice chimed in.

Kerry wiped the tears of laughter from her eyes and let her hand come to rest on Dar's belly. "Guys," she said. "I know exactly what you mean."

"Then you are not mad at us?" Mayte asked.

Kerry looked up at Dar's still profile, just the hint of trembling moisture on the lids of her eyes betraying her feelings. "No, we're not mad," she answered for them both. "But listen, you guys keep out of trouble while we're away, okay? We'll take care of that whole situation when we get back."

"All right," Maria agreed. "We will be good."

"Okay, we'll talk to you later," Kerry said. "Bye." She folded the phone shut, then let her head rest again on Dar's shoulder. "Holy sheep dip, Batman."

Dar cleared her throat. "Definitely unexpected," she agreed. "Damn, I wish I'd been there. I'd have paid a month's salary to see that chili go flying."

Kerry snickered. "Me too," she confessed. "I mean...it's not really funny, Dar. You know how ratty that's going to make that next bid meeting for us?" She sighed. "Not that I'm much better than they are. I'm the one who blew them off."

"Ah." Dar shrugged. "They can kiss my ass. Let's worry about it when it happens."

With a frown, her partner scanned the rest of her mail, then shrugged as well. "Yeah, I guess that makes damn good sense." She pushed the laptop from her a little and turned back to her partner. "Have I ever told you how good you look in just a towel?"

Dar sat down in the big easy chair and tugged Kerry down with her onto her lap. She wrapped her arms around Kerry's towel covered body and hugged her. "Hey."

"Mm?"

"If it stops raining, want to go down to Central Park later and take a carriage ride with me?"

Kerry willingly allowed herself to be distracted. "The ones with the horses?"

"Uh huh."

It was a charmingly romantic idea, and Kerry liked it very much. "Maybe we could find one of those little cafes and have dinner," she suggested. "I know Manhattan isn't your favorite place, but I bet we could have fun here."

Dar nipped Kerry's side gently through the terrycloth. She tilted her head up a little as Kerry's fingers laced through her damp hair and they kissed. She could taste the last hint of grape toothpaste on Kerry's lips as she explored them, savoring the gentle touch against her cheek as Kerry traced the skin on her face. "Bet we could have fun right in this here hotel room," she murmured.

"No bet." Kerry nuzzled her, then went back to kissing. "Noo...bet."

THE OFFICE BUILDING seemed quiet. Kerry walked along the hallway taking a quick glance right and left into hushed rooms and stilted, almost empty atriums. Everything was white and gray, and she found it profoundly depressing even by their own office's standards. "Least I have burgundy walls."

A woman working at a pristine white desk looked up as she passed, and Kerry got the impression of wide, alarmed blue eyes before the woman ducked her head again and went back to the pad she was writing on.

Another woman, in a severe gray wool suit stopped by the desk, tapping on its surface with her pencil before moving on, brushing past Kerry and giving her jeans a very disapproving look. "Are you here to deliver something?" she asked, pausing briefly.

"No," Kerry replied, with a gentle smile. "I'm working on a computer problem."

The blue-eyed woman at the desk furtively watched the exchange, her fingers fiddling with the pen she'd been writing with.

"Well, you should tell your company to dress their technicians better then. It's a shame." The woman in the gray suit turned and walked away, shaking her head. "Terrible." She turned again. "What company is it?"

"ILS," Kerry supplied helpfully.

"Oh, really?" The woman put her hand on her hip. "Never mind then. One of your big bosses is here, and I'll just tell her that myself." She marched off in the direction of the conference room, her shoulders fairly twitching with indignation.

Silence closed down over them again. Kerry shook her head and started to turn away, but a hesitant motion from the girl at the desk made her pause. She waited, taking in the short, stylish rust colored hair and the tiny cross earrings with idle interest. "Hi."

"Sorry you're going to get in trouble," the girl said, in a soft voice. "She's in everybody's business."

"It's okay. I'm not worried," Kerry reassured her. "Is she your office manager?"

"Yeah. Hannah Meyer." She hesitated briefly. "So you're a computer tech, huh?"

A brief twinkle entered Kerry's green eyes. "No." She dug her business card from one of her back pockets and handed it over. "My name's Kerry."

"Shawna...oh." The girl studied the card, then looked up at Kerry. "You're a vice president? Really?" Her voice sounded a touch incredulous. "Wow. That's pretty wild." She eyed Kerry's stone washed button flies and crimson short sleeved shirt doubtfully. "I mean, like, Hannah's right kind of. You don't look the part at all. You do look more like a tech person."

"Looks can be deceiving," Kerry advised. "What do you do?" She indicated the spotless white shiny surface of the desk, which contained the writing pad, a cup with two pens in it, and not much more.

"Oh, I...um.." Shawna shrugged one shoulder. "I coordinate meetings. You know, like schedule the conference rooms and stuff like that." One fingertip rolled the pencil she'd been using. "I set up lunch, too, and bring in materials. Collate." The words seemed to trouble her briefly. "It's a good job, and it's a great office in here, really smart, you know? My parents really like me working here."

Kerry felt a very brief moment of resonance with this skewed reflection of one of her own life's possibilities. "My folks would have liked it for me too," she told Shawna. "But I'm glad I picked my own path," she added. "See you later."

She felt the eyes on her back all the way down the hall, until she turned the corner and pushed open the door to the break room.

Once inside she paused, as her cell phone rang. Kerry glanced at the caller ID, then took a seat at one of the tables and answered it. "Kerry Stuart."

"M...Kerry, this is Mayte." Her admin sounded a bit flustered. "There are some...I need to speak with you about a few things. Is that all right?"

"Absolutely." Kerry glanced around, glad she was alone. "Go ahead."

"Okay," Mayte said. "In the first thing, the papers from yesterday, the legal department brought them down for me. I have them here."

"Okay," Kerry said. "Just hold them for me."

"But..." Mayte said. "That man, the Mr. Quest? He has called here several times looking for you. He sounded very upset you were not here."

"Well, that's just too bad, I guess, because I'm not." Kerry rubbed her temples. "What did he say?"

"He said there was something you were going to give to him, yes?." Mayte said. "He sounded very angry that you were not here, and la Jefa was not here either."

Kerry stared ahead, her eyes a little unfocused. Was Quest bluffing? Playing yet another game? Or just demanding the response he'd requested the day before. "I see."

"He said that if you did not want to be serious with him, he would take you from the job?" Mayte continued. "He is not a very nice man."

"No," Kerry mused. "He's not."

"I think it is the papers he is waiting for," Mayte suggested. "Do you want me to bring them to him? I know where the place he said was. The Intercontinental Hotel. It is not far from here."

Give in? Kerry was uncertain which move to make in the odd chess game she'd been playing. So far, she'd worked to keep Quest and his bid at arm's length, not wanting to seem too eager.

Play his game? Kerry briefly considered going to ask Dar, then she shook her head. "Suck it up, Stuart."

"Kerry? Did you say something?" Mayte asked.

"I said, that's really great of you to offer, Mayte," Kerry responded. "I would really appreciate it if you could drop the paperwork off, but would you do me a favor?"

"Of course." Mayte sounded happy. "Anything."

"Grab Mark, or one of the guys to go with you. Just in case you bump into those ladies you and your mom ran into last night." Kerry smiled as she heard her assistant make a sound. "Okay?"

"Okay," Mayte said. "I will maybe put on my brother's football helmet. That should be okay, no?"

Kerry chuckled. "Sounds great. Thanks Mayte." She set that decision aside. "Was there something else?"

Mayte shuffled some papers. "The reporter from yesterday? He called here," Mayte said. "But he did not want to leave a message. I told him you were out of town."

"Okay."

"Also, there was some security reports. Mark said you would want to see them. I have them on our share, is that okay?"

"More than okay, Mayte. Thanks. You're doing a great job there. I really appreciate you following up on all that for me," Kerry said sincerely.

"You are very welcome," Mayte said. "I hope you are having a good time in New York. La Jefa was happy to see you I am sure."

Kerry chuckled. "Hard to say which one of us was happier," she admitted. "Okay, let me go see what Dar's up to. If there's anything else, just give me a call."

"I will. Have a good day, Kerry."

Kerry closed the phone. Then she got up and went to the window, gazing out at the rain.

DAR STRETCHED, ARCHING her back as she wandered down the wall of windows, peering out of them as the rain continued to roll down. She was alone in the conference room. Hans was in a smaller private office talking to his programmers and Kerry was off finding some coffee.

A surge of well being flooded her, and taking a quick look around, Dar took a bouncing step then inverted into a handstand, balancing her weight on her palms as she edged around in a small circle. "Heh heh heh," she chortled softly. "Haven't done this in a while."

Behind her, she heard the door suddenly open, and knew from the clicking of heels that it wasn't either Kerry or Hans. Caught in the act, so to speak, she decided to pretend walking on one's hands was a normal act and turned, spotting a short, somewhat squat figure in gray staring at her. "Yes?" she asked briskly. "You need something?"

Without a word, the figure retreated and slammed the door. Dar hastily let her body drop backwards and flipped up, landing a bit precariously on her heels, but rocking forward to catch her balance before she could fall back and smack herself silly.

With a soft, wry chuckle, she walked back over to the conference table, settling back into her chair and spinning around slowly.

KERRY GAVE THE two men entering the break room a cordial smile as she made her way to the coffee machine. "Afternoon."

"Ah, Ms. Stuart, right?" The older of the two came over to her. "Nice to see you again, but I wasn't aware you were coming out here. Is the problem that complex?"

"Called in the reserves, looks like it to me," his companion said. "Too much for them, I think."

"No, Mr. Godson, it really isn't." Kerry set two cups down and started preparing them to order. "Or, well...to be totally accurate, yes, it's complex, but Dar is more than up to the task of fixing it. I was in the area visiting another account and thought I'd stop by." It was an innocuous enough lie, she thought, and one Godson would have difficulty proving one way or the other.

"Ah, well of course." Godson nodded. "Are they making progress, I hope?"

The other man snorted softly. Kerry correctly deduced his identity and muffled a grimace. "You could say that. The program's being rewritten and we're waiting for the new code to test it. I think we should have this little problem wrapped up by sunset." She gave them both a smile

"Really?" Godson perked up. "Soon as that? See Jason? I told you they'd fix us up. You're too much of a pessimist."

"Well, I'll believe it when I see it, sir," Meyer said. "I still think we need a second opinion," he added. "I asked that consultant I told you about to meet me here today."

Godson looked vaguely annoyed. "Jason, I told you I didn't want you to do that."

"Well, I thought it was for the best," Meyer said. "I have to do what I think is right for the company, don't I?" He picked up his coffee cup. "Excuse me." He left, letting the door swing shut behind him.

Godson frowned. "Sorry about that, Ms. Stuart," he said. "I'm sure he means well."

Kerry smiled briefly. "I'm sure he's looking to get leverage against us for his own reasons," she gently disagreed. "But it's okay. We see that all the time."

The CIO sighed. "You too?" he said. "This is very discouraging. No one seems to be able to get along. I feel very uncomfortable, and on top of that, someone from the news is coming to see me. Says he wants to talk about your company. Do you know anything about that?"

Kerry's brow cocked. "What's his name?"

Godson pulled a piece of paper from his pocket. "Argos? He's from CNN. Seems to think I have something to say about you all? Sounded very mysterious."

Crap. "Well, we do attract our share of attention." Kerry hesitated. "I think that particular reporter is interested in another project we're involved in."

"Ah." Godson gazed at the paper. "Probably wants a reference on you, eh?" He smiled, much more at ease. "Looking for some background I take it. All right then, I'll bring him over when he gets here. On the way now, apparently."

"Great." Kerry pronounced the word, meaning the opposite. "Well, let me go see how things are going. Hope we have good news soon."

"Me too," he agreed. "Frankly at this point, just to shut Jason up. Maybe Dar had a point about him."

He left, shaking his head, allowing Kerry a moment alone to catch her breath and take a sip of cooling tea. "Rats, rats rats," she muttered, tossing the cup in the garbage and heading back out in the hall.

"WE READY?" DAR asked, as she leaned on one elbow and gave her touchpad a nudge.

"Not just yet," Hans replied, busy at his own machine. "I am waiting for a last set of libraries." He spared a quick glance up at Kerry, who was catching up on her mail in the seat next to Dar. "Did your companion have a nice flight?"

"Hm?" Dar brought her attention back from someplace. "Oh, it was fine," she replied. "I'm going to set up some router policies while we're waiting." A softly melodic whistle escaped her as she set to work, her body shifting a little as she locked her legs up behind the chairs.

"Ah hah." Hans regarded her with mild bemusement. Dar's entire attitude seemed very different today, he'd noticed. She appeared relaxed and friendly, quite a contrast from the edgy, threatening, restless woman he'd encountered yesterday.

Was it perhaps that she had been proven right? Hans pondered. That often did put himself in a good mood, just as being wrong often put him in a bad one.

"Hey, Dar. Check it out. Email from your mother." Kerry reached out and gave her partner's sleeve a tug.

Dar straightened. "My mother?" She turned and stared at Kerry. "You got my mother to touch a computer?" She leaned over and peered at Kerry's laptop in disbelief. "No way."

"Yes way." Kerry grinned. "It's not a computer, though. Bellsouth has these little email keypads...so I talked her into getting one." She opened the mail. "That way we wouldn't end up having to run down to the marina if she opened a spam virus."

"Mm...good thinking." Dar peered at the mail. "How come she didn't send me one?" She frowned.

"Possibly because you wouldn't know the recipe for jambalaya," Kerry pointed out. "I don't know, maybe she did. Have you checked?"

Dar went back to her own machine, minimizing her network session and opening up her mail instead. She scanned the lines quickly, her eyes lighting up slightly as she spotted the new address. "Heh...got one." She clicked on it, then blinked. "But not from mom."

Kerry grinned a little, watching her partner lean closer to the screen, her head cocking to one side as she read. "Hey, Dar?" she asked after a few seconds. "Did some woman in a gray suit come in here complaining about me?"

Dar slowly turned her head and looked at Kerry. "Huh?"

"Never mind." Kerry waved her back to her screen. "Tell dad I say hi."

Hans looked between one and the other, grunting as an apparent enlightenment came to him. He pecked out a few keys, then pushed the machine back. "All right, my friend, it is time. Are you ready to try this child of ours?"

There was a long moment's silence.

"Dar?" Kerry reached over and touched her partner's leg, startling her a little from her intense concentration. "I think he's ready to test...you okay?"

"Um...yeah, fine." Dar seemed a bit embarrassed. "Sorry." She turned to Hans and spoke to him in German. "Ready to go?"

"Yes. I am ready. I will warn you, we have not tested this fully. If we put this in now and it does not work, I cannot back it out, and they will be crashed. Do you understand this?"

Dar nodded. "Go for it."

Kerry's eyes flicked between them, not understanding the words, but seeing by the shifts in Dar's body posture that something was about to happen.

"Are you sure?" Hans asked. "Do you not want to tell these people what we are doing?"

"And give them a chance to say no?" Dar leaned on both elbows. "You're the big shot programmer who's always perfect. You have confidence in your stuff? I've got confidence in mine," she said. "So do it, or admit you blew it."

Hans frowned at her seriously. "That is not fair," he muttered. "But I will hold up my end. If it fails, I will point at you and shrug my shoulders." He attacked his keyboard with a furious rattle.

"Is he doing something?" Kerry asked.

"Putting the new program in," Dar told her, watching her screen intently.

"In the middle of a production day?" Kerry protested. "Dar!" She half stood, caught by surprise. "What if we take them down!"

Dar set her filters, and waited, her hands flexing lightly over the keyboard. "I'll risk it. I'm not missing out on a carriage ride and dinner with you for this bunch of nits." She looked at Hans. "Now?"

With a finishing clatter, Hans touched one last key and lifted his hands. "It is done."

Kerry settled slowly back in her seat, holding her breath and crossing everything she could that her trust in Dar's judgment wouldn't fail her...fail both of them, in this most public of circumstances.

Only a few moments would tell the tale.

DAR KNEW SHE was taking a huge risk. In fact, she knew having Hans replace the running program in the middle of the day was more than a risk, it was a shockingly disruptive action, which she'd just ordered him to do.

However, what she'd told Kerry was absolutely true. She had no intention of sitting around in this glass box until after hours just to dump the program when it was least inconvenient to Godson. He was inconveniencing her by having her be here, and she was doing him a favor. Besides, as her note from her father had reminded her — do it, and ask forgiveness later.

Dar opened her network session wide and watched both of her routers with a hawk-like intensity. She saw the data stream abruptly stop, the packets trickling to absolutely nothing but management traffic. "Program's restarting."

"Yah." Hans folded his arms across his chest. "All the sessions went to the bathroom," he said. "They will not be happy, that is for sure."

Kerry laid her hands on the table, drumming its surface softly with her thumbs. She could sense the building tension, and after a moment she pushed herself to her feet and went to stand behind Dar's chair. She laid her hand on her partner's back, giving the skin under the cotton shirt a little friendly scratch before she focused her attention on the screen in front of her.

Dar didn't like to be hovered over, but Kerry felt some of the stiffness in her back relax at Kerry's touch and knew she understood the gesture of support. She watched Dar's fingers flicker over the keys, the gentle spatter of keystrokes almost rhythmic as the patterns were put in place waiting for the data stream to return. "Should it take that long to restore?" she muttered softly.

"I don't know," Dar replied. "Hans..." she added in German. "Do you have to restart the servers?"

"I should not have to."

"Want to check? I don't see sessions coming up."

With an aggrieved sigh, the German programmer bent over his laptop again, just as the door opened and Jason Meyer entered.

"What's going on? Did you take us down?" he snapped. "I've got everyone in the building calling me."

Dar barely glanced up. "You wanted it fixed ASAP," she said. "We try to give the customer what they want."

"Are you insane? How could you do that?" Meyer said. "It's the middle of the business day! Stop whatever you're doing right now!"

"Hans?" Dar ignored the red faced executive.

"Must you always be correct?" Hans replied in a disgusted tone. "They are coming up at this moment."

Meyer advanced on them, and Kerry reacted instinctively to intercept him, circling Dar's chair and putting herself between her partner and the approaching man. "Just give them a minute, Mr. Meyer. It's almost done."

"I am not going to give it a minute. This is totally irresponsible," Meyer responded. "I demand you bring us back up, right now, Roberts!" He tried to move past Kerry but found his way blocked, and realized the space behind the table wasn't big enough to go around her. "Get out of my way."

"Mr. Meyer, please calm down." Kerry stood her ground. "Just let them finish. I know it's a disruption, but..."

"Get out of my way," Meyer repeated, ignoring her words. "I'm not putting up with any more of this crap. Now move, or I'll..." His eyes slid past her, over her shoulder as he cut off his words.

Kerry knew Dar must have stood up behind her. She could almost feel the bristling danger at her shoulder blades, but she kept her gaze focused forward and her tone even. "Mr. Meyer, you've been having this problem since you put in this program. Most of your people can't work during the day anyway. It's so slow the rest of them are frustrated. Why not give us a chance to change all that? It's worth ten minutes downtime."

For a moment, she thought he was going to ignore her. But then he took a half step backwards, his face twitching. He addressed her again, though the shifting of his eyes indicated he was keeping something behind her in his peripheral vision.

"Ten minutes isn't the question," he said quietly. "The issue at hand here is the fact you did this without warning us. I don't find that acceptable, Ms. Stuart. Do you?"

Kerry heard the chair squeak softly behind her and relaxed a trifle even though the man's question was a valid one she had no good answer to. "Well, that's something we can discuss once it's fixed," she conceded. "So why don't we..."

"They're up," Dar's voice cut in. "I'm resetting the filters now. Let's see if we can make this warthog grow wings."

Letting out an imperceptible sigh of relief, Kerry turned, finding her partner once again hunched over her laptop. She took a step forward and let her hand rest on Dar's back again. "See? Less than ten minutes. More like five."

Dar felt her heartbeat start to slow as she forced herself to concentrate on the screen. The adrenaline pumping through her body was threatening to make her hands shake, and she laid them firmly on the palm rest as she silently willed her algorithms to work.

Stubbornly, the stream seemed to be resisting them, giving her no real improvement. Stifling a curse, Dar studied the output, suddenly aware of the tense silence around her, and the expectations weighing heavily on her shoulders.

The heaviest of all being the light, gentle touch on her back.

"I doubt very much that anything's fixed," Meyer stated. "In fact, I doubt very much you people even know what you're doing."

"Dar?" Kerry uttered softly.

"I know," her partner answered. "Give me a minute. I'm looking."

Her eyes spotted an error. With a twitch of her lips, she corrected it, then put the new configuration in place and watched the streams flicker back up, this time to a completely different rhythm. Dar let out a silent breath. The erratic spikes on her gauges dissipated, replaced by much lower, even flow, and the throughput level settled into a comforting green pulse.

"Well, unfortunately for you, but fortunately for your company Mr. Meyer, you're wrong," Kerry spoke up. "Could you please contact one of your remote offices, and let's see how it looks from there? It looks pretty good here."

Hans had gotten up, and now he circled the desk and planted himself over Dar's other shoulder, leaning down and peering at the screen with interest. "Bah," he grunted.

Meyer went to the phone on the conference table and hit a few buttons. After a brief ring, there was an answer. "Bob? This is Jason Meyer in New York."

There was a pause. "Oh...ah, yes, yes, sir," Bob answered. "Is there something wrong?"

Meyer's head jerked back a little. "You tell me."

"Sir?"

With a frown, Jason leaned closer to the phone. "Can you have someone connect to the system and tell me if you see a difference? Not that I expect you to, but we did something here and I'm just checking."

He glanced up as Stewart Godson walked in, with Nelson Argos and a cameraman at his heels. "It seems we were taken down without warning, sir."

Argos pointed to the corner of the room, and the cameraman swung into place, turning on his light and pointing the camera at them. "Josh, make sure you get all of them," he instructed. "This should be a good clip as it plays out."

"Got it," the cameraman said, tightening his focus.

"Eh?" Godson walked over. "We were? Didn't notice." He glanced curiously at the group at the head of the table. "What's going on here? Didn't leave for but a minute." He turned toward Argos. "Brought this fellow in, seems he knows you all."

"Certainly do." Argos gave them both a smile. "Ms. Roberts, Ms. Stuart. I'm sure you won't mind having this on the record."

Kerry felt her heart skip as the big, round lens pinned them. She could see Meyer's angry profile from the corner of her eye, and sensed the tension in Dar's body.

"Not at all," Dar replied, in a deceptively relaxed tone very much at odds with the slight clenching and unclenching of her hands.

"Check the system? Oh, okay, sir," Bob answered. "Hang on."

Kerry shifted her hand, draping her arm over Dar's shoulder instead and moving a step closer, so her hip was brushing her partner's sleeve. Were they about to be hoisted on their own petard? Undoubtedly this would make a very satisfying news clip for Argos' story if the change Dar had made didn't work.

She wondered how Dar felt about it. She could see her reflection in the laptop screen, and for a second, the blue eyes lifted and their gazes met. Kerry grinned a little, and was rewarded with the flicker of a wink.

"I don't think we're going to be pleased at all with these results sir." Meyer shook his head. "And the entire company was disrupted. You know what I think? I think we need to..."

"Sir?" Bob's voice came back. "I don't know what you did, but boy, it's flying here. Wow. The entry people are all pretty excited."

Dar folded her hands together and smirked. "You need that translated, Hans?" she asked the programmer. "It worked."

Godson clapped his hands. "Wonderful! Bob, are you in Arizona?"

"Yes, yes...ah, is that Mr. Godson? Yes sir, we are." Bob sounded confused, but happy. "Are we a test group? I didn't get that email."

"No one did," Jason ground out through clenched teeth.

"That's great, Bob." Godson leaned over the phone. "Can you ask all your colleagues there how it's going? Life's not just one cup of coffee you know!"

"Uh." Bob rattled some papers, then muffled the phone. "Hey!" He could still be heard, though. "You guys try the system? No, I mean like now!"

There was a brief silence, then a yammer of voices. "Yeah, mine too! About freaking time!" He came back on the line. "Looks great here, sir. Big thumbs up."

"Fabulous," Godson said. "Thanks!"

"Of course it worked." Hans sniffed. "You are brilliant, I am brilliant, it is a wonder the room does not melt with the combined brilliance of us. Can we go have a beer now?"

Kerry felt her entire body relax, and she leaned against Dar quite unconsciously. "I have no idea what else he said, but I got the beer part. I'm up for it." She caught Argos watching them and almost stiffened and moved away from her partner.

Almost.

But something inside her rebelled, and instead she reached over and tweaked Dar's ear, giving her boss an affectionate look. "Rocket scientist."

"You want a beer for lunch?" Dar did a subtle little dance of triumph in her seat, shifting her shoulders and bumping Kerry with the left one. "Stewart, can you put a note out to everyone, and let's get a consensus before we close the books on this. I want to know that everyone's happy."

"Absolutely—just hold on a sec." Godson was on his cell phone. "Hello, Harry? Yes...yes, it's Stewart...listen, I think I've got our performance problem cleared up. Want to give it a go? What?" He listened. "It did? You are? Fabulous! Great to hear...what did I do? Oh, well, you know, it was all a matter of getting some of the kinks worked out...you know, new system and all that."

Dar snorted and rolled her eyes.

"Well, thanks, Harry." Godson beamed. "Glad you feel that way, and I hope to continue to earn that respect from you. Listen, if you hear any other feedback, let me know, hm?" He closed his phone and faced them. "Ladies and Gentlemen, so far so good. That was our CFO. He's been one of the biggest critics...he's in Boca Raton."

"We saved his ass," Dar translated for Hans. "Bet he gets a bonus out of it."

"Hah." Hans snorted.

"Well, I'm glad we could get the problem solved, Stewart." Dar continued in English. "Hans and I figured if we threw the change into production now, we'd know by the end of the day if there were any issues with it. If we did it off hours we'd have to wait till Monday to test and we knew you had a lot of pressure on you."

Stewart nodded briskly. "Good plan. Well, Jason? Let's go take credit for this, shall we? I told you it'd all work out. You should have more faith, sometimes."

Meyer looked like he was unsuccessfully trying to swallow a peeled lemon. "Yes, sir," he eventually got out. "I guess you were right," he admitted. "But I think we need to discuss how we put together our outsourcing contracts, to make sure we have more control over what this process is." He turned and walked off, without pausing to wait for his boss. "I won't forget how it was accomplished, regardless of the result." He left, and the door slammed shut behind him.

Godson chuckled. "He should lighten up." He glanced at the reporter. "That's what I was telling you about, see? These people? The best." He pointed at Dar. "I called 'em up, they came right here and fixed everything. Wonderful."

Dar smiled.

"He could mention I did some work also." Hans frowned.

"He could mention it was all your fault." Dar eyed him, with a grin.

"Details, details." Hans sniffed. "I will pretend I work for you then, so I can get some of this glory."

"Yes, I've heard a lot about how ILS operates," Argos said. "Maybe we can discuss it in your office?"

"Absolutely." Godson pointed to the door. "And I'll order in some lunch. Time to celebrate!" He led the way out, clearly expecting the reporter to follow.

Argos did, but he paused in the doorway and looked back at them. "I'd be curious to know how many rabbits you can pull out of your collective hats."

"Rabbits are prolific," Dar remarked. "They make their own supply."

Argos studied her. "You've kept ahead of me so far, Ms Roberts. You can't do it forever. There's a stink in your Danish pastry and I'm going to find it." He switched his focus to Kerry. "Nice to see you taking care of business, Ms. Stuart."

Kerry met his eyes squarely. "I'm not here for business." She let her hand rest on Dar's shoulder.

The reporter cocked his head, then he disappeared through the doorway and left them all in peace.

They were all quiet for a few minutes, Dar's fingertips tapping lightly on the table. Then Kerry finally sighed, and patted her lover on the back. "Let's go find a bar."

Hans looked over at her. "I understood the part about the bar," he told Dar in German. "And I am all for it."

"Me too." Dar leaned back, feeling the tension drain out of her. "Me too."

THE RAIN HAD finally stopped, and a pallid sunset was brushing the windows of Stewart Godson's office as Dar formally ended their visit. The executive was seated behind his desk, his hands behind his head, looking very pleased with himself, and consequently also pleased with Dar. "Well, Dar, I realize it was a tough spot, but it all worked out, didn't it?"

Dar aligned her forearms on the chairs precisely. "It did," she acknowledged. "Not the way we like to do things, but the bottom line is it got done and now you can move forward."

"You bet," Godson agreed. "Everyone I've heard from so far is very pleased, and I think now we can even find a way to really work with Hans' company if something like this comes up again. So, thanks, Dar. I owe you a big one."

There were times to gloat, and times when it was better just to be gracious. Dar didn't much like being gracious, and it was undeniably more fun to gloat, but she'd laboriously gained a small sense of propriety over the years and didn't like to waste it. "Glad I was able to work it out for you, Stewart."

He waved a hand at her. "Never doubted it," Godson said. "I've had people come in here, pitching me deals to do what you do cheaper, but I know when my keister's in a pickle, you people have always come through for me. Means a lot, and that's what I told that reporter fellow."

"Well, Stewart, you know we value you very much as a customer." Dar went through the requisite dance steps stolidly. "So I hope we'll always be there to come through for you."

"Me too." Godson got up and paced a little. "But what in the world did you do to get old Jason so miffed at you? I got an earful the size of the Empire State after we left that room." He sat down on the edge of his desk and looked curiously at Dar. "He's really got a problem with what he views as your ethics."

"My ethics?" Dar indicated her chest with her thumb. "Stewart, the man's got stock in a competitor of mine, and he wanted us out so he could bring them in. He talks about *my* ethics?" She half shook her head. "You better watch out for him. He's after this office."

A furrow appeared over Godson's brow. "You really think so? He's a good guy, Dar. Very sharp."

Dar sighed. "Stewart, he's a rat. You don't have to believe me, but at least watch your back because I sure as hell don't want to be negotiating with him when our contract comes up for renewal. We won't have a chance."

Godson looked doubtful, but he nodded anyway. "Well, I'll keep it in mind," he answered diplomatically. "You know we all can't be as friendly working together as you and Ms. Stuart are."

Dar lifted an eyebrow.

"But then you girls usually are chummier than us fellas are," Stewart continued. "Anyway, don't let me hold you up, Dar. I know you've got things to do and more people to help. You flying out tonight?"

"No." Dar got up and extended a hand, gripping Godson's when he took it. "Us girls are going out for a romantic dinner together then heading for a show at Radio City Music Hall." She released his hand, watching his jaw drop as he processed her statement. "We're leaving tomorrow morning. But thanks for asking. Have a great day."

"Bu..." Godson half stood as Dar turned and walked to the door, his hand still outstretched. "Ah...bye?"

The door closed behind Dar's tall form, leaving the room far emptier without her vibrant presence. Godson let his hand drop to his knee and snorted, shaking his head slightly into all that silence.

KERRY STUCK HER hands in her pockets as she waited on the ground floor of the big office building. The tall granite walls reminded her a little of their office in Miami, but she found the slate gray even more impersonal and cold than the copper and bronze shades they used down south.

She was glad the weather had cleared up, even though the hazy sun promised a muggy heat. At least they'd be able to go for their carriage ride and find someplace to have a nice, lazy dinner. The show that night was an opera, which neither of them were really partial to, but Kerry didn't care. They had good seats, and Dar had promised to take her strapless gown shopping.

Life was very good. She exhaled. At least, her personal life was very good. Although they'd fixed the problem, she had gotten the feeling there was trouble under the surface here. She knew for sure Meyer was going to be a thorn in their side from now on.

What would she have done in Dar's place, she wondered. Played it safe? Involved the client in the decision, and scheduled the testing based on their needs? Would that have been a better long-term solution?

Kerry sighed, and leaned against the glass, watching the traffic go by outside. What Dar told Godson about testing during business hours was quite accurate, in point of fact, and she knew it. But she also knew Dar's decision hadn't really been based on that at all—she'd simply wanted the problem over and done with because she had, in her view, better things to do.

From a business perspective, Kerry had issues with that. From a personal one, since she was the better thing, it was hard to argue with it since she really had no urge to spend the night sitting around in this building either.

Rats. Sometimes she really hated the duality of her life.

Hans cleared his throat slightly, and leaned next to her on the glass, giving her a polite nod.

Kerry nodded back, and added a tentative smile.

"Kerry, yes?" Hans said.

"Right," Kerry answered. "You did a great job." She wasn't sure exactly how much he'd understand, but nice words never hurt anyone regardless of the language. "Thanks for working with Dar on getting it fixed."

He seemed to get the gist, because his face eased into a smile. "It was much pleasure," he stated carefully. "Your Dar has strong talent."

My Dar. Kerry reckoned he didn't actually mean that in the literal sense, but she was glad to accept the compliment anyway. "Thanks. Yes, she is very talented."

"Also of good taste," Hans commented, blinking placidly at her.

Kerry stared at him for a second before she realized he could possibly be referring to her. "Ah...thanks," she replied, belatedly. "Thanks very much."

"You are very welcome." Hans watched as the cleaning staff started through the building, carrying buckets and mops, content to relapse into silence.

Kerry exhaled, her eyes flicking to the lobby elevators as she spotted Dar exiting from one and heading their way. Her partner appeared relaxed as she ambled across the marble floor, her characteristic slightly rolling walk almost succeeding in returning a smile to Kerry's face.

"We're outta here," Dar said, as she reached them, repeating the sentiment in German for Hans. "You ready for that beer now?" she asked Kerry, giving the back of her hair a little ruffle. "We've got time for that, before we have to go grab real clothes and head for culture world."

The touch reassured her. Kerry nodded agreement, indicating the door with one pointing finger. They walked outside, into the moist heat and started off down the sidewalk together.

"I think I embarrassed your girlfriend," Hans told Dar, in a bemused tone, after they'd walked about a half a block in relative peace.

Dar glanced at him. "She's not my girlfriend."

Hans colored visibly, a somewhat startling sight against his pale skin. "Then I have embarrassed myself and I must apologize," he said. "I assumed..."

"She's my wife." Dar draped an arm over Kerry's shoulders. "You're not embarrassed by that, right?" she asked Kerry in English.

Kerry shifted the strap on her briefcase, having suspected she was being discussed. "By what?"

"Being married to me?" Dar repeated the question in German.

She almost stopped walking. "Did you get some hallucinogenic in that last cup of coffee? Of course not," Kerry replied. "What made you ask *that*, you goofball?" She hooked a finger inside Dar's belt loop and tugged it, to take any sting from her words. "Just because I don't have my 'I'm with her' shirt on today?"

Dar chuckled. "Hans thought he embarrassed you back there," she explained. "He assumed you were my girlfriend."

"Oh."

"So I corrected him."

"Eh." Kerry gave her a sheepish look. "Yeah, I was being a little obvious upstairs. Sorry about that. I wonder if those other guys noticed it too...maybe that's why Meyer was being so obnoxious."

Dar cocked her head in a puzzled attitude. "Huh?"

"Oh wait, there's my T-shirt." Kerry pointed. "That one, right there."

Dar peered at the window. "My girlfriend can beat up your girlfriend?" she asked, with a snort of laughter. "Jesus, Kerry."

"Pick one. I'd rather be Kerry," her partner replied. "Jesus was a sweet guy, but I don't have a thing for suffering and splinters."

"Hang on." Dar slowed down. "What did you mean about you upstairs?" She lowered her voice a little.

Dar hadn't noticed? Kerry wondered, then conceded she hadn't either. A bus roared past, spitting the scent of diesel. "Never mind. We'll talk about it later." Kerry bumped her partner with her hip. "Where are we going?"

They stopped at a corner and waited for the crossing light to change. Hans stuck his hands in his pockets and looked around, then turned inquiringly toward Dar. "Hotel bar is good for you?"

Dar had wandered toward a street cart, sniffing the air. "Yeah, that's fine," she called back over her shoulder. "Ker, want some nuts?" She walked over to the stand and examined its contents, pointing at the cinnamon covered pecans as she dug a few bills from her front jeans pocket.

Having had nothing since breakfast save several cups of coffee, Kerry found the nuts sounding pretty darn good. "Sure." She joined her partner at the cart. As they paid for their purchases, a familiar voice trickled through the surrounding bustle and Kerry turned to see Jason Meyer standing at a pay phone nearby arguing into it. She gave Dar a poke and jerked her head toward him.

Dar turned, putting a nut between her teeth as she looked inquiringly in the direction Kerry indicated. "Ah." She grunted. "Jerk doesn't even believe in cell phones? Now there's a technologist."

It was curious, Kerry knew. Cell phones had become so woven into society it seemed very odd to see a man who had any number of them, and an entire corporate PBX at his disposal using a street side pay phone in the middle of a Friday afternoon crowd in Manhattan.

Why?

"Look! I don't care what you do! Just do it!" Meyer yelled, and then slammed down the phone. With a disgusted look he stalked off, hauling up as he came very close to crashing headlong into Hans. "Excuse me."

He brushed past and kept going, apparently not recognizing the programmer. Hans stared after him, then looked at Dar and Kerry. He shrugged both shoulders and held his hands out in a universal message, which they returned in equal measure.

They rejoined Hans at the corner, and watched Meyer head back toward the entrance to his company's building. He shoved rudely ahead of a woman carrying two boxes, and nearly knocked her down, but didn't even look back as he let the door close behind him.

"What in the heck flew up his butt?" Kerry wondered. "You know, I talked to him a few months ago, Dar. He seemed fine then. Wonder what happened?"

Dar chewed her nut and swallowed it. "Beats me." She nudged Kerry in the direction of their hotel. "Who knows? Maybe I happened. He stepped on my last nerve the second I got there and I went off all over him." She started across the street with Hans at her side, going with the flow of heavy foot traffic. "Maybe he's just a jerk."

"Huh." Kerry followed her, idly nibbling her treat. "Maybe he's related to Shari. Same kind of backwards jackassedness."

Dar stopped short and looked at her. "Been talking to my father again, huh?" she drawled, giving Kerry a very playful grin. "That sounds damn bizarre in a Midwestern accent."

"Heh." Kerry chuckled under her breath. "I'll become Southern yet. You wait and see."

Chapter
Eighteen

KERRY GLANCED AT herself in the mirror and grinned impishly, adjusting the strapless front of her dress with careful fingers. The one nice thing about New York was, if you wanted fast, stylish shopping, you had it in spades all around you. She and Dar had gotten in and out of the stores in under forty five minutes, and now she was reviewing the results.

"Nice," she complimented herself. The dress she'd found was a deep, forest green silk with a tiny embroidered pattern, classic and plain, reaching just down to her knees. It was sleek, and fit her curves nicely, and even the prospect of sitting through an opera couldn't put a damper on her mood. "Hey, sweetie?"

"Yes?" Dar's voice floated out from the bathroom.

"How about we find us some place to dance after the show?" Kerry asked. "Go out and party. I think we're due it, after your brilliant solving of the problem here."

Dar poked her head out of the bathroom. "You consider dancing with me a party?" she asked in a quizzical tone.

Kerry looked over at her. "You are not a bad dancer," she stated. "So don't give me that. C'mover here."

Obediently, Dar eased around the door jamb and came over to join Kerry in front of the mirror. She was dressed in a snazzy blue number an inch or two longer than Kerry's, but with much the same cut. "But sure, if you want to, I'm game." She picked up Kerry's brush and started brushing her partner's pale hair. "That looks really good on you."

Kerry turned her head and looked up. "Likewise, and thank you." She smiled warmly. "Shall we go the opera, madame?"

Dar tossed the brush onto the dresser and gestured toward the door with a grand flourish. "After you." She picked up the small clasp purse that held her wallet and electronics, and followed Kerry as she half walked, half danced toward the hallway.

"Heh."

Kerry turned as they reached the elevator. "What's so funny?"

Blue eyes blinked innocently. "Nothing."

The doors opened. "Uh huh. Go on." Kerry indicated the opening.

"Oh no. Ladies first," Dar drawled. "Please."

Kerry gave her a suspicious look, but she entered the brass and glass lined car and waited for her partner to join her before she pressed the button for the lobby. They started down, and halfway she found herself having to equalize her ears. "Oh, egh."

"Mm." Dar pressed her thumb behind her right earlobe. "I don't like having to do this without getting wet." She looked up in time to see a very devilish expression on Kerry's face. "What's that look for?"

Kerry closed the distance between them and leaned against Dar as she laid a hand on her cheek and kissed her on the lips. "Mm."

Dar forgot about being in a hotel elevator. She slid a hand around Kerry's side and continued the kiss, allowing the passion to build between them even as the car slowed, and bumped gently to a halt.

They parted just as the doors did, and the echoing buzz of the crowd in the lobby filtered in. Kerry licked her lips and took a step back, taking a steadying breath before she dared look up again.

Dar's face had a definite flush to it, and her eyes held a dark twinkle that came very close to making Kerry simply punch the button for their hotel floor and forget all about the damn opera. "Well. Made me forget all about my damn ears," Dar commented. "Shall we?"

Kerry half reluctantly exited the elevator, giving the small group of people waiting to get on a polite smile. She waited for Dar to catch up to her, then they both continued on toward the door to the street. "Dar? Have you ever been to the opera?"

Dar simply laughed.

"I went a few times," Kerry admitted, as they emerged into the warm night air. "I have to admit I missed the popcorn and Raisinettes."

Dar led the way to the curb, bypassing the hard working door man who was busy getting cabs for people. She fixed her gaze on an oncoming yellow cab and hailed it.

The door man gave her a respectful look and hurried over to open the cab door. "Ma'am?"

"Thank you," Dar responded graciously, ducking inside the cab and scooting over as Kerry joined her. "Radio City Music Hall," she instructed the driver.

"You got it," the man responded cheerfully, pulling away from the curb and into the busy traffic flow with little regard to either oncoming cars or the lives of anyone in his own.

Kerry slid her hand into Dar's and clasped it, settling back happily into her seat to watch the city go by. "Boy, I'm glad you got that problem cleared up. I'd hate to have been spending the night in that office."

"Uhm." Dar removed a small case from her purse and offered Kerry one of its contents. "Even though I took them down in the middle of the day? I saw you squirming over that."

"Well..." Kerry selected a small candy and put it into her mouth, grimacing a moment later. "Flamingos on a shoestring, Dar...you could have told me that was sour."

Dar sucked on her candy contentedly. "Sour tangerine," she

agreed. "They had lemon, too."

Kerry resolutely swallowed the offending bit of confection. "It wasn't the choice I'd have made," she admitted. "But you know that. I tend to be...a little more conservative than you are."

"Conservative." Dar reached up and traced around Kerry's tattoo, cheekily visible over the line of her dress. "Uh huh."

"Mm." Kerry grinned a little. "But anyway, you're right. I was squirming. I knew you'd make it come out right, but I really thought you were taking a big risk there."

And she had been. Dar felt the warmth of Kerry's fingers curled in hers, and felt herself at peace with her decision. "I've always been a risk taker," she said. "And to be honest, I didn't really want to spend any more time there myself. So it worked out."

"It definitely worked out," Kerry agreed. "And our friend, the reporter, didn't get his paycheck shot."

Dar chuckled briefly. "That could have gone the wrong way." She sighed. "We got lucky," she added. "Hopefully we can keep it that way. He's going to be sniffing at everything during this damn bid, and we need to win it."

"Because you promised Alastair?"

Dar glanced at her. "No, damn. I didn't tell you," she said. "Slipped my mind, I guess...or maybe I..." She fell momentarily silent. "Anyway, some big shot in the cruise industry called Alastair. He's got almost a hundred ships...wants his tech updated and is going to look at whoever wins this one to do his."

Kerry almost stopped breathing. "That's big bucks, huh?" she finally uttered.

Dar snorted softly. "Alastair thinks it'll save our quarter." She glanced out the window. "Funny how a chance meeting in Orlando turned out."

Kerry stared at the back of the taxi driver's head behind it's Plexiglas protection. "Dar, I almost blew Quest off yesterday and didn't file the bid paperwork."

Dar turned her head completely to one side and looked right at her. "Almost?"

Kerry nodded faintly. "I was pissed off because he kept calling and harassing Mayte. I almost told her to toss the paperwork in the drawer and go home."

"But you didn't?"

"I didn't. She offered to take it over to him and I said to do it." She exhaled. "But it was more important to me to get up and see you. I wasn't interested in Quest." She paused. "Or my job." She turned and met Dar's eyes.

They were twinkling. "Good." Dar leaned forward and kissed her. "Considering I almost blew off a major client and got us both in hot water because I wanted to have dinner with you."

"Is that fair to the company, Dar?" Kerry asked in a quiet voice.

"No. But it's fair to us." Her partner leaned back. "And besides, we won the gamble anyway."

"Mm." Kerry found she wanted very much to accept that answer, and not argue the subject. She often made very different decisions than Dar did as part of their daily work life, and they'd come to understand that their approaches to things were, despite their obvious compatibility, different.

Which was okay. She often learned things from how Dar worked, and she knew sometimes Dar picked up a trick or two from her. Kerry put her head down against Dar's shoulder and fell silent, content to watch the bright lights of the city flash past as the cab driver wound his way through the heavy traffic.

Then they were there. Dar had already handed the driver his fare before Kerry could even so much as grab her wallet, and she reflected that in one area, preplanning, Dar really did have it all over her on a very consistent basis.

They got out and joined a stream of people heading for the doors. The range of dress was amazing, and Kerry found herself almost goggling at the sight of actual mink wrapped around several women's necks despite the summer heat. "Yikes. I'd croak."

Dar spotted a counter nearby. "Want a drink?" she offered.

"My turn." Kerry tapped her on the hip with her purse. "Get us some programs?"

Programs. Dar spotted a woman handing them out, and she headed in that direction. She waited to catch her eye, then accepted two of the handbills. "Thanks."

"No problem, ma'am...can I see your tickets? Maybe I can direct you..." the usher asked helpfully. "It's a big place."

Dar tucked the bills under her arm and fished the tickets from her purse. "Yeah, sure." She handed them over. "That what you're looking for?"

The woman smiled. "Yes, ma'am, these are easy. Go right down front, and it's in the very middle of the row. Best seats in the house." She handed Dar back her tickets. "Enjoy the show!"

"Thanks." Dar studied the tickets in bemusement before tucking them back in her bag. She took the playbills and headed off, intercepting Kerry who was carrying two glasses of wine. "I'm told we have good seats," she informed her partner, trading a playbill for a glass.

"Oo." Kerry opened the booklet. "The Mikado—I'm trying to remember if I've...hm." She read the synopsis. "No, I've never seen this one."

Hearing her name made her look up to see an older woman approaching them, waving one hand. Kerry had to rack her brains to place her, but fortunately she did just before the woman reached them.

"Hello, Ms. Patrick."

"Kerrison! How amazing it is to see you here! My gosh, it's been years!" the woman blurted. She was perhaps in her fifties, with silver gray hair and a sophisticated sequined silver gown. "Are you living up here now?"

"No." Kerry shook her head. "I live in Miami. I'm just in the city for a few days on business." She half turned. "Ms. Patrick, this is Dar Roberts, my partner. Dar, Ms. Patrick was a professor of mine in college."

"Nice to meet you," Dar replied politely. "Professor of..?"

"Computer Science," the woman supplied. "What kind of business, Kerrison? I know when you graduated you said you wanted to do something in management, but..."

And she'd been quite sure, Kerry suddenly recalled, that Kerry wouldn't end up in anything like that at all. "I work for ILS." She tasted a deep sense of pleasure in the words.

"Do you? How marvelous!" Ms. Patrick looked vaguely surprised. "In what area? I seem to remember you really liked design."

"I'm the vice president of global operations."

The woman blinked at her in silence for a long moment. "Oh," she finally managed to get out. "Isn't that lovely?"

"I think so," Dar interjected. "Best vice president we've had in years."

The woman looked up at her in puzzled silence for a moment, then a visible light bulb went on over her meticulously coifed head. "Oh my...are you *that* Dar Roberts?"

Dar merely looked at her, refusing to dignify the question with the obvious answer.

Ms. Patrick backed away. "Well, isn't that great...nice to have seen you, Kerrison. Have a nice time at the show."

Dar waited for the woman to disappear into the crowd, before she turned to her partner. "Enjoy that?"

"Uh huh."

"Good."

They took their drinks and headed into the main hall. Just inside the doors, after surrendering their tickets, they both had to stop and look around in frank wonder.

"Holy catfish." Dar craned her neck and peered around at the vast, grand, art deco infrastructure. "This is gorgeous."

"Uh huh," Kerry agreed, blinking at the bright sunset themed colors, which reminded her unnervingly of Key West. "C'mon." She took Dar's arm and lead the way down the aisle.

They settled into their seats, and now that she didn't have to worry about bumping into mothball smelling matriarchs, Dar was free to take in the immensity of the theatre, from its delicate stage arch to the sloping seating. It was an amazing place, and she found herself looking forward to watching whatever it was that was about to start going on.

The Mikado. Dar studied her program. Ah. Japanese intrigue. Maybe there would even be a sword fight. She stretched out her legs, pleased to be in the front row with all the extra room.

Life was good. She glanced aside at Kerry, who was merely sitting, her program in her lap, and a benignly contented look on her face. "Quarter for your thoughts?"

Kerry chuckled, folding her hands over her stomach and exhaling. "I was just thinking about what my family would give to have front row center seats at Radio City," she admitted. "Going to the theatre in Manhattan was the be all and end all of anyone's social agenda where I came from."

"Ah." Dar wiggled her fingers. "Getting into the X-rated movies for free was where I came from," she responded, with a droll grin. "I got really good at picking the locks on the movie theatre back door."

Kerry started laughing. "Do you realize the first X-rated movie I ever saw was in your living room?" she whispered, catching the stern looks from their neighbors despite the fact that the show had not yet started. "Jesus, people...chill out!"

"Well." Dar leaned closer to her. "Would you be talking about X-rated movies in front of your family?"

Kerry hastily covered her eyes with one hand and bit her lip. "Didn't think so."

A short time later, the house lights began to lower. Kerry tucked her fingers inside Dar's once more, and settled down to watch, resolving to enjoy the moment, the night, and the sense of occasion, even if opera wasn't her favorite thing on earth.

IT SEEMED ONLY a few minutes later when the lights were coming back up, and the show was over. "Wow," Kerry murmured. "That was pretty cool." She joined the audience in enthusiastic clapping. "What'd you think?"

"I liked it," Dar agreed. "Funny story, catchy tunes," she added. "And pretty girls. What more could you ask for?"

Kerry chuckled. "Hm...with a lead girl character called Yum-Yum, I should have known you'd like it."

Dar half turned and gave her a mock outraged look, putting one hand on her hip. "Kerrison!"

Green eyes batted their lashes at her with devastating Midwestern innocence. "Yes?"

"Let's go get ice cream." Dar stood up and extended her hand to her partner. "I think you need cooling off."

Kerry accepted the aid, and was lifted gracefully to her feet by a smooth contraction of Dar's arm. "Why thank you, ma'am. After you?"

They walked out hand in hand, going along with the slow flow of the audience as it filtered through the tall, beautiful entranceways and out into the lobby. There was a buzz of conversation, and Kerry found herself smiling as she took in a crowd once very familiar to her. "Honey, I'm going to go use the restroom...meet you by the bar, there?"

"Nah. I'll go with you." Dar laid a hand on her back as they edged through the press of bodies. "Know what?"

"You're hungry," Kerry replied without missing a beat. "I hear you growling back there even over this circus." She jumped a little as Dar growled in her ear, ending the noise with a rumbling purr. "I'm fairly sure there's at least one restaurant around this place."

Dar chuckled, as she pushed the bathroom door open for both of them, extending her arm easily past Kerry's body. "This was really nice," she commented. "Remind me to send Alastair a box of cookies or something for it, will you?"

"Sure." Kerry found herself a partition and entered. She idly listened to the conversations around her as she went about her business. She heard Dar's low, vibrant voice exchange a mutual excuse me, and then a sharp, very New York accented tone complain bitterly about the quality of toilet paper.

Kerry pulled off a few sheets and examined it. "Hey, Dar?"

A soft throat clearing nearby. "Yes?"

"You see this here fancy napkins they put in here?" Kerry put as much of a drawl as she was capable of into her tone and was rewarded with a muffled snicker. "I'm going to take me some of these and put them on the table back home."

"Okay, Forrest," Dar replied through a rumble of laughter. "You do that."

Kerry finished up and went to the sink, washing her hands while still chuckling under her breath. She wiped her fingers dry and turned to wait for Dar, exchanging glances with a tall redheaded woman also standing by waiting.

"That's a gorgeous tattoo," the woman commented, with a faint nod toward Kerry's chest.

Kerry blinked, suffering a moment of bewilderment before she looked down at her shoulder and realized the woman was talking about her. "Oh. Thanks," she murmured, peering back up with a bit of sheepish look. "Haven't had it that long."

"You have it done here?" the woman asked, turning her arm to display the point of her shoulder, which had a cobra on it. "I had this done last month."

The cobra was nice, but Kerry noticed it lacked the vibrancy of her own decoration. "No, I had it done down in Miami," she replied. "There's a guy there who's a really good artist."

"Yeah, no kidding." The woman leaned closer. "That's very cool." Her eyes studied the mark. "Who's Dar?"

"That would be me."

Kerry resisted the urge to look up and over her shoulder. The redhead didn't, however, and she straightened up and took a step backwards when presented with Dar's towering intimidation.

"Well, anyway, congrats on a nice tat." The woman retreated further, grabbing a napkin off the counter before she left the bathroom, taking her somewhat disappointed looking cobra with her.

"Ready?" Kerry gave Dar a smile as she led the way out of the bathroom with her sauntering lover behind her. "You know, that was nice."

"What was, the TP? I'll get you a double case of Charmin at Costco when we get back, okay? You can keep some in your desk drawer."

"That lady liking my tattoo," Kerry said. "But I'll remember that offer. I don't know what the heck the facilities people were thinking last month, but the stuff they changed to reminds me of grocery bags."

They walked outside, accepting the shock of going from icy chill to muggy heat as something natural. "What's your poison?" Dar asked. "I had Italian last night, but I'll do it again if you want."

Kerry licked her lips. "Mm...let's walk down a little bit and see what we find. I don't know if I'm in the mood for that."

The streets were busy around them in a way Miami never was. Their hometown had no central downtown area and was in no sense a walking city. It was far more a huge urban and suburban sprawl, extending up and down the coast for three counties made up of clusters of shopping surrounded by clusters of residential areas.

This was a nice change, really, Kerry thought. It reminded her a little of the trips she'd occasionally made to Chicago with her debating team, when they'd get away for the afternoon and roam the downtown near their hotel, finding anything that didn't smack to hell of home.

Like Garrett's popcorn. Kerry licked her lips in memory, even after all these years. Or the pieces of thick pizza they'd shared on the sidewalk, looking up at the huge, towering buildings. It had been very different than her few trips to Manhattan with her family, that's for sure.

Ah well.

Dar took her hand again as they strolled along, passing brightly lit store fronts and places that became suddenly familiar to them from television. "Hey, look." Kerry pointed. "That's where you always see people standing with signs looking like goofballs on the Today show."

"Uh huh," Dar agreed. "Isn't that where that huge Christmas tree goes?"

"And the ice skating rink, yeah," her companion said. "Can you ice skate?"

Dar pondered the question briefly. "Yes," she finally admitted. "Chinese?" She directed Kerry's attention to a storefront one level up. "I could go for something spicy."

"Sounds pretty darn good to me." Kerry led the way over to the restaurant. They had just gotten seated when first hers, then Dar's pager went off. "Oh, pooh."

Dar removed her device from her purse and keyed it. "Ops center. Never good news."

Kerry sighed and lifted her cell phone, speed dialing and holding the device to her ear as she listened to Dar order for them both. "Hi, it's Kerry Stuart," she said as the line was answered. "What's up?"

"Oh, hi ma'am," the voice answered. "This is Jason. Sorry to bother you, but Mark said I should page out. We had a big forced entry attempt here a little while ago."

Dar's eyebrow cocked up as she caught the tinny sounding words from the phone Kerry was holding a little ways away from her ear.

"Successful?" Kerry asked.

"Ma'am." Jason managed to sound politely scandalized. "If it had been, you'd be talking to Mark right now, not me, that's for sure. No offense."

Dar snorted softly.

"Does Mark have a culprit?" Kerry asked. "Any ideas, or..."

"He's got some stuff he's tracking down. He wanted me to tell you to tell the boss someone was trying to call her bluff."

Dar's eyes narrowed and the planes of her face shifted into a dour expression.

"The boss knows," Kerry said. "If he finds anything, tell him to call us."

"Will do, ma'am."

Kerry folded her phone up and tapped it on the table. "I don't much like the sounds of that."

Dar eased back in her seat, giving the waiter a nod as he delivered two chilled glasses of plum wine. She picked one up and sipped from it before she answered. "It was excessively stupid of me to make that damn claim."

"Oh, well, that's not what I meant..."

"Kerry, it was," Dar interrupted her. "Regardless of whether it was true or not, pissing into an open fire hydrant is just plain idiotic. Mark's going to be cleaning up after that for months." She glared at her wine. "Bah."

Kerry patted her partner on the leg. "It got us good press, sweetie. If Mark can keep them at bay, we can get even better press out of it. I have faith in him, and in your infrastructure."

"Hmph." Dar looked mollified, however. "Maybe if he's got a lead on who they are, I can go back on them and nail 'em," she suggested. "That'd be fun."

"There you go." Kerry smiled at the waiter, who appeared with two bowls of steaming hot and sour soup. "Mm...that smells great."

Dar had removed her PDA from her purse and was scribbling on it. Kerry watched her as she picked up a spoon and sipped her soup. "Mark?"

"Yeah."

"You know what would be cool?"

"What?" Dar glanced at her.

"If we had software that could not only detect stuff like this, but proactively go out and find the jerks trying it and turn the tables on them," Kerry said. "Couldn't you write something like that, Dar?"

Dar tapped her stylus idly on the edge of her PDA. "I don't do coding anymore," she demurred. "I haven't even looked at some of the newer languages..."

"Sure you do," Kerry disagreed. "You write little things all the time. My dancing gopher, that program that keeps track of our expenses, that database thing Maria uses...those are all yours."

A half shrug. "That's just little stuff, like you said." But Dar's voice lacked real conviction.

"Wouldn't it be cool?" Kerry repeated. "That would be such a killer app, if you could have it go out and snag these losers. Find a way through all those backdoor portals and all that masking stuff."

Dar's eyes went briefly unfocused. "Hm." She made a noise deep in her throat, low and thoughtful. "That would be cool," she admitted. "Might fit in with some of the heuristic stuff I was looking at...maybe I could take a look at what the structure might need..."

Ahh. Kerry smiled inwardly. Caught that mind, I think. "It would be awesome."

Dar scribbled several notes, then keyed something, and scribbled several more. Then she hit send and closed the device, folding her hands over it. "So." She turned her attention fully to Kerry. "What were we talking about...toilet paper, right?"

"Toilet paper, and tattoos." Kerry lifted her wine glass, and touched it to Dar's. "And pretty little girls named Yum-Yum."

Dar returned the toast, and they both took a sip. "You know..." Dar looked around. "New York's not so bad after all."

"Hear hear," Kerry agreed, with a smile. "I'm glad I had a chance to play here with you."

The blue eyes lit as a returning smile appeared. "Me, too," she replied. "Ker, I really appreciate you coming up here. I...um..." Dar's gaze dropped briefly, then lifted again. "I really do."

Kerry put her glass down and reached over to cover Dar's hand with her own. "Any time, sweetie. It made me so happy to do it. I about did somersaults in the airplane aisle," she reassured her partner. "I loved being here."

Dar lifted her glass again, and they touched rims, then impishly, she leaned much closer and twined her arm through Kerry's. They drank from each other's glass, and took advantage of the restaurant's trendy dimness to share a kiss that lasted one heartbeat short of a scandal.

Ah well, Kerry reflected, as they parted and picked up their spoons.

If anywhere on earth could handle that, it was New York. It was big enough to handle just about anything.

OTHER MELISSA GOOD TITLES

Tropical Storm

From bestselling author Melissa Good comes a tale of heartache, longing, family strife, lust for love, and redemption. *Tropical Storm* took the lesbian reading world by storm when it was first written...now read this exciting revised "author's cut" edition.

Dar Roberts, corporate raider for a multi-national tech company is cold, practical, and merciless. She does her job with a razor-sharp accuracy. Friends are a luxury she cannot allow herself, and love is something she knows she'll never attain.

Kerry Stuart left Michigan for Florida in an attempt to get away from her domineering politician father and the constraints of the overly conservative life her family forced upon her. After college she worked her way into supervision at a small tech company, only to have it taken over by Dar Roberts' organization. Her association with Dar begins in disbelief, hatred, and disappointment, but when Dar unexpectedly hires Kerry as her work assistant, the dynamics of their relationship change. Over time, a bond begins to form.

But can Dar overcome years of habit and conditioning to open herself up to the uncertainty of love? And will Kerry escape from the clutches of her powerful father in order to live a better life?

ISBN 978-1-932300-60-4

Hurricane Watch

In this sequel to "Tropical Storm," Dar and Kerry are back and making their relationship permanent. But an ambitious new colleague threatens to divide them --- and out them. He wants Dar's head and her job, and he's willing to use Kerry to do it. Can their home life survive the office power play?

Dar and Kerry are redefining themselves and their priorities to build a life and a family together. But with the scheming colleagues and old flames trying to drive them apart and bring them down, the two women must overcome fear, prejudice, and their own pasts to protect the company and each other. Does their relationship have enough trust to survive the storm?

Enter the lives of two captivating characters and their world that Melissa Good's thousands of fans already know and love. Your heart will be touched by the poignant realism of the story. Your senses and emotions will be electrified by the intensity of their problems. You will care about these characters before you get very far into the story.

ISBN 978-1-935053-00-2

Eye of the Storm

Eye of the Storm picks up the story of Dar Roberts and Kerry Stuart a few months after Hurricane Watch ends. At first it looks like they are settling into their lives together but, as readers of this series have learned, life is never simple around Dar and Kerry. Surrounded by endless corporate intrigue, Dar experiences personal discoveries that force her to deal with issues that she had buried long ago and Kerry finally faces the consequences of her own actions. As always, they help each other through these personal challenges that, in the end, strengthen them as individuals and as a couple.

ISBN 978-1-932300-13-0
1-932300-13-9

Red Sky At Morning

A connection others don't understand...
A love that won't be denied...
Danger they can sense but cannot see...

Dar Roberts was always ruthless and single-minded...until she met Kerry Stuart.

Kerry was oppressed by her family's wealth and politics. But Dar saved her from that.

Now new dangers confront them from all sides. While traveling to Chicago, Kerry's plane is struck by lightning. Dar, in New York for a stockholders' meeting, senses Kerry is in trouble. They simultaneously experience feelings that are new, sensations that both are reluctant to admit when they are finally back together. Back in Miami, a cover-up of the worst kind, problems with the military, and unexpected betrayals will cause more danger. Can Kerry help as Dar has to examine her life and loyalties and call into question all she's believed in since childhood? Will their relationship deepen through it all? Or will it be destroyed?

ISBN 978-1-932300-80-2
1-932300-80-5

Thicker Than Water

This fifth entry in the continuing saga of Dar Roberts and Kerry Stuart starts off with Kerry involved in mentoring a church group of girls. Kerry is forced to acknowledge her own feelings toward and experiences with her own parents as she and Dar assist a teenager from the group who gets jailed because her parents tossed her out onto the streets when they found out she is gay. While trying to help the teenagers adjust to real world situations, Kerry gets a call concerning her father's health. Kerry flies to her family's side as her father dies, putting the family in crisis. Caught up in an international problem, Dar abandons the issue to go to Michigan, determined to support Kerry in the face of grief and hatred. Dar and Kerry face down Kerry's extended family with a little help from their own, and return home, where they decide to leave work and the world behind for a while for some time to themselves.

ISBN 978-1-932300-24-6
1-932300-24-4

Terrors of the High Seas

After the stress of a long Navy project and Kerry's father's death, Dar and Kerry decide to take their first long vacation together. A cruise in the eastern Caribbean is just the nice, peaceful time they need — until they get involved in a family feud, an old murder, and come face to face with pirates as their vacation turns into a race to find the key to a decades old puzzle.

ISBN 978-1-932300-45-1
1-932300-45-7

FORTHCOMING TITLES
from Yellow Rose Books

Piperton
by Carrie Carr

Sam Hendrickson has been traveling around the Southwest for ten years, never staying in one place long enough to call it home. Doing odd jobs to pay for her food and gas, she thinks her life is fine, until fate intervenes. On her way to Dallas to find work for the upcoming winter, her car breaks down in the small town of Piperton. Sam's never concerned herself over what other people think, but the small minds of a West Texas town may be more than she bargained for — especially when she meets Janie Clarke. Janie's always done what's expected of her. But when she becomes acquainted with Sam, she's finally got a reason to rebel.

Available September 2009
ISBN 978-1-935053-20-0

Storm Surge
by Melissa Good

It's fall. Dar and Kerry are traveling — Dar overseas to clinch a deal with their new ship owner partners in England, and Kerry on a reluctant visit home for her high school reunion. In the midst of corporate deals and personal conflict, their world goes unexpectedly out of control when an early morning spurt of unusual alarms turns out to be the beginning of the shocking nightmare that was 9/11.

Available May 2010

OTHER YELLOW ROSE TITLES
You may also enjoy:

The Sea Hawk
by Brenda Adcock

Dr. Julia Blanchard, a marine archaeologist, and her team of divers have spent almost eighteen months excavating the remains of a ship found a few miles off the coast of Georgia. Although they learn quite a bit about the nineteenth century sailing vessel, they have found nothing that would reveal the identity of the ship they have nicknamed "The Georgia Peach."

Consumed by the excavation of the mysterious ship, Julia's relationship with her partner, Amy, has deteriorated. When she forgets Amy's birthday and finds her celebrating in the arms of another woman, Julia returns alone to the Peach site. Caught in a violent storm, she finds herself separated from her boat and adrift on the vast Atlantic Ocean.

Her rescue at sea leads her on an unexpected journey into the true identity of the Peach and the captain and crew who called it their home. Her travels take her to the island of Martinique, the eastern Caribbean islands, the Louisiana German Coast and New Orleans at the close of the War of 1812.

How had the Peach come to rest in the waters off the Georgia coast? What had become of her alluring and enigmatic captain, Simone Moreau? Can love conquer everything, even time? On a voyage that lifts her spirits and eventually breaks her heart, Julia discovers the identity of the ship she had been excavating and the fate of its crew. Along the way she also discovers the true meaning of love which can be as boundless and unpredictable as the ocean itself.

ISBN 978-1-935053-10-1
1-935053-10-8

Twenty-four Days
by Janet Albert

Sometimes life forces us into uncharted territory, as Dr. Miranda Ross discovers when circumstances lead her to seek employment on a cruise line specializing in all lesbian cruises. Although she's single and surrounded by women, she has little time to socialize and even less inclination. She's made promises to herself, promises she intends to keep.

And keep them she does, until she meets the ship's head fitness trainer, Jamie Jeffries. Jamie has the kind of body and good looks most people only dream of and unfortunately, a reputation to match. The buzz on the ship is that she can have anyone she wants and often does.

Miranda fights valiantly to avoid Jamie and the unwanted attraction that seems to have a will of its own. She's strong and determined...but a lot can happen in twenty-four days.

ISBN 978-1-935053-16-3
1-935053-16-7

OTHER YELLOW ROSE PUBLICATIONS

VISIT US ONLINE AT

www.regalcrest.biz

At the Regal Crest Website You'll Find

- The latest news about forthcoming titles and new releases

- Our complete backlist of romance, mystery, thriller and adventure titles

- Information about your favorite authors

- Current bestsellers

Regal Crest titles are available from all progressive booksellers and online at StarCrossed Productions, (www.scp-inc.biz), and many others.

Printed in the United States
220089BV00001B/33/P